BAKER'S DOZEN

BAKER'S DOZEN

NATHAN LEE TRAUTENBERG

WAGGLY DESSERT
PRESS

First edition: December 2025

Cover design and illustration by Eli Klein

Printed in the United States of America

ISBN 979-8-9991078-0-0 (paperback)
ISBN 979-8-9991078-2-4 (ebook)

Visit the author's website at www.nathantrautenberg.com

Waggly Dessert Press
Arvada, Colorado 80002

 Formatted with Vellum

I dedicate this book to Nitsa, the sweetest girl there ever was. Keep my rug warm, wherever you are.

This novel takes place during a time when trains existed but marijuana was still illegal.

PROLOGUE

The aliens took off their safety harnesses, set the computer to autopilot, and rushed to the litterbox to relieve themselves. They stepped onto the rainbow pellets filling the container—which resembled a playground ball pit more than a potty tray—and wiggled their tentacles in excitement. A little bit of goo came out. Having been stuck inside for weeks, the prospect of leaving their ship made the aliens restless, and their bladders overactive.

When they returned to their pilot stations, the aliens pushed a square yellow button on the console. Three struts extended from the undercarriage of the ship and the foot pads kissed the earth. A big smooching sound followed as the ship exhaled a plume of hot steam. They pushed another button, a green triangle, and a hatch opened on the underside of the hull, folding out into a long metallic ramp. As it lowered, the compressed air from inside the ship reacted with the colder air of the planet, forming a mist that cloaked them as they advanced down the sloped walkway.

They stepped off the ramp onto hard dirt. As one, they breathed in the cold, crisp air. Even though the atmosphere from this planet contained unhealthy levels of smog and other particulate matter, it was a refreshing change from the stale recirculated air aboard their ship.

Feeling rejuvenated, they lifted their heads and scanned the horizon. The lights of the city burned like the incandescent haze they had encountered on Titan weeks ago. Some were orange, some were green, others flashed blue and red. Many were as white as the house on the hill they had flown past. Even the trees were wrapped in what seemed to be coats of lights to keep them warm during the winter. Everywhere the aliens looked there were incandescent, fluorescent, neon, and halogen glows—together, they turned the sky burnt orange.

Amidst the dazzling spectacle, the aliens also noted shimmering skyscrapers rising upwards into space like fingers grasping for the stars, forming a skyline of several hands which the space-travelers mistook for a bioluminescent living entity. Darkness was not welcome here; whatever lifeforms that had built this city loved constant stimulation. *They* were okay with that. They had visited planets full of nyctophobes before, but none whose fear of darkness quite matched this one. Nevertheless, it offered a nice respite from traveling through the emptiness of space and time for so long.

After taking in their new surroundings, the space-travelers decided this was as good a place as any to continue their search. They hoped to find something to spark their imagination and bring joy to the predictable, lonely calculus of their being. The more they explored the big, dark universe, the more they found life to be as cold and desolate as space. Maybe this planet and its lifeforms could offer them something to lighten their spirits and add fire to their hearts.

As if it had sensed their arrival, a faint but warm and welcoming aroma wafted their way. With their flat noses they took a whiff, and their mouths quickly watered. In all their travels, they had never smelled anything like it. The scent was so foreign and novel, they hadn't a clue what to compare it to. But even so, they could tell it was most definitely yummy. Captivated, they decided to find the source.

They trudged single file across the frozen dirt field like a train of shadows in the night. The dirt transformed into asphalt, and they jaywalked across the avenue, oblivious to the designated pedestrian-crossing zone. They turned right on the sidewalk and followed the scent another hundred yards before being confronted by a locked door.

Undeterred, they pointed their tentacles at the lock. Instantly, it began to change colors. A red patina developed that rapidly morphed into a turquoise-green hue before turning dark brown. The lock magically disintegrated, leaving a pinkie-sized hole beneath the knob. The aliens pushed open the door and stepped over the threshold that would forever change their lives.

It was love at first sight. Never had the aliens seen anything so beautiful, so precious, as the neatly arranged baked goods in the display. The aliens rushed forward to huddle in front of the pastry shelves, pressing their tentacles against the glass and peering inside like wide-eyed children who had just witnessed magic for the first time. The magic was there, on a plate in the display, illuminated under dim yellow lights like a priceless museum piece.

Dozens of baked masterpieces lined the shelves, each wrapped in fancy burgundy wax paper dotted with small gold fleur-de-lises. Perfectly browned, their muffin tops expanded outwards like mushroom clouds from a nuclear bomb, an atomic explosion of taste waiting to detonate in their mouths.

One of the aliens extended a tentacle over the glass and reached into the display. It gently wrapped its suckers around a lemon poppyseed muffin and lifted it out. The alien's brethren crowded around it as it brought the pastry over to their side of the counter. The alien elongated its tentacle until it was ultra-thin like a knife, then effortlessly sliced the treat into twelve equal pieces to share, each identical in mass down to the microgram.

The aliens sunk their pebble-like teeth into the fragrant mound of sugar, butter, and dough. As the browned top touched their eager, sticky tongues, the aliens froze. The muffin was better than anything they had ever tasted. It was airy. It was moist. It was the perfect balance of sweet, buttery, and flaky.

"Mmmm!" they cooed in unison as they swallowed the first bite.

With great voracity they devoured the rest of the muffin, then licked the crumbs off each other's tentacles. When they were certain no specks remained, they began to hum with excitement. A small amount of goo shot out from their tentacle tips and soared over the display, landing inside the milk frothing pitcher next to the espresso machine. The aliens locked eyes and nodded in mutual understanding: after eons flying through cold and lonely space, scouring thousands of galaxies both sweet and savory, they had finally found the inspiration they were searching for.

CHAPTER 1

Rosaline dipped her palms under the sink's running water and washed the last tray from the morning's batch of pastries. When she finished cleaning, she set the tray on the drying rack, then wiped her hands on her apron. Afterwards, she hoisted herself onto the kitchen counter and looked at the clock on the far wall. It was 5:40 a.m.

Good. Twenty minutes to myself before customers show up.

She took out a joint from her apron pocket, turned on the stovetop next to her, and lit the paper with the flame from the burner. She inhaled deeply and held in the smoke.

In the stillness of that moment, she heard a faint sound, like a humming generator.

Is it the oven again? It's always breaking…

She blew out the smoke and hopped down from the counter to check. She opened the door and put her head inside, but everything was quiet. She pulled her head out of the oven and paused, wondering if it was her imagination.

The humming continued, like the buzzing of a pesky mosquito. She checked the microwave next to the pantry, but it too was quiet.

Where is it coming from?

Rosaline closed her eyes and listened. The sound seemed to come more strongly from her right. She opened her eyes and tiptoed in the sound's direction until she neared the doorway. As she crept closer, she realized the sound wasn't coming from the kitchen but the storefront.

She took another hit of her joint, leaned over the trash bin beside the doorway, and peeked her head around the corner. As she exhaled, a wave of acrid smoke obscured her view. She raised a fist to her mouth and coughed, then uncurled her hand and gently swatted the smoke away from her face. When it cleared, the most unexpected scene greeted her: a dozen aliens stood in front of the display, gazing intently at the selection of muffins, all humming in what sounded like gastronomical arousal.

Rosaline recoiled and opened her mouth in shock, and the joint she held loosely in her lips tumbled into the waste basket at her feet. "What the fudge?" she whispered to herself. She vigorously rubbed her eyes, but when she opened them again, the aliens were still there.

Rosaline jerked her body into the kitchen and threw her back against the wall. She lifted her left hand over her heart, which thumped like crazy. Anxiety surged through her veins, sending goosebumps racing across her skin. She took several deep breaths, attempting to calm the whirlwind of emotions inside of her, before cautiously peering around the wall in disbelief.

The aliens were still there, paying her no attention.

"You're just high, Rosaline, you're just too gosh dang high," she muttered to herself.

With a mixture of apprehension and incredulity, she boldly stepped one foot into the storefront, hoping to get a better glimpse of them. Although they were too short to peek over the counter, Rosaline could see their gray bodies and unusual features refracted through the glass, which made them appear even more other-worldly.

There were twelve aliens in total. Each stood three feet tall and had long, slender legs and arms, flat noses, and enormous saucer-like eyes. Their lower front teeth slightly overlapped their upper front teeth when their mouths were closed; this gentle misalignment created an endearing and distinctive appearance, making them look irresistibly charming if not for every one of their other physical characteristics. Instead of hands and feet, they had flexible double-pronged squid-like tentacles. Although their belly buttons were huge, they had relatively small torsos through which their ribcages stuck out slightly, giving them a malnourished appearance made worse by the fact their skin was the same shade of gray as an over-cooked hamburger. What Rosaline found most notable about them, however, was their unusually large, bald, egg-shaped heads.

She watched, mesmerized, as one of the aliens lifted a tentacle off the glass. Its suction cups produced a popping sound as it reached over and plucked a muffin from the case. Rosaline, realizing these creatures might not be figments of her imagination but real-life aliens pilfering pastries from her bakery, began to panic. Hurriedly, she backed into the kitchen, her eyes locked on the aliens, whose lips contorted into what would have been hideous, grotesque smiles if not for their diminutive underbites as they brought the muffin to their side of the counter.

Rosaline, transfixed by the sight, didn't notice the fire until a flame reached up and licked her leg, singeing her hair. Only then did she jump, look down at the blazing wastebin, and let out a silent scream.

What did I do to deserve this? she lamented, pressing her fists against the sides of her head. *Aliens and a fire… and it's not even 6 a.m.!* Dread flooded her as she realized there was now a second, more immediate threat she had to deal with.

Heart pounding with adrenaline and THC, Rosaline scanned the countertops for the first item she could find to throw onto the fire. Her eyes landed on a bag of all-purpose flour in front of the magnetic knife holder, an arm's length from the drying rack. She reached out her hand and grabbed it, but with a hurried yank, the bag tore open, and a cloud of white powder billowed into the air as flour cascaded onto the floor like snow. Ignoring the mess, she hastily scooped up a handful of flour and dashed toward the waste-bin. She dumped the flour inside, but it only caused the flames to grow brighter as they began to climb the already peeling wallpaper.

Panicking, she reached for the phone on the counter, only to remember that she had moved it into the storefront the day before. "Ungh…" she groaned, realizing she was going to have to sneak in front of the aliens to retrieve it. Bravely, she took a deep breath, crossed her fingers that the space creatures were still distracted by the food, and tiptoed in a low crouch around the corner.

The red rotary dial sat idly next to the cash register. Carefully, she crept forward, sliding her feet inch-by-inch so as not to make a sound on the creaky wooden floors, until the phone was in reach. She extended her fingers toward it, stretching all the way out until she felt her arm pulling uncomfortably at her shoulder, then reached just a tiny bit further until they wrapped around the base. Once secured, she tucked the phone in her arm and retreated into the kitchen. As she moved backwards, the aliens' attention remained on the muffin which they had ripped into bite sized portions and were stuffing inside their little mouths. A rush of relief washed over her; the aliens still hadn't noticed her, and if the tales from the monster movies were anything to go by, she hoped to keep it that way, lest she be torn into pieces like delicate puff pastry.

She slinked through the doorway, mindfully towing the phone cord so she didn't accidentally unplug it from the socket, and placed the base down on the kitchen island a handful of feet behind the glowing wastebin. Hastily, she punched three numbers into the dial, pressed the handset to her ear, then glanced at the fire caused by her joint, which was rapidly advancing up the wall. At that moment, an intrusive thought crossed her mind: *I can't let the police get involved. I just got off probation.*

Rosaline let out a strained sigh. Softly, she set the receiver down, using both hands to stifle any sound, then, with frantic urgency, she scanned the room for something to extinguish the growing confla-gration. *Come on, Rosaline, think. What's something that can put out a fire?* Her eyes darted from one object to another until they landed on the sink, where an enormous forty-quart stockpot sat drying. In an instant, a solution crystallized in her mind.

Rosaline dashed toward the sink. As she crossed the kitchen, however, she slid on a patch of flour, and her flailing arms knocked a set of pots and pans off the overhead rack. Rosaline managed to stay on her feet, but that small victory was short-lived as kitchen-ware loudly clattered to the floor around her.

Rosaline paused, rigid as a cutting board. The cacophony of metallic cookware ringing throughout the kitchen was so deafen-ing, it was impossible that the aliens hadn't heard it. Slowly, fearfully, she twisted her head and glanced over her shoulder, certain that the aliens would venture into the kitchen to investi-gate, but when she set her eyes on the doorway, the aliens weren't there. She took a deep breath and exhaled the tension building inside her chakras. Instinctively, she reached for the joint in her apron to help calm her nerves, but then she remem-bered it was at the bottom of a flaming trash can. Stepping over the fallen utensils, she redirected her focus toward the sink and continued her quest to put out the fire. Cleaning up the mess could wait; right now, her priority was preventing her bakery from burning down.

She turned on the faucet and placed the oversized stockpot under the running water. Seconds seemed to pass like hours as the water level rose at a snail's pace. When the pot finally filled, she turned off the faucet, grabbed the handles with both hands, and lifted. In one deft motion she swung it around, the water sloshing inside, then dropped it as she caught sight of the aliens staring at her. The heavy stockpot crashed onto the floor with a loud bang, its contents spilling in every direction.

Rosaline's heart stopped as she beheld the aliens, whose expres-sions were utterly unreadable. They stood side-by-side, like a foot-ball offensive line, between the island and the counter. They blocked her exit with their formation, but she wouldn't have been able to flee even if she had a clear escape. Whether from fright or mysterious powers, she was frozen in place. Water filled her shoes, soaking her socks as she stood there, motionless, holding her breath, waiting to die.

Suddenly, one of the aliens bent down to lick dry flour off the floor that hadn't yet mixed with water and turned into dough. At the same moment, thick, dark smoke began to fill the room as the fire gained momentum, reminding Rosaline that she needed to protect the most precious thing in the entire world, more valuable than her own life—her bakery.

With newfound determination, she regained control of her body and leapfrogged over the crouched alien licking flour. It raised its head as she vaulted over it, and she could see its face plastered with white powder. She sprinted past the aliens until she stood empty-handed before the fire which had promptly quadrupled in size. Flames covered the doorway, preventing her egress. Embers scorched the calcimine ceiling and wood floors, turning them black. The heat and intensity made it too dangerous to cross into the store-front. Trapped inside the kitchen, Rosaline could do nothing other than gaze hopelessly at the burgeoning inferno as its fiery fingers extended into the storefront, threatening her cherished livelihood.

She curled her hands into fists and pressed them against her temples in fright and confusion.

What should I do?

Amidst the chaos, an unexpected image fluttered into Rosaline's mind: a butterfly net and a swarm of bugs. "Eugene!" she exclaimed, a surge of hope rushing over her. Once again, she grabbed the red rotary phone and furiously punched away at the digits.

Something egg-shaped moved out of the corner of her eye. She turned to shield herself, expecting flames to whip at her, but it wasn't fire that reached her. Moving fluidly, the aliens extended their flour-coated tentacles toward her with an unworldly grace.

"I'm going to die! Oh God, it's happening!" she shouted as scorched fragments of ceiling fell to the floor.

The aliens touched her arm.

Rosaline shrieked.

CHAPTER 2

Eugene sat in his father's favorite brown-leather chair in what used to be his father's office on the top floor of what used to be his father's business. It was Eugene's business now, and his office was huge—two thousand square feet in total.

Lining the left side were twenty-foot-tall floor-to-ceiling windows overlooking the Fairgrounds. Pressed against the opposite wall were two old wooden cabinets, faintly redolent of moth balls, that housed Eugene's bug collection. An emerald-green carpet, featuring the yellow initials "T.S." encircled in the middle, covered the floor. On the wall behind the oversized mahogany desk hung an oil portrait of Theodore Schumaker, Eugene's father. The painting smelled like a polished shoe. The distinguished man depicted in it had a long foxlike face accentuated by a strong angular jaw and high cheek-bones. His short blond hair was in the process of turning white. He wore a perfectly tailored black suit with a dark purple tie that brought out the jade-green in his eyes.

Theo, as he was known to his friends, was the founder and CEO of Schumaker Trains and Oil, one of the largest freight train busi-nesses in the nation. Theo took the company from inception to a peak valuation of two billion dollars just before his premature demise. He was not only a jovial man, full of laughter and positivity, but also a philanthropist whose tax-deductible donations established a soup kitchen for the city. It was hard not to like Theo.

"I hate your father," Eugene's mother once said to him on their way back from a little league baseball game. "All he does is work, work, work. He never spends time with us, but he has time to donate money to homeless people? That doesn't make sense. Does he care more about vagrants than his own family?"

Eugene hadn't known what to say, so he looked out the open backseat window in silence. All his mom ever did was talk about money; all his dad did was earn it. But Eugene didn't care about how well-off his family was; all he wanted was to spend time with his dad, who had been too busy to make it to his baseball game because he was working again. He'd probably show up late for dinner, too, if he showed up at all.

"Some people wouldn't know a good thing if it hit them in their face," his mom continued. She was the good thing she was referring to, but at that moment, a beetle flew through the window, struck Eugene's cheek, and fell into his lap.

He scooped it up with his baseball glove as if he were fielding a grounder and raised it to his face so that he could see it better. The metallic gold bug, less than a centimeter long, had two teensy black antennae protruding from between its large ovoid eyes. Its semi-transparent shell flushed reddish orange.

"Just remember, Eugene, don't be like your father, okay?" his mother said. "Promise me you won't turn into him."

"Okay, Mom," he'd agreed perfunctorily.

Eugene glanced at the clock above the door to his office. 6 a.m. The first rays of sunlight hadn't yet appeared on the horizon. He put his hands together behind his head and leaned back in his chair. There was a stack of papers on his desk, including the blueprints of the new train models he needed to order. *Those can wait.*

Eugene stood up and walked over to the cabinets that lined the wall on the right side of his office. He opened the top drawer and pulled out a glass case. Inside was an assortment of desiccated bug specimens. He peered at a small gold bug that looked like a cross between a scarab beetle and a ladybug preserved in amber. "*Chari-*

dotella sexpunctata," he murmured, gazing nostalgically at the golden tortoise beetle. It was the same one that had struck him in the face when he was a kid. Eugene had pinned the carcass in the middle of the collection case labeled "Chrysomelidae," or leaf beetles. The bedazzling insect was the first specimen he ever collected and the impetus that sparked his interest in entomology.

Eugene's heart sank. Looking at the collection reminded him of a future that could have been. For years he had aspired to be an entomologist. He had dreamed of exploring the world, documenting new species, and becoming a reputed expert on bugs. Instead, after that fateful day his parents were killed, he was forced to drop out of Cornell's entomology program to manage his father's freight-train and oil business.

It was a lot of responsibility to run one of the largest train and oil-producing companies in the country, and Eugene was overwhelmed. Schumaker Trains and Oil transported millions of gallons of petroleum every day, almost all of which the company produced itself in its quest to control the supply chain. Eugene had no previous experience running a business, let alone one worth billions of dollars. Scurrying around the woods didn't teach him leadership skills or how to interact with others, and bugs taught him nothing about money. Although he dutifully tried his best to fulfill his father's wishes to grow the company, it tanked on his watch. Its valuation sank by a quarter in the first year he took over. Investors pulled out, contracts were terminated, and the board became increasingly displeased. Eugene felt ashamed and miserable leading the business. *I just don't know what to do.* His lip quivered thinking about it. He wanted to cry, but a knock on the door interrupted his moment of self-pity.

"Come in," he called out lightly, trying his best to hide the heavy sadness weighing on him.

Alfredo entered and quietly shut the door behind him. Alfredo was a tall, slender man in his late sixties who had heavily gelled gray hair, compassionate brown eyes, and a perfectly tailored charcoal-gray suit. His cologne, which he always applied in excess, smelled strongly of sandalwood and Mediterranean musk. Alfredo was not only Eugene's butler, but also his accountant, assistant, and a member of the board.

"Has TrackTek sent over the blueprints yet?" Alfredo asked, referring to the company's train engine manufacturer.

"Yes, they sent it this morning." Eugene pointed at a rolled-up print resting on top of a hulking stack of documents on his desk. "The designs for the ten new caterpillars we ordered are right there." That's what Eugene called the company trains: caterpillars. He referred to the oil from the refineries as "beetle juice," a pun on Betelgeuse the star. Using entomological jargon to describe the company's system of operations helped him to understand his father's business.

He unrolled the blueprint for Alfredo to see. The specifications showed the new train engine, a rectangular box with small, slanted windows at the front, standing fifteen and a half feet tall and seventy-two feet long.

"They call it the JD-52BC, an improvement over our old JD-52AC model. It has five thousand two hundred horsepower and one hundred and sixty thousand pounds of tractive force. An absolute monster. It's an AC powered, six-axel, sixteen-cylinder diesel. The price tag on each is $1.8 million, so…" he said timidly, unsure how Alfredo would react, "that means ten engines will cost us eighteen million dollars."

"I think this will be a great investment. Your father would be proud of the fine work you are doing," said Alfredo.

Eugene felt his shoulders drop, and a warmth filled his chest. Investing in new locomotives was one of the few financial decisions he had made since taking over the company, and although it wasn't much, he felt more confident knowing Alfredo supported it.

"Thanks, Alfredo. I'm trying to be a better CEO."

"It takes time to master. Don't be so hard on yourself."

"I struggle with indecision."

"It's a new skillset you're learning to develop."

"My 'development' has cost the company a quarter of our market share."

"A small price to pay for your ontogenesis as CEO."

"…It's half a billion dollars."

"We'll make it back soon enough. I believe in you, Eugene, as did your father, and he faced similar struggles early on."

Eugene tried to smile, but his lips turned downwards. He worried that the better he performed, the more trapped he'd become working at a company he didn't want to lead. With every investment he made into Schumaker Trains and Oil, he felt the future he longed for slip further and further away.

"Alfredo, could you help me with something?" said Eugene, retrieving a tape measure from his desk drawer.

"Certainly. What do you need help with?"

"Measuring the cabinets. I'd like to order another one for my bug collection."

"That sounds easy enough."

Alfredo held the end of the tape measure while Eugene pulled out the roll. "Twenty-six inches deep." Eugene pulled a pen from his pocket and looked around for something to write the dimensions on.

"Hmmm…" Eugene strode over to his desk and grabbed the JD-52BC blueprint. "This'll do." He wrote down the dimensions, scribbling over the engine specifications. He recorded the height, width, and depth of the cabinets, as well as the number of drawers, their model number, and name.

"I can order these for you," said Alfredo, gently extracting the blueprint from Eugene's hand. "I'll return this once I finish."

"Thanks. I appreciate it."

He watched Alfredo leave, then crossed the office to peer out of the windows at the Fairgrounds below, wishing he was down there. The dirt lot was a prime location for catching centipedes and other arthropods. *I'll go beetle hunting this weekend,* he decided, making a mental note to ask his friend Winston to join him.

He glanced at the railyard to his right at the edge of the Fairgrounds where a handful of dilapidated trains rested on the tracks, their oil cars waiting to be filled from the adjacent refinery. Eugene shifted his gaze there next. A disconcerting amount of white smog billowed from its smokestacks and disappeared into the sky. Orange halogen lights dotted both the railyard and refinery, their luminescence bright enough to be seen during the day.

As the sun rose over the horizon, a sharp beam of reflected light bounced into Eugene's eye, momentarily blinding him. He pulled his head back and blinked rapidly. When his vision recovered, he spotted a metallic silver disc in the middle of the Fairgrounds that hadn't been there yesterday.

Are they setting up for the May Fair already? It's only March…

With a resigned sigh, he returned to his oversized mahogany desk. He looked at the mountain of documents in front of him and felt his throat tighten. *Don't cry,* he told himself. He wanted to give the company up, but he was afraid of letting his parents down. He had promised himself he would continue his father's legacy. *After all, I'm the reason he was killed. But I hate it. What can I do?* Dismayed, Eugene shook his head. He didn't have any answers. He was stuck.

If only something were to happen to change my life.

The phone on his desk rang. He reached to pick it up, but then paused. *What if it's work related?*

He smiled weakly at the thought. Winston's contempt for work was beginning to rub off on him.

He picked up the phone. "Hello?"

"Eugene! Come over here right now! Hurry, it's urgent!" The voice sounded rushed and frantic.

"Rosaline, what's going on?"

"The bakery—it's caught fire! And there's… *ahhh!*"

"On fire? I'm on my way!"

A mere moment ago, Eugene's heart beat listlessly, numbed from the unrewarding work that had been thrust upon him. But now, called to action, he could feel it pounding in his chest. Enthusiastically, he dropped the handset and put on his tweed peacoat and butterfly mittens. After fastening all of his buttons, he grabbed the fire extinguisher off the wall next to his bug cabinets and bolted from his office, fully prepared to rescue his friend from the flames.

CHAPTER 3

Eugene heroically burst into the bakery, fire extinguisher at the ready, then promptly froze. Rosaline stood behind the pastry counter, surrounded not by flames but by a huddle of humming small gray extraterrestrials.

"I'm not sure I understand," Rosaline was saying sweetly. Her long, wavy blonde hair cascaded in ringlets, forming spools on the glass as she leaned over the counter to speak to the aliens. The doorway behind her was charred, and blackened fragments of calcimine dangled precariously from the ceiling, ready to fall. "Could you repeat that?"

"Mmmm!" they replied in an adorable high-pitched squeak.

"Mmmm? Like mmmmuffin? Is that what you want?"

"Um, Rosaline…?" Eugene said, his gaze fixed on the creatures. He observed their lithe double-pronged tentacles and oversized egg-shaped heads that appeared to teeter precariously with each movement. The sight filled him with fascination.

"Eugene!" She lifted her eyes from her curious little customers. "Thank you so much for rushing over. I just don't know what to do."

"Who are these creatures, and why does that one have stuff all over its face?" he asked.

"Eugene, don't tell me…"—her eyes grew wide—"you can see them too?"

"Yes, there's twelve little aliens here. Why wouldn't I be able to see them?"

She threw her head back and laughed uncontrollably. "Oh, thank God! I thought I was hallucinating!"

"Maybe we both are," he remarked, sniffing the smoky, marijuana-tinged aroma permeating the bakery. "I thought you said the bakery caught fire?"

"It did. I dropped my joint when I saw these guys, and the wastebin lit ablaze."

"So, you put it out?"

"I didn't, but they did." She pointed at the gray visitors.

Eugene examined the aliens curiously. Amidst all their grayness, they possessed neither a bucket nor a hose. "How?"

Rosaline puckered her lips and shrugged. "They shot slime out of their tentacles and smothered the flames."

Eugene sandwiched his head with both his hands. "I must be dreaming."

"Do you think they're firemen?"

"Rosaline…"

"Eugene!" she retorted, giggling.

"How long have the aliens been here?" he pressed, ignoring her silly antics.

"I don't know *exactly* how long because I've been busy making my tarts and a second batch of muffins. You know, it's not easy running your own business. I guess that's what you've been learning though, huh? Speaking of muffins…" Rosaline gently plucked a lemon poppyseed muffin from the display. As she was lifting it out, she jerked upwards and gasped.

"Where's Winston? You two always come in for breakfast together during the workweek. He should be here by now."

"I dunno. Why?"

"You don't think the aliens… *abducted him?*" she said, mouthing the final two words so that the extraterrestrials standing nearby wouldn't hear.

"I doubt he was abducted, and even if he were, he'd probably be happy to have an excuse to not show up at his office. Besides, I thought he said yesterday that he was going to take today off."

"Is he sick?" she asked, placing the muffin on a small white plate and setting it down on the counter.

"No, he just didn't want to work today." Eugene could understand. Working made him feel sick, too.

He watched Rosaline move to the espresso machine and steam milk in the frothing pitcher. Every weekday Eugene ordered the same: a lemon poppyseed muffin and a hot chocolate. When the milk was hot and pillowy, Rosaline added chocolate and stirred. The steaming beverage turned a decadent shade of dark brown. She poured it into a cup, placed it on a saucer, and set it on the counter for Eugene.

Eugene strode cautiously to the counter, making sure to keep a wide berth around the aliens as he did so. Intrigued as he was by them, he didn't know their temperament, and therefore decided to be safe until he had a chance to learn more about them. Without taking his eyes off them, he lifted the cup handle with his index finger and thumb and took a sip, making a sound like a jet plane engine as he slurped in air along with the hot chocolate so as not to burn his mouth. When he finished, he set the cup back on the saucer and smacked his lips.

"Did you add anything different to the hot chocolate?" he asked, glancing at Rosaline.

"No, how come?"

"It tastes funny today."

"Hmm. Wonder why."

Eugene turned toward the visitors. "Rosaline, could we talk about the elephant in the room?"

"*THERE'S AN ELEPHANT IN THE ROOM, TOO!?*" she screamed.

"No, I mean the aliens."

"Oh… don't scare me like that." She took out a fresh joint from her apron pocket, lit it, and took a hit. "This Starlight Kush is something else," she said, blowing a wave of pungent smoke at the aliens, who had pressed their tentacles against the glass of the display and were hungrily peering inside.

"I think we should tell someone they're here."

"Who? Winston?"

"I was thinking the police."

Rosaline gasped. "We can't call the police."

"I don't want them to be taken away or locked up either."

"No, we can't call the police because… you know…" She wagged the joint in front of his face.

"Oh." He looked through the smoke at Rosaline's eyes. Her emerald irises were surrounded by bloodshot veins. They looked like Christmas.

"I agree we should tell someone, though," she said. "I'm not very good at keeping secrets."

"Hey, I know who we could tell."

"Who?"

"Alfredo."

"Your butler?"

"He'll know what to do."

Rosaline snorted. "Sure, if they need help picking out their clothes and filing taxes."

"Then what about something like the Smithsonian Institute?"

"They aren't bugs you can study and put on display, Eugene."

"What I meant was that scientists should have a chance to study them, maybe run some lab tests to figure out their genealogy. After that, they could learn what they're doing here."

"I already know what they're doing here."

"What's that?"

"Drooling all over the pastry display!" she snapped. Thick goo secreted from their tentacles and dripped off the glass onto the warped, timeworn wooden floor.

"Do you think anybody else knows they're here?" she asked.

"No, or there'd be reporters and policemen and thousands of people flocking here to—"

The aliens resumed their humming, cutting him off.

"What are they doing?" he asked apprehensively.

Rosaline narrowed her eyes. "They must really want something from my pastry display."

"They must have good taste then. Everyone knows your bakery is the best in D.C."

Her round cheeks turned the same deep shade of scarlet as her bloodshot eyes. "Awww, you're too sweet. But my bakery isn't even good enough to warrant an invitation to the BABKA."

"Nonsense. There's no doubt in my mind you'll be invited to compete. It's only a matter of time."

The aliens, ceaselessly salivating from their tentacles, pointed at a lemon poppyseed muffin in the display.

Eugene jumped excitedly. "Rosaline, they're communicating with us! They want a muffin!"

Her jaw dropped. "You can understand what they're thinking? That means you're telekinetic."

"I can't underst… You know what, yeah. I can understand them. They want to try a muffin."

"I thought that's what they were trying to say. Maybe I'm also telekinetic." She pulled out a dozen poppyseed muffins for the aliens and set them on the counter. In unison, they each grabbed a muffin and took a bite.

"Mmmmmmm!" they groaned, shuddering with delight. Their pupils dilated in a sign of gastrointestinal ecstasy.

"I guess these are coming out of my paycheck," Rosaline muttered, leaning over the counter to watch the aliens enjoy their muffins.

With each bite, their hums grew louder, escalating into moans of pleasure.

"*Mmmm!*" A torrent of crystalline goop gushed from the pores on their tentacles.

Eugene chortled with amusement, but Rosaline frowned.

"Oh, great. And now the floor's all wet. I'm *not* cleaning that up."

A concerning thought popped into Eugene's mind. He crossed his arms and glanced sideways at Rosaline.

"What is it?" she asked.

"I think the president should be informed—just hear me out," he added when she opened her mouth to protest. "We don't know why the aliens are here. We don't know if they're here for vacation or if they want to take over the planet. We should exercise caution around them."

"Eugene, no one else is here," she said, waving her arms like a kung fu bug and pointing at her empty bakery, "which means no one knows the aliens are here. If they did, police would be all over, and a crowd would have already gathered to gawk and take pictures. That's not the case, which means the first thing these creatures have done upon arriving to our planet is come to my bakery and eat my muffins. What kind of intergalactic conquistadores would do such a thing? I mean, just look at them. They seem rather wholesome." She turned to admire the little gray visitors, and her pleasant countenance quickly deteriorated into panic. "Eugene!" She pointed, her eyes wide and fearful.

"Yeah?" He looked where she was pointing, but there was nothing there.

The aliens had vanished.

CHAPTER 4

Winston felt as if he had exited the womb for a second time. The meeting room was artificial and clean, much like the hospital where he'd been delivered. Bright fluorescent lights shined down on him, their oppressive glare reflecting off the naked white walls, disorienting him. He wondered how he got here. The marketing team was scheduled to arrive for another meeting, but except for the reclining chairs surrounding the long rectangular table at which he sat, the room was empty.

Just like life.

The conference room door swung open, and a trio of marketers —Mr. Tibbles, Mr. Dinkle, and Mr. Sneffles—waltzed in to take their seats. Winston outranked all of them. He was the vice director of marketing, the second highest position within the entire marketing division. The director, Mr. Bradford, couldn't attend because he was playing golf with the vice president of the United States, John Angryberger.

"Eager to start the meeting, eh, Winston?" asked Mr. Tibbles, striding exuberantly around the table to his usual chair, bouncing up and down like a pogo stick with each step.

"Absolutely," said Winston apathetically. He was early to every meeting—not out of a desire to succeed but because he didn't want to do any work at his desk.

Hopefully, I can do nothing while I'm here, he prayed. He pulled out a piece of recycled paper and continued his doodles. He was midway through embellishing the letters "ABW"—"Anything But Work" was not only his motto, it was exactly the kind of work ethic that allowed him to excel at Bullit Inc. Since joining the marketing team one year ago, he'd quickly soared through the ranks to become the vice director of marketing for the entire company. On his first day of work, recruiters recognized his potential and moved him into the accelerated training lane for highly talented and capable entry-level candidates. Since then, he'd been promoted eight times. Nobody could believe how meteorically he rose to the top. Not even Winston could believe how rapidly he moved up the corporate ladder, and it wasn't any ordinary ladder—the rungs he climbed at Bullit Inc. were direct links in the presidency, because Bullit Inc. *was* the president of the United States.

Bullit Inc. became president two years ago when changes were made to the Constitutional requirements to become commander in chief. Corporations won a pivotal lawsuit, spearheaded by the aggressive lawyers of Schlossberg Law LLC, that recognized corporations as people, granting them the amenities normally reserved for real people. This victory enabled companies like Bullit Inc. to run for president because of their newfound legal statuses as "persons."

However, there was one problem in having a corporation as president: it couldn't make decisions for itself. Therefore, the position of president representative was added. Only a "real" human could become president representative, and it was always the CEO of the president who acted in this role. Even though it was a new political position, neither an election nor an appointment was necessary. It was filled by default. The CEO of Bullit Inc., Brian Adams, became president representative. Similarly, the position of vice president representative was filled by John Angryberger, CEO of Jmart, the second largest corporation in the country and vice president of the United States.

This was largely confusing for non-lawyer folk, so, for all intents and purposes, everyone referred to Brian Adams as the president and John Angryberger as the vice president.

Winston didn't care if he worked for the president or the pope. Working sucked regardless. The mere thought of working, let alone working harder, hurt Winston's back, caused his head to pound in his skull, and made his blood pressure rise dangerously high. His feelings toward work weren't exclusive to Bullit Inc., however. He had always hated doing things for other people.

"I hate working," he used to say to Eugene when they were at Cornell together. "My goal is to never work a job in my life."

"Why?"

"Because it's a waste of my time, and I hate when other people tell me what to do."

Homework was no exception. Every paper Winston had to write drove him mad, even though he got straight A's in his philosophy studies. He would scream and yell in his room as he wrote, throwing tantrums like a man-baby, riling himself up to the point that he'd have to get up from his chair and go take a walk outside to clear his head.

"It's just a paper," Eugene once said as Winston passed by on his way out of the dorm room. Even though Winston was a year older than Eugene, they were roommates for two years—until Eugene dropped out.

"I'm not doing it. It's not worth my time," Winston replied. An hour later, he returned and finished the paper.

"I thought you said work was beneath you?" a smirking Eugene taunted.

"It was, is, and always will be."

"What will you do once you finish college, if you don't want to work?"

Winston shrugged. "I'll probably live in a hut on the beach."

"How will you survive?"

"I'll put up a little sign that says, 'wisdom for food.' Beachgoers can come to me and exchange food for a helpful tip on how to live their lives."

And that's exactly what he did. After he graduated summa cum laude from Cornell, Winston went to live on the sandy beaches of Long Island. He set up a little straw hut on a privately owned waterfront during the month of June. There was no stove, TV, or toilet. He took care of all his bodily functions in the ocean. At first, business started off slow, but it gradually improved as more people arrived for their midsummer vacation. However, the flock of visitors died down in September. For months, the beaches stayed empty. Winston was alone. It was a peaceful feeling being the only person around, surrounded by nature and beauty.

But reality soon caught up to Winston. He ran out of money and could neither feed himself nor afford the rent to his small hut. He was kicked out and left to sleep on the sand, exposed to all the elements, which wouldn't have been so bad except nobody was allowed on the beaches after dark, so he got kicked out again onto the streets of Long Island.

Being a beach bum was one thing, but being a street bum was not a lifestyle Winston was willing to entertain. Unable to afford a taxi or train ticket, he swam the four miles separating Long Island from Manhattan. He washed up on the shore of downtown New York City like a beached whale. Wasting no time, he beelined toward the nearest skyscraper, which, serendipitously, happened to be the New York offices for Bullit Inc. Strutting inside, he demanded to speak with the recruiting agent for the branch. He stood barefoot in front of the receptionist dripping water in his brown cargo shorts and red T-shirt from Mr. Choo's Chinese Buffet, which had been gifted to him by one of his wisdom-seeking patrons. Winston had never been to Mr. Choo's Chinese Buffet, but he hoped to go one day.

As Winston spoke to the fair-haired receptionist, something shiny caught his eye. Over her shoulder, Winston glimpsed a reflection of himself in a large silver plaque against the marbled stone wall on which the date of the skyscraper's completion was engraved: 1924. Seawater dripped from his shoulder-length matted black hair. Over the half-year he'd lived in his hut without shaving cream or a blade, he'd grown a small beard and a thick unibrow. He was moderately surprised by his appearance; he had hoped that after a few months on the beach he would have achieved a hot jobless-surfer look. Instead, he looked like a yeti from Saskatchewan.

His unkempt presence alarmed the receptionist, who called security to remove him from the premises. It was in that lucky moment that one of Winston's philosophy classmates walked into the lobby and recognized the wet guru—an impressive feat, given his six months of dishevelment.

"Is that...? No! It can't be! Winston? Is that you?" he asked incredulously.

Winston turned to see who was asking, but he didn't recognize the individual.

"Yes."

"Oh man! You are such a trip, Winston," said the young man with adulation. "Last I heard you were living in South America or something, and yet here you are. Speaking of which, what *are* you doing here?"

"I'm looking for work."

"The Winston I knew would never go *looking* for work. That's like, antithetical to your whole character. Why are you really here?"

"I need to make money so that I can return to my hut and live out the rest of my life in peace."

The other man laughed. "Oh, Winston," he said, slapping him on the shoulder. "I forgot how funny you were."

"I'm not joking. I need a job that'll pay enough so that I never have to work again. Can you help me...er"—Winston couldn't remember his name—"old friend?"

"Of course, come with me. I'll introduce you to my boss, and maybe we can work something out." He turned to the receptionist, who continued to eye Winston mistrustfully. "Don't worry, he's with me."

"Are you sure?" she asked with concern.

"Yeah, yeah." He gave a nonchalant wave of his hand and headed toward the elevator.

Winston followed him. His bare feet made wet slapping sounds and left wet footprints on the tiles.

Together, they entered the elevator. Winston's former classmate hit button forty-four.

Winston felt trapped inside the tiny metal box as it ascended, creaking and groaning like the body of a geriatric. He clenched his fists and jaw impatiently, waiting for the door to open.

"Where are your clothes, man?" asked the former classmate.

Winston pointed at his red Mr. Choo's Chinese Buffet T-shirt.

"You don't have socks or shoes?"

"No."

"Why not?"

"Long story."

The young man laughed. "I'll bet. Another one of Winston's classic stories. I can't wait to hear it."

"Maybe another time."

"Come on, dude. We have time. I really want to hear about what happened to your socks."

Winston shook his head.

"Come on. Pretty please?"

"Fine," said Winston, hoping that by recounting his recent adventures, it would get his old schoolmate to stop talking. "I put up in a hut in Long Island and became a minimalist that lived off the land."

"Long Island? I thought you went to Brazil. How did you live off the land? Did you catch fish or something?"

"I traded wisdom for food and money."

"Wisdom? How did you trade that?"

"People would come to me with existential questions, and I'd guide them to an answer."

"Oh, I see. You were a bum."

"I wasn't a bum."

"Sounds to me like you were a bum."

"I embodied the change I wished to see, free from greed, selfishness, and exploitation. I no longer wanted to be part of the consumer economy. I wasn't a bum."

"Mmmm, and how did that work out?"

"I got kicked off the island."

"Without any socks."

"Without any socks."

"And now you are here doing what?"

"Looking for a well-paying job so I may return permanently the next time."

"That doesn't make any sense."

"It does make sense. Didn't you read any of Marx's dialectics on historical materialism while we were at Cornell?"

"Are you a Marxist?"

"No, I'm saying that in the same vein Marx argued the transition to a communist society required bourgeoisie capitalism, so too would I require capital to make my own transition to my hut lifestyle."

The elevator doors opened. Winston stepped out to a row of cubicles.

"Oops. This is forty-four," his former classmate called out. "I meant to hit forty-five."

Winston backed into the elevator.

"Let me get this straight: your plan is to work in a very loud, busy city at the world's biggest, most exploitative corporation in order to live in a hut on the beach where nobody can bother you?"

"It's not that simple."

The young man flashed a grin. "I must be missing something, then," he said, playfully punching Winston on the shoulder. "Your intentions were always so pure. I admire that."

Winston grew agitated. This former classmate of his, whose name he couldn't remember, was making him feel and sound like a dope, or worse, a dilettante. He was too small-brained to imagine the beautiful, idyllic world Winston conceived.

The elevator opened to the forty-fifth floor. Winston stepped out and was greeted with more cubicles and offices.

His friend grabbed his arm to lead him somewhere else. "This way to my dad," he said.

"I thought we were going to your boss?"

"Yeah, this way," he said, setting off down the hall. Feeling Winston's stare on his neck, he explained the virtues of nepotism: "If my dad wasn't my boss, how else was I going to get a job? You remember how I preferred beer over books." He turned right down another hallway.

A handful of people gawked at Winston as he passed by, but he ignored them. He followed his nameless friend to an office door at the end of a long row of cubicles. A plaque hanging on the door read, "Mr. Tyson—Regional Marketing Specialist." The young man opened the door without knocking, and Winston followed him inside.

"Patrick. How are you?" Mr. Tyson said, standing up to hug his son. He stopped when he saw Winston, and cast a disgusted look at the man who dripped water on his expensive rug. "Patrick, who is this street urchin you brought in?"

"This is Winston, one of my classmates from Cornell. He was the smartest student in our entire class."

Mr. Tyson surveyed Winston from head to toe with a mix of repugnance and curiosity. "And what is he doing here?"

"He needs a job."

Mr. Tyson's eyebrows nearly flew off his head. "Clearly! The poor man doesn't even have socks for God's sake! Tell me, Winston, what were you doing that you ended up in this state?"

"He was bumming around on Long Island," Patrick interjected before Winston could get a word in.

"Is that so?"

"No," Winston said.

"Yes."

Winston wanted to chop his head off.

"And what made you decide to relocate?" Mr. Tyson asked.

"He wants to become powerful and make a lot of money," Patrick answered before Winston could speak again.

"You definitely came to the right place."

"Well, no, that's not exactly what I want," said Winston.

"Then what is it that you want?" Mr. Tyson asked.

"I want to not be bothered."

"And how will you go about achieving that?"

"By becoming powerful and making a lot of money."

Mr. Tyson nodded his head. "That's as good a reason as any I've heard. If we didn't have to make money to live, none of us would be here. We'd all be living in a straw hut on a beach." He stroked his chin. "Let me make some calls and see what I can do. I believe there was an opening for a marketing associate in the D.C. office."

"Thanks, Dad," said Patrick. He turned toward Winston and looked at him expectantly. "Isn't this great? We'll be working for the same company."

Winston shrugged. He didn't like the idea of spending his valuable time doing work for a corporation when it could be better spent sunbathing.

Mr. Tyson shooed Patrick and Winston out of his office so he could make some phone calls. In the meantime, Patrick led Winston to his cubicle and regaled him with stories of wild parties, financial irresponsibility, and excessive drinking on Tuesdays. It made him want to swim back across the harbor to Long Island.

Mr. Tyson soon came out of the office. "Winston, good news. One of my colleagues—a marketing specialist like me—could use your help at the D.C. branch."

"That's great," said Winston, forcing a smile as his stomach lurched.

Later, he waved goodbye to Patrick and Mr. Tyson, who had given him a voucher for a one-way train from New York to Washington D.C. The commuter train dropped him off at the station downtown. He walked the rest of the distance from the terminal to Schumaker Avenue and the Schumaker Estate, where the one person he knew in the city lived. He knew how to get there because he had visited Eugene for a week the summer before.

It was after dark when Winston finally arrived. He slid through a narrow gap in the wrought iron fence, walked a quarter mile up the driveway that was lined with perfectly manicured nine-foot-tall shrubs, crossed underneath the oversized portico, and moseyed up a set of small steps to the French double doors. He knocked, then waited patiently for the butler.

Alfredo opened the door, recognizing him immediately as Eugene's friend from Cornell. "Winchester, how are you?" Alfredo asked, welcoming him inside.

"Good, Alfredo, and you?" said Winston without bothering to correct him.

"I'm doing just fine, but you are in desperate need of a shower." Alfredo guided him to the guest bathroom. "There's a towel in there, a fresh razor, and shaving cream. I'll leave a change of clothes for you on the bed you can change into before saying 'hello' to Eugene."

"Thanks, Alfredo. It's pretty late, though. Can I surprise Eugene tomorrow morning?"

"Certainly."

Winston showered, shaved, climbed into the silk pajamas laid on his bed, and went to sleep.

He woke the next morning to a gentle rapping on the door.

"Breakfast is waiting for you downstairs," the butler called.

Winston scampered down the stairs and into the kitchen, where Eugene was already eating at the table.

What's he wearing? Winston thought the moment his eyes landed on his former roommate. Eugene, spooning eggs into his mouth, wore a navy-blue striped suit that was a tad too big at the shoulders and a complementing burgundy tie with a Windsor knot riding dangerously high on his thin neck. His short black hair, parted down the middle and textured with pomade, made him look like a fifteen-year-old boy playing dress-up. He looked nothing like the dirt-covered, greasy, citronella-smelling bunk-buddy from two years before.

Winston watched runny eggs fall from the spoon onto Eugene's striped pants. Eugene quickly flicked the yellow semisolids in the direction of Winston, where it hit his silk pajamas, and Eugene's hazel eyes met his own.

"Winston!" exclaimed Eugene, rushing to give him a hug. "What are you doing in D.C.? I thought you were living in Long Island."

"I got a job at Bullit Inc."

Eugene busted out laughing. "I thought you had it all figured out in your hut on the beach."

"I did, but society wouldn't let me live in paradise." Winston took a seat across from Eugene. Alfredo had prepared a generous breakfast for them. There was a large pitcher of freshly squeezed orange juice, a glass carton of chilled whole milk, and plates full of

English bangers, scrambled eggs with cheese, baked beans, English muffins, and various spreads.

Why is life so hard? Winston mused, splitting open an English muffin and spreading margarine and lingonberry jam on each side.

"This is a complete one-eighty for you," Eugene remarked. "Plans change, I guess."

Winston watched Eugene's forehead crease in unease. "How are you doing, bud?" he asked tenderly. He knew Eugene was still adjusting to life without his parents.

"I'm doing alright." Eugene pulled his seat closer to the breakfast table and stabbed a piece of sausage with his fork. "Alfredo has been watching out for me and helping me at work, and Rosaline is still around, so that's good."

Winston felt a twinge of pity. Besides the baker, Eugene didn't have any friends. It didn't help that he worked so much, or that he had geeky interests. *Maybe it's a good thing I came to D.C. after all*, he thought. He could support Eugene, and Eugene could help him, too.

~

Winston leaned back in his chair and looked up at the ceiling. God was somewhere up there watching him. He was always watching and listening, apparently. Winston wondered how boring it must be for the Almighty to tune into this meeting.

Winston slipped his feet free of his flip-flops and rested them on an empty chair across from him. He wiggled his toes, hoping Mr. Tibbles would get a whiff. Winston lost count of how many meetings he'd attended in his twelve months with the company, but he clearly remembered Mr. Tibbles annoying him in all of them.

"Alright, let's begin," said Mr. Tibbles, wrinkling his little button nose. Many of Mr. Tibbles's features were little—he had little brown eyes, little elf-ears, little wrists, little pinkies with Lilliputian fingernails, and a little recession in his hair line, even though he was in his mid-thirties—but his mouth was not one of them. Winston found it big and obnoxious.

"We have two focal points for today," Mr. Tibbles continued. "Bullit Inc.'s retail marketing strategy and Bullit Inc.'s presidential approval strategy. In our last meeting, we acknowledged the need to increase the presence of our brands in stores and in the media. We mentioned it would be helpful for our brand image if someone important sponsored our line."

"Like Mr. Adams," Mr. Dinkle chimed in, referring to the president, who preferred to be addressed as Mr. Adams as opposed to President Adams because he was, as he regularly told his supporters, a businessman first. "It'd be great advertising if he wore Bullit Inc.'s clothing whenever he's on TV or in front of a camera."

"Should he dress in Fine-Line clothes or wear outfits from the more casual Sumner's Fun brand wall?" asked Mr. Sneffles, referencing two of the most popular fashion lines Bullit Inc. manufactured.

"It depends what message we want to convey. Fine-Line says something like, 'I'm adventurous and outgoing,' as if the president were ready for an urban American safari. Sumner's Fun, on the other hand, says, 'I'm hip and laid back, just like you.'"

"The adventurer card or the relatable, hip, and cool approach," said Mr. Tibbles. "Those are both good plays. I could definitely get behind either marketing strategy."

"Personally, I like the Sid's Style brand wall," said Mr. Dinkle, gesticulating wildly for no reason other than to attract more attention to himself.

Winston cringed. Mr. Dinkle suffered from heterochromia—his yellow eye was bigger than the blue one—and he had ghoulish, waxy, pale skin, flappy cheeks, devilishly woolly arms, and bulging veins visible in his head and neck. He looked like the spawn of Beelzebub. Everything he did attracted attention, albeit in a *Ripley's Believe It or Not!* kind of way, and Winston didn't think he needed any more of it. Flopping his arms whenever he spoke certainly didn't help.

"The Sid's Style fashion line is sleek and bold—reminiscent of the 1930s Glam Blanc fashion era," Mr. Dinkle finished.

"What's Glam Blanc?" Winston asked disinterestedly. It sounded like something Mr. Dinkle made up to try to sound smarter.

The other men exchanged looks.

"Are… are you being serious?" asked Mr. Dinkle.

"Completely." Winston was always serious, even when he was joking. "I've never heard of Glam Blanc. What is it?"

Mr. Sneffles shook his shaggy brown head in disappointment. Mr. Tibbles raised his eyebrows concernedly.

"Glam Blanc used to be a thing of the past," answered Mr. Dinkle, "but now it's making a comeback."

"That doesn't explain what it is."

"It's both tender and edgy at the same time, kind of like—"

"Think of it like produce," Mr. Tibbles interjected. "It's a fresh look."

"It makes a statement, like, 'I'm not afraid to get dirty, even though I easily stain,'" said Mr. Sneffles.

"Yes, great example," said Mr. Dinkle.

"That still doesn't explain—"

"Isn't the design team bringing back Glam Blanc in their brand wall next season?" asked Mr. Sneffles, cutting him off.

"I think so," said Mr. Tibbles. "That'll be sure to make the millions of Glam Blanc fashion fans out there excited."

"*Millions* of Glam Blanc fashion fans?" said Winston. "How can there be millions of fans for a fashion I've never heard of? What does it even mean to be a fan of fashion?"

"Unfortunately, the Glam Blanc fashion line won't drop for several weeks, so we can't market it yet," said Mr. Dinkle, ignoring Winston. "Therefore, if we want to dress the president, we need to use our current brand wall. Considering all our best-selling lines, I don't think we want to dress him in anything Freddie Powers. That line caters to the punk and emo crowd, who, despite being loyal customers, aren't exactly the type of people you want represented in society."

"I don't know," said Mr. Tibbles, "that could be a good card to play. The bad-boy president sounds like a great marketing strategy."

"Maybe Mr. Adams could be 'overheard' saying something edgy to make the president's approval rating go up," said Mr. Sneffles.

Mr. Tibbles nodded fervently. "What a great idea."

Winston was amazed at how consistently Mr. Tibbles managed to be surprised by things other people said. It was like adding coffee beans to a coffee machine and being astonished when coffee came out.

I need to get out of this meeting. Maybe if I out-absurd them they'll leave me alone.

"I think Mr. Adams would look best in a two-toned amber-caramel polka-dotted tee from the Sumner's Fun collection," suggested Winston sarcastically.

"It would make his beetle-green eyes pop for sure," agreed Mr. Tibbles.

"We could always accessorize him with some sexy shades from the Sid's Style collection," Winston continued, imagining how ridiculous the president would look if he wore any of the cheaply outsourced apparel that Bullit Inc. manufactured.

"I brought with me the planograms for both brand walls." Mr. Dinkle pulled out the seasonal catalogue for Sumner's Fun and Sid's Style. He placed them in the middle of the table so all of them could see the pictures of what items were currently in season. Winston looked at the sunglasses section of Sid's Style, which included half a dozen pairs.

"I like these black glasses with the white stripe," said Winston, pointing at the image. He envisioned Mr. Adams combining the glasses with an earthy Sumner's Fun shirt and a pair of brown corduroys. With his boyish haircut and receding hairline, he'd look like a middle-aged stinkbug.

"I think that would look very stylish," said Mr. Sneffles. "I'll send a note over to public relations with the SKU numbers to have them put together the outfit for the president to wear during his next media appearance."

"Well then, that wraps up our retail-marketing strategy," said Mr. Dinkle.

"I thought that was our presidential-approval strategy?" asked Mr. Sneffels.

"No," said Mr. Dinkle, "dressing up the president in our brands is a retail plan, not an approval plan."

"An approval plan is a statement, not an appearance," said Mr. Tibbles, backing him up.

"I thought it was both? We dress up the president to increase his ratings while promoting our newest clothing lines as part of our marketing strategy," said Winston.

"A retail plan that appears as an approval plan," exclaimed Mr. Tibbles. "What a brilliant idea."

"But Mr. Adams is going to be dressed up to promote a certain image," said a confused Mr. Sneffles. "Isn't that the same thing as a marketing plan?"

"No, his appearance is the approval plan."

"But you just said the approval plan is a statement, not an appearance," said Winston.

"His appearance *is* a statement."

"Then what is the marketing plan? Is that the appearance?" asked Winston.

"No, it's the statement."

"What's the statement?"

"His appearance."

"But you just said the opposite a moment ago!" exclaimed Winston. He felt like he was losing his mind. He gaped at his coworkers, amazed they had gotten so far in their careers. The fact that they were in the same room as him was testament to what could happen given hard work, perseverance, and a fraternal structure within the company that allowed questionably qualified, more senior people to rise to the top.

"You're going about it the wrong way," said Mr. Dinkle. Think of it like a stance on an issue, something that will keep journalists writing and intellectuals talking."

"An ideology," Mr. Tibbles blurted out.

"Precisely," said Mr. Dinkle, nodding vigorously. "Wearing our brand wall is more than a fashionable appearance or marketing strategy. It's a comment on the way things are today, and the vision the president holds for tomorrow. It's a political ideology, one that will increase our sales, revenue, brand recognition, and market control."

Winston massaged his aching temples. *A fashion statement that functions as a marketing tool to gain economic and political power?* He struggled to wrap his head around what that meant, but he also struggled to care. The crazy things his coworkers came up with no longer surprised him.

He gazed upwards at the ceiling and at God. *If you're up there—which you aren't because you're a fictitious character from an archaic book whose existence defies the universal laws of physics—but if you are, could you do something to get me out of this meeting, please? My plan of saying crazy things to make it through isn't working; my coworkers are too farcical. There's no way they are real human beings, although, unlike you, they are, which, if such fantastical ineptitude can exist, maybe it means you can too?*

Just then, a pimple-faced intern burst through the door, panting.

"This meeting is for the marketing department only!" cried out Mr. Dinkle in protest.

"Aliens!" the intern blurted before buckling over and putting his hands on his knees, out of breath.

"Explain yourself," Mr. Dinkle demanded.

The intern took a deep breath. "Aliens… are in the city."

Mr. Dinkle, Mr. Sneffles, and Mr. Tibbles looked at each other, flabbergasted.

Winston beamed. *There is a God after all.* He stood up abruptly. "Excuse me, gentlemen. This meeting is adjourned." Suppressing his grin, he rushed from the room.

As he stepped into the hallway, he looked up at the fluorescent lights in the ceiling. *Thanks, Big G, I owe you one!*

CHAPTER 5

Judge Willis watched the first rays of sunlight dance across the metallic hull.

John's going to want to know about this.

As he stood there in his black robes, mulling over the implications of a spaceship in the city, a fast-approaching siren wailed in the distance. Its shrill grew louder and louder until a policeman arrived at the scene on his motorcycle.

Judge Willis observed the officer push through the mob of people who had flocked to the Fairgrounds to take pictures of the spaceship. A sizeable crowd of several hundred had already gathered. As more and more people arrived, the last few parking spots along Schumaker Avenue disappeared, so newcomers simply abandoned their cars in the middle of the road. Before long, the Fairgrounds was packed like a rock concert, and if the blaring horns of stuck traffic harmonizing with the hoots and hollers from people trying to get a view could be considered music, it sounded like one too.

This can't be good. The police have a proclivity for rash and impulsive behavior when put on the spot.

Judge Willis held his breath. He hoped the man in uniform didn't do anything rash before John Angryberger had a chance to take advantage of the situation. He watched anxiously as the policeman walked under the metal disc, stopped, and scrutinized the ship's undercarriage, perhaps searching for a door to knock on. *Or break down.*

However, the ship was so seamlessly designed it was impossible to locate the hatch opening. Undeterred, the officer pulled out his baton and rapped on the bottom of the hull five times.

He paused. Nothing stirred inside.

He reached up and banged his baton on the hunk of space-metal once more. "This is the MPD," shouted the officer importantly. "You have been caught flying in a no-fly zone. You must provide me with license and registration, as well as proper flight papers."

When nothing happened, he took a more aggressive tone: "Failure to cooperate with police is a crime unto itself. I will not ask again."

Judge Willis watched with delight as the aliens flouted the policeman's authority.

"Open up or move your ship. You're parked illegally. I will not ask again," the policeman asked again.

"Officer, I think you should cut these gents some slack."

"*Chief,*" he corrected, swiftly swinging around to see who dared belittle his authority.

Judge Willis raised his hands to signal benign ignorance. "My apologies, Chief…"—he glanced down at the name on his badge—"Bagsby. Maybe instead of arresting them, we should welcome them. Who knows? They may be here to help us."

"Or they may be commies sent here to destroy us," Chief Bagsby retorted, placing his hand on his gun protectively. He looked up and down at Judge Willis's satin black robes disapprovingly. "Tell me who you are, civilian."

"But you already know who I am."

"A weirdo?"

"Ha! This"—he gestured at his hems—"is my professional attire."

"You work at a Halloween store?"

"Sometimes it feels like I do, but no, my office is the courtroom."

"That's why you're wearing a black robe."

"It's midnight sapphire, not black," said Judge Willis defensively.

"What's the difference?"

"It's ninety-nine percent black and one percent periwinkle. It's the fashion equivalent of steel, which is ninety-nine percent iron and one percent carbon."

Chief Bagsby squinted his eyes. "Your robe doesn't look steel to me."

"It's not steel, it's periwinkle and black."

Chief Bagsby's face screwed into a grimace. "There's only one judge in this city cockamamie enough to wear something like that. You must be Judge Willis."

"That's right." Judge Willis was the Chief Judge of the Superior Court of the District of Columbia, and therefore one of the most powerful judges in the city. He was known for being fair when it suited him to be fair, and ruthless in every other situation. He was also well connected. Among his best friends were John Angryberger—the vice president of the country—several state and federal Senators and Congressmen, and the city's District Attorney. He hoped that one day his links to many powerful leaders would get him an appointment to the Supreme Court.

"Your reputation precedes you," said the chief acidly. "It makes me wonder what you're doing here. If you're so important, shouldn't you be in your little courtroom with your little wooden bangy-thing?"

"I was on my way to the courthouse when I saw the giant flying saucer. I decided to check it out because, you know, I am so important. I figured the aliens would be looking forward to meeting me."

Chief Bagsby sneered. "You know, Willis, I have your dad to thank for getting me promoted to captain a few years ago."

Judge Willis simply smiled. He knew Chief Bagsby was looking to get a rise out of him, but he wasn't going to let him. He wasn't even mad that Bagsby had shot his father. He knew it wasn't personal; his dad taught him business never was.

Judge Willis's father—Papa Willis, as his friends knew him—was a resourceful, self-motivated man who lifted himself up from the lower middle class all the way to the upper middle class by operating a chain of unusually profitable laundromats, which were fronts for a larger drug-smuggling and hustling operation. Papa Willis convinced his son to go to law school so that he could help with the family business. Before Judge Willis graduated from law school, however, Papa Willis died in a shootout with police while resisting arrest for drug trafficking and tax evasion. The standoff lasted four hours. Papa Willis hid inside his laundromat, fighting off the horde of policeman, until a stray bullet hit the "on" button of the washing machine that he was taking cover in. He drowned to death while being power cycled.

Judge Willis sometimes lay awake at night wondering if his dad would still be alive if he'd hidden in a dryer instead. If so, Judge Willis would most likely still be working at Schlossberg Law LLC. It was only when the District tried to steal his inheritance, on the grounds that it came from illegal, criminal enterprises, that he decided to become a judge. As he prepared his legal defense, he'd realized lawyers weren't anything but glorified debaters, hagglers, and half-baked philosophers. Judge Willis admired a good lawyer, but they didn't have the same power as judges. No matter what he argued, if the judge didn't rule in his favor, he still lost. He learned that the hard way when his inheritance disappeared and he didn't become a proud owner of the laundromat chain overnight. Judge Willis swore in that moment to become the one who wielded real power; he wanted to be the legal and moral authority whose word was final. So, he switched which side of the stand he was on.

"I'm glad murdering my dad worked to your advantage," he said to the police chief, "but don't assume these aliens are as dim as my father. Treating them the way you treated him might get you demoted instead."

Chief Bagsby's face contorted with indignation. "These criminals—which they are because their spaceship is parked here illegally without a permit—are a threat to the city. I'll exterminate these roaches like I did your father. I'll be a hero," he blustered, "a legend for saving the city. Everyone will know my name, like Batman!"

Judge Willis shook his head disconcertingly. "Your ego is so fragile."

"Yeah, well, your father amounted to more than you ever will."

"I bear no ill will toward you, Chief," he said calmly.

Chief Bagsby went purple in the face. He opened his mouth then closed it just as quickly. His beady eyes flickered as his brain struggled to compute what Judge Willis had said.

"Whatever," he replied at last, "but these aliens need to respect the law."

Laws can change, thought Judge Willis, looking up at the spaceship in front of them. Hues of orange and yellow shimmered off the perfectly smooth exterior, casting a warm glow throughout the Fairgrounds.

I wonder what Papa would do if he were alive to see aliens come to Earth.

Papa Willis was a resourceful man. He most likely would have used the aliens' spaceship to transport drugs from one laundromat to another.

Judge Willis felt the corners of his mouth twitch upwards thinking about it. *Everything has a use. These aliens are no exception.*

CHAPTER 6

M r. Adams enjoyed a moment of peace at his stainless-steel desk in the Oval Office. He sipped boiling peppermint tea out of a porcelain cup, which he held between his thumb, index, and middle fingers. His pinky pointed to the sky, the same place his company was headed. In his other hand he held up his bank statement. It was a very big number with lots of zeroes and commas followed by a gazillion more zeroes. Mr. Adams put his tea down and patted his stainless-steel desk affectionately. He liked to look at his statement through the reflection on his desk; it made the number appear twice as big.

He smacked his lips contentedly. Although he was the president, he was a businessman first, and seeing his company booming brought him more happiness than lower taxes. He took pride in being a shrewd, unscrupulous, and successful entrepreneur who understood financial laws and all their loopholes. He was a rule follower at heart—and expected everyone else to be, too—except for when it came to rules that prohibited him from promoting his own self-interests, in which case he rewrote them. Mr. Adams saw the world in terms of black and white; there were things he could do and there were things that he could not legally do. His life experiences had taught him there were consequences to every action, and those consequences grew smaller the bigger and more powerful his company became. Mr. Adams believed so zealously in unregulated financial institutions that he considered himself a religious man and preached the meaning of life at every possible opportunity. The meaning of life could be represented by this universal symbol:

$

As he stared gayly at his bank statement, reflecting on how splendidly his presidency was going, a Secret Service agent burst through the doors. "Sir, there are aliens in the city!" he said urgently. "We need to move you to safety!"

Mr. Adams calmly put down the note. "Yes, I'm aware there are Mexicans everywhere. But I don't think it warrants having to move me somewhere else. I'm quite comfortable in my chair."

"No, sir. I mean there are actual aliens in the city, extraterrestrial beings, the kind that come from space."

Mr. Adams sat up straight. "Aliens, you say? What color are they?"

"Gray."

"Gray! Are you telling me there's *more* of them?"

"There's twelve of them, sir."

"And you're *sure* they aren't orange?"

"Why would they be orange, sir?"

Mr. Adams sighed. "Why do aliens keep landing here, of all places?" He rubbed his temples melodramatically. The idea that there were more aliens in the city distracting him from making business deals hurt his head.

"Are they doing anything bad?" he asked.

"Not that I'm aware of, sir."

"Then just leave them alone for now. I can't be bothered with other problems at the moment. I already have John Angryberger riding my ass on every deal I make. He doesn't think Bullit Inc. should be allowed exclusive government contracts with every country throughout the world. Can you believe him?" He shook his head in dismay. "I'm not going to let John and his company be part of my multinational deals. That defeats the whole purpose of business. Jmart is the second largest company in the world, and it should stay that way. I don't want him competing against me, especially when I'm so close to landing my one-hundredth exclusive trading agreement."

"Mr. President, we need to get you out of here and take you somewhere safe and secure."

Mr. Adams sighed again. "You said it's a spaceship full of aliens, the kind from outer space?"

"Yes."

"Then we're fine. Inform everyone to leave them alone. If it were a spaceship full of Mexicans, however, then I'd be worried…" His voice trailed off.

"As you say, Mr. President." The Secret Service agent turned and left the Oval Office.

Mr. Adams watched him leave. "What a waste of my time," he murmured to himself. "Like I need to protect myself from aliens. What are the little space goblins going to do, steal my money?"

CHAPTER 7

"Where is your mole?" asked John Angryberger.

"On her way," said Mr. Chartreuse.

"I don't like waiting for people who are late." John cracked his knuckles threateningly and stared at Mr. Chartreuse, who licked his lips nervously. Mr. Chartreuse stood six feet, four inches tall, almost all of which were bones and skin. He didn't have an inch of muscle on his body. His sinewy figure and greasy black hair gave him the appearance of a starving wolf, and his long, pointy nose and big ears only accentuated his angular canine physiognomy.

"I'm certain she'll be here any moment now," he said, averting John's gaze.

John turned his attention to the office décor. Every inch of the walls was covered in pictures of trains: some big, some small, some carrying oil, others carrying freight. Some locomotives in the photographs were old, dating back to the 1860s, and looked like senescent grandpas compared to their modern, sleek, and youthful counterparts. The KB Rail logo was emblazoned on all of them. John didn't remember what "KB" stood for. No one did. The reason behind the name of the company had died with its founder, Timothy "Tim" Tymin, the disowned cross-dressing son of train tycoon Cornelius Vanderbilt, seventy-seven years ago.

On the desk where he sat was a picture of the company's president, Mr. Chartreuse, dressed in a zoot suit and piano tie, standing in front of a jumbo train, his arms spread as wide as his grin. John couldn't stomach the photograph, so he made the mistake of looking up at the door, above which hung a dinky black sign with an ornamental white wreath wrapped around the edges. In chalk, Mr. Chartreuse had written the words, "My dream: To be the best train company manager in the world!"

John grimaced. *I don't want to be here any longer than I must.*

Someone knocked on the door.

"Come in, quickly," said John.

The door opened to reveal a mousy woman wearing ladybug sunglasses and a brimmed hat, and carrying a mug filled with sweet tea. Mary-Lou Anne, senior sales manager of Schumaker Trains and Oil, furtively glanced over her shoulder before squeezing through the doorway and scurrying inside. Mr. Chartreuse promptly shut the door behind her.

"Sorry I'm late, Mr. Angryberger."

You better be. The only reason he tolerated her occasional tardiness was because she was unwaveringly loyal, and he needed someone on the inside of Schumaker Trains and Oil to monitor Eugene. "Did you get what I asked?"

"I have it here," she said, tapping her left hand over her right coat pocket. "It was easier to steal than I thought it would be on account of the office clearing out to inspect the spaceship outside."

"Give it to me."

She reached into her pocket and produced a notepad. "I've copied everything from the blueprints into here."

"Fantastic," John said excitedly, flipping through the notepad. It contained numerous sketches and specifications of Schumaker's latest locomotive engines, including personal anecdotes written by Eugene himself. These notes would ensure that KB Rail's new fleet of freight trains were not only of the same caliber but better than the ones Shumaker designed.

"Good work," said Mr. Chartreuse.

Mary-Lou Anne's cheeks pinkened, and her fingers fidgeted with the hem of her sleeve.

John looked up with annoyance at his inferiors' daft sentimentality. "Mr. Chartreuse, I trust you can deliver this notepad to our engineers?"

"Yes, sir."

"I want to be updated when the new order arrives."

"Of course."

"And I want the new order to be delivered before Schumaker gets his."

"Absolutely. I'll tell our engineers that it's our top priority."

John stood up from behind Mr. Chartreuse's desk, walked around to the front, and held out the notepad for him.

Mr. Chartreuse accepted the stolen information from the vice president. "Mr. Angryberger, if I may ask a question… why the sudden interest in Schumaker?"

John looked at him coldly. Wasn't it obvious? But when he saw the genuine bewilderment on Mr. Chartreuse's face, he realized maybe it wasn't. Normally, he wouldn't have taken the time to explain his processes, but today he was in a good mood.

"As you know, Mr. Adams is preventing Jmart from expanding into new markets around the globe," he began, feeling his jaw tighten. "His trade deals exclude all companies except his own from establishing themselves in foreign countries. Until I figure out a way to become part of them, I'm limited to expanding my subsidiaries in America, and, since KB Rail is my largest, it has most of my attention. With that being said, our biggest rival is Schumaker Trains and Oil. Since taking over his father's company several years ago, Eugene Schumaker has made zero business moves, so he must have been plotting something big. Our market share has since passed theirs, as it should, but *that*"—he pointed at the notepad in Mr. Chartreuse's hand—"is his first major investment since taking over his company's helm. This purchase must be significant. If he's anything like his father— intelligent, market-savvy, and conniving—then he needs to be closely watched, and his decisions copied, so he doesn't steal the market back from me." Memories of Mr. Adams usurping his international business swirled like a destructive tornado in John's brain, and he slammed his fist on the desk. "I will not lose anything to anyone else!"

A covetous fire raged inside him. Mr. Adams knew he was a threat, so he was trying to contain him, but John could not be contained. *I'll take over every market, everywhere, and neither he nor anyone else will stand in my way.* He'd figure out a means to end anyone who tried.

John towered over the desk, breathing rapidly and loudly like a human ventilator.

Mr. Chartreuse and Mary-Lou Anne exchanged nervous glances.

"Sir, are you okay?" asked Mr. Chartreuse cautiously.

"Mr. Angryberger, whatever it is, we can help you," Mary-Lou Anne said. "Let me be your best mole, your favorite mole, worthy of helping you achieve your grand ambition."

John took a deep breath and exhaled slowly. *No one can be trusted. Everyone's every move needs to be scrutinized.* He took a moment to recollect his composure, then turned toward her. "Just keep up the façade."

"I won't let you down!"

"Mr. Chartreuse," he said, "when you get word—"

"I'll inform you immediately!" said the president of KB Rail, eager to show his dedication to the cause.

John nodded and stalked toward the exit. Mr. Chartreuse hurried ahead to hold the door open for him. "Good day, Mr. Angryberger."

John flashed a rare smile. "Good day indeed."

CHAPTER 8

Eugene couldn't stop thinking about the aliens. Their arrival was the most exciting thing that had happened over the past year besides witnessing the emergence of billions of Brood X *Magicicada septendecim* under a lunar eclipse. Cicadas swarm D.C. every seventeen years, but aliens come once in a lifetime.

Eugene was so enraptured by the aliens that the next morning he dropped by Winston's flat extra early and dragged him out of bed to introduce him. He was hankering to show off the creatures to his best friend and was disappointed when he found out Winston didn't share the same sentiment. Winston had paused in the doorway of Rosaline's Bakery and glanced at the aliens huddling in front of the display for a brief second before offering a small shrug and moving to the counter to order his breakfast. Eugene observed him, wondering what he thought.

"What does that mean?"

"What does what mean?"

Eugene shrugged. "That."

"I'm hungry and alien meat probably isn't safe to eat."

"That's all you can think about right now, your stomach?"

"Ask me again after I've eaten."

Eugene asked Winston what he thought about the aliens once Winston finished eating a muffin.

"I guess they're kinda cool. A bit freaky looking like all those devilish cicadas you had me get up at midnight to see. Although, in hindsight, I probably could have done with the sleep. I was really tired the next day."

Rosaline finished steaming Winston's hot chocolate and walked it over to him. Before he could take a sip, an alien deftly lifted a tentacle and plucked the cup off the saucer and poured its contents into its mouth. Winston and the alien locked eyes.

"No, Eugene, I take that back. Cicadas are way cooler. And alien meat is now on the menu."

For the rest of the workweek, Eugene had timed his arrival at Rosaline's Bakery to coincide with that of the aliens. He dragged Winston with him, who made a fuss about getting up at the crack of dawn but was happy once there to spend as much time as Eugene wanted observing the aliens so long as it made him late to the office.

As a hobbyist entomologist, Eugene's mind ran in circles wondering if the aliens brought any insects with them, and if so, what insects from other planets would look like. *Are intergalactic insects carbon-based or silicon-based? Do they have hemolymph instead of blood, or something else? Does their planet have an abundance of oxygen like Earth did during the Carboniferous period, and if so, did that cause them to grow to gigantic proportions?*

His curiosity about the aliens and their bugs didn't stop at the end of the day but continued into his dreams at night. He pictured the aliens hiding in their ship and he tried, like a secret agent, to sneak inside and see what bugs hid in the dark corners. Disguised in all-black clothes from Bullit Inc.'s Freddie Powers clothing line, he tried but failed to break into the spaceship. He even tried knocking on the hull, but no one answered. He crept underneath the struts and looked up, wondering if he could climb up one of the ship's legs and enter through a duct. As he gazed upwards, however, a football-sized tarantula with blue eyes and green fangs dropped onto his face.

Eugene shot up in his bed. He reached a hand over his heart, which pounded furiously. *Dang. That would have been such a great specimen.* Feeling too feverish to fall back asleep, he rolled out of his bed and got dressed. Besides, he had to wake up early anyway. It was Saturday and he was going bug collecting with Winston.

Eugene took his time getting ready. He grabbed an empty terrarium from atop his dresser and loaded nets and jars into his backpack in an organized manner. He double-checked to make sure he had everything packed, then triple-checked in case he forgot something. Once he was certain his kit was in order, he applied sunscreen on his face, arms, and legs, then headed to the Fairgrounds by foot.

Winston was there waiting for him.

"Morning!" Eugene called out, his voice bright with cheer.

Winston, eyes half-closed, yawned.

"Let's search in the hedges," said Eugene, referring to the row of shrubs that lined the edge of the Fairgrounds next to his office and railyard.

Winston held out an open palm in the direction of the hedges, indicating for Eugene to lead him there.

As they trudged across the lot, Eugene looked down and noticed the first flowers of spring. *That's odd,* he thought. *It's much too early for flowers to bloom. Stranger, still, that it should smell like spring.* He breathed in the fresh, early-morning air. The loamy scent was his second favorite smell after Rosaline's Bakery. It reminded him of when he was younger, when he would scour the same hedges for bugs while waiting endlessly for his dad to finish work.

He bent down to inspect the flowers protruding from stalks already several inches tall. There were exactly five of them, each five inches across, with four vibrant blood-red petals with dark blotches at their bases. At the center of each flower was a bright green stigma with ten rays, like a radiating star.

What are poppy flowers doing here? And why are they blooming two months early?

As Eugene contemplated their existence, he noticed goo on the ground. He touched it, and as his fingers felt the slime, he also felt faint vibrations coming from the Earth. They pulsed deeply and slowly, like a heartbeat.

Eugene lifted his head and searched for the source. There was only a spaceship and slow-moving trains leaving and entering the railyard next to the Fairgrounds. *The tremors must be coming from the locomotives,* he figured. Watching the lumbering giants in the distance, he couldn't help but notice how old and decrepit his trains looked compared to the high-tech ship.

He turned his attention back to the disc. Over the week it had been parked there, it had drawn less crowds every day, but this early in the weekend morning, pre-dawn, there was no one there to see it except a handful of joggers running along Schumaker Avenue. Morning was the only time the aliens ever left their spaceship, and each time they performed the same routine: go to the bakery, eat, and return to the spaceship. They had done nothing else during their first week on Earth.

Feeling tranquil, Eugene smiled at Winston.

Winston narrowed his eyes. "What?"

"I'm happy."

"I'm sleepy."

Eugene led him the rest of the way to the hedges then stopped. "This is as good a place as any. Let's start here," he said, and gently placed the glass terrarium he was carrying on the ground.

He put his backpack down next to the terrarium, unzipped it, and dug around inside. He pulled out two pintsized glass jars and two handcrafted, top-of-the-line butterfly nets.

"Are we searching for anything in particular?" asked Winston.

"I'd be happy to find either *Charidotella sexpunctata* or *Curculio glandium,* maybe even a member of the genus *Phyllophaga,*" Eugene answered, passing him a jar and net.

Winston tried his best to recall the insect names Eugene had taught him. "I know the first one is a golden tortoise beetle, and *Curculio* is some type of weevil, but what's the other one?"

"*Curculio glandium* is an acorn weevil, to be precise," said Eugene pompously, zipping his backpack, "and *Phyllophaga* is the genus for June bugs." He bent down to re-tie his shoes. His tough brown hiking boots were worn out from all his expeditions tramping around in the dirt. Combined with a tan shirt and wide-brimmed hat, Eugene thought he looked like quite the naturalist.

"You look like a booger," said Winston objectively, as if reading his mind.

"Jealousy's not a good look for you," Eugene retorted. He used both hands to scoop up some loose dirt and dumped it into the terrarium. He filled a fifth of the cube with dirt, then tossed leaf litter and grass on top.

Winston watched him lazily while sipping coffee from his Thermos, which was the only supply he had brought. Helpfully, he picked up a rock and dropped it inside the terrarium. "That's my participation for the day."

"I think that's good," said Eugene, looking at the terrarium's contents with satisfaction. "It looks like a nice home for any bug. Why don't you start searching around here, and I'll head over there." He pointed at the last shrub in the row of hedges along the perimeter of the Fairgrounds.

"Whatever you say, boss." Winston put down his Thermos and sat beside it on the grass, the jar in one hand and the butterfly net in the other. He rearranged his weight until he found a comfortable position. "Ah, perfect."

Eugene set off to his collecting site and within the first two seconds of inspecting a leaf had found a specimen. "Come over here and check this one out," he yelled.

"I can't. I just sat down."

"Don't be lazy."

"Gosh dang it, Eugene. You need to tell me to come over there before I get comfortable." Winston clambered to his feet. Begrudgingly, he ambled over to Eugene. His sandals made wet flopping sounds as they sucked at his heels like blind newborn kittens to a mother's teat.

Eugene held up his butterfly net to show Winston what he'd caught. Inside was an enormous pale green moth with two thick furry antennae. The outside edges of its wings were pink, as were its legs. As the moth flew around the net, they could make out four distinct eyespots on its back.

"It's a luna moth!" exclaimed Eugene happily, pleased with his discovery.

Winston faked a smile. "Neat."

"They certainly are. Did you know that adult luna moths don't have teeth or a digestive system? Their sole life's purpose is to mate and die within seven days."

"That sounds better than my past seven days. I worked for five of them. And no mating in any of them, but plenty of meeting."

"Want to hear another interesting fact?"

"Um…"

"They're so intensely attracted to light that on moonless nights, they'll fly toward man-made light, even if it electrocutes them. They're positively phototactic."

"More like positively stupid."

"It's difficult to comprehend," Eugene agreed. "You'd think that after witnessing so many of their friends being electrocuted by streetlights that they'd learn the difference between moonlight and more dangerous sources of light, and stay away from the latter. In some ways, it's like a tragic love story: the poor souls know how bad the streetlight is for them, but they love it so much that they can't stay away from it, even if it will kill them."

"Sounds more like an unhealthy addiction."

"Are they really that different?" Eugene walked back to the terrarium and gently lowered the luna moth inside. As he did so, a thought occurred to him: *luna moths don't normally emerge until May.* For some unknown reason, both flowers and bugs were appearing months earlier than normal.

"Hey, look at this little guy," said Winston, bending down and picking an insect off a leaf.

"Let me see!" Eugene shouted, darting back toward him.

Winston uncupped his hand. In his palm, he held an itty-bitty land snail no bigger than a couple millimeters. It had a translucent spiral-shaped pale-brown shell consisting of four whorls, on which Eugene could make out numerous small radial striae.

"*Punctum minutissimum,*" he said excitedly, pulling Winston's hand toward his face to get a closer look. "Good eyes, Winston. They're hard to spot, despite being relatively common. That's an excellent specimen. Add it to the terrarium so the moth can have a friend."

Winston walked over to the glass cube, opened the lid, and turned his hand upside down. The tiny snail fell unceremoniously into the cage.

After a moment, it began to explore its new home. Winston watched as it crawled underneath the nearest leaf.

"Eugene?"

"Yeah?"

"We're all just bugs in a jar."

"It's not so bad though, is it?"

As they scoured the foliage for more insects, the sun rose above the horizon, its warm gentle rays illuminating the spaceship and turning its metallic hull into hues of orange and yellow. The sunrise seemed to have scared off the morning joggers. No one else was there besides Eugene and Winston.

"I think that's good," Eugene announced half an hour later after they had collected a handful of beetles, katydids, a single June bug, and a walkingstick—bugs that don't normally appear until Summer.

"Gimme," he said to Winston, holding out his hand.

Winston passed him the jar and net, which Eugene put in his backpack. Once zipped, he slung the pack over his shoulders and gently lifted the terrarium off the ground. Before they began walking, he pointed at the Thermos on the ground, which Winston had almost left behind. Winston picked it up, and the two headed off to get breakfast at Rosaline's.

They'd barely gone more than twenty feet, however, when an eerie clang resounded throughout the Fairgrounds behind them.

The hatch to the spaceship opened, and an inordinate volume of air released from hydraulic pistons within the struts, creating a deep whooshing noise. The aliens marched single file down the ship's ramp. Once the last alien was on the field, the hatch closed, obscuring the interior of their spaceship in darkness. The aliens set off toward Rosaline's, their oversized heads bobbing up and down with each step they took.

Eugene and Winston paused to watch the early morning procession with fascination.

"Should we walk over with them?" Eugene said, rushing to catch up with the aliens before Winston could answer.

The aliens, recognizing the two humans, hummed as they approached.

When he reached the aliens, Eugene tilted the terrarium toward them so they could see. "Check this out."

The aliens twisted their heads and peered inside with their ginormous eyes. Noticing there weren't any muffins in the cage, only bugs, they disinterestedly turned their eyes forward and continued their morning pilgrimage toward the bakery.

Eugene frowned. "Why don't they like bugs?"

"Because bugs are dirt animals," explained Winston. "They're gross and freaky looking. Most people don't like bugs, and these are little people from outer space, so it makes sense they wouldn't like them either. In fact, I bet bugs don't even like bugs."

Eugene lowered his eyes. "Bugs *are* interesting, though. I wish more people would see their value."

Sensing Eugene's downtrodden mood, one of the aliens stepped out of line. It awkwardly approached Eugene and held out its hand. In its palm was a quarter-inch-wide black, white, and brown polyester button. The colors swirled together like vanilla and chocolate froyo.

"A button? For me?" asked Eugene, caught off guard. "Thank you."

The alien ran bashfully back into line.

"Oh, that's nice, guys. Give Eugene a gift, but nothing for Uncle Winston? One of you owes me a hot chocolate. I haven't forgotten."

Eugene held up the button for Winston to see. "Did you see that? That alien is like me, but instead of bugs, it collects buttons."

Winston thought about it for a moment. "Has it occurred to you that maybe, instead of studying bugs, you should study aliens?"

Eugene pursed his lips. "That... that's a great idea. No wonder they like you so much at Bullit Inc. You keep coming up with good ideas."

"Never talk to me about work on the weekend, Eugene. You know that."

They followed the aliens to Schumaker Avenue, on the other side of the Fairgrounds. A yellow Volkswagen Beetle raced down the street from their right. Eugene and Winston stopped to wait for the car to pass, but the aliens continued their mechanical march forward onto the road, ignoring the approaching vehicle.

"Watch out!" Eugene cried out, but the aliens ignored him like they did the car. Instead, as they stepped into the path of the speeding automobile, the alien at the front of the line pointed a slender tentacle at the car. Instantly, the Beetle stopped in its tracks as if it had collided with an impenetrable, invisible wall.

Eugene and Winston exchanged glances, dumbfounded.

"Was that magic?" Eugene asked.

"I think so…"

The aliens turned back to them, motioning with their tentacles for the humans to follow.

"How did they do that?" Eugene asked. "Is that even physically possible?"

Winston shrugged. "They're aliens. I guess they can do a lot of things we can't."

An unsettling thought crossed Eugene's mind: *If they can make a car stop instantly by pointing a tentacle, could they blow things up? Could they kill people? No, they wouldn't… would they?* The idea made him shudder.

With trepidation, he followed the aliens across the road and into the bakery, cautiously maintaining a gap between himself and the last alien in line.

The place was quiet except for an elderly gray-haired couple sitting at the tabletop counter facing the Fairgrounds. The man wore a white and blue striped button-down shirt and navy shorts, giving him the appearance of a sailor from Nantucket. The woman wore a white floral dress that paired well with her lilac nails and mallard-green lily-of-the-valley brooch she wore on her left shirt breast. They turned around when the aliens entered the bakery, and their eyes bulged wide with fear and surprise.

"I knew they did things differently in the city, but this is just crazy," Eugene overheard the lady whisper to her husband. "Are those things the A.I. I keep hearing about?"

"A.I? Those are E.T.," the husband whispered back.

"Hello, my cuties," said Rosaline, who had been waiting expectantly for the aliens and had already set out twelve lemon poppyseed muffins for them.

One by one, they took their breakfast from the plate on the counter, then moved aside to make room for the next. When the last alien had grabbed its muffin, they formed a perfect circle and took a bite in synchronicity.

"*Mmmm!*"

"Hey, Rosaline," said Eugene and Winston simultaneously over the drone of mmm-ing.

"Good morning!"

"You've been very nice to the aliens," remarked Eugene, noticing how their regular breakfast had been laid out ready for them, unlike his own. "Are they paying now?"

A grin slid across Rosaline's face. "Not as much as the BABKA will."

Winston looked at her blankly. "The Bob-ka?"

"I know! I can't believe it either. The BABKA is coming to D.C. It was just announced yesterday."

Eugene gasped. "Don't tell me you've been invited to the BABKA?"

"What's that?" asked Winston cluelessly.

Rosaline put her hands on her hips. "What's that? What do you mean, 'what's that?' Haven't we been over this a dozen times?"

"I apologize. I've been stressed at work doing nothing all day and tuning out my obnoxious coworkers. I must've forgotten some of what you told me about this Bob…thing."

"I thought we weren't talking about work today?" Eugene said, grinning.

Winston stared at him with half-open eyes.

"The Best All-Around Baker Kaleidoscope Award is the most prestigious award a baker can earn," Rosaline informed him. "The competition is held in a different city every four years, and it features the best bakers from around the world. Given the elitism and the fact that it's a long time between contests, those who win become baking legends. The baking goddess, Kaleidoscope Brown, won it four times in a row—every time she participated. She crushed every chef the French threw her way. Nobody has won it more than once except her, which is why the competition was renamed in her honor after she retired from competitive baking. And not just anybody can try to break her record; the BABKA is invite only. The competition is exclusive to the best of the best."

"So, were you invited?" Eugene asked excitedly.

Rosaline walked behind the counter. She bent down to open a drawer beneath the register, and pulled out an envelope, which she handed to Eugene.

Eugene set the terrarium he was holding down onto the counter so he could open it. Hungrily, he unraveled the envelope and dived into its contents. His mouth curved upwards into a humongous smile as he read the invitation.

"Rosaline! You're going to the BABKA!"

Her face turned bright red, and she beamed from ear to ear.

"This is amazing! You've always dreamed of going to the BABKA."

"Not just going but winning. I finally have a chance to become the best baker in the world."

"You're going to do it. In no time you'll be on stage proving to the world why you're the queen bee of baking."

Rosaline exhaled heavily. "That's the problem."

Eugene furrowed his brows. "What?"

"There's simply no time. The competition is scheduled for the second-to-last weekend of April, which is just under one month away." Rosaline reached her thumbs above her ears and rubbed her temples. "There are so many recipes I need to practice and get perfect. I might have to lay off the kush for a little while so I bake more quickly. Did you know each round in the BABKA is timed?"

Eugene nodded. "Do you know what you'll be baking? If so, you could focus on those recipes and save time," he suggested.

Rosaline shook her head. "We won't know what we're baking until we're onstage during the event."

"That's not ideal, but you're very inventive so I know you'll do great." He paused for a second, then asked—"By the way, is the competition looking tough?"

"It is," said Rosaline, her joyfulness waning, fading into a quiet, somber tone. "François Rivier will be there."

"Oh, no. Not François," said Eugene.

"Who?" asked Winston.

Rosaline huffed. "Winston, you're seriously out of the loop. François is only the biggest name in the baking community and the best baker on the planet. He's been ranked in the top-five baker standings every year over the past eight years and number one for the past three years in a row, according to *Baker's Top 100 Magazine*. People travel to France just to visit his bakery. He won the last BABKA four years ago, and is hoping to repeat this year, a feat only Kaleidoscope Brown has accomplished before, if you remember."

"Then he better get ready to be disappointed because you're going to beat him," declared Eugene.

"Aww, Eugene. That means a lot to me."

"I mean it. Your muffins are the best. Everyone in the city knows it. On all the reviews for bakeries, you're always at the top. You've won every local and regional baking award for the past few years, and no other bakery in the metropolitan area is rated thirteen muffins." He turned to Winston. "That's the highest rating a bakery can get."

A soft glow spread across Rosaline's face. "You're too sweet. Let me grab you two boys your muffins, so you can enjoy them before the rest of the city does."

While Rosaline got their breakfast ready, Eugene lifted his terrarium off the display and carried it to the counter next to the older couple who remained transfixed by the sight of the aliens. They jumped at the sound of the insect cage clinking against the marbled surface as he set it down.

"What is that?" asked the older man with alarm.

"It's a terrarium," boasted Eugene. He pushed it toward the couple so they could see.

"That's nice," the man said apathetically, returning his gaze to the aliens.

"Gerald," stammered his wife, "you told me the spaceship was an amusement park ride."

"Well, what were the odds a real spaceship full of real aliens would just be sitting out in the open?"

"As of right now, pretty darn good."

"How was I supposed to know that, Gertruda?"

"If you didn't know, you didn't have to make things up."

The man shrugged. "Well, what I want to know now is what those things are doing here."

"Where's your faith, Gerald? They've obviously been sent here by a higher power for a reason."

"Oh, not with that again…" He stared intently at the aliens, who were dripping thick globs of goo onto the floor as they licked their tentacles clean of the last vestiges of muffin. "I can't believe I'm saying this"—he glanced at the terrarium—"but those bugs are not the most disgusting things in this room."

"What did you say about me?" said Gertruda, her voice rising.

"Here you go," said Rosaline as she carried two hot chocolates and two muffins to Eugene and Winston. She peered over Eugene's shoulder into the terrarium. "Oh! What a pretty butterfly," she cooed.

"It's a luna *moth*."

"How lovely!"

Eugene raised his freshly baked muffin to his mouth and took a bite. He smiled serenely as it travelled down his gullet, warming his soul—it warmed his soul a tad too much, however. Something hot burned in the back of his throat. He coughed, and the butt of Rosaline's morning roach tumbled from his mouth.

"Oh, I'm so sorry, Eugene. I was wondering where I put that."

"That explains why the muffins here are so good," Eugene remarked sarcastically once he finished gagging.

The older couple, who had been bickering while Rosaline brought Eugene his ashtray of a muffin, turned to face him.

"Excuse me," said the old man to Eugene, "but how are you so comfortable with the aliens?"

"Welf," said Eugene, caught mid-bite, "over the week they've been here, they've been nothing but docile and polite. I don't think they bear any ill intentions." As he spoke, the image of the aliens halting the car flashed through his mind. He shook his head as if to push the thought away. "They're just happy, gooey, hungry creatures."

"I see. Are you their caretaker?"

"Me? No."

"Then how do you know so much about them? Are you a scientist?"

"Yes, I am. Or, rather, I was studying to become one, but through an unfortunate series of events, I ended up the president of an awfully large train and oil company instead."

"How unfortunate."

"Yeah."

"What kind of scientist brings a box of bugs into a bakery?" Gerald asked, gesturing at Eugene's terrarium. "Doesn't that violate health codes?"

"I was studying to be an entomologist, and to answer your second question, as long as the bugs are caged, I don't think bringing them in violates any health or safety laws."

"If you were to study the aliens, you'd be an alienologist," inserted Winston playfully.

"Astrobiologist," Eugene corrected him. "Alienologist isn't a real thing."

Winston's features morphed into a scowl. "You know, sometimes you can be a real know-it-all."

The old man pointed at the tiny snail glued to the wall of the cage with its sticky snail slime. "I've always wondered where snails get their shells from."

"That's a great question," Eugene said. "Hmm, let's see, where to begin? Or, I guess more accurately, when to begin? Half a billion years ago, all life was underwater. Various fish, invertebrates, and sponges developed scales, calcareous spicules, or platelets to protect their bodies from the highly salinated water and extreme deep-sea pressure, as well as to protect them from predators. Over time, platelets in mollusks fused together to form a single shell. Animals and their shells continued to change form and structure over millions of years, developing into the long conical shells as seen in the nautilus and tubular shaped conch shells, until eventually one evolutionary line developed into this guy here." Eugene gestured at the tiny snail on the glass.

"That's a neat story and all," said the old lady, shifting her weight as she leaned closer, "but the Bible says otherwise. The book of Leviticus says that God gave snails their shells to keep warm."

"That's not what I heard," said Gerald. "I heard that snails stole the idea for shells from a wise, old hermit crab. According to legend, the hermit crab used his entrepreneurial spirit to hollow out rocks, which he turned into shells. He made a business selling them to other animals, such as the turtle and the snail. He even sold his invention to non-animals, such as the pistachio. That's why the hermit crab is widely regarded as the most successful businessman of all time."

Eugene's face contorted into an expression of total confusion. "That's not... *what?* For starters, pistachio shells are an encasing, not a true shell. Secondly, a hermit crab doesn't *grow* its own shell; it uses shells from other animals—"

"Did you know that hermit crabs help each other find their shells?" Winston interjected. "They're nice, hermit crabs."

"Thirdly," Eugene continued, "a snail's shell and a turtle's shell are two different types of shells. A snail's shell is an exoskeleton made from calcium carbonate. In contrast, a turtle's shell is an endoskeleton, an irremovable part of the turtle grown from within, and contains blood vessels, tissues, and cells."

All the talk of snails and their shells must have tickled something in Rosaline's mind, because she burst into song:

> *I'm the inner layer, the butter-dough swirl*
> *Some call me nacre, others mother-of-pearl.*
> *Outside me, the ostracum forms the middle*
> *Calcified and hard, just like peanut brittle.*
> *Furthest from my center, exposed to the air*
> *The outer uncalcified periostracum layer.*

Rosaline finished singing her entomological nursery rhyme and nonchalantly returned to the display counter.

Eugene was flabbergasted, and he wasn't the only one—even Winston had paused snarfing his muffin to stare at her. While he was looking away, his hot chocolate disappeared.

"How do you know about the structure of snail shells?" Eugene asked her.

"She's smarter than you," the old man jibed.

Eugene ignored him. "Where'd you learn that?" he pressed.

"My cookbook. I learned the structure of a snail's shell in the recipe for snail's bread in *The Baker's Bible* by Kaleidoscope Brown. It's the only cookbook that specifically mentions the biology of gastropods. Kaleidoscope believed that the more knowledge a baker has, the better his or her pastries will turn out. 'Remember' Kaleidoscope wrote in her recipe, 'just as a snail's shell has three layers, so too your snail's bread should have three layers—a buttery roll surrounded by flakey dough coated with a layer of cinnamon vanilla glaze.'"

While Eugene stared at Rosaline in awe, the lady poked her husband with the sharp lilac nail of her index finger. "See, Gerald? You're not right about snail shells."

"Well, it's not like you're any righter than me, Gertruda."

Eugene returned his attention to the couple, whose quarrelling provided him with another opportunity to showcase his recondite and completely impractical knowledge of bug evolution. "Believe it or not, Gertruda's argument that shells keep snails warm holds some empirical truth. During periods of cold climate, such as during ice ages, snails would spend most of their time inside their shells to retain moisture and prevent themselves from drying out. In this state, they barely move or expend energy, which greatly reduces their need to eat and drink. It's a snail's form of hibernation, known as aestivation."

"So, I'm right then," concluded Gertruda. "God did give snails their shells."

"No, neither of you are right. What I'm saying is that between two wholly inaccurate claims on the origin of snail shells, yours is more plausible, but that doesn't make your argument any truer than his. God didn't create snails and their shells. Snails, like turtles and crabs, evolved to form shells through a process of natural selection, not through the intervention of an invisible supernatural deity."

"Oh, is that so?" said Gertruda defensively. "Well, if you don't think God is responsible, then who do you think sent the aliens to Earth?" She pointed at the dozen aliens huddling in the corner, who were now passing around Winston's mug of hot chocolate. "Were they just 'naturally selected' to come here?"

Winston looked from the aliens to his empty saucer. "Hey…"

"They came here on their own accord," answered Eugene matter-of-factly.

"You're wrong again! God obviously sent them here to deliver us from our sins. How can you not see that?"

"Why would God send us muffin addicts?" asked her husband, shifting to face her.

"Nobody has seen inside their ship. For all we know they could have huge powerful lasers in there capable of destroying the planet," said Winston, egging everyone on. "Maybe the aliens are scoping us out right now, waiting for the perfect time to launch their attack."

"There's no empirical evidence to support your claim that a higher power sent them here," argued Eugene, ignoring Winston. "You're positing an untestable hypothesis based on religious fallacy that has no value to the scientific community. If anything, we should be asking where they're from and how they got the technology to travel through space. Those questions are more useful."

"About as useful as knowing how snail shells evolved," quipped Gerald.

The old lady looked at Eugene with pity. "You sciencey folk are all the same. You only try to understand the facts of the world, not the reason behind everything. You probe and prod only to come up with explanations of how something happened but never *why*. You can't find motive, and how could you? It's impossible to find out through science alone. For that you need faith. As a scientist, you don't leave room for belief. Without it, you're simply a man lacking direction and purpose in life—a shell of a person."

That last comment hit home. Eugene's stomach knotted into a ball and a twinge of sadness panged his heart. Eugene felt trapped by obligations to fulfill his parents' wishes instead of having his own life. He felt like he was wasting away, knowing what he wanted to do but not being able to do it.

"That's enough, you guys. Any of your theories about the aliens could be right," said Rosaline from her post at the counter, trying to de-escalate the tension. "Nobody knows why they're here, and we probably never will."

Rosaline, Eugene, Winston, and the elderly couple looked at the aliens who had piled in front of the display counter, covering it in gooey secretions. They leaned against it in a state of comatose euphoria, their eyes glazed over like donuts.

In that moment, an epiphany came to Eugene. *It all makes sense! The reason why the aliens came here is obvious. The way they marvel at Rosaline's display case, the way they lick each and every crumb off their fingers, the fact that Rosaline's pastries are the only reason they leave their spaceship each and every morning, and the blooming of poppy plants outside...*

"Shells," said Gerald unequivocally. "They came to Earth for shells."

CHAPTER 9

Winston wasn't born Winston. He was born Teofilo Trujillo. His parents named him after a locally famous homesteader near the Sand Dunes of Colorado. Teofilo, who owned the largest sheep herd in the bucolic San Juan valley, was frequently attacked by cattle ranchers who fought him over grassland. But Teofilo didn't cave to their threats and intimidation tactics; as a result, the cattle ranchers burned down his house and stole all his money. Unfazed, Teofilo built a new house and continued to raise sheep, until eventually his sheep took over the entire valley, destroying the native ecosystem in the process. Inspired by Teofilo's steel nerves, Winston's parents named their child in his honor.

Teofilo's (the Bullit Inc. marketer, not the sheep herder) parents were Romani Mexicans who settled in a nudist colony near Crestone, Colorado. While he enjoyed the freedom his family's lifestyle allowed, he wasn't fond of being labeled as a hippie with its negative stereotypes. People didn't take him seriously without clothes on, nor when he told them his name was Teofilo Trujillo. So, Teofilo got dressed and changed his name to Winston Perry. Winston Perry sounded smart. Winston Perry sounded resilient. Winston Perry sounded like a name that commanded respect.

"Winston, could you make a thousand copies of this for me?" said Mr. Tibbles, dumping a stack of spreadsheets on his desk.

"Thanks," he added in a thankless voice, and waltzed out of Winston's office and down the hallway before Winston could respond.

Winston pulled out his trashcan from under his desk. Using his arm like a broom, he swept Mr. Tibbles's documents into the bin.

I hate Mondays. Where does the time go? The weekend had come and gone and with it, March. April was here.

Winston made sputtering noises out of boredom. He glanced at the calendar on his desk, wondering what was scheduled for today. *Oh, would you look at that, more meetings.*

His first one was with the marketing team to evaluate the branding plan for summer's line of goods, immediately followed by a conference with the teams from logistics and production. Winston expected those two meetings to run through lunch, after which he had seven more. In addition, there was a mandatory training by human resources on how to resolve conflict in the workplace.

He looked up toward the ceiling. *I need another intervention or I'm going to lose my mind.*

As if on cue, there was a knock on his office door.

"Come in," he said gratefully, happily putting his calendar aside.

A lady he'd never seen before sauntered in. She had silky, straight black hair that extended past her shoulders, radiant bronze skin, and wore red square-framed glasses behind which her dark eyes shined brightly. Her white button-down blouse had artsy black blotches on it like a Dalmatian, which was quite modish compared to her restrained gray business pants. On her feet were woven leather clogs the color of straw.

"Hello, Winston Perry. My name is Jenny Jane. I'm the secretary for Dominic Miller," she said, referring to the vice president of Bullit Inc. "He sent me to come get you. He'd like to speak with you right away."

"Why does the vice president want to speak with me?" Winston asked, puzzled.

"It's a private matter he wishes to discuss with you personally. He said it's very important."

Winston stood up from his desk. "Well, let's do this quickly. I wouldn't want to miss any of my meetings."

Together, they strode past rows of cubicles that stretched out endlessly like a languishing sea. As he walked down the dreary, colorless hallway, Winston couldn't help but feel like he was trapped inside a bad dream. *Some things are worse than death. This hallway is one of those things.*

When they reached the elevators at the other end of the floor, he exhaled in relief. The woman inserted a special key and hit the button for the top floor. They rode up in awkward silence, neither of them making eye contact. Finally, the doors opened, and Winston was immediately taken aback by what he saw. The penthouse hallway shimmered as water cascaded from the ceiling to the floor, flowing down the Italian black and blue tiles along the walls. Winston stepped out from the elevator and passed an enormous ivory washbowl perched on top of a granite counter. Behind it, a marble beam rose upwards like the trunk of an oak tree.

Secretary Jane led Winston to a pair of elegant onyx-lacquered double doors. To the right of the doors was a placard which read "Dominic Miller – Vice President of Bullit Inc." in gold letters. The wall outside the office featured ornate mahogany wood inlays with intricately carved geometric patterns.

Winston turned to the secretary. "Where's the president's office? I thought he'd be up here too?"

"The president works from home."

Winston understood. "Home" was a euphemism for the White House.

Ms. Jane knocked on the onyx-lacquered doors while Winston waited patiently behind her. The brass knobs were so finely polished that he could clearly see his reflection in them. He twisted his head left and right, stretching his neck like a boxer before a fighting match.

"Come in!" bellowed a stentorian voice from within.

The secretary opened the door and gestured for him to go inside.

Winston entered the humongous office. A beautiful crimson rug covered the floor, illuminated by the enormous bronze and glass empire chandelier above. Lavish floor-to-ceiling windows lined three sides of the office, providing an impressive view of the city below. Winston could see the Lincoln Memorial, the Washington Monument, and Eugene's railyard in the distance, as well as the spaceship that reflected sunlight so strongly it caused Winston to squint.

"Winston Perry, it's so good to finally meet you," said Dominic Miller, standing up from behind his desk and extending his hand. As the vice president of Bullit Inc., Dominic Miller was the second-most-powerful person in the world. He was an ugly but well-dressed man in his early fifties. He wore a fine black pinstriped suit that epically failed to hide his pudginess. A bright green tie hung from his neck, which, along with his unusually far-apart eyes, gave him the appearance of a reptile. His dark black pupils betrayed a deep, insatiate hunger. Whether he was hungry for another meal or for something else, however, Winston couldn't tell.

"It's a pleasure to meet you, Mr. Miller," said Winston, devoid of emotion.

"Mr. Miller? Ha! That makes me feel old. Call me Dominic."

"Okay, Dominic."

"How are you?" he asked in his booming voice, gesturing with a hairy hand for Winston to sit in one of the leather chairs across from him.

"Seeing what it's like up here made me feel worse than I did down there," Winston answered, taking a seat across from the vice president.

"Good to hear," Dominic said absently. "Now, do you have a moment to talk?"

It was a rhetorical question; Winston had no choice. "No," said Winston, pushing his luck.

"Excellent. I have bad news, and I have good news." He looked at Winston for some sort of reaction.

Winston sat there motionless, anaesthetized, apathetic. *Only twenty-seven thousand, six hundred seconds to go* he calculated, counting down the time until 5 p.m. He took a massive breath and held it, hoping that doing so would slow down his heart rate and induce a state of aestivation while he waited for the VP to tell him what the news was.

"The bad news," the vice president said gravely, "is that the director of marketing, Mr. Bradford, is no longer with us." Once again, he looked at Winston expectantly. When Winston didn't ask what happened, he added, "He's dead."

"That's too bad."

"It is indeed." Dominic shook his head mournfully. "But at least he died a happy man."

"It's always good to die when the chemicals are in your favor," said Winston.

A silence came between them.

"Don't you want to know how he died?"

"How did he die?"

"In a bad golfing accident. He swung his driver, and the golf ball exploded in his face, sending shrapnel through his eyes and into his frontal lobe, killing him right there, on the thirteenth hole—a par five."

"That's a terrible way to go."

"Yes, I know. He was a tremendous golfer and an even better marketing director. He will be deeply missed by all of us at Bullit Inc. The only respite from our mourning is knowing that he died while doing what he loved."

"I thought he loved work."

"He loved that too."

"Then the real tragedy is that he couldn't die twice—first in a golfing accident and then while working."

"It saddens me deeply," said the vice president without a morsel of remorse, "but, without death there cannot be life, just as there cannot be good news without bad news."

Winston sunk deeper into his chair. "What's the good news?"

"We need a new director of marketing."

"You want me to be the new director of marketing?"

"We want you to be the new director of marketing."

"Why me?"

Dominic let out a booming laugh. "Most people wouldn't question a promotion. Well, let's see. A few reasons come to mind. You're adept at leading those bumbling knuckleheads in the marketing department. Every report you've delivered has been succinct and easy to read—directness is a great quality to possess in a fast-paced work environment. You may not have much initiative, but you're prompt and proficient at completing tasks. What I need isn't a freethinker but someone who can follow directions to a 'T'. Someone like you, Winston."

Winston closed his eyes. He hated being promoted. Promotions required him to learn new things he didn't want to learn. They also came with expectations of a more spirited work ethic. *Why does this always happen to me? I just can't catch a break!*

Winston opened his eyes. "I refuse."

The vice president let out another booming laugh. "It wasn't a choice, Winston."

Winston let his head fall forward in defeat.

"There's one more thing." Dominic reached into the lower left drawer of his desk and pulled out an envelope. "This is for the director of marketing. It's yours."

Winston plucked the envelope from Dominic's hand. It was addressed to Mr. Bradford.

"This doesn't have my name on it."

"Never mind who it's addressed to," he said, waving his hand dismissively. "The important thing is that it gets to the person occupying the position, and that would be you. Besides, the dead guy wouldn't have wanted to go anyway. He didn't like parties."

Winston flipped the envelope over and unsealed it. He pulled out an ivory-white invitation. In gold letters, it read:

BULLIT INC. CORDIALLY INVITES YOU TO

THE GALA UNDERNEATH THE SPACESHIP

JOIN US FOR A NIGHT OF NETWORKING, LIVE MUSIC, AND DELICIOUS TREATS CATERED BY ROSALINE'S BAKERY TO

CELEBRATE BULLIT INC. ACHIEVING ITS 100TH EXCLUSIVE
TRADING AGREEMENT. THERE WILL ALSO BE A CHANCE TO
MEET SOME VERY SPECIAL GUESTS—OUR GRAY FRIENDS FROM
OUTER SPACE!

SATURDAY, MAY 1ST
8 P.M. – MIDNIGHT

THE FAIRGROUNDS
(OFF SCHUMAKER AVE)

PLEASE CONTACT JENNY JANE TO RSVP.

Her phone number was printed along the bottom in smaller print.

Winston looked up. "How many people were invited?"

"Two thousand five hundred of the top businesspeople from all over the globe."

"May first… that's in less than four weeks."

"One week after the BABKA."

Winston blew out air like a deflated balloon. "Do I have to go?"

"Yes, and you'll need to RSVP."

"Can't I just tell your secretary that I'd like to attend on my way out?"

"Is that what it said to do in the invitation?"

Winston glanced at the letter. "It gives her phone number."

"Then call her."

"But I could just tell her right now…"

"As director of marketing, it is more important than ever that you follow the rules rather than trying to do your own thing," Dominic warned. He stood up and extended his hand. "Congratulations on your promotion, Winston. We hope you continue serving Bullit Inc. with gusto."

Winston shook his hand. *Only if it helps get me to my straw hut on the beach sooner.*

"Ms. Jane will see you out."

The secretary rose from her desk when she saw Winston exit the onyx double doors and led him to the elevator.

"The vice president will send you more information regarding your duties in the upcoming days. As director of marketing, you will now report directly to him. He'll meet with you and other department heads bi-weekly to check on your division's projects and performance."

"More meetings… how lovely."

The door to the elevator opened and Winston stepped inside. "You know, Winston, it's truly amazing how fast you've risen through the ranks in such a short time."

"Yes, how truly amazing for me." He hit the button for his floor, and the doors began to close.

Unexpectedly, Ms. Jane leaned into the elevator. "You're close to the top," she whispered. "Don't slip now."

Winston recoiled, caught off guard. "What does that mean?" But it was too late. The elevator doors had already closed.

CHAPTER 10

The next morning, Eugene lay on his back with his hands behind his head, gazing happily at the underside of the space-ship as he waited for the aliens to emerge. *Maybe the football-sized tarantula from my dream will drop on my face,* he secretly hoped.

A familiar whoosh of cold air sounded from the pistons within the ship, and the hatch opened. Eugene sat up excitedly, reached down, and felt the fanny pack around his waist. *Tape measure, note pad, pen, magnifying glass, scale… all there.* He felt a teensy bit nervous and wanted to make sure he was prepared for his first day as, what Winston called, an alienologist.

He moved aside as the aliens walked down the ramp one after the other like models on a runway. They watched him with an air of disinterest mixed with mild annoyance; it was as if they knew he was about to bother them.

"Hey, guys. Would it be okay if I took some measurements today?" Eugene asked energetically, taking out his tape measure.

The aliens didn't stop.

"It'll only take a moment," he called out, but they ignored him.

"Alright, I guess I can get your heights while you walk," said Eugene, moving next to the line of aliens and invading their personal space. He pulled out the end of the tape measure and held it to the ground as the aliens marched past. "Three feet, two inches." He scribbled the measurement in his notepad.

The second to last alien stopped at the tape measure and held out a tentacle for Eugene. He noticed something in its palm.

"What's this?" He picked it up and inspected it. It was a worn four-holed orange sew-through button.

"Another button? Thank you," said Eugene affectionately. "Maybe I should call you 'Buttons.'"

The alien let out a nerdy smile.

The alien behind it pushed it forward.

Eugene sprinted toward the front of the line and took out a pocket-sized scale Rosaline had lent him. Even though the scale was small enough to fit inside a fanny pack, it was a top-of-the-line balance able to mass bulk loads up to twenty kilograms. He tossed it down in the path of the lead alien.

"Eighteen kilograms. About the mass of a five-year-old child or a medium-sized dog."

The alien cast a dirty look at Eugene and stopped walking. All the aliens behind it did the same.

"Thanks for stopping. Now let me see your tentacle arms," he said, blissfully nescient of their feelings.

He reached forward and touched the alien's double-pronged arm, then turned it around in his hand until the suction-cup-like suckers were facing him. He counted how many there were, then used his tape measure to record the size of each sucker.

"Twenty-four cups per arm, about a half-inch per cup, located mostly at the end of the appendage, not along the forearm. Confirmed tentacles, not arms." He looked up from his notepad and bent the alien's tentacle backwards in a loop until it touched itself. "That doesn't hurt, does it?" he asked gaily, staring into the alien's black saucer eyes. "No? Definitely no bones, then."

After jotting that down, Eugene looked up and asked, "you guys have special powers, right? Could you show me?"

The alien in the front of the line moved so quickly Eugene didn't have time to react: it plucked the pen from his hand and flung it into the sky. Eugene watched with horror as it sailed above his office building and flew out of sight over the city.

"Hey! That was my favorite pen! It's okay, though, I always carry two in case something like that happens." He pulled out another one and jiggled it tauntingly in front of their faces.

The aliens swarmed him. They took his tape measure, fanny pack, notepad, and backup pen and threw them as far as they could in various directions so Eugene would never find them again, everything except Rosaline's pocket scale which one of the aliens cradled carefully in its tentacles to be safely delivered to its owner.

Eugene put his hands on his hips and puffed the air melodramatically. "Was that necessary? Alright, I get it. You don't want to be studied like animals. Fine. Let's go get muffins." He fell into the back of the line and followed them as they marched toward the bakery. "But would it be okay if I went inside your ship to see if there are any bugs from outer space that you inadvertently brought to Earth?"

The aliens rolled their huge eyes.

"Wow, I didn't realize you were such divas. Maybe I should tell Rosaline that you want your muffins gluten-free."

One alien lashed out its tentacle at Eugene and slapped him across the face. Its suckers stuck there.

"Ahh!" Eugene shouted, staggering backwards.

His recoil sent the alien flying over his head like a punted football.

"Mmmm!" it squeaked gleefully as it sailed through the air across the Fairgrounds. Goo secreted from its tentacles drizzled over the field like a sprinkler. As the sunlight struck the crystalline droplets, a rainbow appeared.

Eugene continued to study the aliens every morning for the next two weeks. He was unable to conduct any experiments or take any measurements, however, without risking his equipment being thrown away and destroyed. He had already lost five tape measures, two fanny packs, a bundle of syringes, a camera, various swabs and test tubes, and a collection of petri dishes. He had even lost one of his favorite hats—a tan wide-brimmed hat with a flap in the back to protect his neck from the sun—when an alien slung itself off his face and accidentally catapulted the hat into the horizon as it flipped through the air like a gymnast.

Before long, Eugene's study of the aliens became limited to simple observations that he could jot down in his notebook. The aliens didn't let him touch them, measure them, or collect anything off them—not even swabs of their tough, rock-like skin or crumbs of muffins they left behind. Anytime Eugene found a crumb, which might contain a saliva sample, an alien ate it before he could secure it in a tube, vial, or dish. After several days of resistance and thousands of dollars in lost laboratory equipment, Eugene gave up trying to be an active experimenter and settled for passively observing the aliens.

Nevertheless, he still thoroughly enjoyed it. He treated the aliens like they were a new bug discovery, and relished in the novelty of their features and habits. He had written several pages in his notebook documenting their appearances, recording everything from general characteristics of their faces and bodies to speculations on the mechanics of their gait (he wondered how their strong, bony hips could support the fluid movements of their tentacles). He also noticed that a couple of the aliens had slightly different interests than others. There was, of course, the alien who brought him a button every third day or so (which he documented and traced in his notebook in its own section aptly titled "buttons"), as well an alien that loved to harass Winston. Eugene noticed that whenever Winston was at the bakery with them, a particular alien kept glancing discretely in his direction, waiting for him to look away. When he did, the alien would steal something from him, normally his drink or his food, but other times money from his wallet and even his car keys (the latter Winston only found out about when he watched his car drive past the bakery with twelve aliens crammed inside). The same alien also somehow once managed to remove a button from Winston's pants; it must have given it to the button-loving alien because the next morning Eugene received it as a gift.

The aliens rarely spent more than an hour at the bakery before returning to their ship where they remained for the rest of the day. That was the worst part of Eugene's morning, as it signaled time for him to return to work as well. Without fail, a knot would form in his stomach as he watched the aliens traipse across the street and disappear into their ship. The fun of being a scientist disappeared as quickly as they did, and he would say goodbye to Rosaline and Winston and trudge into his office with a feeling of emptiness inside of him.

On this particular day, as Eugene sat at his desk readying himself for hours of work he didn't want to do, he felt a surge of jealousy upon realizing he was surrounded by friends who, unlike him, had a clear plan for their lives. Rosaline had her bakery and her dream of winning the BABKA; Winston was grinding forty hours a week to ensure he would never have to work another day once he made enough money to live out the rest of his life in a hut on the beach; and the aliens, whatever they were doing here, clearly enjoyed their established routine. Everyone looked forward to their future, except him.

I hope my purpose in life is more than managing a train company, he reflected somberly. The thought of spending the rest of his life in his father's shadow filled him with apprehension. He hoped it wasn't his destined path, but he didn't know how to leave it. The anxiety of an unknown future slowly gnawed at him.

Eugene shuddered. He didn't like to dwell on his future because it made him feel uncomfortable. Instead, he thought about the only things that brought him happiness anymore—the mornings. As long as they were filled with aliens and muffins and friends, Eugene didn't need to wrestle with dark, scary feelings. He could ignore them and look forward to tomorrow morning instead.

CHAPTER 11

John Angryberger looked at his feet so he wouldn't trip as he stepped over another set of tracks, careful to avoid a loose spike that was angled in his direction. He continued forward another ten feet, following Mr. Chartreuse through KB Rail's railyard, before stepping over more tracks.

"There," said Mr. Chartreuse, pointing in front of them.

Forty yards away, their first new locomotive rested on the track, the acronym "KBR" painted in black and red on its sides. Attached to it were one hundred fully-loaded black oil cars, each carrying over thirty thousand gallons of crude. They formed a long line that extended nearly half the length of the railyard; the train was set to begin its first voyage from D.C. to Virginia.

"Is this where she's meeting us?" asked John, nearly tripping over the train track as he surveyed the train instead of watching where he was walking.

"Yes, she should already be here—ah, there she is."

Mr. Chartreuse waved at Mary-Lou Anne who was sitting on a coupler between oil cars, sipping sweet tea from a ceramic mug. She stood up when she saw them and set off in their direction.

She got up just in time. The locomotive's horn blared loudly, causing them to cover their ears with their palms. It lasted for several seconds before dissipating into the air. A momentary silence followed, then metal clinked as the couplers became taut with tension, and the wheels started to move.

"The conductor is running a bit ahead of schedule," Mr. Chartreuse remarked, glancing at his stopwatch tucked in his coat pocket. "But don't worry," he reassured John, "we're still surrounded by hundreds of train cars, so nobody will see us. Besides, the noise from the train will drown out our conversation."

"That's a relief," said Mary-Lou Anne, peeking over her shoulder with evident paranoia.

John, however, remained indifferent to being seen or heard. His thoughts were consumed by a series of setbacks he had faced over the past three weeks, a fixation he found himself unable to shake. Mr. Adams continued to stonewall him on international trade deals, and to add insult to injury, he had appointed a new marketing director, Winston Perry, who happened to be close friends with Eugene Schumaker. Despite consulting with Judge Willis for potential legal workarounds, John learned that nothing could be done about Bullit Inc.'s situation. Mr. Adams's actions were entirely within his legal rights as president and businessman. All John could do was wait for a potential illegal move by Mr. Adams, but there was no certainty if that would ever happen. To compound his woes, the president decided to flaunt his triumph by throwing a party after securing his one-hundredth exclusive trade deal, with Egypt marking the milestone agreement.

Turning from Mr. Chartreuse to Mary-Lou Anne, John inquired, "Mr. Chartreuse mentioned you have an update? I hope it brings good news; I could really use some."

"Um, well, it's not necessarily good, but it might not bad either," she said, fidgeting with a brown leather bracelet on her wrist.

John crossed his arms impatiently. "What is it?"

"You know how you told me to monitor Eugene's movements?" she began, then paused, waiting for his confirmation.

He said nothing, only stared.

"Yes, well, I noticed he has been coming in slightly late to work each day for the past two weeks. I was suspicious, so this Monday I decided to investigate his tardiness by climbing onto the roof to search which direction he came to work from, and at what time. He parked in the lot an hour before he entered the building, but instead of heading into the office, he rendezvoused with the aliens at their ship. Together, they trekked the block to Rosaline's Bakery. Using my binoculars, I spied him through the bakery's windows taking an extra-long breakfast, but he wasn't just eating, he was also studying the aliens. He hovered around them while they ate, writing down observations in the notebook he keeps in his pocket. When the aliens left, he followed them from the bakery to their ship. It was only after they boarded their ship and the hatch closed that Eugene finally entered the office. I continued to spy on him each morning for the rest of the week, and his routine remained the same—alien observations over breakfast until they left, and then head to the office late for work."

John felt the muscles around his eyes tighten. "That *is* interesting." He knew his rival was keen on collecting and researching bugs having dropped out of Cornell's entomology program—Judge Willis provided him with Eugene's background information—but he wondered if there might be some other motivation for the young CEO to study the aliens.

"Should I do anything about it, sir?"

"Continue to watch him and inform me at once if his studies—" John searched for the right word—"*progress.*"

"You think he might do something more than study the aliens?"

"It's possible he has a reason to get close to them, but I haven't determined what it might be."

"Maybe he wants to get his hands on their technology and make the ultimate train company," suggested Mr. Chartreuse.

"Oh my God," said Mary-Lou Anne. "We must stop him and get our hands on it first!"

John felt a lightbulb go off in his brain as he surveyed his underlings. They had just connected two dots he didn't know existed. If what they were saying was right, then Eugene was much more calculating than he had realized. John would have to figure out a way to get a hold of the aliens' technology before him.

John shifted his attention to the train in the distance. It had left the railyard and was gathering speed as it headed south out of the city.

"At least the new locomotives have arrived," he said, watching the train meander down the track. It made a big right-hand turn, and John could see the locomotive in front pulling all the oil cars behind it.

"It's beautiful, isn't it?" said Mr. Chartreuse, his eyes twinkling.

It's the one good thing I've got going on, thought John. The train wasn't just pulling one hundred oil cars; it was also pulling KB Rail even further ahead of Schumaker Trains and Oil.

The train continued its sweeping turn until it was fully perpendicular to the railyard. As they watched it, a tiny orange light appeared at the front of the train on the locomotive's nose. John squinted, trying to make out what it was. At first, he thought it was the reflection from the sun, but the orange glow quickly grew brighter and larger until it was the size of the entire locomotive.

The train suddenly came to a stop. The conductor, a tiny, faraway speck, jumped from the driver's cab.

A moment later, the locomotive erupted into flames. John watched in horror as smoke rose into the sky. Thick, bilious black clouds formed as the orange fire grew bigger and brighter.

"He needs to run," said Mr. Chartreuse, whose eyes had become as big as the inferno.

Mary-Lou Anne's face turned white. She swung toward Mr. Chartreuse. "You don't think he made it?"

"It's not whether he made it, but if he will *make* it."

"What do you—"

Mr. Chartreuse didn't have time to explain because it happened so quickly. The locomotive exploded, and a deafening bang resounded throughout the area. A split-second later, the lead oil car also exploded, but with an even greater intensity than the locomotive. A second bang, and then the second oil car exploded, followed by another thunderous shock, then the third car, and so on until the entire train was one long burning carcass.

John's blood was already hot when he showed up to the railyard; now it was perfectly scalding. As his insides smoldered, a miracle happened, something John thought impossible—his anger reached its limit. He couldn't possibly become any angrier, so he became numb instead, and his blood turned to ice in his veins.

The only good thing to happen to him over the past few days was gone.

Schumaker. The name popped into his brain at once. *He must have known. He must have tricked me.*

He cast his back on the conflagrant train and headed out of the railyard. He could hear Mr. Chartreuse whispering behind his back to Mary-Lou Anne: "No, don't ask how he's doing. Let him walk away. You don't want him to channel his rage at us, do you?"

He made a mental note to call Judge Willis. *Schumaker will pay for this.*

CHAPTER 12

"This is a toothpick," said Rosaline, holding the slender pointy-stick in her hand. "A plain, brown one you can buy in bulk. Now, what you do is gently push it in… no, not into your friend's arm, into the muffin. Yeah, there you go. Okay, now slowly pull it out, and if it looks clean like this—" she held up the toothpick which didn't have any batter sticking to it—"it means the batch is ready. We can pull them out of the oven and put them on a cooling rack by the apricot bread."

Rosaline, squatting in front of the oven, looked around for her oven mitt. She spotted it on the head of one of the aliens who wore it like a hat. Rosaline pulled it off its head and put it on her hand so she could take out the muffin tray without burning herself. After she put the tray on the rack, she returned the mitt to the alien who put it back on. He only wore it for a second before another alien with a pair of tongs pinched it off his head and ran away with it. Rosaline watched them with amusement as they chased each other in circles around a baking rack.

The doorbells jingled in the storefront. Rosaline poked her head out from the kitchen; twelve little heads followed suit and peeked out from underneath her apron. Together, they watched Eugene and Winston enter the bakery.

Winston closed the door behind him, then looked toward

Rosaline and raised his eyebrows at the sight. "What's going on back there?"

"I *told* you it was strange the aliens didn't come out of their ship this morning," said Eugene. "They were already here."

"I'm teaching them how to bake," Rosaline answered, exiting the kitchen alone.

Behind her, an alien pressed its tentacles into the spongy center of a muffin. While it was distracted, another alien crept up from behind and threw flour in its face. The flour-covered alien lunged at the other, resulting in a cascade of clanking pans bouncing off the kitchen tile.

"There goes their third batch of muffins," said Rosaline, laughing. "The previous two didn't turn out so well, either."

"Have they been helping all morning?" Eugene asked.

"Yup. I've been showing them how to measure and cut things. They helped me mix the ingredients and pour them into the muffin tray. Their flexible tentacles made the process quick and easy." She folded her apron and tucked it into a cubbyhole.

Eugene recoiled at the potent aroma of marijuana wafting off her clothes. "Did you also teach them how to hit a joint?" he said, raising his eyebrows suspiciously.

She grinned. "Their sticky tentacle goo is really good at holding papers together. Isn't that right, my cute little puff pastries?" The kitchen aides looked up at her affectionately with bloodshot eyes.

"What did you bake for us today?" Eugene asked. He and Winston had been her unofficial taste-testers for the past couple weeks as Rosaline practiced her recipes for the BABKA.

"Another of Kaleidoscope's recipes. Here, I'll show you."

Rosaline retreated into the kitchen, which resembled a warzone. She stepped over pots and pans scattered on the floor like children's toys. Her shoes left footprints in the lake of flour covering the kitchen tiles. When she reached the counter on the other shore, she reached for the shelf above her workbench where she kept a small collection of cookbooks. She pulled down her favorite one. On the cover was an image of Kaleidoscope when she was in her early sixties, pulling a fresh loaf of bread out of the oven, a giant spliff hanging from the corner of her mouth.

Rosaline looked at the photograph and smiled. She attributed her interest in baking at an early age to *The Baker's Bible*. The three-hundred-page cookbook did more than teach how to make croissants and crème brûlée flambé; it was also full of recipes on morality, tolerance, love, and open-mindedness. It's no wonder, therefore, that the hemp-bound compendium became an international bestseller, retailing even more copies than culinary staples like *It's Fine Just Eat it*, *Little Kitchen Big Mess*, *Oops I Burned it Again*, *Ganja Gumbo*, and *Friends with Benedicts*.

Rosaline opened *The Baker's Bible* to the table of contents. Beneath the chapter on snail's bread, she found her favorite section, the only one she had drawn hearts by: muffins. She flipped the pages until she came to the recipe for lemon poppyseed muffins, the ones she baked daily. She had no shame in using Kaleidoscope's recipe exactly as written. As far as Rosaline was concerned, it was flawless. Nothing needed to be added or taken away. There were no shortcuts to be found; baking one degree Fahrenheit more or less than intended would make the muffins turn out worse. It was a perfect recipe, and it looked like this:

<u>Ingredients</u>:
    $\frac{1}{2}$ cup sweet, creamy butter
    2/3 cup sugar
    2 large eggs from a Zen hen
    $1\frac{1}{3}$ cups flour
    1 teaspoon baking powder
    $\frac{1}{2}$ teaspoon baking soda
    2 tablespoons poppyseeds
    2 lemons, grated into zest
    $\frac{1}{4}$ teaspoon salt from the Great Salt Lake, a perfect place for spiritual awakening
    $\frac{1}{2}$ cup buttermilk
    2 tablespoons lemon juice

1 teaspoon Mexican vanilla
1 gram of Starlight Kush

<u>Directions</u>:

1. Preheat oven to 350°F
2. In a large bowl, mix the butter and sugar until thoroughly blended.
3. Add the egg yolks, beating after each addition. Save the whites of the eggs in a different bowl and mix those until they rise.
4. Combine the poppyseeds, lemon zest, and Starlight Kush, and stir with love until thoroughly mixed.
5. Add the buttermilk, lemon juice, and vanilla. Stir.
6. Add the egg whites. Whisk vigorously for two minutes until solution is aerated and light.
7. Spray the muffin trays with nonstick cooking spray. Spoon the batter into each hole in the tray, adding it until each spot is ¾ of the way full.
8. Bake for 25 minutes. The muffins will be done when a toothpick inserted into the center is pulled out clean.

At the bottom of the recipe were comments by Kaleidoscope:

There's an adage in science that when looking for an explanation, the simplest answer is usually the right one. Culinary scientists also abide by Occam's Razor. Oftentimes, it's not the most complex pastry that tastes the best, nor the one with the most exotic ingredients, but the simplest meal. Even after my long journey exploring the deepest, darkest, and most esoteric corners of the baking world, I always find myself coming back to the simple pleasures of a Starlight Lemon Poppyseed Muffin. Nothing feels more like home. Nothing is easier to love.

Rosaline brought the book from the kitchen and set it down in front of Winston. He opened to a random page and began browsing the photographs of food, not bothering to read the recipes.

While he flipped through *The Baker's Bible* as if it were a picture book, she returned to the kitchen and transferred a loaf of apricot bread from the cooling rack to a plate and cut it into slices.

"Try this and tell me what you think," she said a moment later, rounding the kitchen corner and passing the boys a slice.

"Wow! This is amazing," said Eugene.

"Exceptionally scrumptious," said Winston without looking up.

Rosaline found herself blushing. "You two are too nice. How does it compare to the scones from yesterday?"

"I don't know how you can compare them. They're both so different," said Eugene.

"I mean, which one did you like better?"

"I liked them both equally."

"Me too," added Winston unhelpfully.

"You guys. If one is better than the other, I need to know so I can prioritize accordingly."

"They're equally delicious," said Eugene.

"I equally agree."

"You're no help," she said, slightly annoyed with them but feeling flattered nonetheless.

The aliens left their mess in the kitchen and scurried over to Eugene and Winston's table where they pulled on Rosaline's leg impatiently.

"Give me a second," she said to Eugene and Winston. She returned to the kitchen where she took a second loaf of apricot bread from the cooling rack. The aliens followed her. Rosaline exited with a loaf in her hand and twelve aliens bumping into her heels grasping for the bread just out of their reach. Rosaline waited until she was standing next to Eugene and Winston's table before handing it to them. Effortlessly, the aliens tore the loaf into twelve identical clumps and shared it amongst themselves. As they took their first bites, their tentacles congealed. Goo dripped onto the floor like rain pattering a window.

"I'll get the mop..." Rosaline muttered, accustomed to the morning cleanup routine.

As she was mopping up the puddle, the doorbells jingled a second time, and a middle-aged man in black satin robes entered the bakery. "So, this is the popular establishment the aliens frequent," he remarked, turning up his nose. "A tad dingy if you ask me."

Rosaline paused what she was doing. She stood with the mop in hand, the twelve aliens huddling around her like kindergartners. The visitor scanned the shop before resting his eyes on her.

"You must be Rosaline," he said. His eyes shifted down to the aliens and then to the puddle of fluid at their feet, and he cringed. "Clean that up," he said disgustedly.

Rosaline scoffed. "Excuse you?"

Winston flipped a page in the recipe book. The motion caught the attention of the visitor, who fixed his stare on him. "Ah! What a surprise this is," the man said, ignoring Rosaline. "Winston Perry. Congratulations on your promotion."

Eugene cocked his head. "You got promoted? Why didn't you tell us?"

"It's not necessarily a good thing," murmured Winston, tracing the swirls in a photograph of a cinnamon roll with his index finger.

The visitor looked from Winston to Eugene. "I was told you would most likely be here too, Schumaker. How fortunate."

Eugene furrowed his eyebrows. "Do I know you?"

"No, but you will," said the man ominously.

Rosaline put down the mop, then corralled the aliens behind the counter. She eyed the robed man warily—there was something eerie and off-putting about him, as if he inherently couldn't be trusted. She stood in front of the checkout register, putting herself between the aliens and the visitor.

"Excuse me, but who are you?" she asked.

"I am Judge Willis."

"That explains the black robes," said Eugene.

"They aren't black, they're midnight sapphire."

"Hold on," said Winston, closing his picture book and joining the conversation. "Willis? Like the notorious drug smuggler, Papa Willis?"

The man wagged his finger side-to-side. "Now, now. It's not nice to compare me to my father. He was a businessman. I'm a judge."

"Clearly. You've been nothing but judgmental since you entered," quipped Rosaline. "Who do you think you are, insulting my establishment?"

"Yeah, judges are supposed to be impartial," added Eugene.

"If you're not getting breakfast then what are you doing here?" said Winston bluntly.

The visitor's lips curved upwards. Rosaline felt her shoulders tense as she observed him. She couldn't help but feel as if he was egging them on.

"Relax, Winston. I'm not here for you. Not now, anyway. I'm here for Rosaline. As a matter of fact, I have something I want to give her." He pulled out an envelope from his back pocket.

"Are you a mailman too?" asked Winston snarkily.

Judge Willis flashed a sly, devious grin as he handed Rosaline the envelope. "This one is for you, *mademoiselle.*"

Hesitantly, she took the envelope and opened it. Inside was a letter, which she promptly began to read. As she did so, she felt the blood quickly drain from her face, and she grew lightheaded. Clumsily, she put the letter down on the counter and stepped back, clutching her heart.

"Rosaline?" asked Eugene, alarmed.

"My bakery!" she cried out as the room began to spin.

"Rosaline!" shouted Eugene, rushing over to her.

Her legs felt weak and leaden. If Eugene hadn't put his arm around her shoulder to steady her, she would've fallen. As she leaned into him, she tried to regulate her breathing, but her chest felt heavy, like something was crushing her.

"It's okay, I got you," said Eugene.

She looked at him, then at Winston, who stood protectively in front of her. He picked up the letter she had put down and read it silently. As his eyes flicked back and forth, he clenched his jaw and the veins in his neck throbbed with anger.

"You can't!" he shouted.

"What is it?" Eugene asked.

"It's a notice to shut down the bakery indefinitely."

"I worked so hard to get it, and now it's gone! And right before the BABKA. How am I going to achieve my dream? Ahhh!" Tears poured from Rosaline's eyes. She wanted to yell at Judge Willis and make him leave, but the pressure in her chest suffocated the words before they could leave her lungs. All she could do was observe Eugene and Winston through her teary eyes as they defended her from the unwelcome visitor.

"What did you do?" Eugene demanded of Judge Willis.

"He came here to shut down Rosaline's Bakery."

"How can he do that?"

Winston scanned the notice. "It's because of the aliens. They aren't humans."

"What does that have to do with anything?" asked Eugene frantically.

Winston perused the document. "He's citing ordinance 4100.1.b, whereby any food service establishment that serves animals is in violation of municipal law for proper health and sanitation codes and is subject to penalties, including fines and closure.'"

"I don't understand what that means."

"What it means," Judge Willis said, "is that because Rosaline serves the aliens breakfast every day—aliens which are not human and must therefore be some type of animal—she is in violation of District of Columbia health codes. As a result, she has been issued a notice to shut down immediately."

Rosaline wailed even louder and fell to her knees. The aliens squeaked in alarm and zoomed around the counter to rub her back with their gooey tentacles to comfort her.

"You dirtbag!" Winston yelled, standing up and clenching his fists.

Judge Willis turned to leave. "Mr. Schumaker," he said over his shoulder, "let this be a lesson to never mess with KB Rail or any of Jmart's businesses again. The last thing you should ever do is get in Vice President Angryberger's way."

"What on Earth are you talking about?" said Eugene, his voice quivering. "I don't understand!"

"Don't play dumb. We know you sabotaged the blueprints. You're trying to claw back the market share that you've lost. And now your refinery is making a pretty penny since the cost of oil rose after the explosion."

"What explosion?"

"But we know what your *real* motivation is," continued Judge Willis, disregarding Eugene's question. "And we'll beat you to it. We are on to you."

Judge Willis opened the bakery door.

"Is this what you do with your time?" Winston yelled after him. "Rather than doing something that could benefit people, you make draconian laws classifying aliens as animals?"

Judge Willis spun around. "It does benefit people."

"Who?"

"Jmart."

"That's a business."

"Corporations are people, too," said Judge Willis mockingly.

"You sleazeball. How is Rosaline supposed to prepare for the BABKA competition this weekend without her bakery?"

"Oh, is that this weekend?" he asked, feigning ignorance. "How could I have forgotten that, especially since Jmart is sponsoring the entire competition. But don't worry, Rosaline never had a chance of winning against François Rivier anyway. Did you hear about his new chain of bakeries, Muffin Magic? They're the new best thing in the city. I suggest you give it a try. You might even learn a thing or two from eating there."

"She'd never eat at a garbage place like—"

"Oh, and did I mention Jmart is Muffin Magic's biggest investor?" said Judge Willis, interrupting him. "It's part of John Angryberger's portfolio diversification and expansion project. With that in mind, I can say with complete certainty that your chances of winning the BABKA are exactly zero percent." He tauntingly waved goodbye over his shoulder. "Au revoir, les nuls."

CHAPTER 13

By the time Eugene arrived at his office he was sweating. He had sprinted as fast as he could from the bakery once Rosaline had stopped crying. In the hour spent consoling her once Judge Willis had left, he had recalled a train explosion printed in the news two days before. Eugene wanted to find the newspaper and see if there was any information hidden within that would give clues as to what was going on.

John Angryberger targeted Rosaline, but why? What did Judge Willis mean by "never mess with KB Rail"?

Eugene wiped the sweat from his brow and frantically sifted through the papers on his desk. Freight contracts, purchase orders, weekly statements—he pushed them all away to the far edge, revealing a red envelope underneath addressed to him from Bullit Inc.—an invitation to the Gala underneath the spaceship.

This isn't what I'm looking for. Eugene scratched his head. He moved swiftly from his desk to his bug collection. He bent down next to the cabinet where he kept a stack of old newspapers for use as bedding in the terrariums. He hastily rummaged through them. *I know I've seen it somewhere. It was on the front page.*

"Aha!" he exclaimed, unfolding Tuesday's paper.

"KB Rail's Newest Locomotor Explodes Carrying 100,000 Barrels of Oil."

Eugene eagerly dove into the article.

KB Rail's newest engine, carrying close to one hundred thousand barrels of oil, exploded on its maiden voyage. According to investigators, the explosion was due to a manufacturing error. Misaligned dimensions for the motor head and catalysis engine caused immense pressure to build, blowing out the engine and setting off a chain reaction that caused the oil cars to explode.

Eugene frowned. *None of this makes sense. Why would John Angryberger think I caused this? I had nothing to do with it. Even if I had, why retaliate against Rosaline instead of me?*

He scanned the rest of the article then stopped when he came upon a picture of the locomotive with Mr. Chartreuse standing in front of it, smiling at the camera. The caption below it read: "The new engine just before its perilous maiden voyage."

That looks oddly identical to the ones we ordered, Eugene thought, puzzled. He examined the image more closely. The locomotive's windows were identical to the ones Eugene had ordered. So were the wheels, the axles, and the nose. In fact, everything appeared exactly the same, even the embossed sketch of a goldbug on top of the conductor cab. The only noticeable differences were the logo and the color—red and black instead of blue and white. *How could that be?*

Eugene didn't understand what that was happening. First his friend was targeted, and now his trains were surreptitiously copied. He didn't know why, he didn't know how, but most importantly, he didn't know what to do about it.

He looked up at his father's portrait for guidance. *What am I supposed to do, Dad? The vice president of the United States is angry at me for some inexplicable reason and taking his frustration out against my friend.* Images of Rosaline sobbing uncontrollably on the floor of her bakery flashed before his eyes. He clenched his fists with indignation. *None of this would have happened if I'd pursued entomology as a career like I wanted! This company has been nothing but a burden. I wish Judge Willis would shut down this company instead!*

He strode to the floor-to-ceiling windows overlooking the Fairgrounds and ran a hand through his hair. As angry and upset as he was, his problems could wait. *Right now, the most important thing is Rosaline and getting her ready for the BABKA...*

Eugene froze. A ghastly realization came to him as he recalled Judge Willis's baiting comment about Rosaline having zero chance of winning the competition. He suddenly discerned what that meant. Jmart wasn't just sponsoring the competition; John Angryberger had paid off the judges. The BABKA was rigged. Eugene ground his teeth in resentment. *This guy is trying to take away Rosaline's Bakery and cheat her out of a fair competition. Just who does he think he is?*

Eugene wanted to punch something, but he also shuddered at the prospect of having the Vice President of the United States as his enemy. Despondent, he looked at the spaceship below. He imagined an alternate reality where none of this had happened, where he wasn't burdened by familial obligation, where Rosaline wasn't ordered to close her bakery, and where he could do something to change their situation.

That's it! he realized, staring at the ship's highly reflective metal coat. *There's a spaceship full of magic-wielding aliens. Maybe I can't help her, but they can.*

Eugene rushed out of his office, sprinted to the elevator where he repeatedly smashed the button for the lobby as fast as he could—not that it made the metal box move any more quickly—and dashed outside. He raced across the dirt-filled Fairgrounds in his polished dress shoes until he reached the spaceship. Its hatch was perfectly fitted so that it was impossible to tell where the entrance was. Unperturbed, Eugene reached up to knock on one of the spaceship's strutted legs. Before he could, however, a rush of air hissed from the hull, and the hatch began to lower.

Did they know I was coming?

Ksssh! A piston sounded once the hatch touched down.

Eugene stood in front of it, waiting for the aliens to come out. Seconds passed, then a minute, but no one emerged.

Am I supposed to go up?

Nervously, he put a foot on the hatch, then quickly recoiled. His foot gripped the extraterrestrial metal better than anything he'd walked on before. He steadied himself, then stepped forward with his other foot, inching closer to the dark interior above.

"Hello?" he called out.

Nobody responded.

Apprehensively, he ascended the ramp, his feet moving effortlessly upwards, until he reached the top. His head passed into the threshold of darkness inside the ship. "Hello?" he called out a second time. His voice tapered off in the gloom. *How odd. A round, hollow chamber—how come there wasn't an echo?*

Once again there was no response. He spun around trying to see what was inside, but he couldn't make out anything in the pitch blackness.

"I'm here to ask for help," he said. "Not for me, but for Rosaline. She needs help at the baking tournament this weekend. The integrity of the tournament has been compromised, and her chances of winning are slim due to no fault of her own. It wouldn't be fair for her to lose because of that. I can't do anything about her situation, but maybe you guys can. You can do magic, after all."

Eugene turned slowly in every direction, hoping to see one of the friendly foreigners, but they didn't show their faces. "Is there any way you guys can help?"

Desperate, he took a step forward into the darkness, but tripped on something. The grippy floor wasn't grippy enough to keep him on his feet, and he crashed down, elbow first, onto the hard metal.

He lay on the foreign surface for what felt like an epoch, feeling lower than he ever had. As his cheek rested on the floor, he remembered his dream of boarding the spaceship to search for bugs from far away planets. *That's not what I'm here for right now.* With great effort he pushed himself off the cold floor and onto his feet. "If you can hear me, please help her. She's suffering immensely, but she's done absolutely nothing to deserve it," he said, hoping that something, anything could provide Rosaline with a fighting chance of achieving her dream of becoming the world's best baker.

"Please!"

Nothing stirred.

Defeated, he trudged down the hatch back outside to the Fairgrounds. As he stepped off the metal and onto the dirt, he turned back to look one last time into the spaceship.

"Mmmm!" someone squeaked from within the darkness.

And the hatch closed.

CHAPTER 14

John Angryberger sat cross-legged on a midget-sized sofa abutting his walnut-framed fireplace tucked within the recesses of an inglenook. Ash from frequent fires had turned the iron-rich red-terracotta brick lining the fireplace sooty black. Carved into the walnut beam above the fireplace was the Seal of the Vice President. A campanulate light suspended from the ceiling bathed the space with soft yellow light. It was a perfect nook for reading.

The gentle *katink katink katink* of a car driving on fine gravel liberated John's attention from the book he was skimming. He rose from the petite sofa, tossed Schuyler Colfax's memoir, *How to Be a Good Vice President of the United States of America*, into the fireplace, and headed toward the front door. He strutted through the central hall past a tall glass case that housed Asian antiques on its many shelves and out the ultra-thick oak double doors to the driveway.

"Welcome to Number One Observatory Circle," he said, greeting Judge Willis.

Judge Willis shut the door to his black Cadillac, pulled up the hem of his robes so it wouldn't drag on the little rocks, and scooted around the front of his car.

"You said you have an important update?" the judge asked, not wasting any time with perfunctory small talk.

"Yes, join me over here," said John, guiding Judge Willis up three stairs to the porch.

The Queen Anne Victorian-era house had an impressively broad wrap-around veranda flanked by a curved white railing.

John led Judge Willis to two white patio chairs, their Civil War era wooden frames made more comfortable by vile key-lime cushions. The chairs faced the immaculately trimmed thirteen-acre lawn.

John cleared his throat. "As you know, my mole at Schumaker's, Mary-Lou Anne, has been watching the young CEO's every move."

"What did he do?"

"She reported seeing him go into the spaceship."

"Did she?" Judge Willis exclaimed, sitting up. Realizing his tone was out of place, Judge Willis quickly followed up with a more somber response. "That's awful news. I remember you said it would be bad if Schumaker ever—"

"It's fantastic."

"I beg your pardon?" asked Judge Willis. "I thought you said it would be bad if Schumaker got a hold of the aliens' technology before you did."

"That's not why he went in there."

"I don't follow."

John smiled sadistically. "Going into their ship was *exactly* what I expected him to do. And now, thanks to Mary-Lou Anne, I won't have to worry about the aliens defending their ship when I go there to empty what's inside." He threw his head back and laughed manically. *What a stupid, stupid boy!*

Judge Willis blinked rapidly. "You *wanted* him to go into their ship?"

"To convince them to leave, yes. After what you did to Rosaline, that was his only play."

Judge Willis nodded slowly. "I think I understand now. If Eugene persuaded the aliens to go help Rosaline, their ship will be left unguarded, and you'll be able to steal their technology."

"Precisely. Just to be sure, however, I had Mary-Lou Anne install clandestine surveillance cameras on the roof of Schumaker's offices, all facing the spaceship. This way I'll be able to monitor when Eugene visits them again, and when the aliens leave their ship."

"I know you didn't call me over just to tell me good news. What do you need from me?"

"A permit to search the ship without disruption or intrusion."

"Does it matter what the permit is for? I could draft something about lack of identification, documentation, violation of no-fly-zone laws, possessing an unregistered flying object (UFO), or unlawful use of public fairgrounds" said Judge Willis, rattling off possible ideas. "Those are just some off the top of my head. How specific or general does it need to be?"

"Anything is fine so long as it gives me access and prevents anyone else from snooping."

"Okay," said Judge Willis, smacking his hands on his thighs and leaning forward. "What's in it for me?"

"I'd like to invite you to be part of the boarding party."

Judge Willis gave a quick, satisfied smile. "We have another deal."

CHAPTER 15

Rosaline returned to her bakery while the full moon was high in the night sky. It had been three days since Judge Willis informed her that it was to be shut down. She put her pink and purple cupcake backpack—complete with rainbow sparkles—on the counter and let out a long, deep sigh. Even though the health inspector put closure notices over her windows, she was still free to use the kitchen to practice for the **BABKA** tournament two days away, so long as she didn't sell food to customers.

A spoon clanged in the kitchen, causing her to freeze. No one was supposed to be there except her.

She stood still as a statue, listening intently. At first, she heard nothing, save the rapid beats from her heart pounding against her inner ear, but then she heard muffled dripping, like a feeble adagietto of water trickling from a loose pipe. She turned her ear toward the sound and heard faint sobbing.

Cautiously, she edged toward the wall connecting the kitchen with the storefront. Back pressed tightly against the wall, she slid her right foot forward, carefully inching to the corner. When she made it to the doorway, she peered her left eye around the wall, keeping the rest of her body hidden.

A disturbing scene unfolded before her. Pots and pans had been scattered across the floor. Every drawer had been pulled open, and their contents removed. Dozens of bags of flour, sugar, and baking soda had been ripped open, and empty egg cartons had been tossed willy-nilly on the ground. Utensils had been flung every which direction, some into the ceiling where they hung like stalactites. Sobbing and whimpering in the middle of the mess was an alien with its back to her.

"What have you done!" Rosaline cried out, stepping out from behind the wall.

The alien tried to turn around but only flailed its arms instead, unable to move its body.

Rosaline covered her mouth in shock when she saw why. The once scrawny alien now had chipmunk cheeks, and its tentacles looked tiny compared to its now large, spherical body. It had devoured everything in her pantries, cupboards, and drawers; her inventory was gone, replaced with this massive potbelly. The alien tried to push itself up but failed. It began to cry in humiliation.

"You poor thing! Were you stress eating?"

The alien nodded in shame. It slumped forward, and its jowls slid to a stop against its swollen belly.

Rosaline sighed. She joined the alien on the floor, sitting cross-legged next to it. It reached its stubby tentacles out for affection. Rosaline hugged it. Its paunch spread around her arms and wiggled like flan. While the alien's body ebbed and flowed like the tides, her socks became soaked with water as the alien's tears puddled on the floor.

She gently pushed the alien off. "Are you upset the bakery isn't open anymore?"

The alien nodded, then burst into more tears.

"Don't worry little—big?—fella. It'll be okay." She gently rubbed its tentacles. "And so will you. Come on, let's get up. Oof, you're heavy! How many eggs did you eat? Two hundred?"

Rosaline helped the alien onto its feet; its stomach hung to the floor. She held its hand and led it to the front of the store. The alien, struggling to walk, trundled like a roly-poly. By the time they made it out of the kitchen, the alien had stopped crying. Happy to be with

Rosaline, it secreted goo, leaving wet and sticky train tracks in its wake.

When they reached the door, Rosaline dropped to one knee, held the alien by its shoulders, and looked squarely into its puffy eyes. "As long as you're safe, my preparations for the BABKA don't matter," she said, then muttered too quietly for the alien to hear: "It's only something I've dreamed of since I was little girl attending elementary baking school."

The alien let out a toothy grin.

"Now, go back to your ship. Don't worry about me; I'll be fine." She turned the door handle, pulled it open, then gently pushed the alien outside. "You take care of yourself, and maybe install a treadmill in your spaceship."

Smiling, dripping, it waddled into the night like a fat, happy Buddha, leaving a trail as deep as a trench in the dirt as it dragged its belly back to the ship.

Rosaline watched it disappear into the darkness, then shut the door and locked it. "Whew," she exclaimed, wiping her brow before marching into the kitchen to assess the damage.

She tip-toed over the empty bags of flour and sugar, avoiding the substantial puddle in the middle of the floor, and made her way to the pantry. Almost all the boxes and jars had been upturned and emptied. She reached into the very back, stretching and straining, until she pulled out an old flour sack with a hand-written label on it: "Starlight Baking Flour – 420 oz." She thought it was a clever place to hide her marijuana flowers. Hastily, she unfurled the sack and peered inside.

It was empty. The alien had consumed everything, including her secret stash.

She screwed the lid back on and delicately set the can on the shelf in front of her, then bit her lip and nodded.

"Yep, I'm doomed."

CHAPTER 16

The day of the BABKA had finally arrived. Tens of thousands of people filled the stadium, eager to watch history unfold and another legend be crowned the best baker alive. Banners hung from the ceiling with the names and pictures of the thirty-two contestants. Streamers were affixed to the sides of the arena and displayed the names, pictures, and dates of each year's Best All-Around Baker Kaleidoscope Award winner since the tournament's inception eighty-eight years ago. Every seat in the stadium was filled; the event had sold out the day it was announced. The collective excitement of the hundred thousand people in attendance was palpable.

Unbelievable, Eugene thought, looking around the arena in awe, taken aback by the size and décor of the venue. *Rosaline is finally getting the attention she deserves.*

People from all over the world had come out to support the bakers of their countries. There were throngs of Argentinians, Spaniards, Belgians, Mexicans, Japanese, Chinese, Brazilians, Bolivians, Peruvians, and French people. Many spectators dressed in the traditional clothing of their country. An entire section wore red and green djellabas and waved Moroccan flags. The contingent of Greek fans sported togas. And the Americans, who filled the largest portion of the stadium, were decked out in quintessential American clothing, such as loose-fitting t-shirts depicting eagles, Harley-David-sons, and guns painted in the colors of their flag.

"This is us," said Winston, gesturing for Eugene to follow him to their seats amongst the other Americans.

They sat dead-center in front of the stage, twenty-eight rows back. On the stage were thirty-two work benches, each accompanied by a shelf stocked with ingredients. Spice purveyors from India had shipped the finest cardamom at daybreak; foragers in the Amazon sent bananas, mangos, and acerola on boats that docked the day before; and mycologists from Macedonia had delivered morel mushrooms that morning. Within the past twenty-four hours, all the world's most exquisite hand-picked sweets, flavors, spices, and seasonings had arrived in D.C.

Without warning, the lights dimmed. Thousands of people roared in excitement as the master of ceremonies walked onto the stage. A spotlight followed him as he crossed, waving to the crowd.

"Ladies and Gentlemen," he announced in a deep voice. "The day is finally here. The day you've all been waiting for. Are you ready? I welcome you to the best competition in the galaxy—the Best All-Around Baker Kaleidoscope Award!"

Screams erupted from the audience. "Let's get baked!" someone cried out. Chanting rang out in multiple languages as the spectators cheered on their favorite bakers.

Eugene pulled out his program. Of the thirty-two competitors, six were from Mexico, six from France, three from the United States, three from Japan, two from Argentina, two from Belgium, and one each from Spain, China, Brazil, Bolivia, Peru, Greece, Australia, Scotland, Denmark, and Morocco.

He skimmed the biographies of the contestants, hoping that François Rivier was Rosaline's sole competition. The more he read, however, the more concerned he became.

Oh boy. Rosaline is competing against some real aces.

All the bakers were internationally distinguished and held impressive accolades that put them in a league of their own. Kambu Mbuto of Morocco, a Rastafarian whose sobriquet was "Haile Selassie Flour-Rise," had won the African Masters of Baking

Competition three years in a row; Zeus Aujus of Greece had invented seventy-eight new kinds of pastries over the past decade, including the Dionysus Delight, a cross between a diple and a saragli soaked in enough wine to cause even the most Herculean of alcoholics to become dangerously inebriated after eating only six of them; Peruvian Chichi Lobito earned a top-three finish at the South American Everything Made of Corn Bakers Heritage Cup eight years in a row; and Mr. Choo, famed for his infamous "red cookies" which literally explode in the mouth, won the Heart of the Communist Party of China, as well as five hundred and sixteen Chinese baking awards, trophies, and assorted plaques, in recognition of his talent and national zeal.

"We would like to thank each and every one of you for coming out to this historic event," said the announcer. "This is the eighty-eighth year of the BABKA, and we couldn't do it without you, the fans. Give yourselves a round of applause."

After the audience congratulated themselves for being there, the announcer continued: "And let's give a round of applause to our sponsor, Jmart."

The audience clapped again, but not as loudly as they had clapped for themselves.

"Now, without further ado, here are the bakers for this year's competition. Representing sixteen countries, nominated by their culinary peers, and selected by internationally renowned food critics, these are the thirty-two best bakers in the whole world. Please welcome the contestants from Argentina. Julius Sandro-Ramos!"

A tall, middle-aged man with a well-trimmed beard walked onto the stage to a thunderous roar. He waved sheepishly to the crowd.

"Barbara Sosa!"

A petite brunette sauntered onto the stage, waving more enthusiastically than her colleague.

Eugene nudged Winston on his shoulder. "I'm getting nervous."

"Why? You aren't onstage."

"Thinking how stressful it must be for Rosaline is stressing me out."

"Eugene, Rosaline has, um, *methods* for reducing stress," said Winston reassuringly. "I'd wager she's feeling quite copacetic."

"I hope you're right."

"Our contestant from China, Mr. Choo!"

"Mr. Choo?" said Winston, intrigued. He leaned in toward Eugene. "Is this the same Mr. Choo that owns a buffet restaurant in Long Island?"

"I dunno… Hey, look!" he exclaimed, spotting François coming out of the tunnel that led backstage.

The Frenchman had satin-black hair styled in a bowl cut and a thick handlebar moustache that twisted upwards on either end. Like the other competitors, he wore a white apron and chef hat, but his wasn't a regular white-pleated chef hat like theirs; instead, it was brown and gold, and embroidered with gold fluff, which projected out of the top, exploding outwards like a mushroom cloud. The hat was also much taller than everybody else's. It gave Eugene the impression that he wore a great big muffin on his head.

"He looks like a regular Parisian," remarked Winston.

"Let's welcome the one, the only, the legend himself," the announcer cried, "François Rivier!"

The audience erupted as François crossed the stage.

Eugene stuffed his fingers in his ears to prevent the booming cheers from rupturing his eardrums.

The French compatriots in attendance screamed.

"Allons François!"

"Flambé leur cul, François!"

"Donnez-moi vos bébés!"

The uproarious applause continued for several minutes, drowning out the announcer as he welcomed other greats onto the stage, like the Scot Mordon Mamsay and the Moroccan Kambu Mbuto. Only when he arrived at the end of the alphabetical list of countries did the audience settle down. "Last but not least, the three competitors representing the United States of America: from Columbus, Ohio, Guy Gruyieri! From Lancaster, Michigan, Fobby Blay! And, representing your hometown of Washington D.C.—you all know her; we've all been to her bakery before it was closed for health-code violations—Rosaline Browning!"

Rosaline stepped forth onto the stage to earsplitting applause. Beaming, she waved at the crowd, which stood in ovation in support of the hometown heroine. Eugene thought she looked like an angel in her white apron and white chef hat. Seeing her surrounded by other distinguished bakers, he felt as if he was seeing her for the first time. She had outgrown her local bakery; she was part of the global stage of elite pâtissiers.

"Let's go, Rosaline!" Eugene and Winston cried out together.

She took her position behind her workbench, continuing to wave and smile at the crowd, her rosy cheeks glowing brighter than normal. Eugene had never seen her so excited. She didn't look nervous in the slightest.

"Gosh, I hope she wins," Eugene stammered without taking his eyes off her.

"How much are the prize earnings?" Winston yelled just to be heard over the cacophony of applause.

"Winner gets a quarter of a million dollars," Eugene yelled back. "Runner-up gets one hundred thousand. Semi-finalists each get fifty."

"Let's hope she finishes top four."

Eugene gaped at Winston with the same incredulity as if he'd been told to sing two songs at once. "Top four? She's going to win!"

"I'd now like to introduce our five distinguished judges for the competition," boomed the announcer. "Each judge's palette is highly refined, sensitive to the smallest microgram of flavor. From Quebec, Alphonse Tebor! From Madrid, Patricia Uno! From Singapore, Xie Tai Qing! From England, Sir Terry Mayflower! And the great Mongol-Mexican palette, Genghis Juan!"

Eugene clapped politely with the rest of the audience, even though he didn't know the judges, nor did he care about them.

"Ladies and Gentlemen," the announcer said as the lights inside the arena turned off, "we're ready to begin the first of four baking challenges."

Eugene turned toward Winston and shook him. "This is it!"

"For the first round, each baker will have exactly three hours to bake three different things, which will be announced in just a moment. Of the three different kinds of baked goods, the contestant must make at least three varieties of each. For example, if one of the challenges is to bake a pie, then each contestant must bake at least three different pies, such as cherry-rhubarb, apple, and mudpie. Gosh, I do love a good mudpie with a moist, sludgy-fudgy center. Mmmm." He smacked his lips loudly over the microphone.

"The preliminary round will be longest. This is because our champions will need more time to prepare and bake the pastries due to their complexity. Baked goods will be judged on the four following criteria: aroma, taste, preparation, and creativity. When it comes to identifying a truly exceptional pastry, our five judges are unbeatable. With their distinguished palates, they'll dissect each dish and decide which baker advances to the next round and which gets cut based on the tiniest missed pinch of salt or the unnecessary addition of a single grain of sugar.

"It will be tough, it will be emotional, and it will be full of flavor. There are thirty-two competitors, but three hours from now, only eight will remain. Are you ready?"

"Yes! Start the show!" someone yelled.

"Can I hear you scream?!"

The audience screamed.

"I can't hear you!"

The audience screamed louder.

"Set the timer for three hours."

The giant timer hanging over the stage lit up with the three-hour countdown.

"Are you ready? Then here we go! For this initial challenge, the three baked goods are…"

The audience became deathly silent. Everyone held their breath, waiting to hear what the bakers would make.

"Cake! Bread! Pie!"

CHAPTER 17

John Angryberger and Judge Willis convened inside a very large white tent, so large, in fact, it completely covered the aliens' spaceship with plenty of additional space for trucks carrying sophisticated drilling equipment to park inside. The tent was roped off by "Do Not Cross" police tape, so John and Judge Willis could work privately without anyone snooping.

Judge Willis turned toward John. "It's bold doing this in daylight, and on a weekend no less."

"The whole city is either at the BABKA or watching it on television. Nobody will bother us. And if anyone tries, they'll be arrested immediately."

"And if someone from Bullit Inc. arrives?"

"Just flash them the warrant. The police have a right to search the spaceship under suspicion of criminal activity."

At the mention of the word "police," Chief Bagsby shuffled over to them.

"Chief," John said, "I don't think I've thanked you for assisting with the investigation yet."

"No thanks needed. I'm doing this to protect the city I love. I don't trust those little gray creatures. I have a hunch they're up to something nefarious, and I want to find out what it is so I can lock 'em away."

"Let's just make sure we get everything we need from their ship before we put them behind bars."

"Yeah, sure, as long as I'm the one who gets to take these pint-sized monsters down to the precinct."

An earsplitting boom rang out in the tent. A moment later, the lead engineer rushed over with a worried and dejected expression.

"What is it now?" asked John sternly.

"I'm sorry, but nothing's working. We can't break through the hull. We even acquired C4 cartridges from your black-market dealer and tried blasting it, but that didn't work either."

"Why do you have a black-market explosives dealer?" Judge Willis asked John.

"In case I need to send someone a message," he answered vaguely.

Judge Willis opened his mouth to inquire further, but before he could the lead engineer cut in.

"We are running out of options and time. With your permission, can we try the bug gun?"

John sighed. "Yes, whatever it takes. Just get the hull open."

"The bug gun?" asked Judge Willis.

"Just watch."

The lead engineer gave his team a thumbs up. Two of the men hurried over to the tent flaps, held them open, and signaled an armored government truck idling outside the tent. The truck skirted past the tent flaps and parked in front of the spaceship.

The driver stepped out and went to the back of the truck, where the engineering team waited. He opened the door, and the lead engineer hopped up and disappeared inside. A moment later, he exited holding a meter-long orange device with green metal spokes poking out at seemingly random intervals. It looked like an octopus-themed grappling hook. Several holes lined the cylindrical frame like inverted suction cups. On the back of the gun rested a dodeca-hedron-shaped button with an unidentified symbol on it.

"What is *that*?" asked Judge Willis.

"The bug gun."

"Everyone, please move back," shouted the lead engineer.

When everyone was a safe distance away, he aimed the barrel at the ship's hull and pressed the dodecahedron button. A steady radioactive-green beam of high-powered cosmic photons channeled from the gun, penetrating the spaceship's harder-than-diamond exterior. "It's working!" he yelled, as the beam slowly made a hole in the side of the ship.

"Where did you get that thing?" Judge Willis asked John.

"Roswell."

"New Mexico?"

John nodded lazily.

"What happened in Roswell?"

"Have you heard about the two aliens that landed on Earth two years ago?"

"No."

"Of course not. There was no way you could have known. Only top military and government officials have access to that information."

"Are you implying these aliens landed here two years ago?"

"Not *these* aliens, no. Different ones. They piloted a golf ball-shaped vessel the size of a bathtub that crash-landed in New Mexico. The aliens were knocked unconscious from the impact. Unfortunately, their ship was irreparably destroyed in the crash, so we couldn't retrieve anything useful from it apart from the bug gun. Nonetheless, we resuscitated the aliens and moved them into a secret facility underneath Edwards Air Force Base in California. That's where we ran all sorts of medical tests to figure out what they were."

Judge Willis's eyebrows rose. "Amazing. So aliens have come to Earth before. What did you learn about them from the tests?"

"They had highly viscous blue blood, which solidified immediately upon contact with air. None of our syringes could successfully extract it, unless the aliens' veins were cut wide enough to let thick goo globs out. Unfortunately, we haven't been able to learn a whole lot more."

"How come?"

"While being subjected to examinations, one of the aliens died. We had to suspend tests on the surviving subject."

"That's a shame."

"Yes."

"The alien that did survive, where is it now?"

"Officially, Mr. Adams let it go."

"But unofficially, the alien is…?"

John smirked. "Somewhere I can continue to run tests on it."

"Does Mr. Adams know?"

John looked at him like a father might look at an estranged son. "What do you think?"

Judge Willis frowned. "The President doesn't seem particularly concerned about aliens."

"Mr. Adams uses people. If you have no purpose to him, he has no interest in you. My assumption is that he couldn't figure out a way to negotiate a business deal with the alien, so he found it useless."

"So, this pair of aliens that arrived on Earth two years ago, were they the same species as the ones that came in this spaceship?" he said, gesturing at the metal disc.

"No. They looked nothing like these disgusting little… gray octopus-people. The ones from Roswell were orange, had bilabiate frills below their mandibles and shifty little eyes, and they were more… globular."

"Globular?"

"It's hard to describe."

A metal screech resounded throughout the tent, followed by a loud pop. The lead engineer sprinted back over to them.

"Excuse me, sir, but we've breached the hull!"

"About time. Show me."

John, Judge Willis, and the chief of police followed the engineer toward the ship.

Three engineers stood by the hole in the hull, one of whom held the bug gun.

Without hesitating, John put his arms against the opening and pulled himself up.

"Sir, I wouldn't do that if I were you," warned Chief Bagsby. "We haven't checked for traps or dangerous devices. The aliens could've rigged their ship."

The hole was no more than a foot and a half foot wide. Nonetheless, John slipped inside effortlessly like a snake entering a vole's burrow.

Aliens are harmless, he thought. *History has proven that to be true twice now.* He looked around the interior of the ship, but it was too dark to see. "Come here and give me a light," he called to the team outside.

"I'm going in next," Chief Bagsby blurted out before the engineers could pass a flashlight to John.

Once the chief had crawled inside, all three engineers followed. Judge Willis went in after them.

The judge stood up and banged his head against the ceiling. "Ouch!" he shouted, rubbing his head. "These ceilings are low."

"What did you expect?" John remarked, annoyed. "The aliens are three feet tall."

One of the engineers handed John a flashlight. He turned it on and scanned the interior.

"No..."

"What is it?" Judge Willis whispered from behind him, sounding terrified.

The flashlight beam jittered as John's hand trembled with shock, and then shook even harder as his mercurial temper roared back. His heart beat furiously, pumping choleric blood into his face, heating his cheeks and neck.

The ship had been torn apart from the inside. Innumerable screens, buttons, switches, dials, and machinery had been ripped out of the console surrounding the circular control room. Wires littered the floor, and all the circuits had been disconnected.

John brimmed with apoplectic rage. *What the hell happened here?*

"Why has the interior been destroyed?" asked Judge Willis, confused.

John didn't respond. Even he was stumped. *Did Schumaker outplay me? Did he know that I knew he'd ask the aliens to help Rosaline? Was he two steps ahead of me this whole time, emptying the aliens' stores while they were gone, all the while pretending to be at the BABKA spectating?*

He kicked a golden rod across the room. "Take as much stuff as you can!" he barked to his engineers. "Whatever looks useful or interesting. And get someone here who can figure out what the hell happened. I want to know who ransacked this spaceship!"

"Is it possible the aliens sabotaged their own ship?" the lead engineer asked.

John scoffed. "Why would they do that?"

"Maybe they knew we were coming?"

"Impossible," said John. "There's no way they could have known that."

He shook his head, but an inkling of doubt remained. *Could they have known?*

He took a step backwards and felt something crunch under his foot. He shined his flashlight and noticed a plastic baggie on the ground. He bent down and picked it up, then held it up to the light so he could see inside.

The bag was labeled "Starlight." Inside were several buds of weed.

"Chief."

"Yes?" said Bagsby, crouching next to him.

He handed the bag to the chief of police. "I believe this is your domain."

Chief Bagsby looked down at the kush in his hands. "Starlight...?" His eyes lit up. "This must be how they power their spaceship."

John smacked his hands over his eyes in exasperation. "Smell it."

"It smells just like weed."

"That's because it *is* weed."

Chief Bagsby's brain was slow to turn on. "If the ship is flower-powered, that must mean... the aliens are space hippies! I knew they were up to no good."

John ignored him and turned to the others. "Search every inch of the ship. Don't leave anything unturned. We need to figure out what happened here. Don't rule out anything until we have firm evidence otherwise."

"Yes, sir."

John paced anxiously while his underlings searched the ship. Someone must've done this, but he'd been monitoring the ship ever since Mary-Lou Anne saw Schumaker enter, and the surveillance cameras hadn't detected anyone gaining access. Schumaker was the only person that had been inside, but he wasn't in the spacecraft long enough to do this. *That leaves the aliens, but there's no reason they'd destroy their own ship.*

He smashed his fist against a disassembled computer console next to him, cutting his hand. Blood trickled onto the metal floor.

"Damn Schumaker and damn the aliens! They won't get away with this!"

CHAPTER 18

Rosaline and François stood on opposite ends of the backstage kitchen during their half-hour respite before the final round. He leaned against the wall, his head drooping over his left shoulder. Rosaline, from her perch atop the workbench, looked at him curiously.

She reached inside her apron and pulled out a doobie. It was her last one, the only weed that survived the sad alien's raid on her kitchen. Fortunately, the alien didn't check the cash register. She always had a spare joint for emergency situations like this. From her pants pocket, she pulled out a match, put the jay to her lips, and lit up. She took a long puff and exhaled, relaxing deeper into the workbench as she did so.

She had breezed through the quarterfinals, which saw Fenna Lekke, Chichi Lobito, Zeus Aujus, and François's fellow Frenchman, Normand Chevre, eliminated after poor performances in the flaky croissant challenge. That left Rosaline, François, Mr. Choo, and Kambu Mbuto in the semifinal's cookie bake-off.

Mr. Choo crafted star fruit, red-bean, and passion-boa cookies. Unfortunately, the judges marked him down because his three types of cookies all looked the same—red rectangles with yellow star glaze resembling the Chinese flag. His zealous nationalism was his undo-ing. Kambu Mbuto also struggled to make cookies that appealed to the judges. The Moroccan baking king's cookies were either too dry or too moist: his powdered butter cookies simply disintegrated to the touch, while his plain vanilla cookies were too gooey.

Rosaline's cookies, on the other hand, were masterfully prepared and shaped. She made cubed lemon-merengue, teardrop-shaped lavender-infused pear, and octagonal peanut-butter oatmeal cookies. Expertly treading the line between consistencies, her cookies were the perfect balance of flavors. She proved without a doubt that she was qualified to be a finalist. Similarly, François advanced with his classic macadamia nut, snickerdoodle, and the more exotic tangerine-plum-and-mango-whipped-butter-dehydro-genase cookies.

Rosaline let out another puff, then reached into her apron pouch and pulled out a circular, light brown disc with orange and yellow swirls on its surface: one of François's tangerine-plum-and-mango-whipped-butter-dehydrogenase cookies she had swiped before leaving the stage.

She took a bite and immediately spat it out. She coughed profusely as her body rejected the sour, inedible cookie.

"Disgusting!" she exclaimed in horror, gagging and clutching at her throat. Instinctively, she took another hit from her joint to get the pungent taste out of her mouth.

She turned toward the Frenchman, who continued to lean against the wall with his arms crossed over his chest. "Your cookie tastes horrible," she said. "It's not even edible. How are you a finalist?"

François laughed derisively. "You're funny, mademoiselle. As if baking ze best cookie makes one a winner."

"Excuse you?"

"I could make cookies out of Playdoh and still win. What I bake does not matter, not when ze judges are being paid by Jmart."

"But this is a place for real masters of baking, not for sellouts like you. You're no better than Chef Boyardee," Rosaline retorted, her voice faltering.

"My cookies have a richness to zem zat you will never under-stand. Enjoy today while you can, for zis is ze last time you will ever set foot in ze kitchen. Your bakery was closed because your pastries are only fit for a-leons."

There was a rattle in the ceiling. Rosaline looked up.

"Zere's probably rats." François pointed at the air duct above his head. "Why don't you feed zem? Rats will enjoy your cuisine, I'm sure."

The air vent came loose and bonked François on the head, and he fell onto the hard tile floor. One by one, eleven aliens tumbled from the ceiling onto the Frenchman, using his body as a landing cushion.

Rosaline watched, stupefied, while flakes of vermiculite showered gracefully onto the floor.

The aliens rolled off François and dusted themselves off before clambering around Rosaline. They encircled her legs and hummed with joy.

"This can't be happening," she mumbled. She ignored the aliens and rushed to François, who was lying face-first on the floor. "Get up," she said, shaking him.

François stirred. "Ungh. What happened?" he asked groggily, sitting up and reaching for his muffin hat, which had fallen off his head. His hand grazed the leg of an alien by mistake. He winced and pulled his hand tightly to his chest as if he'd touched an infected wound.

"Who let zeese animals into ze kitchen?" he shouted.

The aliens let go of Rosaline and each pointed a tentacle tip at François.

"Don't you dare point your fingers at moi!" François pushed himself off the floor and grabbed the nearest bread knife. He held it with two hands in front of his chest, pointing the blade at the aliens. "I will slice each of you into half-loaves!"

Huffing and puffing, the tubby twelfth alien squeezed into the air duct using its slime to slide like a snail and fit through the narrow passage. It fell like a bowling ball on François's head. A loud crack resounded throughout the kitchen. François collapsed onto the floor unconscious. The knife he was holding tumbled from his hand and slid underneath the sink. The alien also collapsed, its tummy spilling out like flapjack batter on a hot griddle. Wheezing, the chubby alien lifted a finger and pointed at the ceiling. The duct cover magically flew back into place as if nothing had happened.

The rest of the aliens left Rosaline's side and hunched over François's body, forming a circle around him. One pointed at the muffin hat and summoned it toward him. The hat zoomed through the air, and the alien caught it in its tentacle.

"Zzzzzrrrrrooooooof! Zzzzzrrrrrooooooof! Zzzzzrrrrrooooooof!" the aliens began to chant.

"Don't kill him," Rosaline urged. "Even though he's a fraud, he doesn't deserve death."

Brrrrrng! The twelve aliens disappeared.

Rosaline looked wildly around the room, but they were gone. All that was left was the muffin hat.

"Where did you go?!" she called out.

"Mmmm!"

She heard them, but they were nowhere to be seen. "Where are you?"

"Mmmm!"

Rosaline kept calling out to them and listening for their replies. Each time, she edged closer to the source of the sounds, as if playing a game of Marco Polo. Rosaline followed the squeaks, which seemed to be coming from François. She looked at the floor near his head and gasped; the aliens had miniaturized themselves until they were only a couple of millimeters tall. They waved to Rosaline, who stood there, dumbfounded.

"No, this isn't happening. I must be dreaming," she said. "All the excitement from the BABKA must've gone to my head."

Single file, like tiny tentacled ants, the aliens marched up into François's ear. They scurried into the ear canal, past the tympanic membrane, and into his brain.

His eyes flashed open, and he sat up. His pupils covered the entire surface of his eyeball. Slowly, he picked up his muffin hat and awkwardly rose to his feet.

"François, are you okay?" Rosaline asked. "Little aliens just crawled into your brain. Or maybe they're hiding in your ear canal." She put her index finger in her mouth to lubricate it and then poked it into his ear. She wiggled it around but didn't feel any aliens.

"No, they definitely crawled all the way up there."

"Mmmm!" the Parisian squeaked, swaying slightly as if drunk.

Ding-dong! the buzzer sounded. The final round was about to begin.

François adjusted his muffin hat and walked past Rosaline. He winked at her, then headed out of the kitchen toward the stage, leaving her to wonder, *What the flour just happened?*

CHAPTER 19

"Ladies and gentlemen, let's welcome our two finalists: François Rivier and Rosaline Browning!"

The audience hooted and hollered as the two competitors took the stage, but Rosaline barely heard them. She was so confused by what she had just witnessed that she was hardly aware of anything happening outside her brain. Her mind replayed the scene from the kitchen over and over again, like a broken record, trying to make sense of what had transpired.

How do they even see in there? How do they breathe? Oh gosh, I'm asking sciencey questions like Eugene, how embarrassing. Oh, no, here's another one: if they crawled into his brain, could that mean I have aliens in my brain? Are we just a collection of aliens inside a bigger brain, and that brain's, like, the universe?

"As with the past two rounds, the contestants will have one hour to complete this culinary challenge. However, there's a twist. This time, both contestants must bake the exact same pastry. Are you ready folks? Here we go! The final challenge is… lemon poppyseed muffins!"

Those last three words magically snapped Rosaline back to reality. She blinked, and the tens of thousands of people in the audience came back into focus, roaring as the timer countdown began.

Thank God. I didn't know where I was for a second.

She sprinted to her pantry. Rosaline grabbed poppyseeds, flour, butter, sugar, baking powder, baking soda, and salt from the Great Salt Lake, a perfect place for spiritual awakening. She filled the space left in her hands with eggs from a Zen hen, lemons, and buttermilk from the refrigerator. She carried the ingredients to her workstation, preset the oven to three hundred and fifty degrees, and began to butter the muffin sheets.

She took a moment to glance at François, who whisked sugar and butter in a bowl. The mixture spilled all over the workbench as he struggled with his basic motor skills.

Rosaline grinned as a whisk flew out of his hand and nearly took off the announcer's head. "The aliens must be struggling to pilot him," she murmured to herself.

After a couple of minutes, utensils stopped flying around the stage as the Frenchman regained his legerdemain.

Rosaline periodically peeked at her rival to keep track of what step he was on. She watched him add egg yolks, buttermilk, lemon juice, and lemon zest to his mixing bowl, fold in the poppyseeds, then poured in a teaspoon of the finest vanilla extract from Mexico. The tantalizing aroma of fresh vanilla beans wafted toward Rosaline, who momentarily closed her eyes and inhaled deeply, allowing the scent to transport her to a calm, faraway tropical paradise.

She opened her eyes and returned her attention to her own bowl. Having finished homogenizing her mixture, she whisked in egg whites. She vigorously beat the eggs until the mixture was lemon-yellow and the same consistency throughout. After thoroughly stirring it, she poured the batter into the muffin tray, carefully filling each mold to the same height. Then she tenderly tucked the muffins into the oven and set her timer for twenty-five minutes.

Seconds after Rosaline shut her oven, she heard the clang of François's oven closing across the stage. They both squatted in front of their ovens, attentively watching their muffins, making sure that heat was being distributed evenly. Without blinking, they stared at the batter through hundreds of little black dots on the oven glass. According to Kaleidoscope Brown, who knew just as much about baking appliances and equipment as she did ingredients, those black dots were called frits. Frits assisted in reflecting heat, increasing baking efficiency in the oven, and creating the perfectly browned muffin.

The timer on Rosaline's oven beeped. She pulled out her muffins and placed them on the stovetop. They were marvelously browned, and their muffin tops expanded outwards like atomic mushroom clouds bursting with flavor. She inserted a toothpick directly into the center, careful to avoid any poppyseeds, and pulled it out cleanly.

Rosaline let the muffins cool for five minutes before lifting them out of the tray and wrapping them in intricate gold and brown pastry paper.

"I couldn't have made them any better," she muttered proudly to herself as she finished plating the last muffin.

"And… time! Finalists, please step back from your workbench and bring your muffins to the judges' table."

Rosaline confidently picked up her muffins, inhaling their sweet fragrance as she carried them to judges. François followed suit. Rosaline noticed him pocket a muffin to save for later.

"Well, ladies and gentlemen, this is the moment of truth we've all been waiting for. Without further ado, let's hear what our judges have to say. Rosaline Browning, please step forward."

Rosaline stepped in front of the judges, who each took a bite from her muffins. Their pupils widened in gastric ecstasy as the flavors hit their tongues. "Mmmm!" they moaned.

Then something strange happened. Something never seen before at the BABKA. The judges didn't stop eating after one bite—they ate the entire muffin.

Unashamedly, they licked their plates clean. When they finished, they exchanged contented looks amongst themselves. Their eyes said what their mouths wished they could: if they hadn't been paid seven figures to vote for François, Rosaline surely would've won.

"Where do I begin?" said the first judge, Xie Tai Qing. "I thought the lemon poppyseed muffin looked extraordinary. I was expecting it to be wonderful, but I wasn't expecting it to be this good. It's perfectly browned, perfectly moist, holds the perfect shape, and tastes better than I could've imagined. It is the biggest regret of my life that I don't have the words to describe this taste—no, this experience. All I can say is that this was the best muffin I've ever eaten."

The audience roared.

"That's true to my feelings as well," echoed Sir Terry Mayflower.

"Truly stupendous," agreed Alphonse Tebor. "The color, the flavor, the smell—que c'est bon."

"Rosaline, we've seen your magic throughout the day. You started out well, performed better each subsequent round, and now, in the finals, you've demonstrated that you are truly a master," said Patricia Uno.

Genghis Juan looked down reflectively at his empty plate. "Muffin. To most, the name means 'morning cake.' But you, Rosaline, have turned 'muffin' into a six-letter word for love."

The audience erupted. Every section rose to their feet to give Rosaline a standing ovation. Nobody in the history of the competition, save Kaleidoscope Brown, had ever received such an astounding response.

"What glorious reviews from our judges!" boomed the announcer. "Now, it's time for the current BABKA title holder to step forward."

A slightly frazzled-looking François took his place before the judges, as though he had just come off a roller coaster, his face flushed and his clothes splattered with batter. The judges, with looks of nausea, hesitated to pick up his muffins. They'd already been forced to stomach his inedible baking three times today.

"Okay, judges. Have a muffin. Don't just sit there admiring them," said the announcer, grinning. "We want to know what they taste like."

Sir Terry Mayflower lost a rock-paper-scissors battle to Alphonse Tebor under the table. With an expression of repulsion, he picked up a muffin and took a bite.

The other judges watched, horrified, expecting him to gag, but he didn't. Instead, his eyes lit up, and he nodded enthusiastically, signaling that the muffins were safe to consume.

The other judges lifted a muffin to their mouths. Daringly, they bit in, their trepidation softened by the thought of their massive paychecks. Like Sir Mayflower, they were pleasantly surprised. The muffins didn't taste like François's baking—or at least, they didn't taste like the pathetic excuse for baking they had come to expect from him over the past few hours. They were steamy, delectable, and delightfully crumbly flavor-bombs. The judges inhaled François's muffins with such gusto that their plates were cleared in an instant.

Xie Tai Qing spoke first once again: "After eating Rosaline's muffin, I didn't think I would need to taste yours, François. I knew from the moment I tasted hers that she was our clear winner. But now, having savored yours, I no longer think that's the case. What you have created, François, is not just a muffin. It is something magical—a bridge connecting stomach to heart. I'm at a loss to say which is the better muffin."

Sir Terry Mayflower nodded in approval. "Exceptional, François. You've outdone yourself."

"You have made it awfully difficult for us," said Genghis Juan. "Your muffins are divine."

"François, this is the best thing you've created all day. How fitting it should be for the finals," Alphonse Tebor chimed.

Patricia Uno spoke last, "You have proven why you're a legend, François."

The audience applauded and cheered for the Frenchman. He walked away from the judges' table to stand by Rosaline, beaming.

Rosaline glanced at him. She couldn't tell if it was François who was happy or if it was the happiness of the aliens disseminated throughout his body that caused him to smile. Whatever the case, she smiled back. She was happy for the aliens, her protégés, to have received such distinguished praise.

The judges consulted for a few minutes, and then the announcer asked, "Judges, have you selected a winner?"

"We have," Patricia Uno said into her microphone. "By a three-to-two decision, the winner is…"

The audience held their breath. The silence was deafening.

"*Françoisssss Rrrrrrivier!*"

The walls shook with the wild cheering that rang out from thousands of seats. Blue, white, and red confetti fell from the ceiling, and French supporters sobbed uncontrollably.

"For the second time in a row, our winner is François Rivier!" bellowed the announcer, handing François a check for two hundred and fifty thousand dollars and a gold trophy shaped as a chef hat with pastries of all shapes and sizes embellished on the folds.

"What are you going to do with your prize money?" the announcer asked, slapping him on the shoulder.

"Mmmm!"

The announcer chuckled. "Someone's certainly happy." He walked over to Rosaline. "Now let's give a round of applause to our runner-up, Rosaline Browning." He handed her a check for one hundred thousand dollars and a silver trophy that was also shaped like a chef hat but smaller than François's. She held it up to applause from the audience. "What an amazing performance. You have cemented yourself as the second-best baker in the entire world. Tell us, Rosaline: what comes next?"

"I'm going to find a way to reopen my bakery."

"That's the best idea I've heard all day. Let's give it up one more time for François Rivier and Rosaline Browning!"

The audience erupted. François and Rosaline waved to the crowd for several minutes before being escorted backstage to change outfits and prepare for post-tournament interviews.

Rosaline sat against the wall and took off her toque with a satisfied sigh. François approached her, reached into his pocket, and pulled out a muffin. He held it out for her.

Rosaline laughed. "I saw you pocket that muffin." She put her hands into her pocket and pulled out a runner-up muffin. "I thought we could enjoy these after the show."

Then, without warning, François collapsed onto the ground. His head made a nasty cracking sound as it hit the hard ceramic tile. Blood trickled from his nose. The aliens washed out from the nosebleed as if they were riding a water slide. Once free from the nostril, they used their powers to return to their normal size.

Rosaline turned her gaze to the man lying unconscious on the floor. "Is he going to be okay?" she asked with concern.

The aliens nodded. Not only would François regain consciousness in a couple of minutes, but the aliens had taken the liberty of filling up the empty muffin-shaped hole in his amygdala where his once great love and passion for baking used to be with muffin batter. In a few days, the batter would coalesce and transform into brain tissue, completely restoring his amygdala. François Rivier would become the legendary baker he once was once again.

Relieved, Rosaline tore a small piece from the bottom of her muffin and handed the rest to the aliens. She watched as they divided it amongst themselves. They then split their own muffin into thirteenths and gave a portion to her.

Rosaline took a bite of the aliens' muffin. They looked at her expectantly, waiting for her to tell them what she thought of their culinary creation.

"Mmmm!" she cooed as the muffin dissolved in her mouth. The sweetness from the buttery bread zapped her palette with electrifying tang, followed by a wonderful zing of lemon and a firm, delightful crunch of poppyseeds.

Rosaline licked her fingers. "Absolutely delicious. That was something special that would amaze even the legendary Kaleidoscope Brown."

The aliens hummed in delight.

She looked at the piece of her own muffin in her other hand. "Let's see whose is better."

She playfully popped it into her mouth. Piquant lemon, vanilla, and almond-like flavors tickled her tongue. The browned texture from the crust of the muffin contrasted wonderfully with the soft, flaky insides. Rosaline could have been eating a cloud of euphoria.

"Our muffins taste exactly the same."

The aliens hummed in agreement.

"In the brief time I've taught you, you've already become baking masters. God knows how good you'll be with more than just a couple weeks of practice. Heck, with muffins that good, you could open your own bakery."

The aliens exchanged cryptic glances.

Rosaline let out a contented sigh. "I may have lost, but I still feel like a winner. You are my protégés, so in a way those are my muffins, too. I can't believe how well you performed out there, and how quickly you picked up my recipes. I'm so proud of you."

"Mmmm!" the aliens squeaked, jumping on top of her and smothering her with hugs.

She laughed and smiled contentedly. "Mmmm indeed!"

CHAPTER 20

John Angryberger hid inside the tent covering the spaceship, peering through a gap between the flaps. A flock of reporters had gathered outside. Per John's orders, Chief Bagsby had reached out to media correspondents immediately after the BABKA ended about a dire threat that needed to be brought to the city's attention. The reporters, who had rushed from the stadium to the dirt lot, loudly gossiped about the finals as they waited to hear the police chief's important message. The armored trucks, team of engineers, and Judge Willis had departed before the journalists arrived to avoid attracting unwanted attention. All that remained was a perimeter of police cars securing the empty dirt lot in an overly dramatic and superfluous display of force.

It's a shame I could only have one victory instead of two today, but this should cut down on my losses.

He turned to Chief Bagsby who was busy reading John's handwritten statement. The chief's brow furrowed. He appeared to be having some difficulty with the text.

"Everything okay?" John asked.

"There's some big words in here," said Bagsby without looking up.

"They're ready for you."

Chief Bagsby nodded. He looked at John uncertainly and took a deep breath.

"It's just reading," said John reassuringly.

"It's not reading that bothers me, but public speaking. There isn't anything more difficult than getting up in front of a bunch of random people and saying words." Chief Bagsby shivered. "I'd rather be in a shootout."

John held the tent flap open for him. "Pretend your words are bullets and your mouth the gun."

"Oooh. Well, when you put it that way…" His arrogance reappeared in a flash, and he ducked through the opening and stepped up to the temporary podium John's team had erected outside the tent.

"Thank you for coming here today," the chief began, diving into the script. "Earlier this morning, a team of investigators, including myself, used a search warrant to inspect the alien spaceship. We had reason to believe the aliens were smuggling drugs due to several reports of a marijuana stench emanating from the spaceship. This would also explain their predilection for morning pastries.

"When we breached the hull and entered the ship, it became immediately clear that something was awry. Bound, gagged, and stowed inside the hull were two aliens, evidently kidnapped and held against their will. Unlike the dozen gray aliens that look more like octopuses than people, these two aliens are orange and globular.

"We released them from their chains and searched the ship, which we found to be in a state of ruin. The interior was destroyed. We believe a fight broke out between the two types of aliens, leading to the gray aliens incapacitating the orange ones.

"Unfortunately, one orange alien was badly wounded in the altercation. We rushed it to the nearest veterinary hospital, but it succumbed to its wounds. The other is being treated at a private location and is in stable condition.

"As a result of these events, we've determined that the gray aliens pose a serious threat to the community and the country. It's imperative that the public be informed that these 'harmless' aliens are in fact intergalactic kidnappers and drug traffickers. Consequently, the aliens shall heretofore be declared as criminals, and they are wanted by the MPD. If you see them, do not engage. Call local law enforcement to handle the situation. They are deadly and not to be trusted.

"Vice President Angryberger has requested a more thorough investigation of the spaceship in order to assess whether it poses a threat to homeland security. We don't believe it's dangerous to people, but just to be sure—we can't take any chances—we'll continue searching the interior of the ship before dismantling it. Due to these circumstances, the spaceship, and the Fairgrounds in which the ship is located, are off-limits to the public. That is all."

CHAPTER 21

Eugene shook uncontrollably as he finished reading the article. Fuming, he balled up the newspaper and threw it at his trashcan as hard as he could. It made a dull *clang* as it hit the rim and bounced out. *First John Angryberger steals the BABKA from Rosaline, and now he declares the aliens as criminals and seals off their ship?* He slammed his fist down on his desk. *This is completely unacceptable. Whatever he has against me, it doesn't make it okay for him to target my friends.*

Incensed, he reached for his phone.

"Hello?" Winston answered.

"Winston, I need a favor."

"Oh gosh, I hope it's quick," he said. "I wouldn't want to be away from work one second longer than needed."

"Do you happen to have the phone number to the White House?"

"Obviously. Our boss works from home there. Let me find it… Here it is. You got a pen to write this down?"

He read out the phone number slowly then had Eugene repeat it back to him.

"Why do you want Mr. Adams's home phone?"

"I don't—I need John Angryberger's."

"Ah. That makes sense. His office is at the White House too. Are you reaching out about Rosaline's Bakery or about the aliens being criminals?"

"Both."

"Alright, well just remember there's nothing you can do about the vice president or his cronies. They are more influential than you and have the full power of the U.S. government at their disposal. Try not to upset him."

"Thanks for your wisdom." Eugene hung up and entered the new number into his dialer.

"Hello, you've reached the White House," began the robotic, automated messaging system. "Press one if your business lies with the president, Bullit Inc.; press two if your business lies with the vice president, Jmart."

Eugene pushed the number two. His receiver rang for several seconds before a woman answered.

"This is Jmart. How may I help you?"

"Hello, I'd like to speak with Vice President Angryberger, please," he said politely, stifling his rage.

"May I ask who's calling?"

"Eugene Schumaker."

"Just a moment." She put him on hold. Engelbert Humperdinck's tinny swing music played while he waited.

The operator came back on the line. "Vice President Angryberger will take your call. I'm putting you through now."

After a moment of silence, he was patched through, and Eugene heard the oleaginous voice of the vice president on the other end.

"Well, well, well. If it isn't the young *Schumaker*. To what do I owe this pleasure?"

The vice president's flippant greeting triggered Eugene, and he responded in like manner before he could control himself. "Cut the nonsense, *John*. You know exactly what you did."

"Oh, is that so?

"You cheated."

"You'll have to be more specific. Which occasion are you referring to?"

"The BABKA. As if Judge Willis shutting down Rosaline's Bakery wasn't enough, you also needed to steal her crown."

"And? Your point is…?"

"How could you do that to her? She's done nothing to you."

"You're right," he said. "My issue has never been with her; she was merely a means to get back at you."

"To get back at me?" asked Eugene, baffled. "Why?"

"You know exactly why."

"I don't have any idea what you're talking about."

"Don't play stupid, Schumaker. You know exactly what you did."

"I haven't done anything!"

"You blew up my train."

Eugene felt his eyebrows climb his forehead and disappear into his hair. "What on Earth are you talking about?"

"The KB Rail explosion. I know you caused it."

"*What?*"

"Drop the innocent act. You purposefully changed your motor specifications to sabotage me. You knew full well I would copy your designs and that my engines would blow up."

"I don't know you're talking about." Eugene felt his mouth grow dry. He licked his lips nervously. "When did you copy my designs?"

"Just admit it. You want to get your market share back, and not only that, you want to take all of mine, too. You'll do anything for it. In that regard, you're just like your father, aren't you? Trying to make your train and oil business the biggest in the country. That's why you blew up my train—you knew you'd come out ahead while putting me behind."

"None of that is true. There's been some huge misunderstanding."

"Your coy-boy façade doesn't fool me, Schumaker. I see how cutthroat you are—just like your father, just like Judge Willis, and just like me."

"I'm not like my father, and I'm definitely not like you. I would never hurt people the way you hurt Rosaline, taking away her livelihood and her pride, all to get back at me for something I never did.

I bet it was you who made the chief of police issue warrants for the arrest of the aliens, too. How could you do that to them? They're peaceful, fun-loving creatures who have no intention of hurting anyone."

"I don't care what they are. I needed to get you away from their ship."

"Why?"

"You're going to act dumb again? Is that the only card you know how to play?"

"I genuinely have no idea what you're talking about."

"You and I both know what this is really about."

"I don't."

"Business."

"How are the aliens 'business?'"

"I know you're trying to fold their technology into your company, but I'm going to steal it first."

"Don't you dare!" said Eugene angrily, his frustration mounting. "Leave them out of this. They've done nothing wrong. You've already hurt my friends enough. If you hurt anyone else, I'll have no choice but to hurt you back."

"Oh? And how will you do that?"

Eugene thought of the only thing he knew that had upset the vice president. "I'll... I'll blow up your trains for real this time!" he blurted out before he could stop himself. The phone slipped from Eugene's hand and fell to the floor as he slapped his palm to his mouth as if trying to shove the words back in.

Eugene picked up the phone again. There was a long tense pause.

"Are you threatening me?" John asked. His tone was different. His playfulness was gone, replaced with a cold calmness that made Eugene shudder.

"I'm sorry, John, I didn't mean that," said Eugene, panic in his voice. "I'm just so upset that I word-vomited. You don't honestly think I would do that, do you?"

"You've done it once before. I'm sure you'd do it again. I thought you'd learn your lesson after all this, but I guess you just don't get it, do you? I'm coming for you, Schumaker, and I'm taking back what's mine."

"John, please, let's talk this out," Eugene began, but the vice president had already hung up.

Dread twisted in Eugene's gut. His heart hammered furiously as the gravity of the situation hit him. *Oh no, what have I done?*

CHAPTER 22

"What does my idiot vice president think he's doing?" whined Mr. Adams. He tossed the newspaper onto his desk then picked up his coffee mug and took a sip.

"Sir?" asked one of his Secret Service agents.

"The main attraction of the Gala—which is in five days mind you—*is* the spaceship. That's the centerpiece I'll use to bring in foreign business. 'Hi, you're from Switzerland and have the biggest chocolate factory on the planet? Here, look at this cool spaceship. Now, let's do business so you can sell those chocolates exclusively at my stores.' But no, John *must* make himself a thorn in my side. Always throwing tantrums, that one. It's always about him." He shook his head melodramatically. "He does this to spite me."

The Secret Service agents exchanged awkward glances.

Mr. Adams rubbed his temples. "Now I need to call Chief Bagsby and override John because *I'm* the head of the executive branch and therefore of the police—not him. I'll need to send out a memo letting everyone know that the spaceship will be there. We aren't getting rid of it just because John doesn't like the fact that little gray people have a bigger parking spot than he does."

"But sir, what if he's right?" asked one of the agents. "What if they are dangerous? The police chief reported they had drugs and weapons on board."

Mr. Adams rolled his eyes. "Aliens are as harmless as butterflies. Trust me, I've met them. John Angryberger, on the other hand, he's a bit more problematic." He sighed and ran his hand through his bristly gray hair. "I really, *really* don't want to talk to him, but I guess I have no choice. He's like a dog without a leash, and I need to remind him of his place. He needs to know that I'm the one calling the shots here in this city. That intergalactic-disco-ball-of-a-spaceship stays."

CHAPTER 23

Five lugubrious days had passed since the aliens were declared criminals. The aliens had disappeared—fled from the city, most likely—leaving Eugene feeling sad and empty. Everything seemed colorless and gray; he was still disappointed in the results of the BABKA, and worry from his phone call with John Angryberger lingered in the back of his mind. The arrival of one of his new locomotives had done little to lift his mood. He no longer had mornings studying the aliens to look forward to, and no matter how many times he had distracted himself by looking through his bug collection, time seemed to pass at quarter speed. It was a nice respite, therefore, when he and Winston found themselves at the Gala. Even though it was a work party, Eugene viewed it as an opportunity to have fun with his friends and get a load off his mind, which he desperately needed.

As they arrived at the Fairgrounds, Eugene was taken aback by how remarkably different it looked from the dirt field he was used to. A wide red carpet adorned the Schumaker Avenue sidewalk; red velvet ropes, strung between faux-golden posts, swayed gently in the breeze. String lights stuffed inside lace ball-shaped doilies illuminated the Fairgrounds, zigzagging overhead like a canopy, transforming the normally barren landscape into a magical evening. A live band could be heard playing from a stage inside. Police cars blocked the streets while their drivers manned the perimeter, and snipers perched atop the surrounding roofs to protect the affluent attendees.

"Look at this place," said Winston disapprovingly. "Top executives from all over the world gathered here tonight to promote their own self-serving interests. What a waste of my time." He picked at his collar, like a dog trying to scratch that one spot on the side of its neck. His black blazer, white button-down, green tie, and tan pleated dress pants made Winston look stiff and uncomfortable. Of course, he still wore flip-flops.

"Remind me again, why are we here?"

"You have to be here."

"Yeah, but *you* don't. If I were you, I'd be as far away from here as possible."

"I came to support you. Plus, Rosaline's catering. We can hang out with her. Besides, we might actually meet some interesting people."

Winston sighed. "Fine, but I'm leaving early."

They proceeded down the red carpet to the entrance, where they flashed their identification to the guards manning the check-in booth. Security patted them down.

"Welcome, Mr. Schumaker, Mr. Perry. We hope you have a pleasant evening."

As they entered the Fairgrounds, they were greeted by a massive event map. The itinerary was listed next to the legend, detailing the entertainment for the evening. The festivities were divided between two colossal pavilions: the Blues Club—a dance hall containing a jazz band, linoleum dance floor, and open bar—and the dining pavilion, where patrons could sit and discuss corporate affairs over a lavish seven-course meal.

Servers meandered through the crowd of global elites, carrying trays of hors d'oeuvres. One of them passed Eugene and Winston, who each took a petite spoonful of carpaccio off the tray.

"Let's go find Rosaline," said Eugene, his mouth full, gesturing to the dining pavilion.

Eugene and Winston set off down the makeshift promenade,

lined with smaller tents containing meeting rooms complete with locking doors, whiteboards, long fake-wood tables, and mildly uncomfortable plastic swivel-chairs. The tents allowed the hundreds of well-heeled businessmen, lawmakers, and other professionals in attendance to conduct business in private.

At the epicenter of the Fairgrounds was the spaceship, lit up by huge spotlights to look like a giant disco ball. A ray of light reflecting off the shiny metal disc illuminated the ground underneath, and Eugene spotted a pocket patch of prospering poppy plants. As they walked past, Eugene looked for the hole in the hull where John and his cronies had drilled to get inside, but he couldn't find it. The ship was hole-less. *The aliens must've repaired it before going into hiding*, he thought, and he felt himself relax slightly.

As they approached the dining pavilion and Rosaline's station within, scents of cinnamon apple tart and vanilla custard cream wafted toward them. The aroma was intoxicating. Even with his eyes closed, he'd be able to find Rosaline amidst the multitude of businesspeople in their suits; all he had to do was follow the wonderful perfume of her pastries.

Before they reached the pavilion, however, he heard a familiar name being mentioned in the crowd: "…if you need anything. It's been my pleasure, Mr. Adams."

Winston heard it too because he stopped walking to listen.

"Give John my regards, Willis," Mr. Adams replied, evidently annoyed.

"You could have told him yourself, had you invited him."

"He was disinvited for a reason."

"Why? Afraid he'd make friends and become a larger threat to you than he already is?"

"He needed a reminder of who calls the shots around here."

"Mr. Adams, you underestimate John. He doesn't need to come to a Gala to network with other less successful businessmen. No, he has bigger plans."

Winston ducked behind Eugene and lowered his head.

"What are you doing?" Eugene asked.

"Hiding."

"You don't need to be afraid of Judge Willis," said Eugene, nervous himself.

"I'm not hiding from *him*. I'm hiding from the president."

"Why?"

"He might recognize me. I'm his new director of marketing, and I don't want to talk to anyone from work while I'm here."

"Oh." Eugene took a step sideways, so that he was no longer blocking Winston from view.

"Hey, you," said the president. "Aren't you my new marketing director?"

Eugene grinned as Winston froze like an igloo. "If I don't move, maybe he'll lose interest," Winston whispered so only Eugene could hear.

The president, who was wearing tan short-shorts, a tan hiking vest, and a pith helmet, walked over and poked him on the shoulder. "Hey. I'm speaking to you."

"Yes, sir," Winston replied with obvious effort.

"Congratulations," said the president. "Dominic told me you were the perfect candidate for the job."

"That means a lot, considering the other fantastic prospects on the marketing team."

"You're here because you've got potential. When I look at you, I see greatness."

Eugene cocked his head. He surveyed Winston's rumpled shirt, three-day old scruff, and worn sandals.

"I'll try not to let my greatness spill out. Wouldn't want to flood the place," said Winston, clenching his teeth and forcing a grin.

Eugene giggled with amusement as Winston suffered pleasantries with his boss, who was dressed like he was ready to go on an African safari. *Winston wasn't lying when he said his marketing strategy meetings involved picking out the president's clothes each day.*

"I'll catch up with you later," said Eugene. He spun around to dart off toward the dining pavilion and bumped into a monstrously large, muscular man.

"Oopsie! Ahh'm real sorry 'bout that," the man apologized in a thick Southern drawl.

"No worries," exclaimed Eugene, marveling at the sight of him. The giant was dressed in an ultra-white tuxedo, silver loafers, and a white leather belt equipped with a Texas-sized buckle. His crinkly brown hair jutted out from underneath a white top hat, and tattoos covered his neck. The man's boyish smile expressed innocence, but the lines around his face indicated a mature level of life experience and wisdom.

This man is an enigma, thought Eugene. His fashion sense coupled with his jolly Southern demeanor was at odds with his intimidating size and fierce display of tattoos. If Eugene hadn't met actual aliens, he'd have thought this man was a Martian.

"Ahh'm Cecil-Lee," said the man, extending a hand to Eugene.

"Eugene Schumaker," he replied, shaking it. The giant squeezed with a bear-grip that nearly crushed Eugene's bones.

"Schumaker? Don't tell me yer the—"

"I'm the president of Schumaker Trains and Oil."

"Well, Ahh'll be darned. That's quite the oil an' freight bisdness yew run."

"One of the largest train companies in the country," Eugene boasted.

"Last Ahh heard 'bout the train industry was when that freighter exploded the other week without even enlistin' mahh help."

"You must be referring to the KB Rail incident—wait, what do you mean? What is it that you do?"

"Ahh'm an explosives expert. I op'rate the biggest supplier of explosive equipment in the country, providin' products an' services t' the milit'ry an' other companies."

"What services, exactly?" Eugene asked, narrowing his eyes.

"Well, it's mostly dem'lition work, like destroyin' old buildin's or helpin' t' bomb a mount'n fer coal minin' op'rations, but once every blue moon there's a nut who comes t' me askin' fer help sabotagin' their competitor's or ex-lover's company."

"Have you ever done business with John Angryberger?" Eugene blurted out.

"That's an oddly specific question," chuckled Cecil-Lee nervously. "Ahh don't give out personal information 'bout mahh clients, but Ahh will tell yew that Ahh haven' ever worked with the vice prezdint. Here, whahh don't yew take mahh bisdness card, an' if yew want, we kin talk 'bout all this nonsense later. Rahht now, Ahh need food. Heck, Ahh'm so hungry Ahh could eat an entire cow."

"I was about to head over to the dining pavilion myself," said Eugene. "My friend is catering the pastry portion of this event. Why not go over together?"

"Whatever's comin' from that tent smells finger-lickin' good. Let's check out whatever yer friend's makin'.'"

"Where are you from?" Eugene asked after they had set off.

"Murchison, East Texas, but Ahh live in D.C. now."

"They have some great wildlife down there," said Eugene, thinking about the plethora of bugs that live in the humid swampland.

"Ain't that the truth. Lotta gators an' snakes an' fish. See these?" Cecil-Lee pulled up his pant leg and showed Eugene his silver loafers. Looking closely, Eugene could make out thin scales. "Gator-skin loafers. Ahh killed the big boy mahhself durin' a fam'ly fishin' trip t' Louisiana a couple years ago. Mama was rowin' an' Ahh was puttin' together dy-no-mite sticks t' blast the fish outta the water when we came 'cross this big ol' gator hangin' out underneath a mangrove tree not twenty feet away. Ahh said t' my cousin, Ahh said, 'Hey, Tigris'—he's named after the river in Africa, see— 'gimme that shotgun there so Ahh kin bag that 'zerd.' An' that's exactly what Ahh did. One shot t' the head an' bam! He was belly-up. Afterwards, Ahh brought the gator t' mahh cobbler, an' he fash-ioned these beautiful loafers here fer me."

"That's quite the story."

"Yessir, me an' Mama an' all the cousins enjoy fishin' trips, an' then afterwards we have a big 'ol feast an' celebrate bahh eatin' Mama's famous 'zerd chowder."

"That sounds like quality mother-son time."

"Catchin' critters is a big part of mahh life, a big part of who Ahh am bein' from East Texas an' all. Hey, check this out."

He pulled up the sleeve of his white tuxedo to reveal an alligator tattoo covering his forearm. A spiky black tail wrapped around the backside of his forearm to the front side where it grew into a thick scaly body with a long flat face that tapered to a point. Lying parallel to it was a dome-shaped reptile with a short beaklike mouth.

"It's an alligator an' an alligator snappin' turtle wrapped 'round mahh arm."

"That's strikingly well done."

"The one on mahh back is even better. It's a giant stick of dy-no-mite, but Ahh won't take off mahh shirt t' show yew durin' a fancy party like this." Cecil-Lee let out a chuckle and pulled down his sleeve, covering his tattoos. "Do yew like huntin' an' fishin'?"

"I've fished a couple times with my butler when I was a kid, but I was too young to remember if I liked it. My main hobby is collecting bugs though. Before taking over my dad's company, I was studying to be an entomologist."

Cecil-Lee nodded approvingly. "Ahh have a good friend who likes collectin' bugs. He's an avid birder, too."

"What does he do?"

"He's the curator at the Tyler Texas Museum of Natural History."

Eugene felt a quiet melancholy creep in. "I wish I was doing something like that."

"It's never too late t' change yer mind."

"Yeah…" He looked down at his black tuxedo and tie. *Cecil-Lee's stories sound so fun. I wish I was out in nature having fun too.* He plucked at his lapel. *Instead, I look like a fool at this fancy party, completely out of my natural habitat. I should be wearing Mr. Adams's outfit instead.*

As they entered the dining pavilion, Cecil-Lee stopped in his tracks, and Eugene bumped into him a second time.

"Holy smokes," Cecil-Lee said. "They don't have this kind of décor in the boonies, that's fer shore."

Glass orbs of various colors hung from the gabled ceiling at different heights, like balls of fruit floating in the air. Beneath them, and filling out most of the pavilion, were hundreds of circular tables that fit up to eight diners each. Impeccably white four-hundred-thread-count Egyptian cotton tablecloths covered their tops, and the white seats were wrapped with ribbons of thornless white roses. Dozens more rectangular tables lined the far side of the tent where the local culinary talent displayed their goods. There were towers of croquembouche, platters of mille-feuille, and six-tier cupcake stands on top which sat assorted cakes, brioches, croissants, and Hamantaschen cookies, all begging to be gormandized. In the middle of the pavilion was an ostentatious chocolate fountain with five levels of cascading fudgy falls; guests could take glass cups hanging from a nearby glassware tree and fill them with molten chocolate.

Eugene stared at the fountain with great interest. *It's big enough to play in.*

"Eugene!" Rosaline called out. She sauntered toward him, wearing a dirty apron and a tall white toque, carrying a tray of muffins.

"I'm so glad to see you." She held the tray to her side with one hand so she could give him a hug with the other.

"You must be working hard," he said, surveying the many stains on her apron.

"It's been super busy all night. We've made hundreds of pastries, crème brûlées, sconces, sorbets, tarts, tortes, and so on and so forth. It's a madhouse, but I don't mind. It's great publicity for the bakery."

"How so? I thought your bakery was shuttered?"

She let out a huge smile. "I can reopen it!"

"That's fantastic!" exclaimed Eugene. "How did you manage that?"

"Since the police announced the aliens are wanted criminals, they've fled the city. I contacted the health inspector informing him that the aliens are no longer in my bakery or in D.C. He came by yesterday and saw that the bakery was perfectly sanitary, then asked if I would serve the aliens if they ever returned. I told him I would not."

Eugene cocked his head. "You really wouldn't feed them anymore?"

"I wouldn't hesitate to feed them again! I just had to say that to the inspector to get my bakery back. Anyway, after I told him that, he gave me a passing grade on the inspection and said I could reopen as soon as two months from now, although I have to pay a fine."

"How much is it?"

"Twenty thousand."

"That's a lot."

The tray Rosaline was carrying rose and fell as she sighed. "Yeah. I had planned to put my BABKA earnings toward renovations, but now I'll need to allocate some of it to the city inspectors."

The toque on her head twitched.

Eugene squinted. "Rosaline, is there something you aren't telling me?"

She grinned cheekily. "Eugene, don't be rude. Who's your friend?"

"You're right. Where are my manners? This is Cecil-Lee," he said, playing along.

"Pleased t' meet yew," said Cecil-Lee.

"Nice to meet you, too, Cecil-Lee. Would you like a muffin?" She extended the tray she was carrying toward him.

"Yes, Ahh absolutely would." The Southern giant plucked a muffin from the tray. His absurdly huge man-hands made the muffin look more like a crumb than a meal. He tossed it into his mouth. "Mmmm! That's darn good."

Rosaline blushed. "How do you and Eugene know each other?"

"We just met, actually," said Cecil-Lee.

"Well, that's what this Gala is for, isn't it? Meeting new people."

"Yes, ma'am. It's funny how things work out. First bumpin' intuh Eugene, then meetin' yew, the best baker in D.C. from the taste of these muffins. Seems like fates at work t'nahht."

"Hey, guys," called out a familiar voice. Eugene turned to see Winston swimming through the crowd toward them.

They greeted him, and introduced him to Cecil-Lee, who tipped his white top hat forward a smidgeon.

Winston looked the giant man in the shining white suit up and down. "What are you wearing?"

"Glam Blanc."

"Of course I'd meet someone wearing Glam Blanc."

"It's makin' quite the comeback."

"Tell me about it," Winston said. "Bullit Inc.'s about to release their new line of Glam Blanc next week."

"Ahh know. Ahh already pre-ordered one of everythin'. Ahh'm so excited."

"It'll be a moment we'll never forget."

"Yep," said Cecil-Lee with dreamy eyes, which fell like shooting stars and landed on Winston's exposed toes in his flip-flops. "Do yew like high fashion?" he asked with genial haughtiness.

"No, I only like meetings," said Winston without skipping a beat.

"How did it go with Mr. Adams?" asked Eugene, butting in.

"Ugh, you'll never believe what happened."

"Mr. Adams, as in the prezdint?" asked Cecil-Lee, raising his eyebrows.

Winston clicked his tongue. "That's the one. Apparently, he's traveling to Morocco next week."

"And?" said Eugene.

"He invited me to join him."

"Winston!" exclaimed Rosaline. "That's amazing! You were just promoted to marketing director, and now you're already taking trips with the president."

"It was either that or suffer through more meetings with the marketing team."

"How come you're going and not the vice president of Bullit Inc.?" asked Eugene.

"He has a meeting scheduled with vice president Angryberger during that time, so Mr. Adams invited me to join him in his place."

"I've heard so many wonderful things about Morocco," said Rosaline. "They've got world-class beaches. Probably world-class beach huts, too. I know you'd like that. They also have amazing food markets with some of the world's best citruses and spices."

"It won't be a vacation unfortunately. Mr. Adams told me if anyone asks about the trip to lie and say we are going for 'oil security,' but the real purpose is to inspect Bullit Inc.'s newest and largest factory and finalize a multibillion-dollar exclusive trade deal with Morocco. He wants me to travel alongside him and create a post-release marketing campaign of Bullit Inc.'s newest Glam Blanc fashion line for the U.S. and North Africa."

"Okay, so oil security," said Eugene.

"Yeah. He said I should blame it on the KB Rail explosion, which raised the regional cost of oil by two cents per gallon."

"The dem'lition-economics causal chain of events is what we in the industry call Demonomics," said Cecil-Lee.

"Is that what you do?" asked Winston. "Are you a Demonomics expert?"

"No," said Cecil-Lee, chuckling. "Ahh'm a dem'lition expert, but Ahh studied Demonomics at school."

"Instead of English, I can see," said Winston dryly.

Cecil-Lee threw his head back and roared with laughter. "Yew sure like t' put yer good sock over yer bad foot."

Winston made a face. "What does *that* mean? I'm not wearing any socks."

As Winston and Cecil-Lee got to know each other, Eugene sidled up to Rosaline's side. "So, about those aliens," he began, leaning in so only she could hear, "you don't have any idea where they might have gone, do you?"

"Not a clue," she replied, plucking a muffin from the tray and lifting it to her toque. Eugene watched as teeny tiny gray tentacles slid out from underneath her hat and greedily pulled the muffin inside.

Eugene smiled. Rosaline beamed back.

BOOM! An ear-splitting explosion rocked the Fairgrounds. The four of them instinctively dropped down, and Rosaline reached for her hat to keep it from falling off, letting her tray clatter to the ground instead. A gargantuan orange fireball shot into the sky. Its brilliance was so intense they could see it through the coated vinyl fabric of the pavilion.

"*What was that?*" Eugene yelled.

"Let's go look," said Cecil-Lee in a deep and serious voice, the kind normally reserved for wrangling alligators.

They rushed outside to see where the noise had come from. Eugene scanned the Gala, but no tents had caught fire or exploded.

"That didn't come from the Fairgrounds. It came from over there," said Rosaline, pointing toward the far corner of the lot. Then she gasped. "Eugene, that's—!"

Eugene's entire body shook as he realized the source of the noise. An incinerated train on the tracks next to the Fairgrounds burned carnival orange, and heavy smoke billowed into the air. "That's my railyard! My first new locomotive just arrived today!" He squared off to Cecil-Lee. "Did you do this?"

"No, of course not," he said, slightly offended. "Ahh'm rahht here with yew. How could it've been me?"

"Then who?"

"Eugene, you wouldn't have happened to upset anyone recently?" asked Winston.

"Me? Upset anyone? Why would you think…" Eugene smacked his hand over his open mouth. He stared at Winston with horror.

John Angryberger! He just blew up one of my trains!

CHAPTER 24

The sun, at its zenith, shined down on the disco-ball spaceship, which was plastered with business cards from the festivities the weekend before. A ray of light danced across the top of the ship and reflected in through the ceiling-high windows of Eugene's office, hitting him square in the eye, momentarily blinding him. Eugene shielded his eyes with the back of his right hand and took a step back. He peered at his railyard, where a gigantic black mark blemished the otherwise brown landscape. It was a sad reminder of his new train's simultaneously inaugural and final journey as it traveled from the tracks to the sky on that unforgettable evening at the Gala.

Eugene had spent his days since the accident finalizing insurance claims, walking through the wreckage with inspectors, and worrying about what would happen to the company. The total losses from the train, the oil it had carried, and damage to the track exceeded eighty million dollars.

He rolled his neck side to side. The stress of everything weighed heavily on his shoulders, forming knots in his trapezius muscles. Dark purple bags had formed under his eyes. He spent his nights tossing and turning as he ruminated on John Angryberger's threats. The vice president's voice haunted Eugene's every sleepless hour: *I'm coming for you, Schumaker, and I'm taking back what's mine.*

Eugene turned from the window and slumped into his seat at his desk. The warmth of the light, combined with the monotony of the day and his sleep deprivation, made Eugene's focus wane. Numbers blurred together on the innumerable statements littering his desk, and the buzz of the ceiling fan began to morph into a buzz that was more familiar and far more interesting.

His eyes fluttered shut for a moment, and when he opened them, a savior appeared before him. It was a beetle—and not just any beetle, but an iridescent creature with a body that gleamed like a polished emerald and wings that reflected the colors of a thousand sunsets. This beetle, unlike its tiny peers mounted in glass cases on the other side of the office, stood proud and tall, its shell a shimmering, knightly armor. With delicate yet determined legs, it marched across the mahogany desk with an air of camaraderie, ready to answer Eugene's call for liberation.

The beetle wielded a sword, formerly a letter opener, and charged valiantly toward the labyrinthine walls of Eugene's desk-prison. It let out a miniature war cry that sounded like a blend of a distant roar and a motivational seminar on personal growth. The beetle's tiny voice reverberated within his mind, whispering words of encouragement. "Break free from your shackles of monotony, Eugene!"

The beetle-hero extended a stick-like leg and, with a well-placed thrust, toppled a strategically positioned thumbtack binding Eugene's insurance receipts. The brass thumbtack, once mundane and overlooked, suddenly transformed into a cosmic portal leading to verdant landscapes of possibility. A gateway to freedom.

The portal shimmered; Eugene felt the excitement of entomology and the pull of adventure beckoning him. The pressures of the freight business waned, replaced by the allure of antennae and thoraxes. With a whimsical grin, he stepped through the portal, leaving the smell of shoe polish and failure behind.

Time became fluid, stretching and contorting as Eugene and his beetle companion traveled across the cosmos. They surfed on rainbows, conversed with hexapods, and danced with boogie-woogie aphids in the aurora borealis. As Eugene gazed around him, the stars in the sky metamorphosed into millions of fireflies whose luciferin-filled abdomens twinkled happily.

In the midst of their frolic, a realization dawned upon Eugene. Perhaps this extraordinary beetle was more than a mere guide; it was the embodiment of his own desire for liberation, a manifestation of his yearning for a life unencumbered by familial guilt and obligation. In this world, there weren't any trains or explosions or businesses.

As soon as he remembered his real life, the daydream began to fade. The fireflies disappeared, and so did his hero-beetle. Eugene plummeted from the cosmos down to his desk on Earth, where he startled himself awake. The symphony of the cosmos was gone, replaced with the buzzing ceiling fan.

Head hanging in defeat, Eugene stood up and drifted over to his bug collection. He opened the top drawer of the second cabinet from the right and pulled out a case of preserved Xyloryctes scarab beetles. In the middle was a two-inch long Hercules beetle he'd found in Central America on a fun-filled collecting expedition in college. Looking at the beetle saddened Eugene. *It's what killed Dad*, he thought, remembering how he'd needed his father to fund the trip.

"What for?" Theo had asked when Eugene had hit him up for the money.

"A business trip," Eugene lied, knowing his dad would disapprove if he found out he was pursuing a career in bugs. "I'm joining the undergraduate business program."

"I am so proud of you for finally doing what I always wanted you to do," Theo rejoiced. "You'll make a great CEO of Schumaker Trains and Oil one day."

Eugene felt ashamed for deceiving his father. It wasn't until he returned from the expedition that he decided to come clean.

"Dad, I want to tell you something," Eugene said over the phone when he got back to campus.

"How was your business trip?" Theo asked enthusiastically. "Did you learn all about exploitation?"

Eugene felt his stomach twist into a knot hearing his dad's excitement. "About that... I'm not studying business. I'm—I'm studying entomology," he stammered.

Horrified, Theo dropped the phone. Eugene later learned from Alfredo that his father had felt so ill after his phone call, he'd taken the rest of the day off and gone to pick up his wife from her manicure appointment to deliver the shameful news.

Eugene could only imagine what his dad had said to his mom.

"Why are you being so spontaneous all of a sudden?" Eugene envisaged her saying when his dad picked her up. "No, don't tell me—are you taking me shopping?"

"We need to talk about our son. He's done something horrible."

The blood drained from her face. "What did he do?" she asked, alarmed.

Theo's expression was grim. "He's not studying business like he told us. He wants to be an endocrinologist."

"To study thyroids?"

"Is that a type of beetle?"

"I think you mean entomologist."

"What are we going to do about our son? He likes to play in the dirt, but he's twenty years old. That boy is throwing his life away." Theo looked at his wife. "How did we mess up so badly?" he asked, sobbing uncontrollably.

"*We* didn't mess up. It's *your* fault. You pushed him too hard by demanding he do something he didn't want to do."

"Our precious son—heir to the family company—is choosing to abandon all of it," he said, ignoring his wife. "Has he forsaken us?"

"*Theo, look out!*"

His eyes, pooled with tears, had failed to see the red light in front of him: he ran the intersection and was T-boned by a truck.

Eugene's parents died before they reached the hospital.

Eugene shook the image of his disappointed parents and their tragic deaths from his mind. He put the case of Scarabaeidae back in the cabinet, turned his back on his bug collection, and walked listlessly toward the mountain of claims, insurance-report receipts, and urgent memos from the board atop his desk.

I can't deal with any of this!

Overwhelmed, he glanced at the portrait of his father hanging magnanimously above him. Anger washed over Eugene like a tidal wave. *Ever looking down on me, aren't you?* He glared. "Well, I never wanted to run your business anyway, Dad!" he shouted. "I hate it! And I'm glad John Angryberger destroyed one of your trains. I wish he'd destroyed more. I hope he blows up everything. That way, I'll be free from the burden you put on me, free from having to pretend to be the son you always wanted."

His lower lip quivered. "You and John deserve each other. Two money-grubbers who value their business more than people." A tear rolled down his cheek. More tried to follow, but he stubbornly fought them back. "I hate you, Dad!"

There was a knock on the door. Eugene hurriedly wiped his eyes and spun around.

A beaming Alfredo burst inside, waving a handful of papers. "I have fantastic news! The train explosion was a windfall in disguise!"

"What do you mean?" asked Eugene, sniffling.

"Here." He handed Eugene a bundle of resolved insurance claims as well as an updated financial statement from the refinery. "Insurance covered the full cost of the trains," he said giddily, "but there's more than that: we reaped a massive profit. The accident spooked oil markets, raising the price of a barrel by two cents on the dollar. As a result, we're poised to make an extra twenty million dollars this month from our refinery alone."

"We made money from someone sabotaging our oil tanker?" asked Eugene, mystified.

"*Considerable* money, yes."

"I don't believe it." For the first time in a week, a smile returned to Eugene's face.

"I thought you'd find the news encouraging," said Alfredo. "You're doing a fantastic job. Don't be alarmed by little speed bumps. You were born to be president of this company." He gave a slight bow and headed for the office door.

Eugene watched Alfredo leave, lost for a moment in contemplation, and then a laugh unexpectedly emerged from the depths of his belly. He tossed his head back and cackled manically. *I can't wait to see the look on Angryberger's face when he finds out. He'll be furious!*

Tears from twisted laughter spouted from his eyes. He wiped them away with his index finger. Smirking, he turned to look at Theo's portrait. "You know, Dad, I was one straw away from quitting this company and this life you forced me into, but why quietly walk away and let John Angryberger win when I can hit him where he'll never expect it, all while making you squirm in your grave?"

Eugene shoved the Matterhorn of claims off his desk with two hands, then opened the bottom drawer and sifted through junk and miscellaneous papers until he felt a rectangular card. He raised Cecil-Lee's business card and showed it to his father's portrait. "Remember how you always desired a son who would turn your cherished company into the biggest train and oil operation in the country? Allow me to show you that I can be the son you always wanted me to be."

CHAPTER 25

The black limousine came to a stop in front of the largest manufacturing plant in Casablanca, the Masnie Almal. Winston, stunned by its vastness, gazed at the monstrosity from behind the car's tinted windows. The titanic factory was the size of twenty-seven football fields, excluding the parking lot for employees, which Winston and the president had passed on their way to the front entrance. Four immense smokestacks protruded from the top of the twelve-story factory. Hundreds of encapsulated security cameras dotted the building's exterior like portholes, monitoring every entrance and exit. It was within this behemoth that Bullit Inc.'s newest line of Glam Blanc fashion was manufactured and produced.

"We're here," said Mr. Adams.

One of the Secret Service agents stepped out from the front of the car. He opened the door to the backseat and extended a hand to the president. Mr. Adams took hold, using his other hand to support himself as he climbed out of the limousine.

Winston watched as Mr. Adams straightened his sand-colored Sumner's Fun T-shirt that the Bullit Inc. marketing team instructed him to wear and affixed his Presidential Seal to the pocket over his left breast. His gelled-back gray hair was parted down the middle in childlike fashion. The seventy-two-year-old president didn't look a day over sixty-eight.

Winston stepped out from the limo after him, flinching at the intensity of the Moroccan sun. He held up a hand to block the solar rays from blinding him, fumbling with his other hand to put on his new gold aviators which were given to him by Salahazzar Boudhin, Morocco's Minister of Foreign Affairs, when he and Mr. Adams landed at the airport.

Mr. Adams put on his sunglasses, too. Together, they waited for Mr. Boudhin to walk over from his government vehicle. They gazed at the factory towering over them, impressed with the sheer size of the building and the magnitude of its operation. Innumerable trucks waited in queues at the factory's loading docks, ready to export the merchandise produced inside to thousands of stores around the globe. The 1,600,000 square-foot facility was like its own bustling metropolis.

"This place looks incredible," said Winston.

"It better be top-of-the-line if they want an exclusive, multibillion-dollar trading agreement with Bullit Inc."

"Imagine if my apartment was this big."

Mr. Adams frowned. "Remember, Winston, you aren't here to daydream. You're here to pay attention so that we can create a marketing strategy for our new fashion line."

"Uh-huh," said Winston distractedly as he stared at the factory with awe. As much as he might like to deny it, he couldn't wait to witness the behind-the-scenes magic of Glam Blanc.

CHAPTER 26

John Angryberger surveyed the long winding driveway for the black luxury sedan transporting the vice president of Bullit Inc., but it was nowhere in sight.

"Where the hell is he?" John shouted, growing increasingly impatient. He crossed his arms, leaned his shoulder against the brick wall, and restlessly tapped his right foot against the hardwood of the wrap-around porch.

"He should be here any moment," replied Mr. Chartreuse, sitting on the stoop at the front of the game lodge.

"Why are you wearing that?" John asked him. "You look like an orange clown."

Mr. Chartreuse wore a bright orange vest, a matching bright orange wool ushanka, a pair of bright orange corduroys, and orange leather boots. Orange-framed sunglasses with reflective orange-gold lenses hid his eyes.

"I don't want to get shot."

"I'm not going to shoot *you*."

John fretfully checked his watch, then looked over with peevishness at Mr. Chartreuse, who took out a stick of peppermint gum and popped it into his mouth. He tossed the wrapper into the bushes next to the driveway and leaned back, rolling out his spine on the hardwood balcony, until he was supine.

"Here he is," said John grumpily, standing over him. "Get up."

Mr. Chartreuse rolled onto his side, let out a grunt, and pushed himself up. Together, he and John watched the black luxury sedan creep down the driveway until it came to a gentle stop at the foot of the stairs.

Both doors opened at the same time. The vice president of Bullit Inc. stepped out from the passenger side, and a man with little elf ears and a button nose—and whose hair was in the preliminary stages of recession—hopped out from the driver's side.

"Sorry I'm late, Mr. Vice President," said Dominic Miller extending a hand as he walked toward John. "I had a pressing meeting that ran long."

"You're here now, that's all that matters," John replied, gripping his hand firmly and trying to crush his bones.

Unperturbed, Dominic smiled gaily at the feeble attempt.

"This is Mr. Chartreuse, CEO of KB Rail," said John, gesturing toward the orange-clad man.

Dominic placed his hands on his hips, which disappeared underneath his belly. "How are you recovering after that explosion from last month?" Dominic asked Mr. Chartreuse.

"We're bouncing back, thank you," answered Mr. Chartreuse pleasantly.

"Good, good." Dominic signaled for his associate and driver to come over. "I'd like to introduce you to Mr. Tibbles, senior marketing analyst of Bullit Inc."

"Senior marketing analyst? I thought your marketing director was coming?"

"Winston? He couldn't make it. He's accompanying Mr. Adams on a trip to Morocco."

"What? Why are they in Morocco?"

"Oil security," Dominic lied.

"He needs a marketing director to help address oil security?"

"It's a covert operation."

John clicked his tongue in irritation. He had hoped to use the marketing director to find out more about Eugene, the aliens, and what had happened to the spaceship.

"In any case, welcome, Mr. Tibbles, to Roxborough Game Preserve," said John unwelcomingly. "A hundred square miles of prime gaming estate a mere two hours outside of the capital."

"I'm excited to be here," said Mr. Tibbles, winking at John.

John stared at him with the warm likeness of obsidian. "Follow me so we can get suited up to go hunting."

The four men walked up the stairs and through the century-old mahogany doors at the entrance. They proceeded through the grand rotunda, which was covered with dark green carpet and oil paintings from the nineteenth century depicting European settlers hunting bison, wolves, and Native Americans.

While Dominic and Mr. Chartreuse took in the infelicitous décor, Mr. Tibbles hung back and sidled up next to John.

"Hey, boss, excited to see me?" he whispered.

"Call me that again and I'll shoot you," vowed John in a hushed tone.

"Whoa! There's no reason to kill anyone."

"That's what you think," murmured John ominously. He looked at Mr. Tibbles, his anger rising. "Why didn't you tell me that Winston was going on a trip with Mr. Adams to Morocco? Why didn't you inform me that you were invited here in his place?"

"I didn't want to spoil the surprise! Besides, Winston never told the marketing team he was going. He's not the best communicator." Mr. Tibbles leaned in toward John and whispered faintly: "I think that's why he doesn't have a girlfriend."

John gritted his teeth. "What's the point of having you inside Bullit Inc. if you don't find out this kind of information for me?"

"But I did find out—he doesn't have a girlfriend."

"I'm going to shoot you."

"You said you had hunting garb for us to wear?" asked Dominic loudly.

"There's a gentlemen's locker room to the right down the hallway," John answered, pointing past the rotunda. "Inside, orange vests and hats have been laid out for you. There's also camouflaged clothing if you prefer to wear that underneath your vest. When you're done, you'll find coffee, tea, bourbon, scotch, whiskey, fruit, nuts, cheeses, and cookies waiting for you in the sunroom. From there, Landon, the game warden, will train us on the proper way to carry and shoot our firearms before we go hunting. That way, nobody gets hurt."

"Sounds good," said Dominic, loosening his tie.

"Great, then we'll see you on the other side."

John leaned sideways toward Mr. Tibbles. "Pretend like you don't know me," he whispered from the corner of his mouth. "We're working. Don't blow your cover."

"Okay, *not-my-boss*," Mr. Tibbles replied, winking. Cheerfully, he headed toward the locker room.

John and Mr. Chartreuse waited for them in the sunroom. It had bright yellow walls which were made lighter by the abundant sunshine that streamed in through the many windows and the glass dome protruding from the center of the ceiling. There was a self-serve bar with two swivel-stools in front of its beautiful, dark birch-wood counter. Two couches, a reclining chair, and an ottoman—all aquamarine—filled most of the room, each with its own side table. It was a happy and upbeat room, and therefore one of John's least favorite places.

While Mr. Chartreuse poured himself a drink, John stopped in front of a window and looked at the woods in the distance. He could hear Mr. Chartreuse pull down one of the glasses that hung above the bar having found an enticing bottle of bourbon to keep him company.

"This should be your next investment," he remarked to John, unscrewing the bottle and sniffing its contents. "A bourbon company."

John pretended not to hear him. He was too busy cogitating on Winston's absence. *Why did Mr. Adams take him to Morocco? What do they have planned? Is Mr. Adams colluding with that damn Schumaker through Winston?*

"Here we are," Dominic Miller announced, stepping into the sunroom with Mr. Tibbles at his side.

John turned from the window to face the vice president. "Help yourself to a drink if you'd like, gentlemen."

Dominic waved his hand dismissively. "I'll pass, thank you."

"What are you drinking?" Mr. Tibbles asked Mr. Chartreuse.

"Bourbon."

"Is it any good?"

Mr. Chartreuse nodded fervently. "It's very smooth. Tastes almost caramel-like with hints of cinnamon and vanilla. You gotta try it."

Mr. Tibbles went behind the bar and poured himself a glass. "This is fantastic," he exclaimed, taking a sip. "You know, Dominic, that's what we should invest in next."

"What's that?"

"A bourbon company."

"That's what I said!" Mr. Chartreuse exclaimed.

"It's a good idea, is it not?" said Mr. Tibbles.

"Not a good idea, a great idea."

"Great minds think alike."

John watched the two of them with annoyance. "Landon is waiting for us outside." He opened the glass doors to the patio. "When you're ready."

Dominic stepped out onto the terrace, followed by Mr. Tibbles, who carried his drink with him, and Mr. Chartreuse, who had drained the rest of his bourbon in one sip and left his glass on the side table.

Waiting for them outside was an older man sporting an orange vest, a pair of clear hard-plastic glasses, and orange headphones. He had an out-of-style white comb mustache that made him look like a walrus. When he saw the four businessmen, he took off his headphones and walked forward to greet them.

"Pleased to see you again, sir," he called out to the vice president.

After introductions were made, Landon said, "If you gentlemen are ready, I'll show you how to shoot. We'll practice on clay pigeons before heading into the woods for real game."

Landon led them toward a table he had set up on the terrace. On it rested a dozen shotguns. He picked up a Browning and twirled it in his arms. "Here's the rundown for beginners," he said, flipping the shotgun in the air and simultaneously catching it while opening the chamber. "First things first, this button right here is the safety." He indicated the tiny knob on the barrel, to the right of the trigger. "This way means it's on, so you can't shoot even if you try. But if you push it in like this"—he pushed the knob in—"then the safety is off, and you can kill."

He flipped the shotgun upside down. "You can pull this flap to open the chamber." He pointed inside. "This shotgun can hold two shells. All these on the table hold two shells, except the semi-automatic shotguns on the end over here. Those can hold up to four. You want to slide the shells in business-end first, with the metal cap closest to you, and then you just"—he quickly lifted the shotgun and jerked it down, causing the chamber to close—"snap it back on, and you're ready to go.

"To carry it around, you want to hold it up against your shoulder with the safety on. That's called the shoulder carry. The other way to hold it is to point the gun down at the ground in front of you. That's called the trail carry. No matter how you carry it, make sure the safety is on, your hand isn't on the trigger, and the chamber is empty. Most importantly, never point your gun at anyone else. Got it?"

"Got it," said Mr. Tibbles.

"Great. To shoot, you'll each need to wear a pair of glasses as well as a pair of headphones. If you don't wear headphones, you'll blow out your eardrums. Now, when you shoot, you want to put the butt of the gun snug against the inside of your shoulder, like this. Rest your cheek against the shotgun so that you can see through the iron sight to aim. I'll step on one of these pedals, which will release a clay pigeon into the sky. Now, put on your equipment so we can get started."

Once everyone had put on their glasses and headphones, Landon tapped one of the pedals with his right foot. An orange disc zoomed a hundred feet in front of him, crossing the field from right to left. He tracked it for a half-second then…*bang!* The loud explosion resounded all around the meadow and bits of clay rained down onto the grass below.

Mr. Tibbles jumped. "What a great shot!"

Landon motioned for them to take off their headphones. "Each of you needs to choose a gun. Then, one at a time, come on up, and I'll show you how to hold and shoot it."

Mr. Chartreuse instinctively reached for a metallic-gray semi-automatic shotgun. Dominic and John each picked up a break-action Browning.

"There's so many choices, I don't know which one I should get," Mr. Tibbles whined.

"How about this one," said Landon, handing him a semi-automatic Remington twelve gauge. "This one's fun. I used to use it on SWAT missions back when I worked for the FBI, after I had finished my service in the Marines. Come up here, I'll show you how to shoot it."

While Landon showed Mr. Tibbles how to hold and fire his Remington, Mr. Chartreuse wandered to the other side of the terrace where songbirds chirped from the trees along the side of the lodge.

John watched his orange-clad underling survey the branches on which a dozen cloudy-gray birds with flashes of white in their wings and yellow on their rumps were perched. They pointed their sturdy bills at Mr. Chartreuse and ruffled their long narrow tails.

Psit tsee chek! Psit tsee chek! the yellow-rumped warblers whistled sweetly.

"Psit tsee chek!" Mr. Chartreuse sung back. He pointed his shotgun at them and pretended to shoot.

Bang!

Bang!

Bang!

Bang!

Mr. Tibbles had shot at the discs Landon released, but he missed. The discs sailed serenely into the distance, gliding down onto the well-trimmed grass, fully intact.

"Aw, shoot!" Mr. Tibbles said. "Can I try again?"

"Yes, you can. Get ready." Landon stepped on the pedal and let several more discs fly out at once.

Dominic watched them with a look of amusement on his face. "Remember when we were young and happy like that?" he asked John.

John pointed at Mr. Chartreuse, who was pretending to shoot birds out of a tree. "Tweedledee and Tweedledum are not taking this seriously."

"They're just having fun."

"They're unfocused. This is a business meeting, not a fraternity party."

"You can't be in work mode all the time."

"I'm always working."

"You can afford to relax for a moment." Dominic slapped John on the arm playfully. "You can be human around us."

"I am human."

"Show me then," Dominic challenged, his reptilian eyes twinkling prehistorically.

John didn't know how.

"Four in a row!" yelled Mr. Tibbles, laughing and high-fiving Landon as the exploded bits of clay scattered into the grass.

"Excellent job, Mr. Tibbles," said Landon. "That was great. Who's next?"

"Me," said Mr. Chartreuse, exchanging places with Mr. Tibbles. He raised his semi-automatic shotgun.

Landon released four pigeons in quick succession.

Bang!

Bang!

Bang!

Bang!

Mr. Chartreuse watched the discs sail away. "Well, I'm rubbish," he said, chuckling with embarrassment.

Landon released several more discs for Mr. Chartreuse, until he managed to hit them. Next, Dominic took a turn, and then John stepped up to the plate. Even though he already knew how to shoot, he wanted to warm up his aim.

Bang!

Two orange discs exploded into fragments with a single trigger pull.

John lowered his gun. "I'm ready, Landon," he said somberly.

Landon locked eyes with him. "So am I."

He turned to the guests. "Gentlemen, let's go do the real thing. I've got plenty of ammunition for us in my pack, along with jerky, water, and bourbon—everything we need for a good time. Let's head down these stairs," he said, gesturing toward the stairwell leading off the terrace to the yard beneath and woods beyond, "and bag some big ones."

CHAPTER 27

Eugene led Cecil-Lee through the railyard, passing hundreds of oil cars as they stepped over dozens of rows of track. Everything smelled like train—a metallic, oily, industrial scent with hints of old wooden planks. The only place in the yard that didn't smell like that was the twisted, banged-up track a hundred feet behind them that was still black from the explosion the previous week. Most of the area had been cleaned up, but there were still bits of jagged and bent steel track lying around as well as hunks of corroded metal from the oil cars that hadn't yet been discarded. The occasional train wheel could also be randomly found far from the explosion, as some of them were blown off the cars and scattered throughout the railyard.

One of them had ended up next to the track Eugene was now crossing. He tapped it with his foot, trying to see if he could move it, but it was much too heavy.

"Somethin' in the way? Here, Ahh'll move it," said Cecil-Lee. He bent down and picked up the wheel with one hand and then tossed it forty feet away as if he were throwing a plastic frisbee.

"Here they are," said Eugene after walking another few yards and slipping between a string of oil cars into an open clearing.

"Would yew look at these beauties," said Cecil-Lee. Nine new sleek and sophisticated JD-52BC models rested on the tracks, their fresh blue and white paint glistening in the sunlight. The burly engines were seventy-two feet long, ten feet wide, and fifteen and a half feet tall. Painted in sky-blue above each train's bullish white noses were the letters "STO," the acronym for Schumaker Trains and Oil. The same letters were painted on either side of the engine.

Cecil-Lee slapped the nearest engine affectionately. "They shore are purdy. An'—mmmm!" He put his probiscis against the paint and took a whiff. "Love that brand-new, fresh-out-the-fac'try smell. How much were they?"

"One point eight million each."

"Dear mama. That ain't cheap." Cecil-Lee twisted his head side-to-side. "Yew shore yew want me t' blow up these expensive babies?"

"Yes."

"Positive?"

"Yes."

"An' yew accept full responsibility fer whatever may happen?"

"Yes."

Cecil-Lee bent down and unzipped the enormous duffle bag he had brought with him. Inside were over a hundred pounds of explosives and wires with which to rig them.

"That's a lot of explosives," remarked Eugene.

"Yeah, an' they ain't the cheap kind either. These are Chinese made, Class B explosives. Virtually impossible t' git yer hands on. Yew cain't find 'em anywhere—nobody sells 'em."

"Why is that?"

"They're illegal," he said matter-of-factly in his sing-songy Murchison drawl.

"If they're illegal then how'd you get them?"

"Ahh'm friends with a gahh who knows a gahh who knows this Chinese gahh who sells 'em. He goes bahh the name Mr. Choo. The explosives are made from the byproducts of a food processin' company in China an' are shipped t' us inside the soles of moccasins from Morocco."

"Mr. Choo? Like the famous baker from the BABKA?"

Cecil-Lee gave Eugene a quizzical gander. "Whahh would a

world-renowned baker moonlahht as a black-market explosives dealer? That doesn't make any sense." He bent down and pulled a dozen rectangular packages from the duffel bag. Each was the size of a loaf of bread and wrapped in black plastic with yellow Chinese characters written on them. Printed on each was an image of a yellow stick figure having his limbs blown off and a big red "X" drawn over his body.

"What are those made of?"

"Oh, the usual stuff," Cecil-Lee answered nonchalantly as he balanced the explosives lazily on his knee. "Mostly zirconium-enriched TNT, RDX, nitroamines, tertiary-butylene an' red phos'phrous, as well as other salts, plasticizers, an' additives. An' let's not forget yellow dahh number five."

"You certainly know an awful lot about chemicals," said Eugene, impressed.

"Not really. That's just what it says on the label." Cecil-Lee pointed at the packaging.

"You can read Chinese?"

"Heck no. But Mr. Choo can, an' that's what he told the gahh who knows my gahh who told me what it says."

"Oh."

Cecil-Lee reached into the oversized duffel bag and pulled out a smaller average-sized duffle bag. He unzipped it and carefully extracted a humongous coil of wires. He looped the coil over his head, freeing his hands so that he could pick up the stack of explosives.

"Ready? Let's go plant mahh babies on yer babies."

They chose the engine in the middle, so the trains surrounding it would prevent unwanted eyes from witnessing their misdeeds. Cecil-Lee gently placed the explosives and the wires on top of the aggressive-looking nose of the locomotive.

"How much does this choo-choo weigh with all the cars attached?" he asked.

"A hundred and fifty-four tons."

Cecil-Lee looked up at the locomotive and cupped his hand over his chin with his index finger resting over his mouth. After a moment of thought, he turned back to Eugene. "Assumin' this steel is an inch thick, we'll need quite a bit of explosives t' penetrate the hull. Yew said this was an electro-diesel motor, rahht?"

"Yes, why?"

"It's important t' know so we can control the explosion. We don't want an investigator discoverin' the train was blown up intentionally based on debris left behind. No, we need to destroy any proof. Therefore, we'll need enough diesel in the tank so that when the explosives blow through the steel, they'll cause the fuel t' react an' set off a chain explosion. If done rahht, the whole thing'll obliterate like"—he snapped his giant fingers—"*that.*"

Eugene nodded. "How many charges do we need to make sure that happens?"

Cecil-Lee stroked his chin. "Ahh'd say ten charges set up directly beneath the fuel tank on either side of the engine. Ahh'll add 'nother couple of charges t' the proximal oil car t' propagate the chain reaction down the line. Once this locomotive here blows, all the oil cars will blow up, too."

Cecil-Lee got onto his knees and crawled underneath the engine, one hand cradling an explosive. Once he located the fuel tank, he flipped over onto his back. He rested the explosive on his belly and pulled out a container of concrete paste from his pocket.

"Where do yew want t' test this?" he called out while gluing the package to the fuel tank.

"Somewhere there aren't any people, so nobody gets hurt."

"Do yew have a place in mind?"

"There's public land a hundred miles outside the city that I've already scoped out. We'll do it there."

"Is the conductor on board with this ahhdea?"

"Ron? Yes."

"Good. Could yew hand me 'nuther charge?" he asked, having already finished sealing the first one to the underside of the locomotive.

"Apart from us and the conductor, nobody else can find out about this," Eugene said, handing Cecil-Lee the second charge. He was surprised by how heavy they were.

Cecil-Lee dragged it under the train like a wolf pulling a carcass into its den. A few moments later, he reached his hand out for a third charge. "How do yew know the conductor will stay quiet?"

Eugene handed him another one. "Ron's been in service to my father since the inception of Schumaker Trains and Oil. When I spoke to him, he said he believed in me and the future of the company, and that he'd do anything a Schumaker asked."

"He must have a lotta faith in yew."

"Sure, or he's crazy."

"Like yew."

Cecil-Lee put out his hand for a fourth charge.

Eugene continued to hand Cecil-Lee a single charge at a time until all of them were set. Then he passed him the coil of wire, and Cecil-Lee connected the charges and blasting caps together.

When he finished, he attached a receiver chip to the initial charge, which would be activated by an encrypted wireless signal from a remote detonator.

He crawled out from under the train and brushed the dirt from his jeans. "She's ready t' go," he said, nodding with a satisfied gleam in his eyes. He stepped next to Eugene, and together they admired the train, now strapped with enough explosives to destroy a small town. "When do yew want t' do this?"

Eugene grinned mischievously. "Ron's already on his way here."

CHAPTER 28

Winston looked over his shoulder, past Mr. Adams who stood next to him in front of the factory, and watched as Mr. Boudhin exited the limousine, said something to his two bodyguards, adjusted his tie, and walked toward them.

"Welcome to Masnie Almal, Morocco's newest and largest factory!" the Moroccan foreign minister exclaimed cheerfully. "It's ready for full-scale production of Bullit Inc.'s newest goods. I believe you'll be more than satisfied with the facility. But before we begin our tour, I'd like you to have a treat from the finest baker in all of Morocco, the legendary Kambu Mbuto." Mr. Boudhin signaled to one of his agents who presented the distinguished guests with a plate full of orange star-shaped cookies. "Almond-orange blossom M'hancha pastries. Please enjoy."

Winston popped the cookie in his mouth. As the sweet, light, citrusy flavor hit his taste buds, he let out an involuntary *mmmm* in pleasant surprise. *This is nearly as good as Rosaline's cookies.*

Mr. Adams smacked his lips. "Good," he said, reaching for another off the plate, "but I've had better."

"Now, if you will follow me, let us go into the facility to see how your newest producer is producing for you," said Mr. Boudhin, doing his best to speak formally.

Winston gawked at the sheer size of the building as they

approached the front doors. Goliath red Arabic letters spelling the name of the facility hung above the entrance. Even though each letter was a whopping twenty feet tall, the words scarcely covered a tenth of the wall.

One of the Moroccan agents bounded ahead to hold open the door. Mr. Adams passed through, followed by Winston and Mr. Boudhin.

"As-salamu alaykum! Hello!" came a loud, raspy voice. A short and squat man with bristly black sideburns and a galumphing gait stepped out from between four women in brown and red worker's uniforms waiting for the Americans inside the reception area to offer a bow.

"Wa-alaykum. Mr. Adams, Mr. Perry, this is Mudir, the factory manager," said Mr. Boudhin, exchanging bows with Mudir.

"Pleased to meet you, Mr. President," said Mudir, "and you, Mr. Perry."

The two girls closest to Mudir stepped forward and offered white canvas bags embroidered with "Masnie Almal" in red letters.

"These are a gift to each of you," said Mudir.

Winston accepted a bag and peered inside. There was a pair of the newest Glam Blanc shoes from the factory, as well as a pair of Glam Blanc socks and a Glam Blanc ball cap. Winston pulled the shoes out of the bag and noticed on the heel of each one was written "GB Moroccasins."

Mudir watched as Winston rolled his finger over the words. "The name is a conjunction of the words Morocco and Moccasins," he explained happily.

Winston lifted the tongue to check the size: U.S. 12.

"Mr. Boudhin informed us of your correct shoe size. Go on, please try them on."

Winston lifted his feet one by one and wiggled off his flip-flops. He took out the Glam Blanc socks from his goodie bag and turned them over in his hand, expecting to find a unique texture or design. There was neither. They were socks—ordinary white socks—with a little white line above the toes that told him which side was up. He looked inside the sock's opening. Inside, in white letters barely distinguishable from the rest of the whiteness, were the instructions, "insert foot here." With ease, he followed the helpful directions before slipping his feet into the white Moroccasins. They were immensely comfortable and fit perfectly.

"How do you like the shoes?"

"They feel great."

"Amazing, isn't it?" Mr. Adams remarked, "given the fact that they cost two dollars and thirty-five cents to make."

"That makes me feel like a cheap Cinderella," Winston joked. He picked up his sandals and put them in the bag.

"Glam Blanc Moroccasins are made out of the finest petro-chemical textile products a low budget can buy," explained Mudir. "The petrochemicals are shipped from Husyuen Chemical, a food-processing plant specializing in rice-based foods in Hangzhou, China. Their leftover chemical processing solutions, which would normally be disposed of at a cost to the producer, are repurposed to provide rigid support in the soles of Glam Blanc's newest line of sneakers. We call it 'liquid sole.' We've turned the waste products into wearable merchandise. Fortunately, *most* people only reported four or fewer medical side effects from walking on chemical waste all day. The products will be sold to Bullit Inc's. subsidiary, Bull's Eye Retail, at no cost to itself. This will maximize your bottom line, because you only need to pay the costs of production, such as purchasing thread, laces, metal ringlets, sheep's wool, and cellulose-derivatives to mix with the food-processing chemicals to make the shoe walls, as well as pay the energy cost to run the factory."

Mr. Adams nodded curtly. "Good."

"Anyway, please, sirs, if you will follow me, I will take you through the factory."

Mr. Adams, Winston, Mr. Boudhin, and a team of security personnel followed Mudir down a long hallway and through the gargantuan complex. After walking the length of a single football field, Mudir turned to point at a door on their left. The cheap black plastic plaque on the door read: "Mudir."

"This is the manager's—I mean, my—office."

He reached into his pocket and pulled out a donut-sized brass ring with a dozen keys on it. He fumbled nervously until he found the one to his office. "Please," he said, opening the door and gesturing for them to enter.

Winston followed Mr. Adams inside the expansive and well-lit office. Mudir's unusually long charcoal-gray desk took up much of the space. Winston counted twenty-four surveillance monitors on the desk, stacked neatly in six columns of four. Behind the workstation, a large glass window wrapped one hundred and eighty degrees, extending from the left side of the room all the way to the far right, about one hundred feet long. The window provided a clear view of the manufacturing operations and workers on the other side, many of whom were operating dangerous heavy machinery.

Mudir pointed at a door tucked away behind cabinets in the back left of his office. "That leads to the factory floor. There are stairs inside the plant which lead to an upper-level walkway that runs across the entire sweatshop. This way, we may patrol workers from above as well."

"Show me," Mr. Adams insisted.

Mudir leapt forward and pushed open the door for the president. Mr. Adams stepped into the manufacturing room followed by Winston, who was immediately greeted by a cacophony of metallic screeching, whirling, fizzing, and buzzing. Pressing machines shrieked loudly as steam whistled through the exhausts. Buzzers rang as shipping doors opened and closed, allowing trucks carrying raw materials ingress and egress for export-ready products. Employees shouted to be heard over the clicking, clacking, clinking, clunking, clattering, and general industrial tintinnabulation of heavy machinery.

The group ascended a long metallic-green staircase that rose six stories. When they reached the top of the stairs and the overhead walkway, Winston looked around. The walkway extended the perimeter of the factory. It crisscrossed like a tic-tac-toe board so that the manager could survey every assembly workbench and every machine, like a warden watching over prisoners.

Winston peered down at the hundreds of workers. "There are fifty workers per workbench, which are organized into one hundred rows," Mudir explained. "Some workers at the benches stitch logos onto sneakers; others fasten bevels and clamps to accessories. Next to the rows of workbenches are gigantic steam presses, forty in total, each operated by four workers."

Winston switched to the other railing and surveyed the rest of the floor. Rows of mighty vats containing milky, tan-colored liquid lined the center, their contents swirling like a witch's brew. Workers wearing protective biohazard suits operated elephantine whisks that mixed the solution inside the vats. The solution itself looked an awful lot like muffin batter. *Must be liquid sole*, he thought, watching the vats gently stir the Husyuen food-processing chemical byproducts, slowly blending the solution and transforming it into the rigid gel-like substance that formed the soles of Glam Blanc sneakers.

At the bottom of each vat was a series of drainage pipes that led to a giant oven, where the liquid was poured into what looked like giant muffin trays and heated until it solidified. After the trays of sole batter were placed in the oven, the workers mixed another batch in the vats. *Baking a shoe is as easy as making a muffin*, he observed.

Winston pointed at the industrialized cauldrons. "Has anyone fallen in?" he asked, imagining what it must feel like to fall into a pool of toxic shoe-based pouf paste while a human-sized whisk swirled him around.

"Not in the past twelve hours," said Mudir.

"Do you like what you see?" asked Mr. Adams, coming to Winston's side and crossing his elbows on the rail.

"I never envisaged it'd be this big."

"If you think this factory is big, wait 'til you see my paycheck," Mr. Adams bragged. "The sales margin I'll make off this Glam Blanc line will be through the roof."

"Good for you," said Winston flatly.

Mr. Adams frowned. "Aren't you curious how I make ginormous profits?"

"N—"

"Textiles and fabric sourced from China and Bangladesh are delivered here to Morocco, where they're woven together to make shoes," he began before Winston could tell him he wasn't interested. "The shoes are then packaged and sorted in the warehouse. From there, they're loaded into containers and stacked onto trucks and driven to port, where they're placed on shipping freighters. The containers are shipped across the Atlantic to the Ports of New York and New Jersey. Then they're shipped transnationally via railroad freight or trucked to Bullit Inc.'s warehouse facility outside Jefferson City, Missouri.

"Once at the warehouse, they're sorted by destination. Some of the goods stay in Missouri to be sold by retailers there, others are sent around the country to satisfy the needs of customers in other states, and a sizable portion are sent abroad—to Morocco, for instance."

"Why wouldn't you just send the goods directly to the stores in Morocco after they come out of this factory?" asked Winston, slightly confused. "Wouldn't that be much simpler?"

"Logistically, it's less efficient."

"How can that be?"

"That's just how the market is. You should know, being a marketing director."

"But how can it be more efficient to send a box of goods to the US from Morocco via boat, transport it by train to a warehouse in Missouri, sort it, send it back to port, ship it on another vessel to Africa, and truck it back to a store in Morocco, than to send a box of goods directly from this factory to the nearest supercenter?"

Mr. Adams nodded. "It's that simple—isn't that amazing? Look at it this way," he said, sensing Winston's lingering confusion, "a single container holds about one hundred thousand dollars' worth of goods. A truck picks it up from the factory and drives it to the port of El Jadida for ten dollars per mile, which comes out to six hundred dollars. From there, a shipping company ferries the container across the Atlantic for two thousand dollars. Once it arrives in New York, it's put on a Schumaker freight train for another three grand. That gets picked up by Bullit Inc.'s own fleet of trucks and delivered to one of our warehouses, where it is automatically and rapidly sorted and separated, then sent back across the Atlantic for the same prices. Factoring in port fees and U.S. Customs fees and tariffs, it costs twelve thousand dollars to get one hundred thousand dollars' worth of goods to the store to sell. That's twelve percent of the gross value of the goods. In other words, a pair of Glam Blanc shoes, which costs two dollars and thirty-five cents to make, only costs three dimes to ship roundtrip from Morocco to the United States and back again."

Winston scratched his ears, which had begun to hurt. He couldn't tell if the primary culprit was the tinnitus from the nonstop whirring and drumming of heavy machinery, the vertigo from being so high up, or Mr. Adams's nonsensical explanation of global logistics.

"In contrast, it's sixty-six percent less cost effective for goods to be sorted in the manufacturing facility and shipped directly to supercenters," Mr. Adams rambled on. "Employees would have to work additional hours to sort everything, and it'd take several hours for one employee to separate a container of shoes whose destination is either Morocco or New York, for example. Those additional hours of work spent sorting packages would be better spent loading finished goods onto trucks or assisting with other functions. If it takes ten hours to sort each shipping container by hand, I'd lose another ten hours from the worker not working on other things. Those compounded hours lost add up to twenty hours lost. Even though the workers are paid Moroccan minimum wage, which is fortunately much lower than what it is in the U.S., it delays the export and sale of merchandise, which is based on the U.S. minimum wage. Therefore, instead of costing thirty-seven dollars of work, it costs two hundred and forty dollars. That's equivalent to one hundred and thirty man-hours on the factory floor. If the factory produces one million dollars' worth of goods per day, then losing that many hours of production equates to losing twenty-one thousand dollars. That's forty-nine cents per pair of shoes, substantially more than the thirty cents it costs me to ship a pair of shoes across the world and back."

"Couldn't you just hire more people so you aren't losing additional man-hours of work?" asked Winston.

Mr. Adams scoffed. "That's not how business works," he said, spittle flying from his mouth over the banister.

"Oh, silly me."

"Don't be too hard on yourself. You don't have a business background."

"Without an MBA, it's hard for me to put my finger on the issue, but something seems wasteful," said Winston sardonically. "All the oil and non-renewable resources it takes to ship a pair of shoes around the globe can't be good for the environment."

"Wasteful? Who are you to talk?" snapped Mr. Adams. "You just wasted my time asking me these dumb questions. Besides, your friend Schumaker operates several oil refineries and an enormous fleet of trains that spews pollution into the air constantly. I don't see you getting pious with him."

Winston frowned. He'd never thought much before about his nature-loving friend running a pollution machine. *That is odd. How can he be okay with that?*

"Most importantly though, look at these workers," said Mr. Adams, pointing to the factory floor with disdain. "They're getting paid one dollar and eighty-five cents per day."

"That's it?" asked Winston incredulously. "How can that be?"

"It's ridiculous," agreed Mr. Adams. "If this sand-shifting government didn't raise the minimum wage three years ago, we could have saved enough money to fill an additional container with goods per day."

"Mmmm," said Winston.

"They should be grateful I'm paying them. Millions of people don't even have jobs." Mr. Adams thrust out his chin and scanned his workers on the factory floor, like a lord surveying his kingdom below. "I don't run a charity," Mr. Adams continued, defending himself from no one. "This is my business and my money. It's mine to use as I want, and nobody has a right to tell me what to do with it. It's not my job to help others."

"There's no written law that says you have to," agreed Winston.

Mr. Adams's expression momentarily softened. "It's good you

understand. With that mindset, you'll have a great future at Bullit Inc."

"How fortunate for me," said Winston. "Maybe one day I, too, can make billions while paying people less than two dollars a day."

Mr. Adams narrowed his eyes. "Winston, do you want to become a successful businessman, or do you want to be one of *those* people who helps others?"

"I just want to be left alone."

Mr. Adams laughed. "You're a lot like me," he said, playfully slapping Winston on the back. "One day you'll have to decide what kind of life you want to lead: one for yourself or for others. I only hope when that day comes, you make the right decision."

CHAPTER 29

The five men headed off into the woods, their guns at the ready. Moving like seasoned hunters instead of business executives, they crept forward silently, crouching, their eyes peeled for any movement in the distance.

"Let's fan out slightly so we aren't clustered together," whispered Landon.

Mr. Tibbles and Mr. Chartreuse nodded. They spread out on either side of the warden, sneaking stealthily through the trees.

John, meanwhile, crept closer to Dominic. "Now that we're in this woodland sanctuary," he said, "I'd like to talk business."

"I figured as much," replied Dominic. "I've never known you to invite someone to Roxborough for a friendly hunt. You're not exactly a social debutante."

"I'm troubled by Bullit Inc.'s discriminatory trading practices in Egypt. The new laws allow Bullit Inc. unrestricted access to factories, ports, raw materials, and markets with zero oversight. Additionally, it gives proprietary rights to imported foreign materials and excuses tariffs from exported manufactured goods. The deal grants Bullit Inc. legislative immunity from trade policies that all other businesses must follow. In fact, if I'm not mistaken, portions of the trade deal stipulate that no other American corporation can do business in the country without Bullit Inc.'s approval. That type of authority is unprecedented and illegal."

"Mmmm. Well, if it were, we wouldn't be doing it. And we already have exclusive trade treaties with a hundred other countries, so I'm not sure why you're getting upset about this particular deal."

"I've been voicing my concerns about Bullit Inc.'s unscrupulous covenants for years."

"Ah, well, there's nothing you can do about them, so if I were you I would stop worrying and focus on the things you can change instead."

"Cut the crap, Dominic," John snapped. "There's no reason why we shouldn't be working together to maximize revenue and market cap for both of our businesses. Mr. Adams and I are president and vice president of this country, for Christ's sake. We should be a team."

"True," said Dominic, looking away from John for a moment to scan the trees for pheasants. "Mr. Adams is president and therefore assumes all presidential duties, including handling foreign affairs. That's not your, or Jmart's, job. As far as we're concerned, the vice president's sole executive function is to break ties in the Senate."

"Are you insulting me?"

"Not at all. I'm merely reminding you that your say in international, legislative, and executive matters is negligible at best."

John felt the veins in his neck twitch. He gripped his shotgun tightly. "You've been intentionally withholding information from me and brokering with international agents for Bullit Inc.'s sole benefit at the expense of free enterprise. If this continues, I'll have the Senate convict Mr. Adams for abusing his power of office."

"Nothing's going to change," said Dominic, swatting John's words out of the air as if they were nothing more than a pesky mosquito.

"I'll mobilize senators and my friends in SCOTUS to begin the impeachment process."

"John, we both know that if you were in Bullit Inc.'s position, you'd abuse your authority to develop the same—if not more—egregious treaties that no amount of money or power could satiate."

John feigned a smile. "Mr. Adams and I work together at the White House. I'm merely wondering why we can't engage in a symbiotic business partnership. There's no reason why we shouldn't collaborate. It might make us better political partners."

"Politically, we have similar interests," said Dominic. "We both want free trade, reduced regulations, less oversight, yadda yadda. But, economically, we're racing against each other, vying for an advantage that shuts out the competition. Therefore, working together makes no sense. Besides, you don't exactly play well with others."

"You need to let me into North African markets," John growled. "I need to expand my freight business, and that's an easy market to take over."

"Why? Is it because you're losing out to Schumaker, so you feel the need to take over somewhere else?"

"You're full of it," John spat, seething. "If you don't give me what I want, I'll expose you. I know all about Mr. Adams's bribery, his underhanded negotiations, and his shady business practices in Egypt and elsewhere. I'm certain he's doing more of the same in Morocco as we speak, forging deal number one hundred and one. Oil security, my ass. I'll impeach Mr. Adams and destroy Bullit Inc."

"Only a hater looks behind the curtain," Dominic taunted.

"I'm going to end you," John snarled.

Dominic let out a booming laugh. "Why don't we just try to enjoy the rest of the hunt? In fact, why not turn it into a friendly little competition? Whoever bags the most pheasants wins exclusive trading rights to Guinea-Bissau."

John put his finger on the trigger.

Dominic chuckled. "Kidding, kidding! We both know those trade deals are exclusively ours, even if you win." He patronizingly patted John on the back before breaking off to the left in the direction he last saw Mr. Tibbles.

"Landon," John called.

The warden, who had stealthily circled back and was now tailing them, moved in closer. "Sir?"

"Do you have the shell?"

"Yes, sir. It's right here." He pulled a maroon and gold shotgun shell from the inside pocket of his hunting vest and held it up for John to see. It looked identical to a shotgun cartridge. Unlike one, however, it wasn't full of pellets; it was an explosive device. "I take it business didn't go well?"

"I'm afraid Mr. Adams won't change his mind unless we send him another message. He needs to know I'm not messing around."

Landon grimaced. "Must it be done?"

John nodded. "Now go."

Landon took off in the direction of Dominic and the others. When the game warden was out of sight, John took a deep breath. *It's not like I didn't try to do this the right way, but they've left me with no choice.*

Gunshots rang out in the distance.

"They must've found a pheasant," John muttered to himself, climbing over fallen tree branches and skirting around thickets of bramble to catch up.

"Would you look at that! We finally got one!" proclaimed Mr. Tibbles as John came within earshot. Mr. Tibbles hoisted the pheasant, whose gorgeous golden-brown feathers were soaked in blood, above his head as if it were a ceremonial flag. "I didn't realize how much fun this could be!" he exclaimed.

"Great shot!" Mr. Chartreuse commended.

"You, too. It was a team effort," said Mr. Tibbles giving him a bloody high five.

"Darn, I almost got the kill, but I guess you can't land everything, isn't that right, John?" said Dominic, jeering.

"Here, I have more cartridges," said Landon, handing Mr. Tibbles and Mr. Chartreuse shells. "Here's one for you too, Dominic," he added, handing him the special shell. They opened their shotgun chambers and stuffed the cartridges inside.

Fully reloaded, the businessmen continued their hunt. Landon carried the pheasant on his back. It swung like a pendulum with every step he took. John watched it, meditatively. He imagined it was like a clock ticking down the time Bullit Inc. had left.

"There," whispered Landon, stopping abruptly and pointing at a pair of pheasants foraging in the thicket.

The group froze, motionless.

"Why don't you take the shot?" Landon whispered to Dominic.

"You don't need to tell me twice," said Dominic, raising his barrel and aiming down the sights.

Mr. Tibbles readied his gun, ready to pull his trigger if Dominic missed.

John looked away. He had already witnessed death many times before. Instead, he gazed up at the gray clouds covering the sky. The weather reminded him of when he was a kid, and he would pretend the clouds were faces. He'd imagine the faces of the other kindergartners whom he hated, and who hated him back. Kindergarten was such a hateful place. He remembered watching jealously as the other children played with their toys.

"You can't play with us, Little Johnny," they once told him.

That had made him mad. "Let me play!"

"No! Get away from us!"

"Come on, let me play!"

"Get out of here, *dork*!"

He waited for them to turn their backs then hit them on their heads. "Those are my toys! Mine! Mine! Mine!" he screamed. The other students cried out in pain and called for the teacher, who yelled at Little Johnny to return the toys to their rightful owners.

Even as John grew older, nobody wanted to include him. Left without a choice, he focused on his interests and himself, until eventually, after achieving success, people wanted to join *his* team. They invited him to luncheons and dinners, asked him out to weekend retreats, and surprised him with lavish gifts in shameless displays of pecuniary courtship. But no matter how many invitations he received, he continued to feel excluded from social circles. These people didn't really want to be around him; they merely wanted something from him.

John hated them and their deceptive pretenses with such fervor it corroded him inside. They didn't care about him, so he didn't care about them. He developed caustic relationships with everyone he met, until hating them became his primary source of motivation, the coal that kept his furnace lit.

As he gazed skyward, he imagined Dominic's face on one of the slowly moving gray clouds. He could make out the vice president's fat round cheeks and long porcine nose. A fold in the clouds looked just like the furrow between Dominic's beady eyes. As far as John was concerned, there was no difference between the middle-aged man who wouldn't share business and a kindergartner who wouldn't share toys. Business executives and kindergartners were equally exclusionary.

John was tired of feeling left out. Today was the day it would change, he decided.

"This one is for Guinea-Bissau," Dominic shouted.

John closed his eyes.

The shot echoed throughout the woods as the shell exploded inside the gun's chamber, blowing a hole in the top of the barrel, sending shrapnel flying. The pheasants, spooked, flew away.

Dominic grabbed his throat in shock. A large piece of shrapnel had struck him in his neck. He opened his mouth to scream for help, but no sound came out. Eyes bulging, he looked toward the other men who simply stood there, dumbstruck.

Dominic pulled his hand away from his throat to signal that he needed help, but as he did so, a fountain of blood spurted out, showering Mr. Chartreuse and turning his bright orange hunting outfit bright red. Dominic's eyes fluttered shut, and he collapsed onto the brambly earth.

A gentle breeze blew, rustling the leaves, and the clouds moved.

CHAPTER 30

Eugene pointed. "There she is."

The blue and white locomotive crept into view on the distant horizon, rumbling down the tracks and leaving behind a plume of white smoke. It pulled eighty DOT-111 oil cars, each carrying thirty thousand gallons of crude, on its maiden voyage from the refinery.

Eugene and Cecil-Lee crouched in the tall grass on the side of a hill overlooking the train tracks. Cecil-Lee's truck was parked on the dirt road at the top. Eugene blended in with the grass in his olive-drab safari pants and safari hat; Cecil-Lee, conversely, looked a tad out of place in his porcelain-white gator boots and swamp vest. They were both equipped with butterfly nets, with which they had caught five monarch butterflies, a meadow fritillary, a *Narceus americanus* millipede, and a pleasing fungus beetle, all in the twenty minutes while they waited to rendezvous with the train. The butterflies, millipede, and beetle explored their new home inside Eugene's terrarium.

"Do yew ever name any of yer bugs?" Cecil-Lee asked.

"No."

"How come?"

Eugene shrugged. "I don't know. I've never thought to name them."

"Whahh not name this millipede here, 'Trainy?'" Cecil-Lee suggested. "After all, the little feller looks just like a train with its long body an' many segmented parts."

"That's a silly name."

"No, it's not. It's a good name. Ahh reckon he likes it, don't yew, Trainy?" He tapped on the terrarium wall.

Trainy crawled on top of a decaying piece of wood and started nibbling on its rotten core.

"See? He likes it."

The train whistle blew, signaling its approach. Cecil-Lee gently tossed his butterfly net onto the ground and stood up. "Ahh'll git the remote."

Eugene watched him head to the truck, open the passenger-side door, and rummage inside the glove box for the detonator. He put it in his pocket and returned to Eugene.

Eugene shifted his attention to the oncoming train. His hands were sweaty in anticipation.

"Ahh reckon she'll be here in five minutes," said Cecil-Lee, licking his lips hungrily. He twirled the remote in his right hand to keep his excitement under control.

As the locomotive approached, Eugene imagined what the explosion would be like. He envisioned it starting a forest fire that took out the whole Eastern Seaboard. He pictured entire subdivisions of little pink American houses burned to a crisp and the families that lived in them forced to evacuate. As if that wasn't bad enough, he imagined the federal government coming after him, seizing his assets, and throwing him in prison.

"I'm having second thoughts," he said to Cecil-Lee.

"Whad'yew mean?"

"I don't know if this is a good idea anymore."

"Don't git all scaredy-cat now. It's a fantastic ahhdea."

"I don't know. I mean, what if—"

"What if what?" said Cecil-Lee with a hint of aggression.

"Oh, I don't know… What if things don't go the way we think they will? And I don't mean with the train," he added, catching Cecil-Lee's defensive look. "I know things will go smoothly when you push that button. I mean afterwards. What if after we do this, things don't happen the way we hoped they will?"

Cecil-Lee chuckled. "When do things ever go as planned?"

Eugene frowned.

As the locomotive crept closer and closer, Eugene found himself forced to choose between two futures: he could continue with his immensely comfortable yet unsatisfying inherited life, or he could blow that fate to bits and pieces and choose the wild, unknown life of an entomologist.

How do I make the right decision?

He turned to Cecil-Lee. "Do you remember when we met a couple weeks ago?" he asked.

"Shore Ahh do. An' how lucky it was that we ran intuh each other. Who knew we'd become bisdness partners as well as friends?"

"Do you think that was planned, Cecil-Lee?"

"Ahh shore didn't have any plans to bump intuh yew. Heck, Ahh didn't even see yew there."

"I know *you* didn't plan to; I'm just wondering if there's something or someone out there that planned for us to meet?"

"Yew mean the aliens?"

"No, not them. Well, maybe. Or someone else. I mean…" Eugene sighed deeply, trying to find his words. "Did our encounter mean anything?"

"Oh," said Cecil-Lee understandingly. "Yew talkin' 'bout fate."

"Yeah, I guess I am."

"Whad'yew think?" Cecil-Lee asked.

"I don't know," said Eugene honestly.

"If yew don't know, then what are yew worried about?"

"I just want to make sure I'm doing the right thing."

"An' what's that?"

"I don't know."

Cecil-Lee thought for a moment. "Ahh think yer askin' the wrong question."

"What do you mean?"

"Does life have meanin'? Is there any purpose t' this?" He pointed at himself. "Whahh me?" He pointed toward the field beneath them. "Whahh this?" He peered into Eugene's fearful eyes. "Those aren't the questions yew need t' ask yerself rahht now. Forget 'bout big ol' ahhdeas like those, 'cuz they aren't questions you'll ever be able t' answer. The only question yew should be askin' yerself rahht now is whether yew want t' blow up this train or not."

"I don't know!"

"Then let fate decide. Ahh'm holdin' up one or two fingers." He hid his right hand. "Guess what number Ahh have behind mahh back? If yew git it rahht, we blow up the train. If yew git it wrong, we don't, an' we walk away from here an' pretend none of this ever happened."

"How will I know you didn't change the number?"

Cecil-Lee grinned. "Yew won't."

"I don't want to make the wrong choice."

"A wrong decision is better than no decision at all."

"But isn't no decision my decision too? And even if I choose wrong—not wrong as in the wrong number, wrong like I made the worst decision for myself—then I'd be deciding my own fate even if I got it wrong. In other words, no matter what I choose, this was my choice all along because... I chose it?" said Eugene, unsure of himself, and even more unsure of his future.

"Yer overthinkin' things. Just pick a number. What'll it be? One or two?"

Eugene looked at the train slowly creeping closer. It was less than a minute away. It reminded him of Trainy.

"One."

Cecil-Lee brought his right hand out from behind his back. He held out two fingers. "Ahh guess we won't blow up the train then." He shrugged. "Oh well."

Eugene's heart skipped a beat. Nothing would change. Tomorrow, he'd go back to his desk and continue to run an extraordinarily profitable train and oil refinery business, and he'd do that for the rest of his life. He'd have everything he could ask for, except happiness.

I can't do that, he thought. *If I go back, I'll live the rest of my life in misery knowing that I never reached for my dreams.*

"No!" he shouted.

"What?" asked Cecil-Lee.

"Let's blow up that friggin' train!"

Eugene marched toward the tracks, trudging with newfound purpose through the tall grass as the train rapidly approached, now only a few yards away. Adrenaline coursed through him, giving him the power to do something he never thought he could do, like be reckless.

The train's pistons stopped pumping and there was a loud *kshhh-hhh!* as it came to a halt in front of the saboteurs.

The locomotor door opened, and an old man sporting blue and white overalls and a matching cap over his wiry white hair hopped out. On his hat was the acronym "STO." In his hand was a fire extinguisher.

"Heya there, Eugene."

"Hey, Ron, how's it going?" said Eugene.

"This must be our demolitionist," said Ron, sizing up the big gruffy man with the tattoos and a detonator who glided to a stop next to Eugene.

"Howdy."

"Howdy howdy right back at ya," said Ron. He looked toward Eugene expectantly. "Are we going do this or what?"

"Absolutely."

"Great, great, can't wait, but, uh, remind me: how's this going to work without me going to prison?"

"Ahh got this doohickey rahht here," said Cecil-Lee, holding up the detonator encased in a glass box and wiggling it before Ron's eyes. "When Ahh push it, the train'll go '*boom!*' The blast radius is huge. We'll need t' head behind the truck if we want t' be a safe distance away when Ahh set this thing off."

"Well, to be honest, I wasn't planning on being anywhere near a giant explosion, so I was going to head to the top of the hill anyway.

Being burnt to a crisp after having my limbs blown off is not my preferred way to go, no thank you."

Ron took off toward the truck, cradling the fire extinguisher in his arms. Eugene and Cecil-Lee followed him up the hill.

"Ideally," Ron said over his shoulder, "I'll die in my sleep when I'm ninety-three. None of that 'exploded by an oil tanker' cause of death. That sounds much too painful. I want to have as little suffering at the end of my life as possible."

"Sounds like you have it all planned out," said Eugene.

"I have a lot of time to think while driving trains. Am I supposed to stand somewhere or something?"

"Just go 'round t' the other side of the truck an' stay down," said Cecil-Lee, leading by example and moving to the passenger door.

Ron lightly kicked the back tire with his toe. "Your tires are shot," he observed. "You need to replace them."

"Dancin's hard on tires."

"You dance?"

"Salsa Thursdays out in Waldorf, Maryland."

Ron raised his eyebrows and glanced at Eugene. "He's my favorite demolitionist."

"Isn't he the only one you know?"

"Yes, but he's also my favorite."

Cecil-Lee opened the door and reached for the glove box. He pulled out three sets of protective headphones and handed a pair to Eugene and Ron and kept the third for himself. "Make shore yew wear 'em, 'cuz once Ahh hit this button, it's gonna git real loud. Without 'em, you'll git tinnitus."

"What?" said Ron. He tapped his headphones. "I can't hear you."

"Keep yer headphones on at all times," Cecil-Lee repeated, putting on his own pair.

Ron turned to Eugene. "What did he say? I can't hear him. Look." He tapped on his headphones again. "I can't hear anything."

"He said to keep your headphones on."

"What?"

Cecil-Lee shook his head and turned to Eugene. "Yew ready?" he mouthed.

Eugene nodded.

Cecil-Lee reached into his swamp-vest pocket and pulled out a tiny gold key. He inserted it into the protective glass box, unlocking the remote inside.

"This is it, boys," he said, smiling with such force that dimples appeared on his cheeks. His finger hovered over the big red button. "Three, two, one…"

"What?" yelled Ron, lifting his headphones. "I can't hear anything you're saying!"

Cecil-Lee pushed the button.

It happened instantaneously: the locomotive erupted in spectacularly bright, hot flames, like a phoenix reborn. The force of the explosion caused the hull to buckle in half and rise into the air, as if an invisible fist had punched it from underneath. Time briefly stopped. The two engine halves floated, suspended in the air. And then, just before they fell back onto the tracks, the secondary charges went off, blowing off the back of the engine in a humongous fireball that ruptured the hull of the proximal oil car, causing it to blow up a split second later and triggering a chain reaction. One by one, like falling dominoes, the eighty oil cars exploded. Some were blown completely off the tracks, and those that weren't melted the tracks beneath.

Even with headphones covering his ears, the thunderous blasts threatened to rupture Eugene's eardrums. Deformed metal from the oil cars skyrocketed into the air. Copious volumes of acrid black smoke billowed from the burning train cars. Oil that hadn't combusted created standing pools of black liquid with bright orange flames dancing on top.

Eugene crumpled his nose as the noxious smell from the burnt fuel and corroded metals wafted toward him. Tremors pulsed throughout his body as the ground beneath his feet shook violently. The heat from thousands of gallons of oil catching fire made the hairs on his skin stand on end. His heart pounded furiously. He had never felt more alive.

John Angryberger and my dad will be displeased! he thought as his lips curved upwards into an expression of uncontainable joy.

Cecil-Lee removed his headphones and indicated for Eugene and Ron to follow suit. "Woohoo!" he screamed, showing off his newfound dimples as he smiled crazily. "Was she a beaut or what!"

Ron shook his head. "Let's temporarily ignore the fact that I might have just lost my hearing and instead, tell me, what do we do now?"

"Let's blow up 'nuther one," said Cecil-Lee, a psychotic gleam in his eye.

"I'm getting out of here," said Eugene matter-of-factly, dusting ash and soot off his hands.

"That's good for you," said Ron, "but I was really asking about me. What should *I* do now?"

"Yew shore yew don't wanna do it again?" Cecil-Lee asked Eugene, ignoring Ron.

"Yes, I'm positive. We need to get out of here."

"Aww, shucks, but that was so fun! Let's blow somethin' else up real quick. Ahh just love blowin' things up."

"I can see that, but we need to go," said Eugene, anxiously looking past his shoulder down the dirt road.

"How 'bout mahh truck? Ahh carry dy-no-mite in the glovebox bahh mahh gun. Ahh can ignite it real quick, set it off within twenty seconds."

Eugene stared at him, growing concerned. "Cecil-Lee, I'm not messing around. Let's go."

"Well, alright, fine," he said, clearly disappointed. Then, under his breath, muttered just loudly enough for Eugene to hear: "party pooper."

Ron cast his palms upwards. "Wh-what about me?" he stuttered. "Did you forget about me? I'm part of this little team, too."

"Ron, you'll need to call the police and tell them the train blew up," said Eugene. "Then, hang out here and wait for them to get you."

"Okay, and after? Are we going to meet to debrief about this at some point? Maybe after I see an audiologist?"

"Of course."

Ron took a seat on the grass. "Well, I guess I'll just sit here by myself and wait for someone to come help me. See ya boys later."

"Just tell the police exactly what we rehearsed," said Eugene.

"Oh, hi, Mr. or Mrs. Officer," said Ron sarcastically. "Fancy seeing you here. You'll *never* believe what happened. The train blew up for *no reason whatsoever*. How lucky was it that I was up on a hill outside the blast zone when it exploded?"

"Try again," said Eugene impatiently. "Take this seriously."

Ron's eyes rolled back as if searching for a misplaced script in his head. "Oh, hi, Mr. or Mrs. Officer. The engine started smoking, so I stopped the train and stepped outside to inspect it. That's when I noticed the engine seals were on fire. I hopped back inside the locomotive, grabbed the fire extinguisher, and tried to put out the fire, but it was too late. It had already spread throughout the engine. I heard loud rumbling noises, so I dashed up the hill to get as far away as possible. I barely made it a safe distance before the entire train erupted. That's when I called you."

"Much better." Eugene looked toward Cecil-Lee. "Ready?"

"Yew shore yew don't want me t' rig the truck? It'll barely take a sec."

"Cecil-Lee…"

"Alrahht, let's skedaddle."

Eugene and Cecil-Lee hurried to the unrigged truck and got in.

"If I get arrested you better bail me out!" Ron shouted as they drove off, leaving the conductor to watch the flames feed on the locomotive's corpse alone.

CHAPTER 31

Winston sat uncomfortably in the chair across from the president in the Oval Office. They had just flown back from Morocco and Winston was happy to be free from Mr. Adams, but much to his dismay, the president summoned him to an emergency meeting before he could call a cab home. Winston surmised the president must have been informed of the pressing matter of Dominic Miller's death the moment they had landed and not an instant sooner. *Otherwise, we could've had this conversation during the eight-hour flight, and I'd already be home.*

"What kind of idiot is he?" asked Mr. Adams from behind his stainless-steel desk.

"*Was* he."

"Was he," he said. "Don't correct me," he added. "I mean, Jesus Christ, who gets killed by a pheasant?"

"The pheasant didn't kill him."

"What do you mean?"

"His gun jammed and blew up in his face."

"Whatever. You know what I was trying to say. Only an idiot gets killed from a pheasant jamming and blowing up in their face. I can't have an idiot as my number two in command. It looks bad for the company."

"Yes, sir."

"The shareholders lose faith."

"We can't let that happen."

"This is just another thorn in my side. Why does this have to happen to me?" he lamented. "Not a moment after we got back from such a splendid business trip to Morocco, I find out about this. On top of that, we're nearing peak summer season, and I need all hands on-deck. Instead, I'm missing leadership. It's just one more thing I don't want to deal with." He sighed. "All these other directorial and managerial dimwits aren't good enough to be my vice president."

"It seems like you're in a pickle."

"A pickle… That reminds me. Do you want to hear something I've never told anyone?"

"Um…"

"I didn't know what a pickle was until I was seventeen years old. Up until that point, I had gone my whole life thinking that a pickle was a just a slightly acidic, shriveled up finger of a green vegetable covered with warts. One day, as I was standing in front of the fridge contemplating what I should eat, I asked my mother, 'Where do pickles come from?' My mom said to me, 'Cucumbers.' Then I said, 'Mom, I'm not talking about cucumbers; where do *pickles* come from?' I thought she didn't hear me. And that's when she blew my mind: 'Pickles *are* cucumbers, sweetie.'"

Winston rubbed his temples. "You're saying you didn't know what a pickle was until you were a teenager?"

"Indeed. That was a pivotal moment for me. I realized they came from cucumbers, which transformed via the process of pickling. That was revolutionary for a seventeen-year-old—the pickling *process*, where one thing I don't very much care for is turned into something that I kind of like." He paused to assess Winston's reaction. "Do you know why I'm telling you this story?"

"I have no i*dill*a."

Mr. Adams stared blankly at Winston.

"…that was a pickle pun."

Mr. Adams rose from his seat and walked toward the window

where he looked out over the lawn. "Winston, I want you to be my vice president."

Winston did a double take. "Excuse me?"

"Don't make me repeat myself. I'm going to give you three seconds to decide. Three…"

Winston let his jaw hang open. *Me, vice president? That will mean so much more work.*

"Two…"

And I don't want to do work.

"One…"

"Unfortunately, I must decline, Mr. Adams."

"I decline your declination. It's not a choice, Winston. I'm making you my vice president."

Winston buried his head in his hands.

"Don't let it go to your head, Winston. It's not that I have confidence in you; it's just that I lack confidence in everybody else," Mr. Adams clarified. He looked at Winston like an estranged father might look at his ostracized son. "Even though I've only known you for a week, it's long enough to know that you'll do fine. You're not a complete idiot."

How I wish I was.

"Come back same time tomorrow and I'll fill you in on your new duties as vice president of Bullit Inc. Unfortunately, I can't get you up to speed today because I have a meeting with the chancellor of England regarding our new trade proposal, and afterwards my cabinet wants to discuss insurgencies in Oman."

"I didn't know that England had a chancellor."

"I don't know. Chancellor, prime minister, führer, whatever. It's all the same. There's two hundred something countries. I can't keep up with who's who in all of them. Their titles and positions change as often as runway models in a fashion show. I've got more important things to worry about than job titles."

Winston nodded, wishing he didn't need to worry about his own job title. He stood up to leave.

"Just promise me one thing," Mr. Adams called out to him before he reached the door.

"What's that?"

"Don't die on me, Mr. Vice President."

Winston didn't think his day could get much worse. He had spent almost the entirety of it traveling, then had an impromptu meeting, and if that wasn't bad enough, had just been promoted. He suffered through so many hardships within the past several hours, he didn't know if he could handle another one. It was with great misfortune then that John Angryberger provided him with an opportunity to test his resolve.

"Winston, I'd like a word," he said in an ophidian whisper, ambushing Winston the moment he stepped foot from the Oval Office.

Winston looked around wildly before his eyes settled on the vice president whose back was hugging the wall so tightly it gave Winston the fleeting impression he might be a gecko. "Have you been waiting there this whole time for me?"

"No, no, of course not," he said, grabbing Winston's arm above his elbow and leading him down the wide hallway toward the end of the West Wing. "Let's go to my office and have a quick chat."

"Please, no. Can we raincheck this? Today has been so hard already."

John smiled through gritted teeth. "This won't take long at all, I promise," he said, clutching Winston's arm more tightly.

Winston, realizing that he had no choice, whimpered in agreement. "Okay, but *quickly.*"

At the end of the hallway, John opened a plain brown door and pushed Winston inside. The room was decorated simply; a small three-foot wide desk with two claret barrel chairs facing it and one black wingback chair behind it. The walls were painted with vertical, alternating stripes of white and navy. A lone potted bromeliad rested on a coffee table in the corner, its leaves flaccid and withered.

John locked the door behind him. "Sit," he said, wearing the same saturnine smile and gesturing toward one of the chairs in front of the desk.

"Thanks, but I prefer to stand. I've been sitting most of the day already."

"Fine." John took his seat behind the desk. He put both his elbows on the surface, then theatrically balled one hand into a fist and caught it in the other so that it made a popping sound. "I have some questions I'd like to ask you," he said, tilting his head sideways so he could see past his hands.

"If this is about poaching me to come work for Jmart, you can forget about it. I've already changed positions once today, and I don't want to do it again for at least another couple of months."

"I wasn't going to ask you that."

"Good. It's bad enough working for—"

"What happened to the spaceship?" said John, interrupting him.

"What do you mean?" asked Winston, caught off guard. He expected John to ask him about Bullit Inc., or even Eugene, but he wasn't anticipating fielding questions about the aliens. "Is it not there? Did the aliens move it?"

"You misunderstand me. I meant, what happened to the *inside* of the spaceship?"

"Oh…well, I have no idea. I've never been in there."

"But Schumaker has."

"He has?" asked Winston with surprise. He gazed at John who eyed him narrowly.

"He must not have told you," said John.

"No, he hasn't." Winston thought it was strange. *Wouldn't Eugene have informed me right away if he had gotten that opportunity?* It sounded like something Eugene would have loved to experience. Why was he hiding it?

"Where are the aliens?"

That question he knew the answer to, but there was no way he would ever tell John.

"I don't know."

"Is Schumaker in possession of any strange artifacts or technology?"

"No, he isn't," said Winston, growing increasingly uncomfortable. "If you have any more questions about Eugene and the aliens, you should ask him, not me. Can I go?"

John's countenance shifted, taking on a grotesque shape as he pressed on. "What about Mr. Adams? What were the two of you doing this past week?"

"We were in Morocco doing some oil security stuff. Look, if you have questions about it, you should just ask him."

"Which country is Mr. Adams going to visit next?"

"I don't know, and I think it's time for me to—"

John stood up from behind his desk. "Are you feeding Mr. Adams information about the aliens through Eugene?"

Winston raised two fingers in a lazy salute and gripped the door handle behind him. With his other hand he unlocked the latch, then spun the knob, pulled open the door, and stepped outside the office. He could hear John continue to question him as he walked away.

"Are you helping Mr. Adams collude with Schumaker? Is that how he knew about the trains? What are you planning next?" John yelled before the door finally shut.

"What a nutcase," Winston muttered, quickening his pace to a jog so he could leave this dark and dreary building as fast as possible.

CHAPTER 32

Eugene swung open the bakery door, put his hands on his hips, and inhaled deeply in anticipation of the sweet, fragrant smell of morning cakes.

He wrinkled his nose instead. The aroma wasn't sweet but glue-like. Rosaline stood near the wall, gluing a strip of brown and gold fleur-de-lis paper onto it. All the old paintings and posters had been taken down.

"Just a moment, I'm almost finished," she called over her shoulder, rolling a squeegee over the wallpaper.

"No worries, we can wait," he said.

"Eugene!" she cried, swinging around at the sound his voice. A look of relief spread across her face. She put down the squeegee and rushed over to him, wrapping her arms around his neck. "I'm so glad you're okay!"

"Why wouldn't I be?" he asked as Cecil-Lee entered the bakery behind him.

Rosaline walked behind her cash register and took out a newspaper she had stuffed underneath. "Look at this," she said, thrusting it at Eugene. "I was worried sick when I saw it."

On the front page was a black-and-white photograph of a burning train. The caption read: "Oil Train Carrying 2.4 Million

Gallons of Crude Explodes." Eugene snatched the paper from her hands and dove in:

An oil train, owned and operated by Schumaker Trains and Oil and carrying over two million gallons of crude, exploded yesterday just after noon, roughly one hundred miles outside the nation's capital. All eighty cars went up in flames, leaving a long trail of debris and smoke. It took two hours for firefighters to put out the fire.

The conductor of the train told reporters that he sensed something was wrong moments before the explosion. He noticed smoke seeping from the engine and felt powerful vibrations inside the cab, which convinced him that something was awry. Less than a minute after he stopped the train and ran a safe distance away, it burst into flames, releasing thick black clouds of smoke hundreds of feet into the air.

"I just can't believe how lucky I am that I didn't get hurt," stated Ronald Lionel, the train conductor. "Not even a single scratch! Although, to be honest, my ears haven't stopped ringing. I think I have tinnitus."

The Inspector General, along with a team of forensic experts, detectives, and policemen, are investigating the accident. As of this moment, there is insufficient evidence to determine the cause of the explosion, though detectives have not yet ruled out arson.

This is the second major accident in the history of Schumaker Trains and Oil since Theodore Schumaker founded the company half a century ago. Their first explosion occurred two weeks ago, when an oil tanker exploded during a Gala hosted at the Fairgrounds. It is not yet clear if the two incidences are connected.

Rosaline looked at Eugene expectantly. "Well?"
Eugene flashed a dumb grin.
"How can you be smiling at a time like this?" she asked,

worried. "What happened out there yesterday? Somebody could have gotten seriously hurt."

"It was a freak accident, and we'll get to the bottom of it," Eugene assured her. "If the problem is with the new engines we purchased, we'll send them back to the manufacturer to have them repaired."

"What about all that oil that caught fire? The cleanup must be costly."

"Government agencies will be responsible for cleanup, although we'll help subsidize the expense. It's not a big setback though, because our insurance covers this type of thing. But never mind me, how have you been these past couple of days?" he said, eager to change the subject. "It looks mighty different in here."

He looked around the bakery walls which were plastered with the new wallpaper. Part of the old hardwood floor and been pulled up, and several bags of thin-set mortar were tucked in the corner near the door. A huge box labeled "Fragile—Tiles" was parked next to them. Propped against it was the old artwork that had been taken off the walls.

Eugene pretended not to notice Rosaline eyeing him uncertainly. He knew she wanted to press him about the incident, but he could also tell she wanted to share about her new decorations and her progress in the reopening process.

"I needed a bit of a change, and not just with the walls—I've been trying out lots of different recipes getting ready to reopen the bakery next month," she said, her eyes lingering on him.

"How are you feeling about it?"

"Amazing. After all the support I got during the BABKA, I can't imagine how well the bakery will do once it reopens."

"It's going to do great."

"Speaking of great, I just made some almond-anglaise infused croissants that turned out wonderfully. Would you like to try one?" she asked.

"Yes, please."

"Ahh'd love one, too," said Cecil-Lee. "They sound dee-licious."

"Of course. And what would you like to drink with that?"

Cecil-Lee pointed his thumb at Eugene. "Whatever he normally has."

"Coming right up." She washed her hands in the front sink, picked up a bakery tissue, and reached into the display to grab a croissant for each of them. She put them on little white plates, then turned on the espresso machine to steam milk for their hot chocolates. She poured the frothy milk into two mugs that were wider than they were tall, added chunks of Venezuelan salted dark chocolate, and stirred gently until the chocolate dissolved.

"What have the two of you been up to?" she asked over her shoulder. "You've been spending so much time together, like two peas in a pod."

"Bug stuff," said Cecil-Lee without missing a beat.

"Oh, that's great. Now you don't have to drag Winston to do those things with you," she said to Eugene. Rosaline passed the mugs of hot chocolate and the plated croissants to the boys. As Cecil-Lee reached to take his, Rosaline asked unexpectedly, "Are you trustworthy?"

"That's a weird question," said Cecil-Lee, wearily gripping his plate and bringing it close to his chest. "Ahh like t' think Ahh'm trustworthy. Whahh do yew ask?"

Rosaline didn't answer, but merely smiled sweetly instead.

Cecil-Lee lifted his croissant to his mouth and devoured half of it in one bite. "Wow, Rosaline, these are incredible."

"I'm glad you like it. These guys do, too." She grabbed a handful of croissants from the display and held them up to her toque. Sensing the pastries' presence nearby, a dozen tiny tentacles speedily reached out and pulled them under.

Cecil-Lee jumped high into the air like a spooked cat. "What was *that*!" he shouted. "Was that what Ahh think it was?"

Eugene grinned. "It's just the aliens."

Cecil-Lee's eyes widened. "Yer harborin' intergalactic criminals!"

"Nonsense. How could things this adorable be criminals? Just look at them," exclaimed Rosaline, taking off her hat to reveal a dozen miniaturized aliens atop her head eating croissants fifteen times their size. One alien, however, was bigger than its croissant.

Cecil-Lee forced a nervous chuckle. "Well, Ahh'll be darned. What're their names?"

"That one is Buttons," said Eugene, pointing at his old pal.

Cecil-Lee and Rosaline glanced at him.

"You named one?" asked Rosaline with surprise. "When did you do that? You never even name your bugs."

Buttons finished eating, jumped off Rosaline's head, and tossed a tiny button to Eugene. He caught it and inspected it—a two-holed wooden button with a fuchsia Japanese maple engraved on the front —and put it in his pocket. Then he took out his notepad and recorded the new addition to his collection.

"Ahh can guess whahh yew call it Buttons," said Cecil-Lee.

"It gives you gifts it finds on the street like a crow. How adorable," said Rosaline. "How many buttons has it given you so far?"

"This one is number seventeen."

"What will you do with them?"

"I was going to make a necklace once I had enough of them."

"Aww."

"What're the others' names?" asked Cecil-Lee.

"I don't know," said Rosaline.

"Whad'yew mean yew don't know? Did yew ask 'em?"

"They don't speak. All they do is point, hum, and drip goo. Besides, even if they had names, I wouldn't remember who's who. They're all identical."

The aliens, having devoured the croissants, jumped from Rosaline's head onto the display case. The rotund alien performed a cannonball somersault and fractured the glass.

Cecil-Lee chuckled. "That one's clearly not identical."

"Hey, be nice!" said Rosaline sternly. "Poor thing got nervous and stress-ate my entire storeroom before the BABKA."

Cecil-Lee reached out a finger and poked the alien in its tubby belly. The alien latched onto his finger and bit him.

"Stop bitin', Tubby," said Cecil-Lee, wiggling his finger and making the alien flop up and down.

Rosaline furrowed her brow. "Don't call it that. That's mean."

"It's a Southern thing. We say it like it is. 'That's the tubby alien,' becomes 'that's Tubby, the alien.' No hard feelin's. Besides, he's the one bitin', not me."

"Buttons and Tubby," said Eugene contemplatively, letting the names roll of his tongue to see if they sounded any good.

At the mention of its name, Tubby jumped at Eugene and clung onto his shirt.

"I don't like it. It's insensitive to name a fat alien 'Tubby,'" said Rosaline.

Once again, at the mention of its name, Tubby jumped from Eugene's shirt onto Rosaline's apron like a monkey swinging from branch to branch. She plucked the alien off her apron and set it on the display with the others, who paid them no heed. They stared at Cecil-Lee, mesmerized, pointing at the markings on his neck.

Eugene followed the direction of their tentacles. "I don't think they've seen tattoos before."

"Oh, these?" Cecil-Lee turned his back toward the aliens and pulled down his collar so they could make out his tattoo more clearly. "This here is a stick of dy-no-mite. Ahh'm an explosives technician, see. Dy-no-mite is sorta mahh thing."

The aliens gazed at the marks, mystified.

"Ahh have more." He unbuttoned his cuffs and rolled up his white dress shirt to reveal the alligator tattoo covering his left arm.

The aliens moved in for a closer look. One of them was so bold as to reach out and stroke the black reptile tattoo, causing Cecil-Lee to flinch at the coldness of its touch.

"Alligators an' alligator snappin' turtles are two reptiles that live near where Ahh'm from," he explained. "Mama, Uncle Jimbo, and Ahh used t' go out an' catch 'em all the time. They're prehistoric creatures. Been 'round fer millions of years."

The aliens' saucer-shaped eyes grew larger as Cecil-Lee explained the connection between alligators and his family. "Ahh reckon yew must be wonderin' whahh Ahh'd do this t' mahh body.

Well, yew gotta understand, tattoos are something yew git t' show people the things that define yew. That's whahh Ahh got a gator an' a snappin' turtle on mahh arm, 'cuz they mean a lot t' me. Similarly, the dy-no-mite 'round mahh neck symbolizes mahh profession, which fills me with pride."

The aliens hummed their approval.

"I think they like it," translated Eugene.

"Well, Ahh'll be darned."

Eugene reached into his pocket and pulled out his trusty notebook. He licked his pointer finger then used it to flick through the little pages until he came upon a blank one. He wrote the day's date at the top.

"Takin' notes?"

"Just jotting down some observations."

"That's yer naturalist bent."

"Hmmph."

"What have yew observed 'em doin'?" Cecil-Lee asked, trying to peek at the notebook.

"Mostly eating muffins, smoking weed, and flinging themselves off my face."

Cecil-Lee threw his head back and laughed. "Fascinatin' critters."

"Truly the pinnacle of intergalactic evolution," said Eugene sarcastically. "Living a simple hedonistic lifestyle seems completely natural to them."

"That don't sound so bad, Eugene. Maybe they're onto somethin'."

"What's that?"

"Maybe the secret t' happiness is doin' what yew want. Yew ever think that?"

Eugene grimaced. *Every single day.* Even though he was in a good mood from yesterday's events, he couldn't help but feel something was missing.

He looked at the miniaturized aliens, who were now playfully tugging each other's tentacles. Some of them slid back and forth on their bellies, using goo expunged from their tentacles as lubricant for the glass countertop slip-n-slide. A pair nearest the register flung Tubby into the air, and he crashed back down, splashing countertop goo across Eugene's face.

Eugene was amused, and a little crestfallen. *They do whatever they want whenever they want,* he thought enviously. *I wish my life were that fun and simple. I wish I hadn't been born a Schumaker. I wish was an alien like them.*

CHAPTER 33

John Angryberger pouted from the plaintiff's table. He sat cross-armed and cross-legged, glowering sullenly at Judge Willis, who sat in the elevated judge's bench across from him. The courtroom was empty, except for them.

"John, I've been meaning to ask you something."

"What?" John spat, projecting his frustrations at him.

"Why are you angry all the time?"

"It's in my name."

"I can change your name."

"To what, John Happyberger?"

"It could positively affect your disposition."

"It sounds like a McDonald's meal. Just let me be Angryberger."

"Whatever makes you happy." Judge Willis gestured at the courtroom. "Now that you're here, what do you think of my office?"

Judge Willis's courtroom was designed in the French fashion of Arts Décoratifs. Sleek and sturdy pillars extended from the floor to the ceiling against mahogany walls. Connecting the pillars were Art Nouveau arches carved with geometric patterns, which paired well with cubist paintings underneath them. A massive mural covered the ceiling. In bright Fauvist colors, it depicted shirtless ancient Mesopotamians laboring to complete construction of their utopian civilization. They carried logs on their backs, pushed massive stone blocks up ramps, and weaved baskets beneath the steps of a towering pyramid. John let his eyes fall from the pyramid to a gold Bakelite statue of an angel directly beneath it. Her wings, narrow and long, curved upwards, and her hair blew backwards in a tube shape, like the exhaust nozzle of a fighter jet. The statue was six feet tall and positioned directly in front of Judge Willis's bench.

"It's nice," said John.

"It is, isn't it? Although, I'm starting to find it a little small."

"You better not be insinuating anything," John muttered under his breath too quietly for Judge Willis to hear.

Judge Willis folded his arms and leaned forward over his podium. "So what do you want from me this time?"

"I'm going to be quick and direct," John said. "Mr. Adams continues to stonewall me. He appointed Winston Perry to vice president after the unfortunate death of Dominic Miller. That's a major problem. Winston and Schumaker are close friends who have spent copious amounts of time amongst the aliens."

"That's a red flag."

"I should mention I briefly met with Winston, but he didn't know that Eugene had boarded the aliens' ship, and therefore didn't know anything about what may have happened to the inside, or where their technology went. He also said he didn't know which country Mr. Adams was going to make business negotiations with next, and he denied collusion between the president and Schumaker to thwart me."

"And you believe him?"

"No."

"I wouldn't either. There's no way Mr. Adams, Winston, and Schumaker aren't scheming together. It's as clear as day."

"Speaking of Schumaker," John continued, grinding his teeth, "it seems the unfortunate train 'accident' in the countryside was nothing but an enormous windfall for him. I'm positive it was his own doing, but he excels at hiding his trail." John leaned back in his chair and folded his arms behind his head. "As frustrating as he is, I do give him credit. I never expected him to be so daring as to outwit me at my own machinations."

Judge Willis wagged his finger reproachfully. "That boy doesn't take a hint, does he?"

"We must deliver a very clearly worded message that is impossible for him to ignore."

"What do you have in mind?"

"I'm going to blow up another of his trains and frame him for it."

Judge Willis banged his gavel against the sound block. "No, that won't work. We'd need concrete evidence that Schumaker blew up his train if we want to incriminate him. Without evidence, the case against him won't stand. The prosecution won't have enough to convict him."

"I can get 'evidence' from Mr. Choo."

"Who?"

"My Chinese explosives expert and black-market dealer. We'll plant Mr. Choo's explosives on Schumaker's trains for investigators to find. They'll presume foul play, and their primary suspect will assuredly be Schumaker."

"It won't matter if you plant evidence to frame him. Independent investigators will perform tests on the explosives, and if the way you sabotage his train doesn't match the way *he* sabotaged his own train, the case will be dismissed. You'll have done Eugene a favor by blowing up another of his trains and making him more money."

John scowled. "Then what am I supposed to do? Just sit back and watch Schumaker destroy his assets and gain advantage over me? I don't like that plan, Willis."

Judge Willis opened his mouth, then quickly shut it. He kneaded the ends of his armchair with his palms and shifted his gaze to the wall on his left.

John watched him impatiently.

"Unfortunately, we must take a backseat on this one," the judge said after what John felt was an eternity, "but only for a while. We'll remain vigilant in the meantime. You need someone to survey Eugene unremittingly. It's imperative we know the next time he plans to blow something up, so we can steal his explosives. Then we'll have Mr. Choo manufacture identical ones, so we can properly frame Schumaker. That's the only way it'll hold up in court."

"I've already assigned Mary-Lou Anne to Eugene-watching duty. She's been told to observe everyone at the office and keep logs of anyone he interacts with. In addition, she scours his trains daily to see if there are any abnormalities or hidden explosives."

Judge Willis shifted his weight in his seat. "Did the inspector find anything substantial that could help us?"

"There's zero proof of any kind that Eugene is sabotaging his own trains. Whoever's doing this for him is a professional."

"I would think so, otherwise he'd be here right now instead of you."

"Schumaker has proven himself to be as devious as Mr. Adams. I can't let my guard down."

"About Mr. Adams—do you have a plan for him and his henchmen? Dominating Schumaker Trains and Oil won't result in significant growth for Jmart unless you escape Bullit Inc.'s stranglehold on international markets."

"I've told Mr. Tibbles to continue monitoring Bullit Inc. He's surveilling both Winston and Mr. Adams's actions and will report back to me. Hopefully, they'll do something stupid enough that'll let me force his hand and finally include Jmart as a part of his exclusive trading deals."

Judge Willis nodded approvingly. "I think Winston is the key here, as he has connections to both Mr. Adams and Eugene."

"And to the aliens."

"Speaking of, where have they disappeared to?"

"Nobody has seen them since the BABKA, which is good because it means their ship is unprotected. However, they not only resealed the hole in the hull, but they reinforced it with material much stronger than before, so we can't re-enter. My engineers tried everything, even resorting to using the bug gun again, but nothing can penetrate it."

"Hmmm," murmured Judge Willis. "If they resealed their ship, they may be hiding somewhere in the city."

"There's only one place I'm aware of that the aliens frequent."

"Would you like me to check there?"

John shook his head. "No. Using them to get back at Schumaker only made him into an even more formidable adversary, and their ship was ransacked, so there's little left that would be of use to me. Besides, Mr. Adams doesn't care about them in the slightest, and he's the true final boss of Jmart. I think it's best we focus our efforts on Schumaker and Bullit's new VP, Winston Perry."

"I agree." said Judge Willis, standing up from his chair. "Inform me the minute you hear a new development, so we can strike accordingly."

"That goes without saying."

Judge Willis grabbed his briefcase and drifted toward a secret door behind his bench that blended in with the mahogany wall. Hand on the knob, he twisted his head toward John. "I'm tired of these superior courts. I'm ready to be one of the Nine."

"Just be patient."

"I have been patient, but now I want to see results."

John glared at Judge Willis. "Don't forget who made you the Chief Judge of the Superior Court of the District of Columbia in the first place," he hissed.

"I remember, but that was years ago. I'm due for a promotion. Let me know when those buffoons make their next step—I'll be waiting."

And with a flourish, he opened the door and slipped through.

CHAPTER 34

Winston's new responsibilities were prodigious. As vice president of Bullit Inc., his decisions affected millions of people around the globe. He had the power to influence the fabric of reality. He could make a difference. He could make a change.

As if I needed another reason not to come to work today.

He rode the elevator down to the eleventh floor where the marketing team was waiting. It was at Mr. Adam's behest that Winston had to attend yet another meeting.

"You enjoy those meetings, don't you?" Mr. Adams had goaded a couple of days prior. Winston had just been promoted and was spending a day with Mr. Adams to learn his new duties as vice president.

"I really don't," mumbled Winston, staring rigidly at the milky white wall behind the president.

Mr. Adams adjusted his Boy Scouts sash—a piece from Bullit Inc.'s Vintage fashion line—which was wrapped diagonally over his topsoil-colored crew neck. The sash came complete with interchangeable patches, of which Mr. Adams wore his favorite four: adventuring, underwater basket weaving, disability awareness, and best-dressed-camper. He noticed Winston's gaze flit lazily to his sash and rest on his patches of pride.

"Wearing this getup is good for business, right?" he asked with a soupçon of self-consciousness.

Winston nodded imperceptibly. *Underwater basket weaving?*

"If it improves business, then we won't change the formula," Mr. Adams said, his arrogance rushing back. "Besides, you were the one who came up with the idea to dress me in this. I want you at another meeting. They can use your genius on the next important marketing project."

"For Glam Blanc?"

Mr. Adams's amber eyes twinkled. "It's a surprise."

"I hate surprises."

The president smiled cheekily. "I know."

Until the day of the meeting, Winston refused to entertain the thought that he was most likely going to be inconveniently and unpleasantly surprised. Dwelling on it only made his suffering worse.

Winston stopped in front of the meeting room door. He heard animated voices forcing laughter on the other side and let out an involuntary whimper. Slowly, he reached for the brass doorknob, caught sight of his reflection in the polished brass, and paused. He stared numbly into his glinting reflection, which made his body appear further away than it was, small and insignificant. As he gripped the knob, he felt his internal energy-battery, already depleted, suck into itself, becoming a void that drained more energy he didn't have.

What am I doing?

Winston hesitated. He took a deep breath then exhaled forcefully, bracing himself for what was to come. *Let's just get this over with. Three, two, one, go.* He swung open the door with the same power and anticipatory fear he might use to tear a bandage off a sensitive and hairy body part.

Mr. Tibbles greeted him energetically. "Welcome back, Winston —Oops! I mean, Mr. Vice President."

Winston ignored him and sat down at the head of the table. "What's the first order of business?" he asked robotically.

"Bullit Inc. is looking to expand its reach in other sectors of the market," said Mr. Sneffles.

"I thought Mr. Adams wanted all the markets in one sector, not multiple sectors in one market."

"Mr. Adams wants all sectors of all markets everywhere," said Mr. Sneffles.

"What does he want to invest in besides retail?"

"He wants to expand his portfolio into 'the essentials,' namely, food. Bullit Inc. already has a stake in certain food-processing companies, like Husyuen Chemical, but Mr. Adams would like more presence in other parts of the food industry. Our research and development team, comprised of our own Bullit Inc. scientists, have begun developing what they refer to as an 'alternative essential product.'"

"What's an 'alternative essential product?" asked Winston.

"Just that: a replacement for something absolutely necessary for survival."

Winston scowled. "If something is essential, then by definition, there can be no alternative."

"That's where you're wrong," chirped Mr. Tibbles. "Our R&D team has identified new victuals to feed people altogether."

"What?"

"Snow."

"Snow?"

"Snow!"

"How do people eat snow? Snow isn't food."

"Dr. Nitzroy can explain," said Mr. Sneffels.

"Who?"

As if on cue, there was a knock on the door, and Dr. Nitzroy's goblin nose led the way into the room, followed by his grimy face. He wore a white lab coat that was far too big for his five-foot-four figure and draped down to his bony ankles. He carried a tarnished brown briefcase and wore thick round glasses with a variegated sterling silver and gold frame. His black hair was gelled backwards, except for the front part, which was styled into a quiff.

Winston scanned him with moderate curiosity. Looking at Dr.

Nitzroy made him feel something, but he didn't know what. He couldn't decide if the sight of the scientist amused, charmed, or repulsed him. *If a scientist, clown, businessman, and cockatoo made a baby together, they'd make a Nitzroy.*

"Hello, I'm Dr. Nitzroy, food expert and one of Bullit Inc's chief investment strategists," he said in a nasally New Jersey accent before taking an empty seat next to Mr. Dinkle.

Winston's lips twitched into a wry expression. "Dr. Nitzroy, I'm not a food expert or anything, but please explain to me: how is snow a substitute for food? I've always been under the impression that snow *isn't* food."

"Well, I *am* a food expert, and I can tell you with certainty that snow *is* food."

"And I should believe you because…?"

"I have a degree in chemical engineering."

"Chemical engineering isn't food science."

"Clams casino!" shouted Dr. Nitzroy in protest. "Of course it is! Almost all the food you eat is altered in some way by chemical engineers. Take, for example, a cool ranch corn chip. Do you know what it's made of?"

"Corn," answered Winston flatly.

"And those little green and red dots that give it so much flavor?"

"I don't know."

"Red and green triglycolysidic alpha-ribomethyloxylamine dimers. Non-chemists call them 'flavor dust.'"

Winston crossed his legs. "What are you saying?"

"My point is that food is no longer grown in soil; it's made in chemical laboratories. Oftentimes, lab food tastes better and lasts longer than 'real' food."

"So, you want Bullit Inc. to engineer food?"

"Well… no."

"Then what's your point?" said Winston. He felt his patience thinning.

"I was merely providing an example of how chemical engineers contribute to food science."

Winston cleared his throat, adjusted the knot to his tie—a new requirement from his promotion—and tugged on the collar of his shirt, which seemed tight. "I'm not following how this is relevant to snow."

Mr. Sneffles came to the scientist's aid. "Dr. Nitzroy is working on a way to turn snow into an edible food source to feed millions of people."

"Our financial analysts have determined it to be a niche area with hundreds of millions of dollars in annual cash-flow potential," added the big-nosed scientist.

"I don't understand the concept of snow being edible. It's frozen, dirty city-sky water. It doesn't have any nutritional content whatsoever."

"I'm afraid you're wrong about that, too," said Dr. Nitzroy. He pulled his briefcase out from underneath his chair. "I have something—here." He handed Winston a packet of papers held together by a clamp.

"That's a report published in the *Journal of Technological Science* six months ago. It was written by several distinguished scientists, including myself. Our studies indicate that snow is, in fact, a nutritious and safe alternative to food."

"Who funded your studies?" asked Winston.

"The National Science Foundation."

"Who funds the NSF?"

"The government."

"Who controls the government?"

"Bullit Inc."

"How much did we give you for this research?"

"Ten million dollars."

"We gave you *ten million dollars* for this study?"

"Don't get your panties twisted in a knot," said Dr. Nitzroy in his street-tough New Jersey accent. "It wasn't our money. It was taxpayer money. And I didn't use all ten million dollars—it only cost a few thousand to bribe the scientific journals to publish the results asked of me."

Winston frantically looked around the room to see if anyone else found what Dr. Nitzroy said absurd. Mr. Tibbles, Mr. Sneffles and

Mr. Dinkle sat forward in their seats, eagerly watching the back-and-forth, as if the scientist's complete disregard for basic morality was part of the entertainment.

"What happened to the millions of dollars that weren't used?" Winston asked with concern.

Dr. Nitzroy shrugged. "I gambled it away in Atlantic City."

Winston shook his head. *I shouldn't have expected anything less from a person born of cockatoo, businessman, and clown.*

"After I published my report concluding that snow can be used as a healthy, nutritious source of food, I began researching the best ways to make snow, as well as what were the healthiest kinds of snow. My conclusions were these: the best way to make snow is to wait until winter, and the healthiest snow is white snow. I presented my findings to sales, who discussed how to maximize our margins. They believe snow will replace food stamps because of its low cost of production and ease of consumption, which means that we can save lots of government money from being spent on public welfare and can instead redirect that money to private industry. If Bullit Inc. enters this business before our competitors do, we'll completely control the market."

"Besides the many, many things that are wrong with this idea," said Winston, "I'd like to point out that it's mid-May, summer is around the corner, and it's seventy-five degrees outside. Where could we get snow?"

"We'll construct a pipeline to funnel snow from the Rockies and glaciers near the Arctic Circle into the continental United States."

"This is ridiculous." Winston glared at the marketing team. "Why am I here?"

"Mr. Nitzroy just told you why you're here," said Mr. Tibbles. "To feed people snow."

"You don't seriously believe I'd approve a pipeline to feed people snow as a substitute for real food, do you?"

Mr. Sneffles's face soured. "But, Winston, you have no choice."

"I'm the vice president of this company—I'm not going to feed people snow." He cleared his throat. "I thought dressing the president in safari outfits was a stupid idea, but this is truly on another level. This will *hurt people*. This is a joke, right?"

"But Mr. Adams already approved the pipeline's construction," said Mr. Sneffles.

Winston clapped his hands together in prayer. "*What?* When?"

The others all exchanged glances. "Yesterday. He didn't tell you?"

Winston shook his head. "No, he hadn't even told me the project existed."

"The reason you're here is not to approve this project, but to help us market it," Mr. Dinkle chimed in. "Mr. Adams told us we need your help advertising snow food to the masses, so they can get behind it, too. He said if anybody could figure this out, it'd be you. He believes you're an invaluable asset to this company."

Winston sighed heavily. *I should quit.*

"You're the best," agreed Mr. Tibbles. "We *need* you."

Winston felt a severe jolt in his throat chakra. Hastily, he looked toward Mr. Tibbles, who smiled with such effulgence that Winston felt nothing but pure terror. As he beheld him, Winston realized he was the furthest he'd ever been from achieving his dream of living in a hut on the beach. *I can't quit, because if I do, somebody else would fill my position, somebody much worse than me, like Mr. Tibbles.*

He was stuck in an impossible position.

"How do you move snow through a pipeline?" Winston asked Dr. Nitzroy, his voice teetering delicately between surrender and resolve.

"The pipeline will be a two-thousand-mile-long chilled conveyer belt."

"That's going to cost a fortune."

"It'll cost two trillion dollars to construct."

"Two *trillion* dollars?"

"Don't worry, it won't come from our pockets," said Mr. Sneffles soothingly. "The lobbying division has applied for public-service grants to fund the operation. The cost will be completely subsidized by public dollars."

Winston threw his arms wide. "Think of how much food you could buy with two trillion dollars!"

"Two trillion dollars' worth!" piped Mr. Tibbles.

"All we're left with is to come up with the best way to market this enterprise to the public and get them onboard," Dr. Nitzroy said. "We'll need to get the Bullit Inc. brand name out there, so people on food stamps won't want snow from any other potential competitor in the future."

"That makes a lot of sense," said Winston caustically.

"The biggest problem jumping out at me is the fact that much of the snow we'd be selling isn't American but Canadian," said Mr. Dinkle. "Sales are forecasting a trend to return to American-manufactured goods. People are sick of their Chinese plastic toys, German sports cars, and Italian food. I think it's important that, as we move forward, we can claim our goods sold at retailers—including our snow—are American in some way. Something like American-Made, American-Manufactured, Assembled-in-America, or Thought-of-in-America.'"

"Could we say, 'American-Processed?'" Mr. Sneffles recommended.

"'Caused by American Climate Change?'" suggested Mr. Tibbles sprightly.

"'Snow for Americans, Made by Americans,'" Winston blurted out, unable to control his impulse for saying stupid stuff when surrounded by stupid people.

"How misleading. I love it."

"You know, when it comes to American snow, I never eat December snowflakes; I always wait until January," remarked Mr. Tibbles.

"We could put out posters as we begin construction of the pipeline and distribute them all over the city, like they did with those BABKA posters," said Mr. Dinkle.

"Speaking of which, I had box seats to the competition," Dr. Nitzroy bragged.

"Ugh, I'm so jealous," said Mr. Tibbles. "I waited three hours in line to get François Rivier's signature before the show, but when I got to the front, he had to leave to get ready. It was such a shame because I absolutely love his cooking. My wife and I watch his shows on the Baker's Network whenever we can."

"François Rivier is overrated," Winston stated, blasé.

Dr. Nitzroy covered his mouth, appalled. Mr. Sneffles shielded his eyes. Mr. Tibbles cast a look of disgust at Winston.

"You're joking, right?" said Mr. Dinkle. "He's the best baker on the planet."

"Not better than Rosaline."

Everyone laughed hysterically.

"Oh boy, that was a good one," chuckled Mr. Dinkle. "The only reason she made it to the finals was to raise viewership. If the judges were fair, she would've been eliminated in the first round. They were obviously paid to advance her to the finals."

"Winston let me put it this way," began Mr. Tibbles with a smirk, "Rosaline is like zucchini bread: not bad, but not your first choice either. On the other hand, François is like a fresh berry tart, or a passionfruit chocolate truffle, or a raspberry soufflé with crème anglaise—just so much more elegant, refined, and better in every possible way."

"If everyone thinks he's so good then why don't we get a guy like him to sponsor our snow?" asked Winston defensively.

Mr. Sneffles eyes met his. "That's… that's a great idea."

"We wouldn't be able to get him, though," said Mr. Tibbles ruefully. "He's already sponsored by Jmart."

"If we're going to feed people something bad for them, like snow, why not have someone bad like Rosaline sponsor the ad campaign?" Winston muttered facetiously under his breath.

"Winston, stop. Your jokes aren't funny," said Mr. Sneffles.

"I've got it," said Mr. Dinkle. "We could run standard ad campaigns explaining how snow will create thousands of jobs, so supporting snow supports local communities."

"We could run promotions advertising the snow as organic," suggested Mr. Sneffels.

"Oooh, I like that! Then we could offer both organic and non-organic snows. They'd be the same thing, but we'll sell them separately to increase the margins with people paying more for organic snow," said Mr. Tibbles.

"Or even an organic and gluten-free variety," said Mr. Dinkle.

"Sugar free, too."

"Organic, gluten free, and vegan."

"And keto."

Winston touched his palm to his forehead. This crackpot conversation made him weary. He felt dizzy, and his throat was constricting. He pulled on his collar again.

"What if we dyed the snow different colors, offering different flavors?" continued Mr. Dinkle.

"We could add red and green triglycolysidic alpha-ribomethy-loxylamine dimers to make cool-ranch–flavored snow," said Mr. Tibbles.

"That sounds tasty," said Dr. Nitzroy.

"What if we made a cartoony character as the sponsor?" asked Mr. Sneffles.

"He could be 'The Snowman,'" said Mr. Dinkle.

"He could be shaved ice," said Mr. Tibbles.

Winston felt a bead of sweat fall from his forehead into his eye. He blinked rapidly, then wiped his eye with the back of his hand, which had turned pale. The room began to spin. He closed his eyes so he wouldn't feel nauseous.

"Winston?"

I can't take it anymore.

Winston rushed from the conference room and down the hall toward the elevator, loosening his tie and gasping for air.

As if anticipating his premature arrival, the elevator doors were already open, beckoning him to enter its sacred space where no one ever spoke about anything, let alone trillion-dollar atrocities. Winston rushed inside.

"C'mon, c'mon!" He repeatedly smashed the button for the sixty-ninth floor.

The elevator beeped and the stainless-steel doors closed. Winston slid down the wall as the elevator ascended. When his bottom hit the floor, he folded at the torso until his face was level with his navy Cape Cod beach shorts. Winston stared at the patterns of whales spurting water from their blowholes around his kneecaps. He pulled them tightly toward his chest.

Sweat dripped from his brow onto his shorts. With the back of his shaking hands, he wiped his forehead. "What am I doing?" he said. "Why don't I ever try to stop this madness?'" He dug his sweat-soaked fingers into his legs so tightly that one of his fingernails poked through a whale pattern and ripped his shorts. Vermillion water from a combination of blood and sweat rose up through the whale's blowhole.

Looking at the whale reminded him of his hut on the beach. *It's not even worth the wait if it means enabling this lunacy.*

The elevator dinged and the doors opened. Secretary Jane stood in front of him with her hands on her hips, bearing an expression of mild anger coupled with protracted frustration. She peered at him over her red square-framed glasses, her eyes piercingly sharp, and in a hardened voice said brusquely, "It's time we have a talk."

CHAPTER 35

Winston rubbed his clammy palms on his shorts which had turned a dark red ochre in the spots where blotches of blood had dried. Secretary Jane had brought him a bandage to cover the cut on his leg, but his shorts were already ruined. Winston didn't mind, however. Shorts were easy to replace, unlike a pair of stiff leather sandals that had been broken-in over the course of several weeks. If it were his flip-flops that were caked in blood and covered in holes, he would've been thoroughly upset and likely have cried. Instead, he gently extended his leg under his desk, wincing slightly from pain, and wondered how long it would be until he could pry off and throw away his tattered garments.

He couldn't do it now because Secretary Jane stood across from him in his penthouse office, refusing to sit. Her black eyes bore into his with an intensity that made Winston's stomach squirm. Her expression was set and determined as if she had been waiting for this moment for a long time, and Winston could sense a fearsome gravitas emanating from her like an aura. As he returned her gaze, he had a feeling that this chat, whatever it was about, was somehow going to be worse than the horror show he had just come from.

Jane spoke first. "Winston, do you know how long I've been the secretary for the vice president of Bullit Inc.?"

"I don't." Winston had barely interacted with her—he had just moved to the top-floor office this week and was preoccupied with his new work requirements, which he valiantly procrastinated against. In the few times they had spoken, it was mostly her who asked him questions: How are you? Can I get you anything? What are your most closely guarded hopes and dreams? She had learned a bit about him, but he knew nothing about her.

"I've been at my station on the other side of this office for twenty years."

Winston felt his eyebrows rise. Secretary Jane was older than him, he knew, but he didn't think she was in her forties, or even fifties.

"I've seen a lot of vice presidents come and go at this company. I'll admit, I'm not sure why the turnover is so high—there's been an unusual number of fatal accidents and firings—but as a result, I've seen quite a few different faces. Some were a little older, some a little louder, but all of them belonged to the same kind of solipsistic, vainglorious, and avaricious reprobate that occupied this high-tower and cast their iniquitous will toward the city below, like dark clouds on what should have been beautiful, sunny, cloud-free days."

Winston wasn't sure where she was going with this, or what half those words even meant, so he kept his mouth closed and listened.

"Mr. Adams is a selfish person—"

Winston nodded in agreement.

"—and so were all the vice presidents before you, especially Dominic." Secretary Jane paused to stroke the edges of her mouth down to her chin with her thumb and index finger. "You're the only one who's not," she said, letting her arm fall.

"Hang on," said Winston in protest, "I am a very selfish person."

"No, you are not."

"Yes, I am. I only watch out for myself. I don't do anything anyone at work who is not my superior tells me to do, and my goal in life is not to be bothered. I just want to be left alone and not have to deal with other people's problems. I might not be on the same level as Mr. Adams, but I think I'm just as selfish as someone like Dominic."

Secretary Jane let out something between a scoff and laugh. "Winston, that's not being selfish, that's being *lazy*."

"Well, I'm also lazy," said Winston, conceding this fact, "but I'm selfish, too."

"No, you aren't," said Secretary Jane, doubling down on her position. "And I don't know why you're even trying to be considered selfish. It's not a good trait."

"Maybe I'm not a good person," said Winston without thinking about what he was saying.

"I think you are, you just don't know how to be."

"That's because I'm selfish."

"No, it's because you're lazy."

A silence came between them. Winston still wasn't sure where the conversation was headed, and he didn't know why he was being defensive about being selfish either.

"You mentioned to me that your goal is to have a hut on the beach where you don't have to work another day in your life," said Secretary Jane.

"Yeah, that's right," said Winston, sitting up a little taller. "A nice straw hut, like one of the little piggies had."

"That sounds very peaceful," she said in a placating tone. "I'd imagine that lifestyle would be calm, free from the chaos and stress of working in the city, providing you with the space to think about and do whatever you want."

"Yes, that's why I want it."

"This hut of yours is—"

"In Long Island," Winston interjected. "Near the Hamptons."

"—*not* a real place."

"It isn't?" asked Winston, confused. "But I lived there for months. I mean, sure, at this point the wind and waves have probably destroyed it, but I can put it back together in one day."

"What I'm saying is that your hut is merely a metaphor for the change you want to see, the idealism of swapping the way your life is now for what you think is a better future."

"Obviously, but it's also a real—"

"Moving to a place like that won't change everything. Bullit Inc.

might be gone from your life, but you'll still have problems you'll want to make better; there will be things out of your control that you will wish you could manipulate. You'll still have your health to watch out for, the weather to deal with, and there's no way you'll be truly left alone and unbothered by other people—it's impossible to be—but your friends won't be there, and it'll be very lonely. Is that what you really want?"

"Well," said Winston, thinking about his experience a year ago, "the friend bit doesn't sound so good, but not having to work is great."

"Winston, you are the hut on the beach," she said with a softness that caught Winston off guard.

He furrowed his brow. "What does that mean?"

Secretary Jane once again uttered that same noise that was somewhere between a scoff and laugh. "You aren't the only one with a picture for a better future. Everyone has their idea of a hut on the beach. I've been patiently waiting twenty years for the materials to build mine, and as it turns out… it's you."

Winston felt his pulse quicken. "Workplace relationships are frowned upon—"

"I'm much too old for you," she said, laughing. "And it's not just my age I'm referring to." She took a few seconds to regain her composure, then wiped the corners of her eyes before continuing. "It's *change*, Winston. We both want to see things change. You want to ameliorate the world, make it more simple, relaxed, and fair. That's the goal you're working toward. I also have a goal, which is to help others—namely, you—realize that change. Do you understand?"

Winston still had no idea what she was talking about.

"You are the first one in this office who has their priorities right, but you are wasting your time by not acting on them. Having this job doesn't matter if you don't do the right things. As you are now, you aren't heading toward a future with that hut on the beach—you are heading for nothing. The future isn't guaranteed. Paradise is now, yet how are you helping to shape it?"

Something finally clicked in his brain, and he understood what she was telling him.

"It's not much of a paradise though, is it?" he asked.

"And whose fault is that?" she said with a strength in her tone that made Winston feel like it was his fault.

"What should I do? I can't do anything about the pipeline," he said defensively. "And all the other things—the Moroccan factory workers being paid two dollars a day, Mr. Adams's exclusive trade deals that are limiting legitimate free competition from honest companies, and asinine marketing schemes—I can't change them. How do you expect me to do anything about any of this? There's nothing I can do." Winston didn't realize his voice was rising, or that he was bending his leg, placing it under his body, and was now pushing off it to stand over his desk, towering and hunched, like a mantling bird. "I'm stuck in this position with my hands tied behind my back. What do you want from me? Why can't you just leave me alone!" he shouted at her.

Secretary Jane remained motionless, her dark eyes studying him while he breathed heavily. Then, the tiniest smirk formed on her face. "You'll know what to do when the time comes."

She whipped around and left him in his penthouse office, a soon-to-be hut in the sky.

CHAPTER 36

"Hand me a Franklin," said Eugene, extending an open palm toward Cecil-Lee who sat at his desk counting the money pyramid.

"Here yew go."

Eugene ferried the hundred-dollar bill to Trainy's terrarium and dropped it inside for him to eat. The millipede scurried out from underneath a stick and crawled across the damp leaf-laden soil to the green paper. It hungrily nibbled on the corner containing the alphanumerical serial number.

Money, everywhere. There was more money flowing into Schumaker Trains and Oil than Eugene knew what to do with. His company had cornered thirty percent of the market from KB Rail within a month. All of Eugene's new locomotives experienced destructive accidents leading to hundreds of his oil cars—each carrying thirty thousand gallons of crude—exploding. Insurance covered the cost of the trains, and, due the price of oil increasing after each incident, Eugene's company realized enormous profit from their refinery. Seeing such spectacular success and imagining the havoc he was wrecking on John and, if he were alive, his father, Eugene decided to blow up many of his older locomotives until his fleet was depleted to half its size.

Investors, attracted by the unprecedented growth of Schumaker

Trains and Oil, flocked to the company, throwing copious sums of money at Eugene. The shareholders were so ecstatic, they unanimously voted to give him a handsome raise.

"I don't think that's necessary," Eugene had said at the company's board meeting the previous week. "I don't know what I'd do with the money. I already have more cabinets than can fit in my office. I have twenty terrariums stacked one on top of the other, not being used. I don't need any more."

"It's not about the money. It's the symbolism of it," said one of the board members. "Your leadership is paramount to the company's success, and we'd like to ensure your tenure at its helm for the rest of your long, prosperous life. That's why we're giving you more money. We want to shackle you to your father's desk forever."

Or something like that. Eugene couldn't remember clearly what anyone had said. His mind had felt fuzzy over the past month, like a tennis ball. He hadn't gone bug collecting in that time, nor had he dropped by Rosaline's bakery to check on her progress with the reopening. He had been so busy sabotaging his own company that he had neglected his friends, his hobbies, and his own health.

Overwhelmed by his own success, Eugene stared, depressed, at the ziggurat of money basking majestically on his desk. Alfredo had brought it in earlier that morning. "A gift from the board. I'm so proud of you, young sir, and your father would be too if he were here," Alfredo had said, his eyes watering.

His kind words only added to Eugene's misery. Blowing up trains was a way to get back at his dad and John; it wasn't supposed to entrap him as company president forever.

"Three hundred an' seventy-four thousand dollars. Holy cow," Cecil-Lee patted the pile of green bills on Eugene's desk affectionately. "Bisdness shore is boomin'."

Eugene wanted to cry. He smiled pleasantly and gave a thumbs up instead.

"Yer doin' the Lord's work makin' all this moolah."

Cecil-Lee's comment made Eugene feel even more discontented. If the Lord's work was for him to become rich, tenured, and adored, then why wasn't he happy? He had exacted revenge against John

Angryberger and upset the ghost of his father, but it didn't feel good. Instead, deep-seated feelings of jadedness trounced the wild thrill of self-sabotage, unsettling him.

If I don't destroy this company, it's going to destroy me, he reminded himself. *I must commit to what I started, or I'll never get out.*

He closed the lid to the terrarium and walked behind his desk where Cecil-Lee was now reshaping the money pyramid into a money cube. He turned to his father's portrait and swung the painting open to reveal a modestly sized safe, about an alien tall and an alien wide, the color of sable-black grapes. The intricate, esoteric glyphs carved along the frame next to the door hinges made him suspect his father had stolen the old safe from somewhere abroad. Eugene entered the code using the large silver knob on the front. After spinning it back and forth three times, he pulled on the heavy metal door with both hands, but it didn't open. He was too weak.

"Can you help me?" he asked Cecil-Lee, his voice as frail as his arms.

"Shore thing." Cecil-Lee abandoned his construction project, gripped the safe with one of his giant hands, and yanked it open with ease. The safe revealed several dozen sticks of C4 sitting in the vault. "So this is where yew keep them goods."

"It's the latest order."

He smacked his lips in approval. "Ahh cain't wait t' rig these up t' yer trains."

"Not to the trains," said Eugene weakly.

Cecil-Lee cupped his hand to his ear. "What's that?"

Eugene shook his head. "No trains."

Cecil-Lee furrowed his eyebrows. "Ahh don't understand. Whatchu callin' me over here for if not fer dem'lition?"

Eugene glanced down at his hands, which glistened with sweat. He wiped them on his trousers. "I don't want to blow up any more trains."

"So, what then?" asked Cecil-Lee in a pushy voice.

"My refinery."

Cecil-Lee's eyes lit up. "Yew want me t' blow up yer refinery?"

Eugene nodded. "More of the Lord's work."

Cecil-Lee shifted his weight nervously, unsure if Eugene was teasing him. "Hold yer horses rahht there, cowboy. Yer tellin' me that yew want me t' rig yer refinery? Yew want t' destroy yer main source of income?"

"That's right."

Cecil-Lee held up his hands like two big stop signs. "Ahh don't understand. The trains make sense, but... yer *refinery*? Where'll the profit come from?"

"From the same source as with the trains," Eugene lied.

"Yew need a refinery t' make money off yer oil trains blowin' up, but yew don't have nuthin' t' make money off a refinery blowin' up," said Cecil-Lee, confused.

"You forget the insurance."

"But you'll lose yer main source of income fer years."

"I'll make a Brobdingnagian profit."

"Yeah, but *how*?"

"Just trust me." Eugene reached into the safe, scooped up the charges into his arms, then dumped them unceremoniously on top of the stack of money on his desk, knocking over Cecil-Lee's cube. "This will be the most rewarding act yet."

CHAPTER 37

John grumbled as his rotary dial telephone buzzed. The muscles in his neck and upper back tensed as he prepared to be annoyed.

"You're only supposed to use this number if you have something useful," he spat instead of the conventional "hello."

"Sorry to bother you, Mr. Angryberger," said Mary-Lou Anne so sweetly and mellifluously John thought he'd get diabetes just from listening to her speak, "but I have news you'll want to hear."

"What is it?"

"I overheard Mr. Schumaker talking to a tattooed man in his office today," she said. "Apparently, they've been using C4 to blow up their own trains. They've been intentionally sabotaging their assets this whole time!"

"Of course they have. Any moron could figure that out from looking at the sheer number of trains that have exploded. Yesterday was train number what, thirty-six? We *know* it's a scam; the only thing we lack is evidence to incriminate him. Please tell me you recovered one of their explosives."

There was a pause on the other line. "No," she said sheepishly.

"Then why are you wasting my time?"

"B-b-but they mentioned what they're going to blow up next, sir," said Mary-Lou Anne, stumbling over her words.

John's ears perked up. "What's that?"

"The refinery, sir."

"The refinery? When?"

"I didn't hear them say."

"Go there, now!" he barked. "We can't let Schumaker get away with this."

"But sir, I don't understand. If he were to blow up his refinery, he'd lose all his oil. Even if insurance covered the damage, he wouldn't see a profit."

Is that right? "No," he said, dismissing the thought entirely, "there's a catch, I'm sure. This is Schumaker we're dealing with, after all. He's a clever weasel, a proper rapscallion, and an obstreperous son-of-a-gun. I'm certain whatever he's planning will be even more lucrative than blowing up trains."

"Could he be doing this because he wants to destroy his company?"

"And what, let me take over everything? Preposterous! He'd never do that."

"He frequently mentions how he'd rather be collecting dirt worms than running a train business."

"That's a ruse he employs to distract his competition. His true motives are as clear as hand sanitizer: to become the most successful businessman in D.C. and surpass me and Mr. Adams. He's an unrepentant, obdurate manipulator who'll stop at nothing to achieve his goal. For that reason, we must stop him from destroying his refinery, no matter what," said John resolutely. "Is that understood?"

"Yes, sir."

"Good. One more question," he quickly added, biting his lip, "did they mention where they get their explosives?"

"From a man named Mr. Choo."

John made a sound somewhere between a snort and hiccup.

"Sir?"

"Mr. Choo, you say?"

"Yes."

John pumped his fist into the air. *This is better than I could have dreamed!* "This is truly wonderful news, Mary-Lou Anne. Great work!"

"It is my honor to serv—"

John hung up on her before she could finish, then quickly dialed Judge Willis's private number.

"John?"

"I have evidence on him—or, rather, I'm about to have some," he rattled excitedly, his heart pumping triumphantly. "Go ahead and make the next move we discussed. It's time we show our hand."

CHAPTER 38

After several weeks' closure, the day had finally arrived for Rosaline's Bakery to reopen. Before business hours, Rosaline heard a knock and saw Eugene, Winston, and Cecil-Lee through the glass panels in the door. They had arrived early to congratulate her before a swarm of customers appeared.

She held open the door, and they stepped inside.

"Oh my gosh," said Eugene as he, Winston, and Cecil-Lee beheld the newly completed renovations. Pink cupcake streamers were strung across the ceiling and an enormous monkey-bread wreath covered the wall behind the cash register. The words, "Rosaline's Bakery Grand Reopening" were written in cinnamon-swirl around the flaky layers of sugary bread.

The Hallmark-card pictures of pastries and other doughy delights that used to decorate the bakery's walls had been replaced with Chibi-style anthropomorphic paintings of the same. In one painting, an irascible blueberry muffin tried to strangle its friend, a smiling, doe-eyed chocolate cupcake, who had speared a lit candle through its head. In another, twelve rascal eggs surfed a silver mixing bowl against a beach background, splashing batter on the counter. The cutest painting, however, was of an adorable baby gulab jamun wearing cardamom blush with hazelnuts as hair ribbons and tossing cinnamon in the air.

On the wall opposite the windows overlooking the Fairgrounds was a poem written in broad, bold letters. It was a mantra Rosaline copied from Kaleidoscope Brown in *The Baker's Bible*, and it went like this:

> *The workbench is my altar,*
> *The oven is my church,*
> *Rolling dough with holy water,*
> *On this pastry shelf I perch.*
>
> *Toiling day after day,*
> *From dawn until dusk,*
> *Endless tasks of the baker*
> *Sate the hunger inside of us.*
>
> *For parents and their children,*
> *The young and the old,*
> *Here's a bite for all to eat,*
> *Good food to warm your soul.*

In addition to renovating the walls and paintings, Rosaline had used her BABKA winnings to replace the creaky old wooden floors with saffron and rose tiles. The white walls had been repainted, and old kitchen equipment had been upgraded with fresh, top-of-the-line models. She employed her new armamentarium to bake her second-place-winning recipes from the BABKA. She had also made carousels of chocolate croissants, a strawberry galette in the shape of a galleon, a pyramid of pies of every kind, a moat of muffins surrounded by a levee assembled from loaves of lemony bread, and a magnificent Chantilly-vanilla cake, which stood tall in the very center of the counter.

"Rosaline, you've done a superb job redecorating. I had no idea it looked this amazing," said Eugene.

"That's because none of you dropped in the last two weeks to check," she said as she loudly shut the door behind them.

"I'm sorry. We've all been so busy with work."

"Yeah, it's been an absolute nightmare how much they expect from me as vice president," echoed Winston.

"Mhmm," sounded Rosaline flatly. She hurried into the kitchen where she grabbed a gazette she had propped against her flour bench. She rolled it up in her hand, returned to the storeroom, and threw it at Winston's head. The newspaper made a dull *splat* sound as it hit him square between the eyes.

"What was that for?" asked Winston, massaging his nose-bridge.

"*I am so mad at you!*" she shouted.

"At me?" asked Winston, while Eugene and Cecil-Lee cowered behind him.

"All of you!" Rosaline yelled, steaming like a fresh-baked buttery brioche bun. "*Read it!*" She pointed her flour-coated finger at the paper on the ground.

Winston picked it up. He didn't need to turn past the front page to see what had riled her. The headline read, "Bullit Inc. Begins Pipeline Construction for New 'Snow Stamps' Project."

"Rosaline—"

"Read it!"

Reluctantly, Winston scanned the article:

Bullit Inc. has begun construction on a trans-American pipeline for its new Snow Stamps project. The project, approved by Mr. Adams and designed by the company's vice president, Winston Perry, will transport snow from the Rocky Mountains and Canada to be sold to people on welfare as an alternative to food.

Winston looked up. "I didn't design it."

"What *exactly* did you do for this project then?"

"I helped with marketing."

Rosaline threw her hands in the air. "What don't you get about this, Winston? You helped market a project that'll feed people snow instead of food," she said, enunciating each syllable slowly and fully, as if speaking to a child. "What were you thinking?"

Winston looked to Eugene and Cecil-Lee for assistance, but they stared at the floor, eyebrows raised, chin muscles retracted in fright. Neither volunteered to help him. Rosaline's scolding was too terrifying.

Winston faced her alone. "Well, you should know, I thought about you during the marketing meeting."

"Oh, really?" she said, her tone candy-cane sweet.

Eugene, who was now crouching behind Winston's leg, groaned. "Ohhhhh, Winston."

"I asked if we could make you a sponsor. It would've made you so much money. You'd be more famous than François Rivier."

His words didn't have the uplifting effect he had hoped. Instead, they caused Rosaline to seize. She felt her eyes roll back, and her body begin to tremor.

"Rosaline, are you oka—"

"How freaking *stupid* are you!" she shouted as molten anger flooded her veins. "Did you genuinely think I would *ever* agree to something like *that*?"

"You shouldn't have said that, Winston," Eugene chirped.

"You have *no right* to tell Winston what he should or shouldn't do!" Rosaline roared, casting her wrath at Eugene instead.

"What did I do? I had no part in marketing snow as food."

Rosaline stormed over to Winston and yanked the paper out of his hands. She tore through the pages until she found what she was looking for, then shoved it into Eugene's face. *"Read!"*

Eugene glanced at the article's header: "Schumaker Trains and Oil Performing Splendidly Well After Series of Accidental Train Explosions."

"We've already talked about thi—"

"Just how oblivious do you think I am?" she yelled. "Do you honestly think I don't know what you're up to? Do you hold me in such low regard that all I am to you is a dumb blonde stoner-baker who knows nothing other than pastries and tarts?"

Eugene crossed his arms over his chest nervously. "No, of course not."

"Then why did you lie to me, Eugene? The first time I heard about your trains exploding I thought it was a one-off accident. But dozens of your trains have been destroyed and you don't seem concerned in the slightest. It's obvious that you and Cecil-Lee have been blowing them up, and for what? Because you didn't want to work for your dad? So, you acted out like a child, throwing tantrums, destroying equipment as if they were toys instead of tackling the real problem, which is that you wanted to work with bugs instead?" She looked at him expectantly.

He remained silent.

"Well?" she prompted.

"I did this to protect you."

Rosaline guffawed. "Protect me?"

"From John Angryberger. He believed I was somehow responsible for his train blowing up, so he lashed out against you for my presumed transgressions."

She put her hands on her hips and leaned forward questioningly. "Were you responsible?"

"No, of course not! But it didn't matter. He sent Judge Willis to revoke your bakery's license anyway."

Rosaline sighed. "I know that, Eugene, but I didn't need you to protect me. Doing so showed you don't trust me to take care of myself. You acted on my behalf without consulting me. I didn't want that from you."

Eugene timidly bit his lower lip. "But John paid off the Judges at the BABKA so you wouldn't win."

Rosaline closed her eyes and took a deep breath. When she opened them, she felt the bubbling anger inside herself evaporate, leaving resignation in its place. "Eugene, I *know*. I sampled François's cookies, and boy, let me tell you, they were awful. There's no way he could've won even an amateur bake-off with them. Of course Jmart bought off the judges—they sponsored the entire event. Not only that, but they're majority stakeholders in François's bakery chain, Muffin Magic. The BABKA being rigged was as obvious as your self-sabotage."

"I had hoped the aliens would help with that."

Rosaline recoiled. "Excuse you?"

"I asked the aliens to help you when I found out that you were being robbed of your BABKA title."

"Oooh, is that why you went in their ship?" asked Winston.

"Yeah, that was why—wait, who told you I went in there?"

"*You're* the reason the aliens came to the BABKA?"

"They showed up? I didn't see them."

Rosaline felt a gut-wrenching pang of disappointment. Eugene must have noticed because he quickly added defensively, "Why does that upset you? I was only trying to help."

"Eugene… that was *my* competition. I wanted to compete on *my* terms. I didn't want any help. Getting aid from the aliens is cheating. I feel humiliated, disgusted, and insulted that you would try to manipulate the competition on my behalf." She looked up at the ceiling. "You know, it's good François won. If I had won knowing what you did, I…" She shook her head.

"Go easy on him, Rosaline," Cecil-Lee interjected, patting a whimpering Eugene on his back.

"*You!*" she exclaimed, turning on him like a piranha in bloody water. In a flash her rage was back. "Look at what you've done!" she said, lifting her hat to reveal the twelve aliens.

Eugene, Winston, and Cecil-Lee gasped. The dozen aliens were covered head to toe in muffin tattoos. Carrot-ginger muffins decorated their cheeks, banana-walnut muffins coated their chests, and twelve-packs of assorted muffins adorned their abdomens. Their arms featured tattoo sleeves of bowls, mixers, and piping bags, while their legs were plastered with black and white ink murals of themselves in a stadium baking muffins before an audience.

The aliens hopped from Rosaline's head onto the display counter where they spun around to show off more tattoos on their backs. From the top to the bottom of their spines were identical giant Milky Way galaxies depicted as cosmically large lemon poppyseed muffins, where each individual poppyseed represented a cluster of stars arranged in the form of constellations. Drawn in the moist center of the lemon poppyseed galaxy was Rosaline's Bakery. It was the supermassive black hole around which all the other muffins revolved.

"Look at them," said Rosaline angrily. "They no longer look cute and adorable. They look hideous, like thugs."

"Rosaline—"

"What have they done?" she lamented. "They're already wanted criminals, now they look the part."

"They don't look like thugs, Rosaline. They're just showin' off what they love, which're muffins," said Cecil-Lee.

"It's not just that. You've led Eugene astray. He's lost, like a sad, dejected puppy. He doesn't want to work at his dad's company—he hates it!—but all you've done is enable his bad choices. He's no longer the sweet, innocent boy he used to be.

"And you," she pivoted toward Winston, "haven't helped Eugene either. You keep getting promoted, and yet you've done nothing except encourage people around you to do the stupidest things. You're the vice president of Bullit Inc., for crying out loud! You're Mr. Adams's right-hand man. Have you made *any* positive changes with your new powers? I mean, if you wanted to feed impoverished people real food, you could've come to me, and we could've engineered a solution, such as bringing my end-of-day leftovers to a food bank. There are other things you could've done, too, like help Eugene rediscover his spark, so he didn't lash out in weird ways that endanger himself and others. Or maybe you could've asked Mr. Adams to decriminalize the aliens, so they didn't have to hide underneath my sweaty hat all day."

She glared at Winston, who simply stared at the floor, averting her gaze.

"I'm so disappointed in each of you," she continued, shaking her head which felt heavy from all the worry she carried around. "Judge Willis shuttered my business, Chief Bagsby took away our space-friends' freedom, and John Angryberger deprived me of any chance to win the BABKA. I'm hurt too, boys, but I'm still moving forward. Today is my grand reopening, and it's supposed to be about me, but you keep stealing my shine and bringing me down to your level. Shame on you! The three of you live such privileged lives —you have money, clothes, food, the ability to do whatever you want—and yet you're so horribly confused and upset, you deliberately bring madness into the world." She pointed exasperatedly at the newspaper. "Are you kidding me?"

None of them looked her in the eyes. All three of them admired the new saffron and rose floor tiles instead.

"And don't think I've forgotten about you lot," she said, towering over the display counter. "All this time you've been mooching off my muffins, getting tattoos, smoking my stash, not doing anything productive. Does nobody remember that poor, scared orange alien Chief Bagsby framed? John and the government are probably torturing it in a secret chamber somewhere. I bet it's in pain, suffering for having done absolutely nothing wrong, all because powerful people, like Mr. Adams, John Angryberger and Judge Willis, want even more power. Those narcissists don't care about anyone but themselves and are ruining so many lives, but what have any of you done about it? You all let your intergalactic brethren endure great distress and tribulation while you got fat off the back of my hard work. Shame on you, too."

Rosaline couldn't stomach looking at any of her friends, human or alien. It hurt her too much. Instead, she cast her gaze at the window, where she caught her reflection in the glass. The skin around her eyes and cheeks hung heavy with disappointment. She looked like a deflated puff pastry.

The doorbells jingled, and Judge Willis entered, as if summoned by the mere mention of his name.

In one deft motion, Rosaline scooped the aliens off the counter, dropped them back on her head, and covered them with her hat.

"Happy grand reopening!" said Judge Willis, beaming.

"What do you want?" asked Rosaline with hostility.

"There's no need to get so excited. I'm not here for you or your second-rate muffins," he said, flapping his hand dismissively. "My business is with him," he said, pointing toward Eugene. He strode across the room, the hems of his black robes billowing behind him, pulled out an envelope, and handed it to its designated recipient.

"What's this?" asked Eugene.

"A subpoena," said Judge Willis brightly.

Eugene's face turned white. "What for?"

"Blowing up your trains, of course."

"Yew have no evidence of that," exclaimed Cecil-Lee.

Judge Willis sneered. "Oh, but we do. Your court case is scheduled for July 24th. That's in four weeks. I'll see you then, obviously." He winked, spun on his heels, and headed toward the exit. The doorbells jingled again, and Judge Willis dematerialized as quickly as he appeared.

"This is what happens when you throw an oil tanker into the fire," said Rosaline without remorse. "You brought this on yourself."

Eugene bolted toward the door, thrust it open, and flew outside, like a bird escaping its cage.

Rosaline shot a nasty glare at Winston. "Well?"

Winston didn't understand.

"He's your friend, you idiot. Help him!"

Winston nodded and rushed after him.

Cecil-Lee quietly followed them. As he was stepping through the doorway, Rosaline called out to him.

"Cecil-Lee?"

"Yes, ma'am?" he said, turning to face her.

"Stay away from Eugene." Her tone was uncompromising and frigid.

Cecil-Lee opened his mouth to protest, then thought the better of it and held his tongue. Quietly, he slid out the door.

Rosaline watched him leave, then lifted her hat and tilted her head forward so the aliens tumbled onto the counter. They looked up at her, and she stared angrily into their big saucer-shaped eyes, which they quickly diverted in shame.

"Yes, you should feel ashamed," said Rosaline sternly. "I don't want to see any of you today either. Go do something useful."

"Hrnnn," they whimpered. Heads drooping, they marched single file out of the bakery.

"So much for my grand reopening," Rosaline murmured as tears streamed down her cheeks. "And I still need to bake my blueberry tarts!" She ducked into the kitchen, steeling herself to celebrate her big day alone.

CHAPTER 39

Eugene's hands quivered as he held the subpoena. *What am I supposed to do with this?* He wanted to throw it away. He wanted to light it on fire, along with the world. Instead, he crumpled the paper in his hand, walked over to the terrarium, lifted the lid, and threw it inside for Trainy to eat.

He watched the millipede as it crawled to the wadded-up ball and began to nibble on it hungrily. Trainy had become skinny and malnourished, far from the plump millipede Eugene had originally found. Its diet of hundred-dollar bills and now, a subpoena, provided as much nutritional content as snow.

"Hey, Eugene," said Winston, knocking on the half-open office door. "Do you have a moment to talk?"

"Leave me alone," said Eugene stubbornly, striding briskly to his chair. "I'm busy. I don't have time for you."

Winston stepped inside the office, then gently shut the door behind him. "Rosaline's right, Eugene. Your reckless shenanigans have upset a lot of people. The vice president and Judge Willis want your head, and even federal prosecutors are investigating your misconduct." He pointed at the balled-up subpoena in the terrarium.

Eugene shrugged. "What's your point?"

Winston's eyes narrowed. "Where's this indifference coming

from?" he said. "It's like you don't care about anything anymore, and it frightens me. I'm worried about you."

"Worry about yourself."

"*Excuse me?* What the heck's gotten into you? I'm here trying to help you, and you act like you don't want my help, let alone need it. You seem to have no regard for your own safety or for the future of your company. You're acting like a spoiled brat."

Eugene's felt his lips tighten and his nostrils flare. "This whole thing is just one big joke."

"There are real-life repercussions for your actions. You need to take things more seriously."

"Who are you, my parents? I don't need a lecture."

"Eugene, talk to me. What's going on? What exactly do you want?"

"I want you to leave!" shouted Eugene.

"Are you trying to sink with your ship?"

"It's what I've been doing for weeks, if you haven't noticed."

"There'll be horrible consequences if you keep this up. Something needs to change."

"Oh? You want *me* to change? That's grand coming from you. You're nothing but a freaking hypocrite."

Eugene could see the veins in Winston's neck throb. "Watch it."

Eugene burst out laughing. "Ha! Getting defensive, are we now? Have you been trying your best at Bullit Inc., Winston? How'd that go? Not well, clearly. Let me tell you something. I'm done trying; I'm getting things *done*. I'm a doer, not somebody else's marionette like you."

"Stop it, Eugene."

"Mr. Vice President," mocked Eugene, "you haven't done anything to help the disenfranchised, marginalized, underrepresented, and oppressed. All you've done is help Mr. Adams make more money for himself. Did it even occur to you to ask Mr. Adams to raise the wages of the factory workers in Morocco when you were there?"

Winston's face turned a deep shade of scarlet.

"Just as I thought. You couldn't be *bothered* to help. You so badly don't want to be bothered that you couldn't even be bothered to advocate for better pay for slave-wage laborers, just like you couldn't be bothered to tell everyone at your office that a plan to replace food with snow stamps is beyond stupid. It's asinine and barbaric. How many people do you think will die so Mr. Adams can pocket billions more? Why don't you go run off to your beach somewhere and hide. You'll do less damage to the world that way."

"What about *you*?" Winston retorted heatedly. "What are you gaining from blowing up trains? Are you not getting enough attention? You've transformed into a megalomaniacal saboteur and a desecrator of woodlands. What you're doing is just as dangerous as feeding people snow stamps. How many bugs do you think died in your train explosions? You love bugs, Eugene. You're the only one on the planet who does. Why would you kill them? It doesn't make sense. Why are you blowing up your trains? That doesn't make sense either. You are putting your billion-dollar company in danger. Do you want to lose the company your dad created?"

"That's it right there," said Eugene, clapping his hands in derisive applause. "My *dad's* company. It's his, always has been. His pride and joy, his baby boy. It's never been mine, and I've never wanted it to be. Truthfully, Winston, I want to be free from it. I've wanted to be free from it since the night my parents died. That night, when I saw their bodies and the crushed car… it's like my dad killed not only my mom, but my future, too."

Eugene felt his lower lip tremble. "I never wanted to take responsibility for the company. All I wanted was to go back to school and become an entomologist, but everyone thinks studying bugs is a waste of time. Nobody cares about little dirt dwellers except me. All people say is what an idiot I'd be to turn down being president of such a large and successful company, but I want to live my life for me, not for the memories of my father or for money.

"But no, everyone told me I just had to do it. 'Take over the company, Eugene. It's the right thing to do. How can your father rest peacefully if his only son turns his back on the family business?' I gave in to all the pressure, and it's made me so unhappy and depressed that I decided to burn the company down. But God forbid it work out the way I want it to."

The emotions that had built-up for years inside of him couldn't be held back anymore. The floodgates opened and tears streamed down his cheeks. "Why didn't you help me, Winston?" he said in-between sobs. "Why didn't you tell me to step down? Why weren't you there to tell me that it's okay to do what I wanted to do? Why weren't you there for me?"

"Eugene, I'm… I'm sorry."

Eugene shook his head. "It doesn't matter. It's too late." He wiped his eyes and stood up from behind his desk. He could feel his shoulders sag and his back hunch forward, as if his body had been tethered to his desk for eons. He turned away from Winston to face the portrait of Theo hanging on the wall and swung it open.

"What are you doing?" Winston asked with a hint of unease.

Eugene ignored him. He fumbled around inside the safe until he pulled out a palm-sized controller. "I'm going to end it all."

"What's that?" asked Winston, his voice rising.

"A remote detonator."

"Hey, let's just take a moment to think this one through," said Winston, his skin turning pale. "We don't want to blow up any more trains, not while prosecutors are after you."

"Is that all you care about—my indictment?"

"No, I want you to be happy, but I don't think that means going to prison."

Eugene nodded. "I'm not going to blow up any more trains."

"Okay! Good! Let's just put that remote down—"

"I'm blowing up the refinery instead."

"*Eugene!*" Winston jumped across the desk and lunged for the remote, knocking over stacks of papers and briefcases full of money. "Are you *mad?*" he screamed, trying to wrestle the detonator from Eugene's hands. "The refinery is one-hundred yards away. Put the remote down!"

"It's mine!" Eugene shrieked, his voice breaking.

"Pushing that button will kill us all."

"I don't care!"

"Give me that!"

"*Never!*" Eugene shrilled maniacally. He pulled on the remote as hard as he could, but Winston pulled back. Eugene lost his balance and stumbled forward. He felt the remote slipping from his hand. *No!* He quickly recovered, planted his feet, and pulled with all his might. The remote came sailing toward him, along with Winston, whose fingers clutched the other end. Eugene lifted his leg to stop Winston from crashing into him and kicked him away.

Winston went sideways. His head hit the portrait of Theodore Schumaker, which came crashing down on top of him. There was a nasty crack, and Winston stopped moving.

Eugene gazed blankly at Winston, who lay motionless on the ground. "Sorry, but this is my only way out."

He pressed the button.

Nothing happened.

"No. No, no, no!" said Eugene. "It needs to go! It all needs to go away!"

He pressed the button again, but there was no explosion.

"Why won't you work!" he screamed, punching the detonator. "*You have to work!* This bad dream has to go!" He smashed the button as hard as he could. Bits of plastic sliced his hand as the controller broke.

He flung it across the room and slid down the wall. He pulled his knees to his chest and curled into a ball, crying uncontrollably.

"Ungh…" Winston rubbed his head and slowly sat up. His temple was bleeding from a gash above his left eyebrow. Blood trickled down his face, collecting into a pool by his hand as it dripped off his chin. His left shoulder hung lower than his right one, dislocated. He needed to seek medical attention. Instead, he crawled forward to hug his friend.

Eugene howled in pain. Snot, drool, and tears fell from his face. He opened his arms and squeezed his best friend. "I'm sorry!"

"It's okay."

"These past few years have been really hard for me," he cried.

"I know, buddy."

They sat on the floor embracing each other, covered in blood, tears, and paint residue, until Eugene, all dried out from crying for so long, gently pushed Winston off.

"What am I supposed to do now?" he asked, sniffling.

"Right now, you're neck-deep in dangerous water, barely managing to keep your head from getting sucked under, and you don't have many good options left. If you don't act quickly, it's likely that you'll go to prison for several years. You've made a lot of money, but the way that your competitors see it is that you stole that money from them. They won't let you get away with it."

"Do you think they have evidence like Judge Willis said?"

"Remember what they managed to do to you, Rosaline, and the aliens *without* evidence? I can't imagine how bad they'd make your life if they did."

Eugene's lower lip quivered. He had made a bigger mess out of things than he wanted. He covered his eyes with his hands as a second rain shower flooded his face. "Why couldn't I just say 'no' from the beginning? I never wanted to do this, and now…" He looked at the portrait of his father lying on the ground, splintered into a dozen pieces. "My dad would be so unhappy with me."

"Eugene, no offense, but your dad wasn't nice to you. He didn't care about you, nor did he support what you wanted to do. He only wanted you to be what *he* wanted you to be, and it's led you to this predicament. You've been nothing but a great son. You've done everything your dad wished, even though you didn't want to, but now it's time to end this the right way, or at least the best way you can."

"What do you mean?"

Woozily, Winston stood up, gripping the desk for support. He opened a drawer and pulled out a pen and paper. "You know, there might be something useful about being vice president of Bullit Inc. after all."

"What are you doing?" said Eugene from the carpet.

"Giving you the only option you have left," he said. "I'm making a contract. You're going to sell Schumaker Trains and Oil to me— er, to Bullit Inc. It's the only thing you can do if you ever want to become an entomologist."

Eugene sniffled and wiped his face with the back of his hand as he watched Winston scribble on the paper. "How did you learn to write a contract?"

"Mr. Adams showed me."

"Doesn't he have to agree to this?"

"I'll offer him a deal he can't refuse. Something that benefits all of us: Schumaker Trains and Oil in exchange for decriminalizing the aliens."

"What about the subpoena?"

"Judge Willis and John Angryberger are in cahoots, but they've never been able to get past Mr. 'Stonewall' Adams. This'll be more of the same. They shouldn't be able to frame you if Mr. Adams is in charge."

Eugene glanced down at his lap in shame. "Why are you helping me? I almost just killed you."

"I'm helping because everything you said about me is true. I haven't accomplished anything meaningful while at Bullit Inc. I'm the vice president of the biggest company on Earth, and I have nothing to show for it. So, starting now, I'm going to do the right thing for myself and those around me. I don't care about Bullit Inc., I don't care about Schumaker Trains and Oil, and I especially don't care about helping Mr. Adams make money. But I do care about you and Rosaline and those rascals from Outer Space, and that means I'm going to help you get out of this situation."

Tears poured from Eugene's eyes for a third time. "I'm thankful to have you as a friend, Winston!"

Winston's eyes watered, too. "I'm sorry I haven't been there for ya, but I'm going to be there for you from now on. We're in this together."

Eugene smiled, rubbed his eyes with his hands, and laughed uncontrollably.

"What's so funny?"

"We've wasted *so much time* doing stupid things we never wanted to do."

Winston grinned. "Well, it's important we don't waste any more."

He extended the pen and paper to Eugene, who was still sitting on the floor.

Eugene took the pen. He could hear his father turning in his grave, but he knew what had to be done.

"It's not that I hate everything, I'm just really frustrated with myself."

"Me too, Eugene. Me too."

CHAPTER 40

"What do you mean you didn't find any charges?" John yelled at Mary-Lou Anne who sat in one of the claret barrel chairs across from him. Annoyed, he looked away from her and glanced at the clock hanging above the door which ticked loudly.

Mary-Lou Anne smacked her lips. "Just that, sir. I spent dozens of hours over the past two days scouring the oil refinery, but I couldn't find a single explosive."

"This doesn't make any sense. You told me you clearly heard him say he was rigging his oil refinery with explosives. Were you lying to me?"

"No, I'd never!"

"Then where are they?"

"Maybe there weren't any? Maybe it was a cry for help."

John shook his head. "Schumaker's not that dramatic. No, this can only mean one thing. Someone else must have stolen them."

"But who would do that?"

"That's what I need to figure out."

The phone rang loudly throughout the office.

This better be important, he thought, reaching for the handset.

"Hi, sir," exclaimed an annoying voice on the other end.

"Be quick, Mr. Tibbles, I'm busy. What is it?"

"Bullit Inc. just acquired Schumaker Trains and Oil."

"You're lying."

"Winston Perry just informed us."

John sat up. "What? When?"

"Mmmm… forty seconds ago."

No. I don't believe it. They can't be that stupid. He cleared his throat. "If this is a joke…"

"It's not. Winston really did acquire Schumaker's company on behalf of Bullit Inc."

John slowly pulled the phone away from his ear and gently laid it on his desk. *This can't be. It's, it's…* He felt the thrill of impending revenge course through every atom in his body. *It's too easy!*

John's eyes searched the room hoping to find something to prove him wrong, something to fret about, something to fill him with rage and agony, but everything was in perfect order.

"Sir?" asked Mary-Lou Anne.

John didn't hear her. The sound of his heart pounding in his chest was too loud. His mouth watered—the taste of victory was near. He already had Schumaker cornered, but now his enemies just fumbled the biggest prize of all, and it fell right into his lap. *Forget the refinery. I need to tell Judge Willis to drop the Schumaker case. A much bigger fish has jumped into the net!*

CHAPTER 41

Winston watched Mr. Adams peer over the report, wondering what the president was thinking. "Keep in mind everything I'm telling you is classified information," said the commander in chief. "In fact, it's so classified I shouldn't be telling you about it."

Winston leaned forward in his leather chair across from Mr. Adams in the Oval Office. Sunlight streamed in from the windows behind the president, reflecting off the stainless-steel desk and making Winston squint. "I understand. Keep going."

"Since fleeing police and district prosecutors two months ago, the aliens haven't been seen. No one has any clue where they went." Mr. Adams cleared his throat before continuing. "That is, until yesterday, when they showed up in Southern California and infiltrated a secret government complex inside Edwards Air Force Base. Using alien magic, they entered the subterranean labyrinth within the facility." He paused. "How they managed to do so without alerting a single guard or tripping a single security camera is beyond me. Anyway, they made it to the lowest level in the complex: the level holding the orange alien. Their magical powers failed to break through the twelve-inch-thick titanium-reinforced walls containing the orange alien, so they strapped several kilograms of explosives onto the walls and blew an enormous hole in them, tall enough for a giraffe on stilts to fit through.

"Every alarm within the complex set off immediately, and hundreds of military troops stormed the facility, but when they got to the basement, the aliens were already gone. All that was left was a leather button."

Winston raised his eyebrows. "A leather button?"

"That's right. From a bomber jacket."

"Huh." Winston thought for a moment. "Was it a two-holed button or four-holed?"

"Two-holed." Mr. Adams eyed him. "You wouldn't happen to know where it came from, do you?"

"No," Winston lied. "I don't know where the button came from."

"I don't care where the button came from; I'm talking about the bomber jacket. We don't make bomber jackets, so I wonder who's manufacturing them. I think there could be a market for bomber jackets in the fall."

A silence came between them as Mr. Adams thought about bomber jackets and Winston contemplated leather buttons. Winston broke the silence. "Why would the gray aliens reclaim the orange alien? What could they want with it?"

Mr. Adams shrugged. "They're criminals, Winston. The same criminals that *you* had me decriminalize."

"I respectfully disagree, Mr. Adams. They aren't criminals."

"What definition of 'criminal' do you use? Breaking into, destroying, and looting a United States military complex falls squarely into my definition of criminal. Even if they weren't criminals before, they sure as hell are criminals now."

Winston had reservations. It didn't make sense. The benevolent gray aliens he knew would never do anything so brazenly destructive without good reason. *Eugene's been too much of an influence on them*, he thought, realizing where they must have gotten the explosives to free their orange friend.

"Where are the aliens now?" he asked Mr. Adams.

Mr. Adams snapped his fingers. "Poof! They disappeared, just like they did two months ago. Your guess as to where they went is as good as mine."

"I hope they don't get into any more trouble."

"You have a knack for befriending troublemakers."

Winston offered a strong rebuttal. "No I don't."

"Everyone you spend time with is a lawbreaker. Rosaline Browning flouted health codes at her bakery, the aliens blasted their way into a top-secret government base, and Eugene Schumaker shamelessly rigged the BABKA, or tried to anyway, if John Angryberger is to be believed. It might do you well to find better, more law-abiding friends before this lot ropes you into their criminal shenanigans."

Winston cocked his head sideways, rested his chin on his thumb, and reflected on Mr. Adams observations. *He's not wrong...*

"Anyway, thanks for the trains, Winston. Just make sure you keep them away from the aliens. Those little buggers will be dead the moment they think of laying a finger or a block of C4 on my business. Is that understood?"

"Yes."

"Good. Now let's keep it clean from here on out. The only concern I want to have is my other vice president. I don't want to add thirteen intergalactic monkey wrenches to the mix."

CHAPTER 42

Mr. Choo's Chinese Buffet was a family-friendly four-star restaurant in Long Island and a neighborhood classic. It charged by the scoop—fifty-cents per—and offered sixty classic Chinese-American dishes. Frequently scooped entrees included the orange chicken, honey walnut shrimp, and Peking duck, among others. The restaurant also had a bakery attached to it. Reviews for the establishment were consistent: the Chinese buffet portion of the restaurant was three-star worthy, but the bakery was five-star, so it always averaged four-star.

The restaurant employed twelve chefs, one hostess, four dishwashers, sixteen bussers, and one baker. At peak hours, there could be over a three hundred people eating and working at the restaurant, with dozens more on a waitlist hoping for a table to clear.

That night, however, there were only two people inside the restaurant. John and Mr. Chartreuse had trained it six hours from D.C. to New York, walked the half-dozen blocks to the restaurant, and entered through the back-alley door using the keypad code Mr. Choo had provided. They had arrived after hours, well past restaurant close. All the patrons and staff were home asleep. Nobody would be there for a couple hours, until the baker got their head start.

"It should be in here," John said, gesturing to the kitchen supply closet. The white door was stained with various greases and sauces, some orangey, some flakey, and some quite congealed. The doorknob shook loosely as John grasped it. The door swung open with a faint creak. There, on the floor, surrounded by shelves of cleaner, towels, rags, napkins, spare utensils, glasses, and a mop and bucket, was five hundred thousand dollars' worth of explosives in a duffle.

John stared at it. Mr. Chartreuse stepped inside the closet next to him, snarfing down a heaping plate of sesame chicken.

"All this for four bucks. Unreal," said Mr. Chartreuse, momentarily pausing from eating to breathe.

John bent down and took out one of the cartridges of C4 in the bag and handed it to Mr. Chartreuse. "They are just like I told you."

Mr. Chartreuse put down his fork and plate on top of a rack of paper towels before accepting the charge from John. He examined it carefully by tracing the yellow Chinese characters with his finger. Intrigued, he brought the charge to this nose and took a whiff.

"Give it here," said John, holding out a hand.

Mr. Chartreuse passed it back to him.

John put the charge in the duffle bag with the others.

"That's more than enough C4 to obliterate Schumaker's—er, Mr. Adam's—fleet of trains," said Mr. Chartreuse.

John looked up. "Haven't I already explained it to you?" he said crabbily. "We aren't blowing up *his* trains. Judge Willis devised a smarter plan that'll frame more than just Schumaker."

"I know, I was just saying…"

John shook his head, annoyed. "Directions are in the bag. Mr. Choo drew pictures illustrating how to wire the charges. They're already synced to the detonator. Judge Willis is moving quickly, so I need this done this week. It'll take a few hours to set up, so you should start the instant you get back to KB Rail."

"Gotcha," said Mr. Chartreuse, rubbing his palms together.

"By the way, you haven't come across a bug gun recently, have you?" John asked abruptly.

"A what?"

"It looks like an octopus-themed grappling hook—orange, with green metal spokes. An unidentified symbol on the back."

"No, I haven't seen that. Why?"

"It's missing."

"Did Schumaker…?"

There was a pause, then John zipped the explosives-filled duffel and handed it to Mr. Chartreuse. "This is the most important thing you'll ever do in your life. Don't mess it up."

CHAPTER 43

Judge Willis walked down the hallway to Eugene's office. He glanced at the black placard beside the door, where white letters spelled out "Eugene Schumaker – CEO." Glittering stickers of ladybugs, caterpillars, and butterflies adorned the placard. Judge Willis peeled off a ladybug sticker, rolled it in his fingers, and let it fall to floor. *Where bugs like you belong.*

He curled his fingers into a fist and knocked on the door.

"Come in."

Judge Willis quietly pushed open the door and stepped inside the office. Eugene was making a goofy-looking necklace out of differently shaped buttons and nylon string. He looked up at Judge Willis, and his eyes grew wide with worry and fear.

"What are you doing here?"

Judge Willis reached underneath his black robes and took out an envelope. He handed it to Eugene. "It's an updated subpoena. The court case for Schumaker Trains and Oil is no longer happening on the 24th of July."

Eugene hesitated before taking the envelope from Judge Willis. "How come?"

"The district is rescheduling the case for the 30th so it can add more defendants under the permissive joinder rule."

"What does that mean?"

Judge Willis sneered. "Think. Who else could be a defendant in the Schumaker case…?"

Eugene's eyes widened. "No!"

Judge Willis turned around, waved goodbye from over his shoulder, and dipped from Eugene's office, leaving the train ravager speechless.

From there, Judge Willis hopped into his car and drove to Bullit Inc.'s headquarters. He arrived at the company's office and presented his ID and credentials to security.

"I'm here for Vice President Winston Perry," he said to the security guard.

The guard scrutinized his glossy black robes and Superior Court Justice identification card. "Sixty-ninth floor," he said. "You'll need a special-access key to get up there. Let me swipe you in."

"Thank you."

Judge Willis rode the elevator to the top floor, then traipsed across the atrium toward Winston's office. Secretary Jane stopped him before he could waltz inside.

"Is Winston expecting you?"

"Yes."

"Just one moment." She withdrew into Winston's office.

While she was gone, Judge Willis studied the lavish atrium with its wonderful waterfall. He went over to it and put his finger under the running water, changing its flow so that it ran down his finger and trickled from his wrist into the basin below. He looked with satisfaction at the narrow, dry column of wall that formed below his finger and extended to the floor. Splitting the water made him feel like Moses.

A moment later, Secretary Jane exited from Winston's office. "You can go inside now," she said.

He entered the office and pulled the door shut behind him with his wet finger. Winston eyed him reproachfully as he walked in.

"Good morning, Winston, or should I say, *Teofilo Trujillo*."

Insecurity flashed across Winston's eyes. "How do you know my name?"

"I had some friends look up dirt on you. Don't worry," he

added, sensing Winston's agitation, "they didn't find anything new or exciting. I already knew you were a son of Mexican gypsies."

"Tell me what you want or leave." Winston spoke calmly, but his tone was full of hostility.

"I've come to inform you that the case against Schumaker has been rescheduled."

Winston narrowed his eyes. "What's the catch?"

Judge Willis drew another subpoena from his coat pocket and offered it to Winston, who impatiently plucked it from his hand. He watched as Winston's eyes flit rapidly back-and-forth across the paper like a typewriter.

"The case now names me, Eugene, and Mr. Adams as defendants," said Winston without looking up. "Why am I named? How does that make sense?"

"Schumaker is the saboteur, so unsurprisingly he must appear in court. I added you as a defendant because you're liable for the acquisition of Schumaker Trains and Oil, and Mr. Adams is named because he presides over Bullit Inc., now the parent company of Schumaker Trains and Oil."

Winston crushed the subpoena in his hand. "You can't do this."

"As long as you and your friends continue to break the law, then yes, I can."

"We've done nothing wrong."

"Then who blew up KB Rail's train last night?"

Winston scrunched his forehead. "What do you mean?"

Judge Willis reached into another pocket and pulled out a folded newspaper clipping. "From this morning." He flicked it like a booger at Winston. It caught him just under his left eye.

Glaring, Winston gently massaged the skin above his jaw. Then, reluctantly, he unfolded the clipping, which had fallen in his lap. "KB Rail Train Explodes," the caption read. There was a picture of a burning train underneath.

KB Rail has suffered another setback after one of its freight trains exploded late last night. It is the company's second train explosion over the past two months. Its competitor,

Schumaker Trains and Oil, has sustained dozens of explosions in the same timeframe. Investigators are searching for clues to determine if all these incidents are somehow linked. Mr. Chartreuse, president of KB Rail, suspects they are. "It's clear Eugene Schumaker has it out for us," he said when interviewed following the aftermath of the accident. "He's obviously jealous of KB Rail's market growth and therefore has decided to intimidate and sabotage us. This was no accident, and we will get to the bottom of this."

Winston looked up at Judge Willis, the lines around his mouth fraught with scorn. "There's no universe in which Eugene would have ever done this."

"Schumaker's biggest competitor wouldn't blow up their own train without a reason, now, would they? This is clearly Schumaker's doing. He destroyed it to get back at John Angryberger, and you knew. You're an accessory to the fact."

Winston rolled his eyes. "This sounds like a dumb scheme John Angryberger devised to retaliate against Eugene for God knows what. I doubt there's evidence indicating Eugene was in any way responsible."

Judge Willis felt a grin tug at his lips. "If you believe you've done nothing wrong, then you shouldn't have anything to worry about; but you ought to remember what we're capable of, even without evidence. And I'll let you in on a little secret…" Judge Willis leaned in. "This time we have proof."

CHAPTER 44

The next morning, Winston found himself reclining in a Victorian daybed in the Oval Office while he waited for Mr. Adams. The bed rested against the far wall of the office, opposite the president's stainless-steel desk and the mustard-draped windows behind it, which Winston had closed to prevent the morning sun's rays from shining in his eyes. Two ugly beige couches sat in the middle of the room like squishy, sun-bleached Yukon potatoes. They were separated by a glass coffee table on which rested a pot of fake lilacs.

Winston reached above his head and pulled a burgundy and blue throw that was dangling off the bed's headboard over himself. Feeling cozy, he rested his hands on his chest and looked up. On the ceiling was an image of an eagle carrying a branch, the motto *E. Pluribus Unum* inscribed beneath it. He rolled his head to the left and inspected the wall next to him, which was adorned with portraits of past presidents, some whom he recognized—George Washington, Franklin Roosevelt, and Thomas Jefferson—and others he didn't. He looked closely at the portrait nearest him. A long, bony, gaunt face with thick sideburns and a black top hat on his head stared back at him.

Two paintings down, the portrait of George Washington swung open, and Mr. Adams hopped out of a secret passage. "Tell me why you manipulated me into buying Schumaker Trains and Oil," he yelled, flouncing across the room and taking his seat behind his desk.

"I thought it would be good for business," said Winston, without sitting up.

"How?"

"Acquiring it would allow us to compete against Jmart directly and eventually beat them out."

"You idiot, you didn't even consult me on this! I'm already squeezing John dry with our government contracts. We don't need to go toe-to-toe with him across the board. What the hell were you thinking?"

"Last time we met you thought it was a great idea. I remember you laughing about it. You said it'd be hilarious to knock John out of business with your own set of trains."

"That was *before* I got roped into a lawsuit. Now, because of you, I have to deal with John Angryberger and Judge Willis. Do you know how much of a pain in the ass those two are?"

"Yes, actually."

Mr. Adams balled his fist and shook it angrily at Winston. "I should fire you."

Winston smiled at the proposition.

Mr. Adams scoffed. "Like I'd let you off the hook that easily. No, you're going to work for me for the rest of your life, until the skin decomposes off your dry, pathetic bones and all that's left is your hunched-over corpse rotting away at a cubicle for all eternity."

Winston put his hands behind his head. "I understand you're upset…"

"I'm not done scolding you!" said Mr. Adams, his voice rising. "You're a sloppy, lazy, thoughtless freeloader who can't distinguish a bad investment from a good one, even if they come with literal bombs strapped on."

"…and while I understand your frustrations, I think we should try to quell our emotions and, instead, use our minds collaboratively to figure out a way we can all avoid being sentenced to jail."

"Jail?" Mr. Adams threw his palms open. "Are you a moron? I'm the president, I don't go to jail."

"But what about Eugene and me?"

"Winston, you might just be the stupidest person I've ever met," he said. "We're businessmen. Rich, successful businessmen. We don't go to jail. That's a place for poor people and people with bad lawyers. Our livelihood, not our freedom, is the only thing at risk."

The phone on Mr. Adams's desk rang, interrupting him. "What's this now?" He lifted the receiver impatiently. "This is the president."

Although Winston couldn't make out what was being said, he immediately recognized the sinister voice hissing from the handset: the vice president.

"No, I don't want that!" exclaimed Mr. Adams heatedly.

Winston tilted his head backwards until he was looking behind himself and admired a surrealist painting on the wall while the president and vice president spoke. The painting, a landscape drawing of D.C. centered around Bullit Inc.'s skyscraper headquarters, was rife with propaganda. The Bullit Inc. logo was drawn on the lone cloud floating across a mildly polluted blue sky. A train with the Bullit Inc. logo on its nose ploughed across the foreground, its paint fresh. Dozens of cheery children skipped on the station platform. Winston squinted to look closer: yes, they were dressed in Glam Blanc clothing. Adults in bowler hats drove gaily down avenues in Bullit Inc. manufactured cars. Even the spaceship hiding behind the single cloud had the Bullit Inc. logo on its hull.

"When you put it that way, I'd *love* to entertain a nice chat with you … Now? Yes, now works for me… what? Why does he want to come? Fine, whatever, bring him. I'll tell Secret Service to kindly refrain from shooting the two of you on sight… It was a joke… just come over. Bye."

Mr. Adams put the phone down and crossed his arms on top of his desk. "Winston, I need you to get out of here. We *adults* need to have a conversation," he said condescendingly. "Now go, before I send you off to Roxborough to end up like Dominic Miller."

CHAPTER 45

Eugene pushed open the door to the familiar jostling of bells. Before he could step a single foot inside, however, Rosaline came running from the kitchen. She shrieked loudly when she saw it was Eugene and Winston.

"Rosaline, is everything okay?" asked Eugene, full of trepidation; he didn't want to be yelled at again.

Instead, Rosaline hugged him.

"I'm so sorry that I shouted at the two of you! If anything had happened to either one of you, I would never be able to forgive myself."

"We deserved it," said Winston.

"I want both of you to be happy—I want everyone to be happy. I was just so upset with how *stupid* you boys can be at times." Her eyes traveled from Eugene to Winston, and she directed her next comment at him: "But I owe you more than an apology; I owe you a thank you," she said, touching Winston's arm.

"For what?"

"For helping Eugene and the aliens."

"I should have done something sooner," said Winston, fidgeting uncomfortably.

"Still, you helped. Better late than never."

"Speaking of the aliens, have you seen them recently?" Eugene asked. "I finished making the necklace, and I want to give it to Buttons."

Rosaline's eyes lit up. "You won't believe it."

"Did something happen?" asked Winston nervously.

"They came by yesterday, but they weren't alone."

"Don't tell me Judge Willis was here again…"

Rosaline shook her head. "Not unless Judge Willis is an orange alien from outer space."

"You're kidding," exclaimed Eugene, instinctively reaching for his notebook. "I must see it."

"It isn't here."

Eugene's shoulders slumped forward dejectedly. "So, they aren't here either?"

"No, and unfortunately, I don't know where they went. The good news is they don't need to hide anymore, now that Mr. Adams decriminalized them."

"Let's hope they stay that way," said Winston.

Rosaline put her hands on her hips and frowned. "What do you mean?"

"Well, they might have, um… how do I phrase this? They broke into a top-secret government facility beneath Edwards Airforce Base and stole the orange alien."

Rosaline's mouth opened wide enough to fit a grapefruit inside. "*What!* Why didn't you tell me about this sooner?"

"I didn't want to alarm you," said Winston unconvincingly, giving Eugene the impression Winston had forgotten about the incident with everything else going on.

Rosaline slapped a hand over her forehead. "Ugh! As if I need any more stress! I'm already worried sick about you two!"

"We'll be fine," said Winston.

"How do you know?" Eugene blurted out. He couldn't stop thinking about the court case, and worried he would lose not only material wealth, but also his freedom. "How do you know we won't be going to prison for years on end? How do you I won't lose everything? How do you know I'll be able to become an entomologist like I always wanted?"

Winston wrapped his arm around Eugene's shoulder. "Mr. Adams assured me."

Eugene pushed him away. "And you trust him?"

"We don't have any other choice. Besides, I heard him on the phone with John Angryberger. I figure they'll negotiate a deal behind the scenes."

Winston's complacency wasn't enough to persuade Eugene, and his anxieties remained. "Then why do we still have to go to court?"

"I think it's going to be okay, too, Eugene," Rosaline said.

Eugene whipped around to stare at her. He couldn't understand how Rosaline and Winston were so calm when all he could feel was the world caving in. "What makes you think that?"

"The aliens." She looked out the window at the spaceship. "I had never seen them so happy. The way they looked at me, beaming with their new orange friend…" She trailed off. She was beaming, too. Her cheeks glowed with fox fire, and her emerald eyes sparkled peacefully. "It was a sign that things are going to be alright. Everything's going to work out, I just know it."

CHAPTER 46

John Angryberger could barely contain his excitement. He had been waiting for this day for years: the day he would break Mr. Adams's stranglehold and could finally begin his quest to conquer every market in the world. Judge Willis had privately dropped by that morning to wish him good luck with his case and to confirm that the courtroom session would proceed as planned. John thanked him, then assured him that if all went as rehearsed, he'd be appointed a Supreme Court Justice. If anything, the case today was as much Judge Willis's victory party as it was his own.

John Angryberger followed the narrow corridor to the courtroom. The bright blue carpet that guided him was illuminated by austere lamps set inside inlays of ornate mahogany walls. He yanked open the courtroom doors, feeling like a rockstar as he walked inside. Everyone turned as he entered. He strolled down the aisle, passing a plethora of journalists sitting in the back, their pens poised, eager to report the session's outcome. Seats unoccupied by news reporters were filled with second-rate businessmen who had paid a premium for nosebleed seats, the cost of their ticket a small price to pay if they could be the first investors in foreign markets. *Fools*, John thought, *the deal has already been struck. There won't be any crumbs for the rest of you.*

He took his seat in the front row, glancing at Mr. Adams,

Winston, and Eugene, who stood behind the defendants' table. Mr. Adams looked like a mountain goat in his Glam Blanc suit. He met John's eyes and nodded.

Standing next to him, Winston and Eugene were both visibly distraught. Eugene's skin was so pale it appeared snow white, which was especially noticeable in contrast to the hideously colorful necklace of buttons around his neck. John squinted at it. A pendant made from a goldbug encased in amber dangled from the garish string. As it caught the light, it cast a yellow glow on Eugene's face, making him appear jaundiced. Next to him, Winston pulled at the collar of his shirt as if he were struggling to breathe. John smiled sadistically. *Evidently, Mr. Adams had not informed them.*

Judge Willis entered the courtroom from a separate passageway behind the judge's bench. He winked at John before sitting in his highchair above the golden winged-angel statue with blown-back hair. That was the cue for the bailiff.

"The Superior Court of the District of Columbia is now in session. Judge Willis presiding. Please be seated," the bailiff called out to the congregation.

The audience rustled as they took their seats.

Judge Willis pulled out the script from his briefcase. He laid it out orderly on the podium in front of him and inhaled deeply and serenely. "Ladies and gentlemen, calling the case of the People of the District of Columbia versus Bullit Inc., president of the United States and parent company to Schumaker Trains and Oil, represented by Brian Adams, president and CEO of Bullit Inc., Winston Perry, vice president of Bullit Inc., responsible for acquisition and portfolio management of Schumaker Trains and Oil, and Eugene Schumaker, former CEO of Schumaker Trains and Oil. Are both sides ready?"

"Yes," said Mr. Adams, Winston, and Eugene in unison.

"Yes, Your Honor," said the district attorney.

"Will the clerk please swear in the jury?" Judge Willis asked.

After the jury was sworn in, he looked toward the plaintiff's table. "I'm ready for opening statements."

The district attorney stood up. "The district has investigated

Schumaker Trains and Oil's recent explosions for evidence of criminal activity. After the initial investigation, we found evidence indicating the train explosions were deliberately caused and orchestrated by the owners and operators of Schumaker Trains and Oil, namely, Mr. Adams, Winston Perry, and Eugene Schumaker. In addition to intentionally destroying their assets as part of an illicit scheme to collect insurance money and benefit from the increased cost of oil, these three individuals sabotaged their competitor, KB Rail, to secure unfair advantage in the freight train market."

John shot a gleeful look at Eugene whose hands had begun to shake. *Serves you right for messing with me.*

The DA took his seat. Mr. Adams rose to speak for the defendants.

"Your Honor, the claims brought against us today are false and unsubstantiated. Winston Perry and I of Bullit Inc., as well as Eugene Schumaker, formerly of Schumaker Trains and Oil, did not destroy our assets, knowingly or otherwise, nor did we destroy the assets of our competitors. I would like to make it clear that we do not condone sabotage and destruction—which is a violation of the law and an endangerment to the public—to secure unfair financial advantage, manipulate insurance loopholes, or for any other gain or purpose." Mr. Adams took his seat.

Judge Willis cleared his throat. "Are there any witnesses to call to the stands?"

"I'd like to call Ronald Lionel to the stand," said the DA.

The congregation turned their heads in unison, like spectators watching a tennis match, as the bailiff escorted Ron the conductor from the back of the courtroom to the stand.

The DA began his questioning. "Mr. Lionel, how long have you worked for Schumaker Trains and Oil?"

"A long time."

"And how many trains that you conducted had mechanical failures or exploded when Theodore Schumaker was acting president of the company?"

"None."

"And how many trains that you conducted exploded over the past two months?"

"Three dozen."

"That seems highly suspicious."

Ron let out a tremendous smile. "Merely an unfortunate string of accidents."

"Did you intentionally destroy any of those trains?"

"No."

"Did you help Mr. Schumaker destroy those trains?"

"Nope."

"Were you complicit in the act of sabotage and knowingly and willingly let the trains blow up?"

Ron's smile grew even bigger. "I would never."

"Mr. Lionel, if you had no responsibility for the train explosions, then how do you explain why thirty-six trains—all of which you conducted—went up in flames?"

Ron shrugged. "Your guess is as good as mine."

"You don't find it at all unusual?"

"No, not really. Nothing seems unusual anymore, not since aliens landed on the planet."

"Just to clarify for the jury, you are stating that you had no part in the train explosions, and you have no idea how or why they occurred?"

"That is correct."

"That's all the questions I have, Your Honor," said the DA.

"Very well. You may return to your seat."

Ron stood up and the bailiff led him out of the courtroom.

Judge Willis addressed the DA. "In your opening statement, you said you had proof that Eugene Schumaker intentionally sabotaged his own company. Do you have evidence to present to the jury that supports your claim that Bullit Inc. and Schumaker Trains and Oil engaged in criminal and unlawful activity?"

"I have numerous photos of the aftermath of the train explosions that I would like to provide as evidence."

"Bring them here."

The bailiff took the stack of photos from the DA and brought them to Judge Willis. Taken from many different angles, they collectively showed the extent of the explosions and the aftermath of the oil cars and locomotive engines.

"What am I looking at here?" asked Judge Willis.

"That first image was taken of a destroyed locomotive half an hour after the fire was put out by the fire department. As you can see, the bottom had holes blown through and was completely melted. If you flip through subsequent images, you can see holes in the bottom of many of the oil cars as well."

Judge Willis flipped through the photos. He paused, holding one up for the courtroom to see. It showed three tanker cars with multiple gaping holes in them like Swiss cheese.

"What do these holes mean?" he asked.

"They indicate that some explosive force generated them."

"That seems obvious enough," remarked Judge Willis, "but is there anything else we can glean from these images?"

"The images show a pattern. The holes are in the same location and are the same diameter and depth in each case. Explosive fuel alone doesn't explain why such similar holes are found on the locomotive engines."

"What do you believe caused them?"

"An explosive device."

"Is it possible that they could have been caused by oil exploding in other cars, setting off a chain reaction that blew up the engine last?"

"We've run simulated models, but the chance of a single locomotive becoming disfigured the way they're pictured occurred in less than two percent of simulations. If you exponentiate the probability by the number of incidences, then the chance for all the engines to detonate by a force other than an explosive device is about 6.87×10^{-64} percent. That's 0.00000000000000000000000-0000000000000000000000000000000000000687 percent."

"That sounds pretty small."

"It's virtually impossible, Your Honor."

"But still possible, nonetheless. Your calculations merely provide a probability of something occurring, but I need evidence that there was foul play involved. Do you have anything else?"

"Yes, Your Honor. I'd like to bring a disarmed explosive cartridge to the judge."

John licked his lips and peeked at the defendants, hungry to see their reaction, and it wasn't long before he was rewarded. Whatever blood was left in Eugene's face drained as the bailiff carried the explosive charge to Judge Willis. His skin turned practically see-through. Eugene exchanged frightened looks with a tattooed giant in the stands behind him.

Of course that's not your charge, you dimwits.

Judge Willis took the explosive out of the plastic baggie and examined it. The palm-sized cartridge was black and yellow. Chinese characters covered one side, and wires protruded from either end.

"Where did you find this?" he asked.

"We uncovered it at one of the train sites strapped to a locomotive, Your Honor. It evidently didn't go off."

"I—I object, Your Honor," Eugene called out in an enfeebled voice. "That thing, whatever it is, is not ours."

"Wait your turn, Schumaker," said Judge Willis lazily. "You can provide evidence for your defense in a moment."

Judge Willis wiggled the C4 in his hands. "What does this Chinese writing say on the charge?" he asked the DA.

"They are directions for use and a warning about proper handling."

"Where did it come from?"

"We aren't sure. Most likely the charge came from a black-market dealer in the city."

"You said you found this explosive charge on one of Schumaker's locomotives?"

"That's correct, yes."

"How come more charges weren't found?"

The DA flipped through his copy of the script for the answer. "We found a second charge, and the photo of that one is within the stack of images the bailiff handed you. After documenting that charge, we used it to test whether its explosive power was enough to cause the damages seen in the photos. Furthermore, we performed a chemical analysis of the charge to determine its properties, which we could use to identify chemical markers on site.

"Our experiments showed that the heat generated by the charge was great enough to melt reinforced steel plates on train cars and engines, as well as capable of completely incinerating the charge itself, getting rid of any evidence in the process. Furthermore, we learned the charge contains numerous chemicals that interact with oxygen and form gaseous molecules, which are subsequently liberated after detonation. These molecules can travel great distances with the wind before settling. As a result, concentrations of the chemical agents aren't found at levels greater than what would normally be detected in the earth. Therefore, it's nearly impossible to determine the cause of explosion from chemical signature alone." The DA paused. "It's quite an ingenious device," he added as an afterthought.

Judge Willis studied the black and yellow cartridge. "This charge is engineered to be undetectable?"

"That is correct, Your Honor."

"How can the jury be expected to believe your claim that Schumaker Trains and Oil sabotaged their company if we can't use soil analysis to detect these explosive chemicals?"

"Two reasons. First, we found two intact charges at the scene. The physical, rather than chemical, evidence is enough to conclude that Eugene Schumaker, Winston Perry, and Mr. Adams intentionally destroyed the trains in question. Second, in our test of one of the charges, we blew up an oil car and found the explosion produced holes identical to the ones seen in the photos."

"I see. Is there any further evidence you can provide?"

"Yes, Your Honor. We found the exact same holes on KB Rail's exploded freight train."

"Are you implying that Schumaker blew up one of KB Rail's trains?"

"No, Your Honor. At the time, Eugene Schumaker was no

longer the CEO of Schumaker Trains and Oil. Schumaker was not responsible for destroying his competitor's train."

"Then who was?"

"Mr. Adams."

"Thank you." Judge Willis turned toward the defendants as the DA took his seat. "Now is the time for the defense to make their case. Eugene Schumaker, please take the stand."

John leaned forward in his chair as Eugene rose to his feet. *This isn't part of the plan. Judge Willis must be taking a few minutes to torture the poor boy.*

"Eugene Schumaker, did you intentionally destroy your trains?" asked the DA.

"No," said Eugene, shuddering.

"Then why did so many of your trains explode?"

"I'm not sure."

"Who is your black-market explosives dealer?"

Eugene briefly peeked at Cecil-Lee. "I don't have one."

"I'd like to remind you that lying under oath is a crime punishable by up to ten years in federal prison. So, I'll ask you again, did you intentionally destroy your trains?"

Eugene's lips quivered. "I, um…" he began, but quickly trailed off. He licked his lips nervously and swallowed. His throat was so dry the entire courtroom heard the clicking of his uvula as it stuck to the back of his mouth like Velcro. He glanced at Winston, who mouthed the word "no."

Eugene burst into tears. "I just wanted to study bugs! I never wanted to take over my dad's company and run his stupid trains!" he exclaimed, weeping into his palms. Eugene bleated and blubbered and heaved uncontrollably. Snot leaked from his nose, adding more wet sounds to the symphony of his despair.

John smirked. *Music to my ears.*

"If you didn't want to run Schumaker Trains and Oil, why did you become its president?"

"My dad wanted me to continue his legacy that he spent his life creating," said Eugene softly.

"Your dad founded his company on the principles of deceit and selfishness. There are a lot of similarities between how you run the company and the way your dad did."

"That's not true. He wasn't like that, and I'm not like him. I don't ever want to be like him."

"So you destroyed your trains because you didn't want to be like your dad?" said the DA. It was more of an accusation than a question.

Eugene whimpered and wept, but he shook his head. "No," he said faintly.

"What about KB Rail? Do you expect us to believe you didn't destroy their trains either?"

Eugene's sniveling suddenly stopped. "Oh, well that I *definitely* didn't do," he answered firmly.

"Alright, Schumaker, you can return to the defendants' table. Winston Perry, please take the stand."

Winston took the hot seat once Eugene had been escorted down.

"Winston Perry, why did you purchase Schumaker Trains and Oil knowing full well Eugene Schumaker's unlawful misdeeds? Were you an accomplice in his schemes?" asked the DA.

"No. I oversaw the purchase of the company because I thought it was a good investment for Bullit Inc."

"Once the purchase was complete, did you set out to destroy Schumaker's main regional competitor, KB Rail?"

"No."

"Why should the jury believe you? Your moral integrity ought to be called into question. The friends you surround yourself with are nothing but lawbreakers; your work involves selling snow to the destitute as a replacement for food; and you dutifully assist the president with formulating exclusionary business treaties that limit free-market competition. Either you are an accomplice in shady criminal practices, or you're the biggest ignoramus I've ever had the misfortune of meeting."

"I can personally confirm the latter to be true," interjected Mr. Adams.

"How does it make you feel knowing that all your hard work has gotten you nowhere other than a spot at the defendants' table and a ticket to twenty years in prison?" the DA continued, ignoring Mr. Adams.

"It makes me feel like I could have played my hand differently."

"What would you have changed?"

"A lot of things, but the one thing I *wouldn't* have changed was convincing Eugene to sell me his dad's company."

"You don't learn from your mistakes, do you?"

"Buying Schumaker Trains and Oil wasn't a mistake."

"Thank you for proving my point. You may return to your seat."

As Winston left the stand, Judge Willis turned toward the president. "Mr. Adams, was there something you wanted to say?"

Without glancing at Winston or Eugene, Mr. Adams rose from the bench and took the stand, bringing his briefcase and stack of papers with him. His attention was focused on the monologue John had typed out for him, which he began to read: "Thank you, Your Honor. As I mentioned earlier, we at Bullit Inc. were not involved, knowingly or otherwise, in the destruction of trains. We've internally investigated the explosions to try to understand why so many of our engines improperly ignited. I'll remind you that the cost of each engine is nearly two million dollars, and if you include the cost of our oil cars, we've lost close to three hundred million dollars in assets, not including all the crude that went up in smoke."

"But Mr. Adams," Judge Willis began, looking down at his ledger and reading his part, "according to Schumaker Trains and Oil quarterlies, despite losing hundreds of millions of dollars in assets, the company received full reimbursement from insurance. The economic impact of the explosions meant that Schumaker profited beautifully from fluctuations in the oil market."

"That's… merely coincidence. We didn't orchestrate a scheme to blow up our trains so that we could profit off insurance and market manipulation. That's not only preposterous but completely unlawful and morally reprehensible. As the president of the United States, I'm fully aware how unethical and illegal those actions are. I've sworn an oath to not engage in fraud or deceit."

"But Eugene Schumaker took no such oath before the nation. Perhaps he manipulated you into buying his company?"

Mr. Adams shrugged. "That's irrelevant to the trial. If anything, that'd mean Bullit Inc. should be suing Schumaker instead of the district suing us."

"Mr. Adams, do you have any proof of your innocence, or is the only defense you offer your word that you didn't do it?" said Judge Willis.

Mr. Adams eyed John over his shoulder before continuing. "I have evidence I'd like to bring before the court." He opened his briefcase, fumbled inside for a moment, and then pulled out a plastic baggie with a familiar rectangular object inside. "I'd like to present a disarmed explosive cartridge to the judge," he said to the bailiff.

The bailiff took the baggie from him and brought it to Judge Willis.

Judge Willis pulled the object out of the bag—a black cartridge with yellow Chinese characters on it and wires poking out of either end. He compared it to the charge the DA had handed him.

They were identical.

Judge Willis looked at the president. "This is the same C4 cartridge as the one the DA brought to me."

"Apparently so, Your Honor."

"You admit that these are your charges?"

"No, Your Honor. Neither of those explosives are ours."

"If it isn't yours, then where did you find it?"

"California."

"Are you implying that your explosives supplier lives in California?"

"First of all, we don't have an explosives supplier, because we don't traffic in illegal weapons. Secondly, going off the first point, we don't know if the peddler of these charges lives in California. If anything, evidence suggests the black-market dealer operates in China, hence the Chinese characters on the charges."

"Then explain why a charge found on the West Coast of the United States is related to events in the nation's capital."

"If the DA found that charge on one of Schumaker's oil trains, then I believe that charge was planted there. However, we didn't do it, and we didn't know who did it until very recently."

"Are you implying someone else destroyed your trains?"

"Not only our trains, Your Honor, but also those belonging to KB Rail."

"If you withheld this evidence from police and federal judicators during their preliminary investigation into the train explosions then that is an obstruction of justice and a felony in its own right."

"You'll remember, Your Honor, that we weren't aware of explosives planted on Schumaker's trains until just moments ago when the DA brought forth the charge he found. When he did, it became evident that the events surrounding Schumaker's and KB Rail's trains are connected to recent attacks on government property."

"What attacks are you referring to? I'm not aware of any attacks on government property."

"I am referring to a previously classified but now, at this moment of my testimony, declassified incident that occurred at a government installation in California. Last week, the dozen gray aliens, who have been sought for arrest by the federal government and whose spaceship remains in the Fairgrounds, invaded a top-secret military compound using their advanced alien technology. However, they were unable to penetrate reinforced titanium walls with their space-powers. When our troops swarmed and surrounded them, they set off explosions using the same C4 you're holding in your hands to blast a hole in the wall and escape."

"What were the aliens doing in a military complex in California?" asked Judge Willis.

"They broke into the facility with the intent to steal back the orange alien that they had previously stowed in their spaceship and smuggled onto this planet."

"How did the aliens know that the other alien was in California?"

"We don't know."

"Where are they now?"

Mr. Adams shrugged. "We have no idea."

Judge Willis held up the black and yellow explosive in his hand. "This charge was found in California where the aliens blew up the military base?"

"They didn't blow up the entirety of Edwards Airforce Base, only the most impenetrable parts of it. I have photos of the damage from the explosions if you'd like to see them."

"I would."

Mr. Adams took out the photos from his briefcase and handed them to the bailiff. The bailiff passed them to Judge Willis.

Judge Willis studied the photos presented to him.

"Ten of the photos, taken from different angles, show the melted titanium-reinforced wall flecked with numerous holes big enough for a tank to drive through," said Mr. Adams. "Others show the hole in the ceiling where the aliens had blasted an exit after kidnapping their bounty. It was smaller than the holes in the wall, but still very large."

"The holes caused by the explosives in these photos look remarkably like the holes in the trains in the DA's photos."

"That's because they used the same charges."

"Let me make sure I'm understanding your story correctly. You're claiming that the aliens broke into and bombed a government facility, as well as destroyed Schumaker's trains?"

"*And* KB Rail's. These aliens, who have a known criminal background and who possess alarmingly powerful weaponry and technology, do not abide by laws set forth by the United States. They are here illegally, and they knowingly and intentionally destroyed government property."

"Then why did you decriminalize them a couple weeks ago?"

"That was clearly an error of judgment, but not relevant to this trial. What we currently know, and what is pertinent to us right now, is that the aliens are a threat to both private interests and national security. Capturing them alive for interrogation and arrest is no longer a safe or possible option now that they have demonstrated what they're capable of."

"What are you suggesting, Mr. Adams?" Judge Willis asked.

"As president of the United States, with the full power of the United States Military at my backing, I am using the authority vested in me by the American people to declare that the aliens are terrorists and enemies of the State."

The crowd gasped. The jury murmured loudly. Pens scratched furiously as journalists struggled to keep up with the juicy details.

"Order!" Judge Willis exclaimed, banging his gavel on the podium.

John stared at Eugene Schumaker who wore an expression of horror. He smiled in delight as Eugene clutched at his chest, hyperventilating, his mouth agape, like a whale gulping a bloom of plankton.

Now you understand what it felt like when you blew up my trains.

At that moment, the door to the courtroom burst open, and a Secret Service agent rushed inside breathing heavily.

"Sir! Your Honor! I apologize for the intrusion, but we need to get the president to safety at once."

"What is it?" asked Mr. Adams wearily. The interruption wasn't part of the script.

"The aliens—they've returned!"

"How do you know?"

"There's a huge green beam shooting from the spaceship. We need to get you to safety, sir! Quickly!"

Mr. Adams looked toward John. They held eye contact for just a moment, but that moment was all they needed to seal the deal. Mr. Adams gave a curt nod. John would have his solatium: Jmart would be allowed to partake in Bullit Inc.'s international deals. The trade document was already signed and dated to go into effect the next day. And Judge Willis would become a Supreme Court Justice. His name was ready to be put forth at tomorrow's executive session in the Senate. In turn, Mr. Adams would keep his company and avoid any sentencing. The DA would get a new car.

Judge Willis picked up his gavel and struck it against the hardwood block. "The dozen gray aliens are guilty of treason, trespassing on government property, conspiracy, arson, terrorism, drug trafficking, kidnapping, and smuggling. But, as a matter of national security, I defer my judgment on this case and instead acknowledge the president of the United States's declaration recognizing the aliens as enemies of the State."

Judge Willis stood up.

"This case is now dismissed."

CHAPTER 47

Eugene couldn't breathe. He clutched his throat and gasped, but his lungs burned more oxygen than they took in. His whole body tremored uncontrollably. He was distantly aware of people moving about, leaving the courtroom, but his eyes were shut and he felt dizzy, ready to collapse at the defendants' table. It was at that moment that a surge of adrenaline shot him into the air like a fish leaping from the water.

"It was me!" he shouted. "I did it! I blew up the trains—nobody else. The aliens are innocent!"

But nobody heard him. The court had already adjourned. Mr. Adams, flanked by a quorum of Secret Service agents, had left the courtroom. The jury, scavenging business executives, and journalists were filing out.

Eugene slumped into his seat. The adrenaline that had given him the courage to speak disappeared, replaced with deep anguish as he realized the aliens had just been sentenced to death.

"Come on, Eugene, hurry!" said Winston, tugging on his limp arm. "We need to get outside and see what the hell is going on!"

He let Winston drag him onto his feet and funnel him toward the exit. Overcome with a profound sensation of hollowness, he barely noticed his body bumping into others.

Winston pushed him through the tightly packed crowd to the

steps outside, where spectators had congregated to stare at an enormous green beam shooting into the sky from the Fairgrounds.

"What is *that*?!" exclaimed Winston.

The green beam, thick as a tornado, pulsated menacingly with electrical energy. Green lightning periodically discharged throughout dark clouds that swirled around it, followed by enormous cracks as thunder roared over the city. Whatever the beam was, it threatened to split the heavens with its wrath.

Sirens blared throughout the city. A caravan of police cars sped past Eugene and Winston on their way to the Fairgrounds.

"Something's about to go down. We need to go," shouted Winston, pulling Eugene in the opposite direction of the aliens' beam.

Eugene touched the button necklace around his neck. He rubbed the pendant made from a goldbug coated in amber—not just any goldbug, but the first *Charidotella sexpunctata* he ever caught. "No, we need to go there," he said weakly.

"Where?"

He pointed at the green light.

"Are you out of your mind?" Winston tugged on him a second time, but Eugene held his ground. "We'll die if we go there."

Eugene stared at the enormous beam. For some inexplicable reason, he felt it calling him, like a summoning beacon. "I don't know why, but I feel like we need to go toward it."

"There's no way we're going toward that interdimensional alien lightning beam," said Winston. "They might kill us."

"Who will?"

"The aliens, the police, the explosions—everyone and everything!"

A huge blast echoed throughout the streets shaking the earth.

"What was that?" screamed Winston hysterically.

A massive ball of fire and smoke shot into the sky near the green light. Eugene squinted in its direction as a long, slender, caterpillar-like object flew into the air, rising with the plume of fire. After a moment, the skyward train reached the peak of its arc and plummeted back to the ground. A boom followed the crash, shaking the earth.

"The railyard!" exclaimed Eugene. "My trains! They're destroying my old trains! Come on, let's go!" He bolted toward the parking lot, Winston at his heels.

They got into Eugene's car and sped off toward the Fairgrounds.

"What's happening, Eugene?" Winston asked.

"I don't know."

"Did you do that?"

"Not this time."

"Did the aliens do it?"

"They would never do something like that."

"They did at Edwards Airforce Base."

"They'd never do that to us, or to my railyard."

"Then who? Is John Angryberger still attempting to frame Bullit Inc.?"

"That doesn't make sense. He and Judge Willis framed the aliens instead of us, expunging us of any wrongdoing at the same time, so why would they bomb the railyard?"

Another colossal ball of orange and black smoke erupted into the air near the first one. The car shook violently as a concussive blast swept through the city, shattering windows in a high-rise apartment complex in front of them.

Winston looked at Eugene in horror. "Was that your refinery?"

Eugene nodded slowly. "It must've been."

"What's *happening?*"

Something clicked inside Eugene's mind. For once, the events unfolding around them made sense. "Winston, I think you're right," he said, fitting the pieces together.

"About what?"

"This *is* John's doing."

"How do you know?"

"He used the aliens to get what he wanted from Mr. Adams, and now, under the pretext of them being national security threats, he's blowing up what's left." He clutched the steering wheel tightly and pressed down on the accelerator. "Everyone will think it's the aliens' doing, so he's using the opportunity to get away with destroying his biggest competitor."

They sped toward the beam, following the trail of flashing red and blue lights, passing droves of people standing on the sidewalk and staring at the sky, mesmerized. Like Eugene, they were attracted by the sight, and had begun to move in its direction, like bugs to a porchlight.

As Eugene and Winston ripped down the road, they passed a giant billboard in which a child, wearing a Glam Blanc coat, played in the snow outside a dilapidated housing complex. "Look, Ma! There's food everywhere!" the child exclaimed. On the bottom right-hand corner of the billboard was the Bullit Inc. logo.

Eugene turned onto Schumaker Avenue and raced toward the office parking lot. He instinctively drifted into his reserved parking spot, jumped out of the car, and sprinted toward the Fairgrounds with Winston right behind.

An enormous horde of bystanders had already gathered around the spaceship, completely filling the Fairgrounds. Eugene and Winston weaved through the crowd, pushing people aside to get toward the metal disc.

As they fought their way to the ship, Eugene spotted Rosaline who, like him, was elbowing people out of her way.

"Rosaline!" Eugene yelled. He twisted and contorted his body to slip through the gaps between people.

She turned at the sound of her name. "Eugene! What's going on?" Her voice was calm but her face betrayed confusion and fear.

He pushed the last set of shoulders out of his way to reach her. "They framed the aliens."

Sirens blared all around them. The National Guard, heavily armed with assault weapons and tactical equipment, had been sent in to help the local police. Armored vehicles surrounded the Fairgrounds. Sirens from dozens of firetrucks at the adjoining railyard and refinery wailed as firemen fought roaring flames. Massive plumes of black smoke wafted upwards, adding to the already dark clouds in the sky.

"Come with me!" shouted Rosaline, grabbing his hand and pulling him deeper into the crowd as thunder crackled above their heads.

They pushed forward until they came upon an opening at the front of the crowd, and the spaceship appeared before them. They couldn't get any closer, however. Police had set up a secure perimeter around the ship. Chief Bagsby stood in the center, gun at the ready.

Eugene, full of worry and unease, leaned against the blue barricades. He could only wonder what was going on inside the ship to warrant such a response. Whatever it was, it was not good.

Suddenly, the spaceship emitted a deep throbbing hum, which reverberated throughout the Fairgrounds, joining the cacophonous melody of sirens and shouts. Louder and louder the thrumming grew until the rhythm of the sound matched the pulsating energy of the green beam. Eugene's eyes followed the beam down and noticed it originated from an orange octopus-themed gun-like artifact mounted on the vertex of the ship. After a minute, the deep reverberations grew so loud that they drowned out the howling sirens, until it was the only thing that could be heard.

Then, without warning, the spaceship's humming stopped, and the green spotlight turned off.

Collectively, everyone in the Fairgrounds held their breath.

And the hatch opened.

CHAPTER 48

With a soft thud, the hatch kissed the ground. A lone light cast the aliens' shadows down the red-carpeted ramp. The aliens lurked inside the stygian black recesses of the spaceship while their amorphous tentacular penumbrae danced—long, ominous, and hazy, like air on a tarmac on a hot day—down the carpet to the ground by the feet of the ship. Without warning, the shadows snaked forward as the aliens paraded down the ramp.

Halfway down, the aliens' silhouettes took shape. Little white Moroccasins appeared, followed by perfectly hemmed white pants. As the aliens descended further, their torsos materialized, and each alien could be seen having paired their white dress pants with white tuxedos and a white apron. Wavy blond wigs and white top hats covered their heads. The aliens were decked in Glam Blanc.

Eugene noticed their tattooed faces and hamburger-gray bodies looked a shade pinker than normal. *Are they blushing?*

As they came closer, Eugene observed one alien wasn't medium-rare-colored like the others; it was carnival-orange and globular, and it had a bilabiate frill beneath its throat, like an Elizabethan ruff.

"Put your hands up!" Chief Bagsby yelled, raising his pistol.

The aliens ignored the police chief's request. They didn't have hands, and even if they did, they wouldn't have been able to put them up. Their tentacles weren't free to raise. They were preoccupied with large rectangular trays pressed tightly against new white aprons on their chests.

"Everyone, get down!" Chief Bagsby commanded. "They're carrying bombs!"

Nobody moved. Everyone was too entranced by the unfolding spectacle.

"Don't take another step or I'll shoot!" said the police chief, tightening his grip.

The aliens defied his command.

He took aim.

And then a scent, like an invisible bullet, struck Eugene. It was the most wonderful, intoxicating smell his olfactory bulbs had ever encountered—warm and buttery, textured and flakey, zesty and lemony. It zapped him like jumper cables hooked up to his nostrils. He recognized the mouthwatering aroma at once. *Muffins! They're carrying trays of muffins!*

The aliens had converted their spaceship into a bakery.

Eugene scanned the crowd, bewildered, to see that everyone was lifting their noses, sniffing the air, and licking their lips hungrily.

The aliens disembarked onto the dirt of the Fairgrounds.

"Stop right there!" ordered Chief Bagsby.

But the aliens paid him no heed. They advanced, tray first, offering muffins to the thousands of customers who had gathered to witness the grand opening of their bakery.

"Nobody take a muffin! There are explosives inside—the same kind they used to blow up the city!"

"Stop this madness!" Rosaline shrieked at Chief Bagsby, bulldozing past the ring of heavily armed police officers surrounding the ship and rushing toward him. "They're just muffins!"

The alien nearest the chief plucked a muffin from its baking tray and proffered it to him with open tentacles.

Even though it was phenotypically identical to the other gray aliens (minus Tubby), Eugene instinctively recognized the alien holding the muffin. There was something inexplicably geeky and awkward about Buttons that resonated with Eugene that enabled him to identify Buttons from amongst all the others. It was Eugene's kindred spirit from another galaxy.

A gunshot rang out throughout the Fairgrounds. Buttons collapsed backwards, head violently smacking the ground. The tray flipped upside down, scattering bloodstained muffins across the dirt.

One rolled to a stop in front of Rosaline.

She screamed.

The spell hypnotizing the horde of onlookers abruptly lifted. The stupefied masses regained their senses and began to flee in terror. Bedlam ensued. A stampede formed. The previously docile crowd was suddenly screaming and shouting and shoving. A thousand people all at once forgot about those titillating, heavenly muffins, and a few unfortunate souls were dragged underneath trampling feet, swallowed alive by the hungry earth.

Eugene stared in shock at the sight of Buttons lying motionless on the ground. *This can't be happening. Not Buttons. I never even got to give it its necklace.* Eugene tried to move toward Chief Bagsby to tell him to stop, but his feet had become heavy cinderblocks. He tried to speak, but he couldn't find the words. He was immobilized by fear. His courage left him. It had left him long ago.

Chief Bagsby faced the rest of the aliens. He raised his pistol again.

The orange alien sensed danger. It tossed away its tray of muffins and fled, slipping through the crowd of people. The other aliens, however, didn't move. They stared at their fallen brethren, mortified.

Eugene put his hand on his forehead. He felt woozy. *I need to tell him to stop,* he thought. *I need to say, 'No, don't do this'...* He shut his eyes hard, trying to expel the abominable scene he had witnessed from his mind, and when he opened them again, watched disjointedly as his dad held a model train and pointed it threateningly at a three-foot-tall, tentacled version of Eugene.

That's not right. Chief Bagsby, not my dad, is wielding a gun, not a train. And he's aiming it at an alien, not at me. Eugene was discombobulated. The scene in front of him was too horrific for him to handle; he began to dissociate, retreating into the safety of his own mind. *Am I an alien?* He tried to fight it. *It doesn't matter. This needs to end. I must say...*

"*NOOOO!*" Rosaline screeched.

But Chief Bagsby pulled the trigger. There was a thud as the second alien hit the ground.

Not to be outdone, the other officers discharged their weapons at the sinister tabernacle of muffin-wielding aliens. A cascade of crimson, blood-soaked muffins rained from the sky like a shower of red-velvet cupcakes.

"NO, NO, NO, *WHAT HAVE YOU DONE!*" Rosaline thundered over the hubbub of sirens and gunfire. Tears gushed from her eyes as she hopped the barricade and rushed forward. "*Murderers!* You killed them!"

"Lady, you need to get away," said one of the officers.

"Don't you tell me what to do!" she roared. She pushed past a row of officers, scrambling toward an alien filled with as many holes as a Schumaker locomotive. She crouched to check its pulse, flinching when she found it lifeless. She covered her mouth with both hands and yowled. "They never deserved this!"

She stood up, faced Chief Bagsby, and slapped him.

He pointed his gun in between her eyes.

"Shoot me, you fucking coward!"

He laughed and holstered his pistol instead. "If you died today, nothing would be different tomorrow."

She turned her back on him, rushed to the next body, and bent down to check its pulse. Dead.

"Rosaline," Eugene murmured. He wanted to console her, but he had nothing to say. His mouth was as empty as his soul. He felt distant, trapped inside a bad dream he couldn't wake from. He could only watch, benumbed, as she raced helter-skelter to every alien lying blood-soaked on the ground beneath the spaceship.

She reached Tubby last. Its head lay sideways on the dirt, smushing several muffins trapped underneath. She reached for its neck to check its pulse and gasped when Tubby shifted its torso.

"Tubby! Oh, poor baby!"

Tubby tried to sit up, but it only managed to raise itself a couple of inches before falling backwards onto the dirt.

"I've got you, Tubby. It's going to be okay."

Tubby cooed. It reached a tentacle into a fold in its belly and brought out a muffin. Tenderly, it tucked the muffin in Rosaline's hand. With another tentacle, it gently wrapped her fingers around the pastry as if it were a small treasure she needed to keep safe and protected.

"Tubby," she whispered, as its tentacles slowly slid off her hand and fell gracefully onto the dirt.

Rosaline opened her mouth with shock. Tears streamed down her cheeks and her eyes sunk into her skull. With two hands, she clutched the muffin it had given her and brought it tight against her chest.

It was too much for Eugene to witness. He looked away from his crying friend, but his eyes found a corpse, so he diverted his gaze again only for his eyes to land on another corpse. It was insufferable. Seconds passed like days as he stared without seeing, feeling nothing. And yet, through the confusion and discordant noise, he heard the faintest cough. Through his peripheries, he caught the slightest motion as something expectorated droplets of blood.

Buttons exhaled a deep, rattling breath.

"Buttons…" The invisible chains that bound Eugene in place magically disappeared, and he bolted toward the sound. In an instant, he was kneeling by the alien's side. He lifted a bloody, bullet-hole ridden tentacle. He didn't expect the alien to respond. But once again, the alien defied expectations and lifted its head when it felt Eugene's gentle touch.

"Oh, Buttons!" he wailed, cradling the alien in his arms.

The alien's eyes fluttered halfway open.

"Please, don't move! Save your energy!"

"Mmmm!" it hummed. The alien reached a tentacle inside the pouch of its apron and pulled out a blood-soaked muffin.

"Now isn't the time for muffins," Eugene yelled frantically, pressing his hands over the aliens' wounds to try to stop the bleeding.

The alien batted his hands away and pushed the muffin closer to Eugene's mouth. "Mmmm," it repeated.

"We need to get you to the hospital!" Eugene tried to lift Buttons, but, once again, it stubbornly pressed the muffin toward his shaking lips.

Eugene cracked. His mouth hung limp with despair, and the alien gently pushed the muffin inside. He chewed between sobs, fighting back convulsions so he could swallow.

Eugene closed his eyes. All the pain and resentment he had bottled up over the past few years disappeared into nothingness. And in its absence, it became clear—so heart-wrenchingly crystal clear—that he had made a great big thing out of absolutely nothing at all. *It was only a muffin,* he realized. *All you ever wanted, Dad, was to share your muffin with me, a simple, harmless muffin.*

He opened his eyes and gazed at Buttons who smiled at him with its adorable little underbite. Eugene touched the necklace around his neck.

"This is for you. I'm sorry I turned it into this mess."

He slipped the sloppily-made handcrafted necklace off his neck and extended it toward his friend, who ever-so-slightly bowed its head, and Eugene put the necklace over it. The colors looked ugly against its gray flesh.

Buttons, humming proudly, looked at Eugene expectantly.

"What do you want me to say?" he asked. "You already know what I think. That was the best muffin I've ever had!"

The alien let out a toothy grin. It reached its tentacle up and ran it across the buttons on the necklace. Its eyes rolled back, and its head gently fell to the ground.

"Buttons! Stay with me. Don't go, don't you dare go!" The alien didn't respond. Eugene looked up at the officers who stared at him with their guns raised. "Help! We need an ambulance. Someone help!"

They didn't move. "The only good criminal is a dead criminal," one of the officers responded.

Eugene's heart sank. He turned back to Buttons. "Please don't go," he whispered.

Buttons, with eyes closed, reached out a tentacle and touched Eugene's hand. Content beyond all measure, the alien hummed one last time.

EPILOGUE

Eugene and Winston stopped in front of the ramp and gazed into the recesses of the spaceship. A warm yellow light reflected off the interior, casting its glow upon them. They basked in its embrace, and the events of the past several months replayed in their minds, until the warm and welcoming aroma of freshly baked muffins tingled their noses, beckoning them to enter.

"I've never eaten at a billion-dollar bakery before," said Winston, his voice gently pulling them out of the silence they'd settled into.

Eugene felt the tension in his body ease. After the massacre in the Fairgrounds, John Angryberger took over the spaceship. He tried to relocate it, but the ship was too heavy to budge. Engineers were unable to dismantle it to move individual parts. To John's dismay, the spaceship was a permanent fixture of the Fairgrounds. Knowing there was nothing of value left inside that would provide him and his corporations with technological superiority over his competitors, he did the second most profitable thing: auction off the spaceship to the highest bidder.

Eugene bid his entire Schumaker fortune and won. He had the government auctioneers write the deed in Rosaline's name.

Today was her bakery's re-reopening in the new space.

"One sec," said Eugene. He turned around and ventured several feet away to the site where the aliens were murdered. It was easy to find because a garden of blossoming poppy plants grew in the places their bodies had bled into the earth. He pulled from his pocket a handful of buttons and threw one into each patch of poppies, like he had done every day since the incident.

After he tossed the last button, he looked at the mostly dark sky. The moon hung full. Beyond it, dozens of stars still shimmered. One of them might have been the aliens' home star. Who knows. The dawning orange light on the horizon began to wash them away.

Eugene closed his eyes for several seconds and breathed in the air. A light wind brushed his cheek and shuffled the poppy flowers next to him. *I miss you all so much.* He opened his eyes and returned to Winston.

"Okay, I'm ready now."

Eugene and Winston climbed the ramp, which hadn't retracted since the aliens last descended, into Rosaline's new bakery. They were early, of course; Rosaline told them to come before the official opening time. Their heads passed through the open trap door which the government had installed because they couldn't figure out how to close the ramp, and Eugene and Winston could see inside.

The circular interior was sectionalized into four quadrants. The first was the bakery storefront containing the ordering counter and display, an espresso machine, a four-gallon glass dispenser filled with cucumber-infused ice water, and the cash register. A sign that read "The Baker's Dozen" hung over the display. Suspended above it were cartoon images of twelve gray aliens in chef hats carrying trays of muffins. On the wall behind the counter, on its own shelf, was a vacuum-sealed glass cube containing a singular bloodstained muffin.

Next to the storefront was the kitchen, which contained every-thing a baker could ask for: an enormous island with a granite coun-tertop, an overhead rack for pots and pans, wide counter space next to a deep sink, several bread and pastry cooling shelves, and a state-of-the-art oven. There were plenty of drawers to store utensils and other cooking equipment, as well as two pantries to store ingredients.

The third section contained several small wooden tables and checkered navy-and-white bistro chairs for bakery patrons to sit and eat. Dodecahedron-shaped centerpieces containing various succulents rested on each table. Signage on the wall indicated a maximum capacity of one hundred and sixty.

Finally, the fourth section contained a ball pit area kids could play in. Nobody was sure why the aliens had put that there instead of something more conventional, like a bathroom.

As Eugene gazed around the interior, he noticed that the wall of the spaceship wasn't an opaque metal like he presumed, but rather see-through, like a toggleable one-way mirror. He could see outside in every direction. From the kitchen, he could see Rosaline's original bakery; from behind the storefront, his office building; from behind the ball pit, the refinery; and in every direction like a panorama, the skyline of the city.

Eugene spotted Rosaline in the kitchen quadrant sliding a large tray onto the cooling rack.

"Hey, Rosaline," he called out.

"Eugene! Winston!" She tore off her apron and hurried over to hug them. "What do you think?"

"You did all of this?" asked Winston.

"I did none of this. The ship was already like this when Eugene bought it. The only addition I made was the showcase," she said, pointing at the glass cube on the shelf behind the counter.

"It's incredible," said Eugene.

"*They* were incredible," said Rosaline.

She escorted them to the counter where she gathered two muffins and whipped up two mugs of hot chocolate. Eugene and Winston ate their lemon poppyseed muffins over the display.

"How's everything tasting?" she asked Eugene and Winston.

"Wonderful."

"Delicious."

Rosaline glowed.

Eugene fidgeted. "How are you holding up?" he asked her

timidly. It was something he asked her every time he saw her, just to check in on his friend.

"I'm doing well. The bakery has generated terrific hype, and I feel… invigorated."

"That's good."

"Yeah… it is. And you?"

Eugene took a folded letter from his pocket and passed it to Rosaline. "I finally did it. That's my re-acceptance letter into Cornell's entomology program. I'm going back to school in a couple months."

"That's wonderful! You're doing what you always should have done."

"Yeah," said Eugene with a twinge of melancholy. He glanced out the window toward his old office, then shifted his gaze to the railyard that had burned down the night of the massacre. Insurance had paid back the cost of the entire facility and all the trains, of course. Next to the railyard, the refinery hadn't fared much better. It had been burnt to a crisp. Metal beams struck out every which way, like an eerie dystopian post-nuclear playground for tetanus-seeking children.

Eugene instinctively ran his fingers over the buttons comprising his necklace. It had become a habit for him whenever he felt scared, nervous, or doubtful. The button necklace gave him strength.

"I'm rid of the burden I put on myself," he said. "I can finally do what I want."

"I'm happy for you."

"Yeah, me too."

"And what about you, Winston?" Rosaline asked. "What have you been up to?"

"Teofilo."

"Excuse me?"

"Teofilo. I changed my name back."

"Wow, that's a big change. How come?"

"I realized who I really am." Teofilo paused, and his eyes searched the room as if seeing things that weren't there. "Winston used to fight against the status quo: I used to seek due regard for my opinions and beliefs, and I wanted to be taken seriously. Then you-know-what happened, and I had clarity. There is no fight to be had with the status quo; the fight was all inside my head. Why did I want others to care about what I had to say? That was my pride fighting, and it wasn't fighting to make positive change in the world. Winston was proud, and he wanted to rebel, but against whom? Not against things out there, but against things in here." He tapped his temple. "Winston is a part of me, but he isn't me. I'm Teofilo Trujillo. Like my traveler parents, I'll find my own path in life. If I respect myself, I don't need the validation and respect of others. That's what I've come to learn."

Rosaline touched his shoulder and gave him a warm smile. "I'm happy for you, too."

"But to answer your question about what I've been up to," he continued, "I resigned my post as vice president of Bullit Inc."

"Good. That evil company wasn't a place for you, Teofilo. What will you do now?"

Teofilo started laughing.

"What's so funny?" Rosaline asked.

"He's not doing anything at the moment," answered Eugene. "He's as unemployed as he was two years ago."

Rosaline looked at Teofilo with a mother's worry. "You don't have any plans?"

"I don't know. More than ever, I have no idea what to do next."

"Nothing at all?"

Teofilo shrugged. "I need time to figure that out. Maybe I'll write a book or something."

"What will it be about?"

"Innocence."

"Will it be a fantasy novel?"

"More likely an anachronistic piece of speculative fiction."

"Will there be any strong female leads, preferably from a minority or disenfranchised upbringing?"

"No, but it will have gender-neutral aliens."

"That's inclusive of you," said Rosaline. "What will you call it?"

"How about, 'Recipe for Disaster?'" suggested Eugene.

Teofilo let out another laugh. "That's not bad."

"Oooh! Oooh! What about 'Space Chefs?' Or 'Muffins from Outer Space?' Or 'Intergalactic Smugglers Who Come to Earth to Share Their Love of Muffins with Us?'"

Teofilo patted Eugene on the back. "You should stick to bugs."

"Well, what title have you come up with then?"

Teofilo thought for a moment. "I'll name it after your bakery, *The Baker's Dozen*."

Footsteps clanked behind them, and Cecil-Lee entered the spaceship.

Rosaline puffed out her chest.

"Before yew say anything, Ahh owe yew an apology, Rosaline," said Cecil-Lee, taking off his white cowboy hat and holding it over his heart. "Ahh hurt yew, Eugene, an' yer friends. Ahh'm sorry. Nuthin' Ahh say can bring 'em back, so if yew don't forgive me, Ahh understand. Ahh just want yew t' know Ahh apologize fer the part Ahh played in all this, an' Ahh promise Ahh will be better from now on."

Cecil-Lee reached inside the inner lining of his jean jacket and pulled out a wrapped box. "Ahh made these fer yew."

Rosaline briskly strode across the bakery to the Texan. She snatched the box from his hands. "You think a gift will make up for everything you've done?"

"No, Ahh don't think it will, an' it shouldn't. But Ahh hope this small gesture will start t' move us forward in the rahht direction."

Rosaline eyed him coolly before tearing the wrapping off her gift. She reached inside the box and held up a cookie cutter in the shape of an alien.

"Ahh got yew a dozen cookie cutters. An' that one there is specially made fer Tubby," said Cecil-Lee, pointing at one lying on the bottom of the box that was five times larger than the others.

Rosaline put the cookie cutter she was holding back in the box and carefully lifted the extra-large one. She held it up to the light. The metal, like her eyes, glistened. "Cecil-Lee..."

"Look, ma'am, yew don't need t' say nuthin'."

"No, Cecil-Lee, you look." She put down her present and rolled up her sleeve. On Rosaline's arm were tattoos of the aliens doing all the fun things they loved: smoking weed, flinging themselves off faces, dripping goo, collecting buttons, eating muffins, and saving their friends. In the center of it all was her bakery.

Cecil-Lee's eyes watered.

Rosaline's lower lip trembled. "Go on, say it!"

"Yew look like a wanted criminal."

"I'm just doing what I love."

Rosaline and Cecil-Lee returned from the kitchen. They had cried so much that Rosaline ran out of tissues and paper towels and had to grab more from the drawer below the sink. She handed Cecil-Lee his muffin, and he joined Teofilo and Eugene at the counter.

"Rosaline, somehow this tastes better than anything yew've ever made us before," he said, taking a bite. "How kin that be? Did yew alter the recipe?"

"No," she replied. "I didn't change anything about it."

"How odd," mused Cecil-Lee. "Those aliens didn't share any secrets or magic with yew when they shared their last meal, did they?"

"I learned something from them that I'd only thought I understood for all those years: how far a little love and a zest for life can go."

"Is that why you reopened their bakery?" asked Eugene.

"I reopened it because I have something to share. It took me three months to realize that. At first, I didn't want to bake anything ever again, but that would be an act *against* the horrors of the world instead of a decision *for* the happy memories of our dear friends, whose only desire was to share their love with the rest of us. That realization made me remember why I wanted to be a baker in the first place. Once I took ownership of my life choices, I could finally understand the world. It isn't inherently bad; we *make* it bad with our poor decisions. But if we can do that, then we can also make it good by making better choices. It's wonderful to know we don't live in a hopeless place. We can change it so that it is full of joy. And love. And even happiness. That's what *they* taught us."

"But they tried that," said Eugene. "Buttons tried that, and it didn't work."

Rosaline smiled compassionately. "I disagree. Remember how happy they were eating my sweets and spending time with us? Compare them to how you felt. You were in a horrible place, and you made things worse as a result. Just because the aliens died doesn't mean they failed to make a difference. They changed us. They showed us that to make the world a better place, you have to go about it the right way, which means doing it *your* way. For me, I can bake. I can bring the same joy, happiness, and love the aliens had for muffins to the rest of the world."

Eugene looked at his feet, discouraged. "What can I do? It's not like everyone loves bugs in the same way people love muffins. I can't give bugs to people. I can't make other people happy because I'm an entomologist."

"That's not the point, Eugene."

"What is?"

She looked at him, dumbfounded. "Have you seriously not figured it out?"

"What?"

"Eugene, it's not about making others happy. It's about doing what makes *you* happy. Look at the aliens. They loved baking so much they turned their spaceship into a bakery. They felt that was more important than being able to get home."

"Or maybe they felt the bakery was their home, an' they didn't need t' go anywhere else," said Cecil-Lee wisely.

"So, it's okay if I become an entomologist?"

"Yes!" Rosaline, Teofilo, and Cecil-Lee exclaimed in unison.

"Eugene, it's not only okay that you become an entomologist," said Rosaline, "the world also *needs* you to do it."

"Oh." Eugene felt strange. It had been so long since he had done what he wanted to do. His body began to shake. He stared down at his plate, fighting back tears.

"What's wrong?" Rosaline asked, rubbing his back.

"It's just… that's all I ever wanted to hear!" he cried out.

Teofilo hugged him. "Oh, bud."

Eugene sobbed uncontrollably on his shoulder. "I just wish I knew all this years ago. I could have saved so much time and been so much happier."

"You're not the only one," said Teofilo. "We all feel that way."

Eugene sniffled. He wiped his face with the back of his hand and stared longingly at the open trap door in the middle of the spaceship floor. He imagined the twelve gray aliens climbing the ramp, and their smiling faces and bright souls parading on in. He pictured them splitting a muffin into twelfths, before devouring it in synchronization. Rosaline would have a mop on stand-by for the inevitable goo puddles, those little pools of happiness.

"I've been wondering something ever since that fateful day," said Teofilo as if reading Eugene's thoughts. "If the aliens were so technologically advanced and possessed unexplainable magical powers, why didn't they stop the police from shooting them?"

"You're thinking too logically," Rosaline replied. "You've always thought too logically. That's why you failed at Bullit Inc."

"What do you mean?" he asked.

"*Of course* the aliens could have stopped the bullets, but they didn't want to."

"Why not?"

"Because they chose to be vulnerable. Their willingness to fall so deeply in love, not only with their craft but with all of us too, meant they relinquished their defensive guards. They didn't want to live in a world without love. I think that's also why they left their spaceship out in the open for anyone to tamper with. They didn't need to protect themselves from us, nor did they want to. From the first moment they visited, they found something here that they couldn't find anywhere else, and it made them loving and vulnerable."

"Muffins?" asked Teofilo.

"It wasn't ever about the muffins," replied Rosaline.

"Ahh'm pretty shore it was *always* 'bout the muffins," Cecil-Lee said.

Eugene clutched his necklace. "They found the freedom to be themselves," he said unequivocally.

A momentary silence fell over the bakery.

Rosaline grabbed a glass from the shelf, filled it with water and powdered sugar to make a gooey solution, and threw it on the floor. "I'll grab the mop!" she said. As she reached for the handle, she began to weep. Teardrops ran down her cheeks and dripped happily onto the metallic floor. "I'll miss those guys!" she howled.

"We all will," said Eugene, who had also begun to cry.

And in remembrance, they all murmured the aliens' favorite squeak—their word for love.

"Mmmm!"

ACKNOWLEDGMENTS

I'd like to thank my editors, Marissa Van Uden and Julie Tibbott, for making my project not only readable, but enjoyable. Thank you Nate Petropoulos, Joshua Hansen, Benjamin Trauner, Thomas Harrison, and my brother, Zeke, for helping me improve various parts of the manuscript. I'd also like to thank Dominic Kallas and Isabel Hoyt for reading through initial drafts and helping to smooth the story. A special thanks goes to Renée Rodgers for many nights spent editing with me—your creative insights, constructive feedback, and words of encouragement were invaluable.